LORI G. ARMSTRONG
SHALLOW
GRAVE

Medallion Press, Inc.
Printed in USA

female characters to come along in awhile, with her simmering attraction to the wild and disreputable Martinez being especially of note. There's plenty of suspense here, as well, to challenge and interest, with the whole package being one glorious adventure, leaving us eagerly anticipating what's next for this uniquely drawn crew of misfits and miscreants."

—*Stephanie Padilla, New Mystery Reader*

4 1/2 STARS!

"Hard-drinking, chain-smoking P.I. Julie Collins has a fascinating, multidimensional personality, as do all the characters in this story. Armstrong's writing continues to be fresh and exciting in the second book of this series."

—*RT BookClub*

"Lori Armstrong provides a fabulous mystery starring an intriguing protagonist with a climax that will stun the audience."

—*Midwest Book Review*

"Hard as nails, a barroom brawler — and a chick! Lori Armstrong's creation is born of the Black Hills. Tough, sensitive and smart, Julie Collins is a welcome addition to the private eye genre. In BLOOD TIES she breaks all the rules."

—*Stephanie Kane, Author of SEEDS OF DOUBT.*

"BLOOD TIES by Lori G. Armstrong is a thrilling roller of a mystery that taunts you to try and solve the riddle. The suspense was superb, keeping you glued to the page. Your subconscious urging you to read just one more page, get one more piece of the puzzle."

—*In The Library Reviews*

Published 2007 by Medallion Press, Inc.

The MEDALLION PRESS LOGO
is a registered tradmark of Medallion Press, Inc.

Typeset in Adobe Garamond Pro
Printed in the United States of America
10-digit ISBN: 1-9338361-8-0
13-digit ISBN: 978-1-933836-18-8

10 9 8 7 6 5 4 3 2 1
First Edition

ACKNOWLEDGEMENTS:

A round of high fives to Helen and Adam at Medallion Press for everything, from kick-ass artwork to their kick-ass support of this book.

Pilamaya ye (thank you) to my *kola* (friend) Craig Howe—for helping me with the snippets of Lakota language, and for not laughing at my mispronunciations or misspellings—any errors in translation are solely mine.

Huge thanks to Dr. Doug Lyle for sharing his vast knowledge on the density of bones.

My critique partner, Mary LaHood, thanks for sticking with me all these years on this journey, and for keeping me (and Julie) heading in the right direction.

To my fabulous kiddos—Lauren, Haley, Tessa—you guys are my life. Special thanks to my husband Erin for willingly subjecting himself to all sorts of "research" ideas I come up with.

My First Offenders blog partners and good friends, Alison Gaylin, Karen Olson and Jeff Shelby, my life is so much better for having you all in it.

A special thanks to every person who has contacted me online or connected with me in person and told me how much they love the books. I appreciate the support more than you'll ever know.

CHAPTER 1

My ass was asleep.

My thighs were as hard and cold as Popsicles.

My nose and Rudolph's? Too close a resemblance for my taste.

And I was so damn hungry I could gnaw off my own arm.

Oh, yeah. The glamorous world of private investigators.

I bounced my feet on the floorboards. A hundred hot needles jabbed my flesh, but didn't drive the numbness from my butt.

"You need a bathroom break?" Kevin asked snidely, without moving the binoculars trained on the ramshackle farmhouse.

"No." My breath puffed out in a little white cloud. Reminded me I hadn't had a cigarette in hours either.

1

"This sucks. These seats suck."

"Quit complaining."

"Can we at least shut the damn window?"

"Your whining will fog it up in about two seconds."

"Jerk."

"Wuss."

He sighed and rolled it up anyway.

My hero.

Three hours of surveillance hadn't netted us one shred of evidence on this case. We were both a little cold and a lot cranky.

Kevin and I were parked in the midst of rusty cars and ancient farm equipment, in a cow pasture smack dab in the middle of Bear Butte County.

Technically we shouldn't be on the owner's property without permission, to say nothing of inside the fence and a 100 feet from the residence. But unlike law enforcement, as investigators we could toe the line without breaking fifty procedural laws and it wouldn't adversely affect our client's case.

I stared out the window. Milky gray clouds cast murky shadows across the grass, flattened and dead, courtesy of the first frost. With amber and scarlet leaves a distant memory, the stripped branches of cottonwood and elm trees in the distance added depth to the endless horizon.

"You see anything yet?"

"Nah. Same old, same old."

"Let me look."

"Have at it." Kevin passed me the binoculars.

I leaned forward and readjusted the focus.

The house was in sad shape; white paint aged to a cheerless yellow, the once red trim faded to pumpkin orange. Windows were coated with a film of dirt. Draperies of an indiscernible color blocked any view of the inside.

On the porch a mangy mutt slept beneath a three-legged resin lawn chair. Several scruffy cats strutted across the bowed porch railings, then dropped out of sight.

Spent oilcans, empty Busch Light bottles, warped 2X4's and a crumpled blue plastic tarp were scattered on the left side of the sagging foundation. Two black garbage bags sat forgotten by the torn aluminum screen door, ripped from the hinges.

And I thought the houses in my neighborhood were bad. "We know this guy isn't violating his worker's comp limitations by cleaning up his damn yard."

"That'd entail him bending over. Wouldn't want him to further injure himself and require additional therapy."

Wow. That was almost snarky, coming from Kevin, Mr. innocent-until-proven-guilty.

The man we were surveilling, Langston "Lang" Everett, was out of commission due to a work related injury he'd received at a local sawmill. Nothing as serious as an industrial-sized saw slicing off his thumb, or a limb getting pinched between run-away logs. Lang had injured his back sweeping. With a plain old broom and dustpan while bending over to clean up piles of sawdust.

His employer, Larson Timber Products, hadn't disputed the claim. Like any responsible company, they'd filed the appropriate paperwork with Rushmore West Insurance, their private workman's comp carrier, and with the proper state agencies.

An occupational therapist started Lang on an intensive physical therapy regimen. At the end of the eight weeks, Lang claimed there'd been no change in his range of mobility. He'd also asserted that because of the injury, he'd begun to suffer from constant, debilitating pain.

His absence put Larson Timber in a bind. Legally they couldn't fill Lang's position as long as he was collecting worker's comp due to an injury. No one was happy with the situation, except Lang, who (according to his employer) was enjoying an extended vacation on their dime.

After twenty weeks, Rushmore West Insurance had demanded a second medical opinion.

The second occupational therapist's diagnosis concurred with the first. Often, the most innocuous injury proved the most difficult to heal. The new expert swore Lang needed an additional six *months* of intensive therapy to gauge the severity and permanence of the damage.

I called bullshit on it, but I was hardly an authority or held an unbiased opinion. An identical situation had occurred in the Bear Butte County Sheriff's Department the first year I'd worked there. The night dispatcher, a woman named Rhea, injured her knee and elbow hauling out garbage. Poor baby suffered through four months of rehab.

When the insurance company received the all clear from Rhea's physician, she demanded a second opinion, which was in direct opposition to the first doctor's diagnosis. She couldn't return to duty because the injury had caused her to suffer from "chronic pain." Rhea expected the county to pay for permanent disability.

She'd been a whopping twenty-four at the time.

The county refused to pay. The case had gone to court.

In response to their extra workload, two fellow employees had called Rhea one night after too many Budweiser's. Questioning the validity of her injuries supposedly inflicted additional trauma on Rhea, spurring her lawyer to seek extra compensation for her "mental anguish."

The county had lost face, money, and the employees involved in what'd been a drunken prank had gotten shit-canned. Rhea collected a pile of cash and was lazing around Florida with her winnings. Probably paid her cabana boy to take out the trash.

At times the perversity of the legal system stunned me.

In Lang's case, two weeks earlier, someone had called the employer with an anonymous tip, claiming Lang Everett was faking his injury. Larson Timber reported the incident to their insurance company and to the state insurance fraud division.

Most insurance companies, especially out-of-state conglomerates, maintain specialized fraud teams. But often it's cheaper for them to hire a private local investigative firm to validate or invalidate the claim.

Kevin had previously worked for Rushmore West on a similar situation. All we needed were two separate documented instances of Lang Everett's questionable behavior.

And what were Lang's supposed infractions? The unidentified caller had seen Lang ripping around on his ATV. Driving was a definite no-no on the list of activities that aggravated his injury. But that wasn't all. Supposedly Lang had been under the hood of his Chevy Blazer, wrenching on the engine block. And the source swore Lang raced his horse down the driveway every day to pick up his mail.

Sour grapes? Or was Lang Everett a big, fat faker?

In staking out the Everett abode, not only hadn't we seen Lang zipping past on a four-wheeler, a mud buggy, or a horse; we hadn't seen Lang Everett, period.

Rushmore West Insurance retained our services for fifteen hours of surveillance. If we didn't deliver the goods in the allotted time, we'd be off the case, unless they ponied up more cash. I was hoping for a quick end to this ho-hum assignment.

Bored, I fiddled with the screen on the video camera.

"Hey, be careful with that," Kevin said.

"I am. When was the last time you used this?"

"Couple of months ago on that employee theft case. Why?"

"Just curious. Don't remember seeing it in the supply closet at the office."

"That's because I had it at home."

"For?"

Kevin looked at me strangely.

With guilt? "Ooh. Didn't know you were into making porn, Kev."

"Jesus, Julie. Get your mind out of the gutter."

I grinned. "But it's so happy there."

"Not everything has to do with sex."

"All the good stuff does."

He directed his scowl out the window. "Can't believe I'm saying this, but I'll actually be *glad* when Martinez gets back in town."

"You and me both."

Kevin didn't understand what I saw in Tony Martinez, my latest paramour, president of the Hombres—a motorcycle "club"— and an all-around, scary, badass dude.

7

Martinez had been in Colorado for two weeks on business. Pained me to admit I missed him, especially when I didn't know if the feeling was mutual. The stupid jerk hadn't bothered to call me. Yeah, yeah, I knew phone lines ran both ways, and it might be juvenile, but I sure as hell wasn't about to call El Presidente first.

"You up for doing anything tonight?" Kevin asked.

Since his girlfriend Lilly's death from cancer, I suspected Kevin spent most nights alone, staring at the ugly-ass walls in his condo. After being together eight hours a day, he didn't push for us to hang out after the 5:00 whistle blew.

"I guess. Wanna get a pizza and watch a movie?"

"Sure. As long as it's not a Clooney flick."

"Then no Cameron Diaz stinkers either."

"Maybe we should stick to TV."

"Great. I think *Queer Eye* is on at eight."

Kevin groaned.

I smiled, readjusting my position. "How many hours are left on today's allotment?"

"Two."

My butt would never recover. And my stomach rumbled like an empty cattle truck. "Got any Twinkies?"

"For the last time, *no*. God. Eat a protein bar. There's a whole box in the back seat."

"Nice try. But I don't see you eating those nasty

things. Why didn't you pack Snickers bars?"

Kevin faced me. "What is up with you? You never care about food when we're on stakeout." His brows lifted. "Christ. You're not pregnant, are you?"

The look of horror on my face matched his. "Omigod, *no*, I'm not pregnant."

Sounds of an engine revving cut his retaliation short and brought our attention back to the Everett household.

Our suspect was finally out in the open.

Kevin swore, picked up the binoculars and rolled down the window as I fumbled with the video camera. Zooming in on the action, I poked the record button.

Lang's wife—June, according to our records—still wore a grubby pink bathrobe and bunny slippers at 2:00 in the afternoon. Even from our secret vantage point I could tell she was screeching at her husband like a barn owl.

Lang shouted back at her.

She stormed down the steps. Snapped off a mean comment, by the sneering set of her mouth. The bunny head on one slipper flopped as she tapped her foot, waiting for his reaction.

Lang's shoulders tensed. His hand shot out and connected with her face.

Not the reaction she'd expected.

She staggered, bringing her palm to her cheek.

"You fucking bastard," I said.

9

Kevin's hand gripped my thigh, an attempt to keep me from jumping out and kicking Lang's ass.

"Easy, Julie."

"He hit her. You saw it."

"I know."

"What are we going to do?"

"Nothing."

"But—"

"Focus on why we're here."

I hated that he was right. I directed my anger on nailing this wife-beating asshole. Maybe I could convince his wife to charge him with assault, since we had proof.

"Come on," Kevin taunted him softly. "Turn around."

Almost as if he'd heard Kevin's directive, Lang spun. Bonus: he'd whirled around fast enough the movement should've caused excruciating pain to his "injury."

"Gotcha," Kevin said, as I clicked a still shot.

Lang climbed onto the dirt-covered four-wheeler, whipped a U-turn, spewing gravel at his wife's feet.

She ran back inside the house.

Without a backward glance, he sped through an open gate and across the field by a decrepit barn.

Kevin started the Jeep. "Whatever happens, keep that camera on him."

"How are we going to avoid him seeing us?"

"We can't." The Jeep lurched forward, hit a low spot

10

in the pasture and bounced us like ping-pong balls. "I'll try to hang back only far enough he stays in sight."

We followed him along a rutted old wagon trail most likely last used by pioneers. The house and barn were no longer visible. But we were out in the open so clearly we should've been quacking.

Lang made a hard left.

"Hey, slow down. The camera is jumping all over the place."

"You've still got sight of him?"

Lang disappeared down a slope.

"Shit. I lost him." A flash of red. "Wait, there he is. I need to get up higher."

In a moment of brilliance, I said, "Can you open the sun roof?" just as Kevin unsnapped the latch with his right hand and slid back the glass partition.

He mumbled something about great minds thinking alike as I wiggled up through the opening and anchored my feet, one on each bucket seat.

Cold wind lashed my face. My ponytail became a thousand little whips. I ignored the sting and kept the video lens pointed at the red jacket bouncing across the bumpy prairie.

"Still see him?" Kevin shouted.

"Yeah. Think we've got enough tape?"

"Not yet."

11

Easy for him to decide. He wasn't up here freezing his nose and ears off.

We zigzagged behind Lang for so long I was sure we'd crossed the state line into Wyoming.

The distance between us had increased. With Lang familiar with the terrain, and us trying to stay discreet, he could easily lose us. I was kinda hoping he would.

"Hang on, I'm speeding up," Kevin said. He didn't wait for my reply before stepping on the gas.

The Jeep struck a pothole the size of a meteor crater. I managed not to let the camera sail from my hands, which were getting colder by the second.

Tears streamed down my cheeks from the bitter wind. I couldn't feel my nose. My ears burned. I braced myself as the Jeep angled down yet another steep slope.

Yet, I kept taping.

Lang kept moving.

I didn't know how much time had passed, an ice age possibly, judging by the frozen state of my fingers.

During that time, Lang hadn't turned and glanced over his shoulder. Not once. Weird. How did he *not* know we were tailing him?

When he cut to the right I realized why: his hot-rod four-wheeler wasn't equipped with a rear view mirror. Or any mirrors at all.

Kevin narrowed the gap.

I figured we had adequate footage. Plus, I suspected I might have hypothermia.

"Back off," I yelled down at Kevin. Didn't care if he thought I was a whiner. I'd had plenty of fresh arctic air today and the wind burned cheeks to prove it.

"You got enough?"

"No. I've been filming the goddamn scenery," I snapped, remembering too late the camera was recording everything, including my colorful observations.

Crap.

Kevin slowed down.

I don't know why I kept the tape running, even after we'd jerked to a complete stop.

But later, I was glad I had.

One second Lang was directly in front of us. The next, I watched on the viewing screen as the ATV hit a hole, pitched sideways, caught air, and sailed off an embankment.

Lang Everett popped in the air like a cork.

Everything in front of me switched to slow motion.

The tires on the four-wheeler spun madly mid-air, and Lang was windmilling his arms in the same manner.

Then both man and machine vanished with a loud crash.

CHAPTER 2

"WHAT THE FUCK JUST HAPPENED?"

"I don't know," Kevin shouted back and again jammed the Jeep in gear. "That thing still on?"

"Yes."

"Don't shut it off now. Hang tight."

The top of my ribcage smacked into the metal housing of the sunroof as we jounced across the field.

Once we skidded to a stop, Kevin took the camera. I climbed down from the sunroof and got out. When my feet hit the ground, he slapped the camera back in my palm and we raced to see why the four-wheeler had become airborne.

Although we couldn't see the machine, a high-pitched ghostly whine of the engine echoed from below. A thin trail of black smoke snaked up, carrying scents of motor oil and burning rubber.

At the vanishing point, I almost stumbled into the hole that'd caused Lang to plunge over the embankment.

Kevin righted me. We looked at each other and then over the ledge.

The ATV was tipped upside down. One of the back tires spun. The engine coughed, smoked, and sputtered before it died.

Was Lang Everett trapped underneath?

Images from my last encounter with dead bodies swam to the surface and I choked on the sour taste of fear.

"Julie," Kevin prompted. "The camera."

"Right." I swept the area until a red jacket came into view.

Lang had landed on his back twenty feet from the four-wheeler.

I watched for movement. None. "You think he's okay? Had the wind knocked out of him or something?"

"Maybe. Do you have your cell?"

I pulled it out of my left jacket pocket and handed it over.

"What's the number for the Bear Butte Sheriff's Department?"

"Hit speed dial number seven."

Beep beep beep. Kevin explained the situation to dispatch. The microphone on the video recorder picked up every word.

"Missy said the emergency crew would be at least twenty minutes. Can you see anything?"

I don't want to see anything.

Even as every instinct inside me rebelled, I focused on the prone form at the bottom of the draw.

My stomach pitched. Lang's eyes were wide open in sightless terror. Blood ran from his gaping mouth, disappearing into his scraggly beard. Part of his bloodied tongue hung out. His right ear touched his right shoulder, making his neck bulge out like an over-stuffed sausage.

No doubt about it. Lang Everett was dead.

Kevin crowded behind me. "Looks like he might've broken his neck." His finger traced the body on the LED; silver ripples further distorted Lang's image. "His left arm is at a weird angle too." He tilted the camera up. "There's only about six minutes left on this tape. Put it on pause until the sheriff gets here."

"Good plan." I let the camera dangle by my thigh. Taping Langston Everett's final indignity seemed wrong. TV news ghoulish somehow.

Kevin sidestepped me to stare over the bluff. No psychic powers were necessary to hear the thoughts whirring in his head. When he said, "I want to go down and take a closer look," I wasn't particularly surprised.

I wasn't particularly pleased either.

"You don't have to go," he said.

"I can't. Not after . . ." I ripped my eyes from his and gazed across the undulating prairie, the once lush green and gold grasses now dead and dulled to brown. Ducks paddled across a half-full stock dam, oblivious to the opening of hunting season. The sun's warmth was hidden behind blue-gray clouds.

I shivered.

In the craziness of the last few minutes, I'd forgotten the cold. I began to shake and pulled my wool coat tightly around my hips, chilled to the bone by the late October afternoon and another up close brush with death.

Kevin, being Kevin, wrapped his arms around me.

I leaned into him and absorbed what he offered.

In the past few months we'd slipped back into our old groove, the rock solid friendship that'd sustained us before we'd become full-time business partners, before Lilly's death. Before I'd hooked up with Martinez.

Contrary to what I'd feared, our bond hadn't weakened in the months we'd separately dealt with our personal traumas and demons. The time apart had strengthened it, and strengthened us in the process.

"You okay?"

No. "Yeah. I think so."

He released me. With the toe of his boot, he kicked an orange dirt clod into the abyss. "Something about this doesn't fit, but I don't know what."

"I know what you mean." I pointed the direction of the farmhouse. "You want me to let Lang's wife know what's going on?"

"No. Stay here. The sheriff can handle being the bearer of bad news. I'll be right back." He turned sideways and inched his way down the steep dropoff, one booted foot at a time. Within seconds his head disappeared from view.

Good thing I wasn't expected to traipse back to that depressing farmhouse and inform the woman her husband was dead. Offering consolation wasn't my bag. Then again, he had smacked her around. Maybe she wouldn't weep and wail about his sudden demise.

Not your business to judge, Julie.

I dug my cigarettes and lighter out of my right coat pocket and lit up. The landscape provided the perfect distraction; a vista of beautiful, rugged, open country, with endless acres of rolling prairie, clusters of cedar and pine trees, a realm unmarred by civilization. I imagined it hadn't changed a whole lot in the last 100 years. Maybe even 200 years.

That thought calmed me somewhat.

Low hanging, colorless clouds obscured the view of the buttes twenty miles to the north. A crooked barbed wire fenceline dipped and wavered with the rocky terrain until it disappeared into the horizon. I squinted at the black specks in the distance. Cattle.

Cows had always outnumbered people in Bear Butte County, but this lonely stretch of land reminded me of how sparsely populated our state is. Not another neighboring ranch or house for miles.

Brought another question to mind: If we hadn't been following Lang, how long before someone would have found his body?

I wandered a few feet, to where our tire tracks intersected Lang's in the dirt. Odd. I didn't see animal tracks of any kind on the bone-dry earth. Just cuts, swirls and gouges of an ATV ripping up every possible square inch of ground.

An icy blast of wind whirled the powdery red dust around me, a sobering reminder of the severe drought we'd suffered for the last few years. No wonder there weren't tracks. Most wildlife had migrated to greener pastures.

I smoked. Crouched, snuffed my cigarette with my bootheel, and set the camera next to my feet.

The ground was cold, but hadn't yet yielded to a hard frost. Small clumps of pale gray-green buck brush had survived without regular precipitation. The plants dropped prickly, oval-shaped brown seeds this time of year. Those irritating burrs would attach to anything: clothes, hair, rubber, even plastic. I leaned back to see if any had stuck on the cuffs of my favorite jeans and lost my balance. Instead of pulverizing the camera, I twisted to the left and fell on my ass.

I wished my butt had still been numb. As I swung around and pushed myself up on my hands and knees, I spied a long, black strand half-hidden beneath a skeletal sage plant.

My fingers tugged at the frayed end until the string untangled from the branches. I held it up for a better view.

Weird. It looked like some kind of braided rope, weighted at the end with unusually colorful beads; the top was a small piece of leather. Although covered in dust, it wasn't faded, which told me it hadn't been out in this harsh environment very long.

Sirens blared. Tires crunched. Reality encroached.

I glanced up at the approaching emergency vehicles.

Two sheriff's department cars followed the ambulance. The swirling red lights gave the bleak day an illusion of color.

I pocketed the spent butt and wound the object into a ball before picking up the camera.

Kevin waited patiently at the edge of the bluff, his shoulders hunched against the bitter wind, his hands toasty inside his sub-zero Northface ski jacket pockets.

The ambulance crew climbed out, assessed the situation and dragged out a stretcher from the back end of the van.

As the crew picked their way down the incline, Sheriff Tom Richards emerged from his car, slapped on his hat and motioned for Deputy Al to stay behind and deal with the Chevy Cavalier barreling across the field.

June Everett I assumed. Probably curious about the commotion, angry with her husband, and clueless her life had changed forever.

The other deputy, one I didn't know, trailed after the stretcher and EMTs.

I swung the camera in position and followed the sheriff.

The sheriff demanded, "What happened here?"

I melted into the background to get Kevin's explanation and the sheriff's reaction on tape.

Kevin provided a summary of our objective and a detailed description of what we'd seen.

One of the ambulance guys shouted. I aimed the camera at him, avoiding shots of Lang.

The blue fringe ball on the man's ski hat bobbed as he shook his head. He touched his watch, signaling he'd call the time of death.

The young deputy snapped pictures, the excitement of the situation an unexpected bonus. He had to be a rookie; his whiskers were little more than dandelion tufts, his eyes clear and hopeful. Even his crisp uniform looked fresh out of the plastic packaging. That youthful optimism would be replaced with cynicism by year's end.

Sheriff Richards sighed. "You sure the man you were following was Langston Everett?"

"Fairly sure," Kevin said.

He removed his radio and told Al to detain Mrs. Everett for positive identification.

My stomach rolled the remnants of my lunch into a hard lump.

"Did it appear he lost control of the machine?"

"Yes, sir. One minute he was in front of us, then airborne, and gone the next."

"So you weren't chasing him?"

"No, sir," Kevin said. "We stayed far enough behind he didn't notice we were following him. In fact, he never even turned around." He pointed to me. "Verify it with the tape."

The sheriff glowered at the camera, then at me. "Collins, what are you doing?"

"Recording the events for our client, sir."

His hackles rose at my *sir* comment. "Shut that thing off."

I complied, only because I had a minute worth of tape remaining.

"You wanna explain why once again you're around when a body turns up?"

Would it be petty to mention I hadn't been around

when my *brother's* body had been found? Probably. I shrugged and clamped my teeth together.

"In the last six months this county has become a regular Cabot's Cove," the sheriff grumbled. "I see more of you now than when you worked for me."

His diatribe was interrupted by a shrill demand. "Move!"

Sheriff Al struggled to contain June Everett by blocking her with his doughy body without physically touching her.

Her clumps of black hair hadn't seen a comb, but she'd replaced the robe and bunny slippers with stained white stirrup pants and an oversized #7 Denver Broncos football jersey. Orange flip-flops with big yellow flowers decorated her bare feet.

My toes curled in my boots. God. Her little piggies had to feel like frozen sausages.

"You can't keep me here. I got rights!" she yelled. "Lemme talk to my husband."

Sheriff Richards doffed his hat and ambled toward her.

I didn't envy his task, though I knew he'd done the duty many times. Despite his intimidating size at 6'8", he was a compassionate man.

"Mrs. Everett? I'm sorry—"

"Damn right you'd better be sorry, Sheriff. You're trespassin' on private property."

"Mrs. Everett. Please listen carefully. I need to ask you to come with me."

"What for?"

"There's been an accident."

"Where?" She fidgeted, shifting from one flip-flop to the other. "What's that hafta do with me? I don't know nothin' 'bout it. I just got here."

"I need you to identify the body the ambulance crew is bringing up."

"Whose body?" She peered around the sheriff.

The low murmurs and grunts of the ambulance guys, the clatter of metal on rocks broke the silence as they hauled up the body strapped to the stretcher.

A body wearing a red windbreaker.

Comprehension dawned in June Everett's eyes. Her face went pallid beneath the cheek that still bore the imprint of her husband's hand. "Lang?"

Sheriff Richards nodded.

"How?"

"Appears Mr. Everett hit a sinkhole, lost control of the four-wheeler and went over that embankment. I'm sorry."

Her knees buckled. The sheriff caught her.

I wanted to turn away. Hell, I was tempted to crawl in the sinkhole and dig my way to China so I didn't have to witness this.

The emergency team called the sheriff. He spoke to

June; she nodded and shuffled behind him reluctant as a death row inmate.

Hushed silence followed. I knew what was coming, but you're never truly prepared for that initial outburst of grief as June Everett's shrieks rent the air.

The day that'd started like any other became cold, dark, and harsh.

Kevin came up behind me. Set his hands on my shoulders and squeezed. "Warm up in the Jeep. I can handle the rest."

"I'm fine."

"Jules . . ."

I shrugged until his hands dropped. "I said I'm fine."

He didn't push the issue.

I hiked to the ledge where the earth fell away. Across the distance mule deer grazed, their velvety ears swiveled to the sound of danger. Sensing none, they returned to foraging.

While the sheriff conferred with the EMTs, June stumbled around the front of the patrol car. She rushed Deputy Al, who'd been standing by as helpless and worthless as usual.

"Show me the goddamn sinkhole," she demanded.

"W-what?"

"Show me the sinkhole that Lang supposedly hit."

Al's cheeks burned bright red and he blinked nervously.

25

She shoved him. "Got no answer, do ya? That's what I thought. No one knows this land better'n me and there ain't no goddamn sinkholes around here! Been too fuckin' dry! So what was it that got my husband kilt?"

Sheriff Richards would slap the cuffs on her regardless of her crazed state of grief. No one pushed around his deputies.

"The hole is over here," I said loudly.

June's head snapped my direction. "Who the hell are you?"

"Does it matter?"

She gave me a wounded look so I gave her my name. "Julie Collins."

Mumbling, she headed uphill until she was close enough to burn me with the full wattage of her glare. "How do *you* know where it is?"

"Because I was here when it happened." I pointed to the hole fifteen feet away. "That's it."

She froze.

"What's wrong?"

She didn't answer right away; she stared in disbelief at the shallow pit. "Who dug that up again?" she said, almost to herself.

But I'd heard it. "Again? You *knew* about this?"

June's outburst with Deputy Al hadn't been an irrational expression of grief. Her observation had been dead on. This wasn't a sinkhole; the red soil at the bottom and around the sides was chunky and moist, unlike the dry dirt surrounding it. This hole had been dug recently.

If June knew the hole had been there, why hadn't Lang?

Her dull blue eyes met mine. Guilt. Fear. Pain. I recognized it and could do nothing to alleviate it in her or in myself.

I refocused. "June, what was in that hole?"

She shook her head.

Somber male voices carried on the wind. At least they weren't laughing and joking like some crime scenes.

Crime scene. Not the situation I'd prepared for when I'd rolled out of bed this morning. And I realized it was no longer my job.

I shouted, "Hey, sheriff!"

June grabbed my arm. "Don't say nothin' to him."

"If there was another reason why Lang—"

"There ain't no other reason. He hit that hole and died. He ain't gonna be any less dead if the sheriff goes pokin' around."

My mouth opened.

"Please."

Without waiting for my response, she peeked over the edge. Took a step and her flip-flops slipped, sending her sliding sideways toward the gaping maw that'd claimed Lang's life.

I lunged for her, grabbed the jersey and jerked her back. "Watch out."

June lost it. She threw her arms around my neck. "Get me away from here. I can't believe the son of a bitch went and died on me! What am I gonna do? Oh, God. Oh, Lang."

Her grief kicked me in the gut. With her clinging to me and bawling her head off like a lost calf, I slowly navigated my way down to the sheriff.

"What's going on?"

I attempted to shake her off; she'd become a buck brush burr, refusing to let go.

"I wanna go home," June wailed.

"I understand, Mrs. Everett. We'll get you there as soon as possible, but we need to ask you some questions." The sheriff's gaze raked her from bare head to bare feet. "Maybe you'd better warm up in the car first."

She released me.

I squirmed away. I didn't get far.

She grabbed my hand. "Don't go."

My initial response didn't make it out of my mouth, fortunately for her.

Did she want me around because I was the only woman present? Or because she thought I'd talk to the sheriff about the mysterious hole while she was warming her tootsies?

I needed a shot of tequila. Better yet, a whole bottle.

The sheriff drifted closer. I had to tilt my head back to look in his eyes.

"Julie, will you stay with her while we finish up?" He frowned. "Wouldn't hurt you to warm up."

Like I could say *no* now. When I attempted a smile, I realized my teeth were chattering.

June scooted into the back seat of the patrol car. I followed. The sheriff slammed the door behind us. Great. We were locked in. When I noticed his smirk through the window I understood that'd been his plan all along.

Bastard.

The police radio in the front seat squawked. June watched the ambulance drive away and sobbed softly.

It'd be less painful to beat my head into the metal partition until my ears rang rather than listen to her desperate, raw cries.

My head fell back and I closed my eyes.

Finally June stopped weeping and asked, "Are you a cop?"

"No, I'm a private investigator."

In the heavy silence, I knew I'd made a mistake.

"You said you saw Lang's accident. That means you were here before the cops. Why?"

Too late to feign sleep.

"Were you investigating Lang?"

Ethical dilemma. Lie? Pad the truth? Avoid? I was all pro at avoidance.

"Were you?" she persisted.

"Yes."

"What for?"

I turned and looked at her. "Insurance fraud."

And she appeared . . . relieved. That was strange.

"I'm not surprised. No one believed he'd gotten hurt at that stupid job. They all thought he was fakin' it."

"Was he?"

June thrust out her chin toward the window and stubbornly refused to answer.

Since she'd brought the subject up, I goaded her. "What did you two fight about before he took off?"

Her troubled gaze whipped back to me. "You saw that?"

"Yep."

"Shit."

After a time she laughed, a bitter grunt. "Ain't it just a kick in the ass that we was fightin' about that—"

My door opened. Kevin stuck his head in. "Everything all right?"

Great timing, Kev.

"Fine. June, this is my partner, Kevin Wells."

"I'm sorry for your loss, Mrs. Everett."

She waved him off.

"Sheriff wants to talk to you."

June and I looked at him. "Which one of us?" I asked.

"Both of you." He stepped aside and we left the warmth of the car.

Sheriff Richards motioned me over first.

"Did Mrs. Everett say anything I should know about while you were in there with her?"

"No."

His eyes flashed skepticism. "I'll tell you the same thing I told your partner; you're damn lucky you've got the tape to prove you weren't chasing Mr. Everett and didn't inadvertently cause his death. If not for that, I'd be carting both your butts to jail."

I blinked slowly. Think I might've pulled off contrite.

"That said, thank you for your cooperation today."

Ooh. So heartfelt.

"We've taken the tape as evidence. After we review it we'll get it back to you."

"What are we supposed to tell our client?"

"Not my problem." His lips twisted in what almost resembled a smile. "Have a nice day, Collins."

CHAPTER 3

KEVIN DROVE. I SMOKED. WITNESSING LANGSTON Everett break his neck had taken on a dreamlike state, which neither of us wanted to talk about. Without the tape, contacting the client could wait. Their case was moot now anyway.

The disturbing events led me to thoughts of my half-brother, Ben Standing Elk. Three and a half years had crept by since his body had been discovered in Bear Butte Creek. And for those years I'd been obsessed with finding out who'd slashed his throat and left him float-ing like discarded garbage.

So far, I hadn't found answers. The shame of that failure ate at me every damn day. The hole Ben's death left inside me hadn't diminished with time. Instead, it'd spread, slowly, like an acid leak that gradually corrodes even the toughest steel.

On a day like today I felt about as resilient as a gum wrapper.

Mired in dark thoughts, I brooded. Smoked some more.

The second Kevin killed the ignition he sprinted into my house. I'd warned him not to drink that last Diet Mt. Dew. But had he listened to me? No. Not my fault his back teeth were floating.

I bestowed an admiring glance on my gleaming new Ford F-150. Okay, it was a couple of years old, but it was new to me.

My crappy Sentra had become scrap metal during a case a few months back. Instead of replacing it with a practical, fuel-efficient car, I'd opted for a big, badass, black pick-up. Chrome running boards, gun rack, towing package, leather interior, sliding "beer window" and a killer stereo; this baby had it all. Minus the naked lady mud flaps. I'd removed those and the "Rodeo Naked" sticker straight away.

I'd embraced my inner cowgirl. Seems fitting to crank up my Gretchen Wilson CDs.

Yee-haw.

I wandered to the mailbox. As I flipped through bills —no cocktail party invitations for me—a car parked on the road between my house and the Babbitt's.

A burgundy Ford Taurus with Arizona license plates. Maybe one of the Babbitt's kids had actually deigned to visit their parents. Maybe they could convince their asshole father to quit beating up their mother.

Not my business, at any rate. I'd nearly made it to my steps when a young female voice called out behind me.

"Please. Wait. I'd like to talk to you."

I turned. Not visiting my neighbors after all. What could she want? The last thing I needed today was a door-to-door salesperson selling junky wildlife art. It boggled my mind why my low-income neighborhood was a magnet for these types of cold call sales. They'd have had better luck selling gift certificates for the local bail bondsman's services.

Instead of pulling out a stack of framed pictures from the back seat, she'd unbuckled a small boy from a car seat and settled him on her hip. He pushed aside her thick black braid, which practically dragged on the ground, and buried his face in her neck as she hustled toward me.

A brightly colored gauze skirt swished around her ankles. Sensible taupe shoes were silent on the gravel driveway. My gaze roamed over the vibrant turquoise and magenta jacket she wore, obviously hand-woven and handmade. Striking, but not practical attire for a harsh South Dakota winter.

The intense hues brought attention to her black eyes, shiny as buttons. She was very young, twenty or so. Native American. I knew she wasn't Sioux, not because of the Arizona plates, but by the roundness of her face and the darker brown of her skin. Not a reddish hue like the Plains tribes, but closer to Mexican. It made me think of Martinez.

A friend of his? My feeling of unease increased.

The plump woman smiled nervously. "Are you Julie Collins?"

"Yes. Do I know you?"

"Umm. No, ma'am."

Ma'am? Made me feel like a geezer. "What can I do for you?"

"We have a mutual . . . umm, acquaintance."

"Yeah? Who?"

She murmured in the boy's ear, set him down on the sidewalk and handed him a toy metal car.

I waited for her to answer.

Apparently she was in no hurry to do so.

With my extremely crappy afternoon, I'd longed to snuggle into my couch with a thermos of Irish coffee— minus the coffee. I suspected I'd be standing here until *Letterman* came on if I didn't force her to get to the point.

"Before you tell me the name of our mutual acquaintance, why don't you start with your name?"

Her words tumbled out in a tangle of consonants.

"Run that by me one more time?"

With her accent, I heard gibberish and made her repeat it slowly a third time.

"Abita Kahlen." She'd pronounced her first name, *A-beet-a*, last name, *Kay-lin*. "That's my son. Jericho."

The little boy, around three, wasn't dressed for playing on the cold, dirty ground. Didn't bother him; he hadn't looked up from racing the Matchbox car back and forth.

"So, Abita. Who's our mutual acquaintance? Or is that a tactic you're using to try and soften me up to sell me something I don't need?"

Her brown eyes clouded. "No. I really am here to talk to you."

"I'm listening."

"Thank goodness. You're the only one who can help me."

My fake smile faltered.

Occasionally clients showed up on my doorstep, hoping if I met them face to face, heard their tale of woe straight from the horse's mouth, it'd compel me to take their case—for free—out of the goodness of my heart. Hadn't worked so far and it immediately put me on the defensive. "I prefer to conduct business at my office."

She frowned. "I'm not here for that. I'm here because—"

The boy shrieked as his car performed a loop-de-

36

loop over the toe of my boot.

Made me think of Langston Everett and I shuddered. I shoved the image aside and leaned down to pick up the purple mini-hotrod. As I handed it to him, the kid finally looked at me.

And I felt like he'd kicked me right in the stomach.

Holy shit.

This little boy had Ben's eyes.

My breath stalled. When my gaze wandered over his face I noticed he also had a hint of Ben's crooked smile.

Blood slammed into my head. Jesus. This was impossible. It had to be an illusion, or projection, or wishful thinking on my part, at the very least.

Didn't it?

My gaze flew to hers. But with my jaw hanging to my kneecaps, and no air left in my lungs, I couldn't speak.

Abita stared back at me. "Uncanny, isn't it? How much he looks like Ben?"

CHAPTER 4

A CHOKING SOUND ESCAPED FROM ME, AND JERICHO glanced up at me with alarm.

Looked at me with Ben's eyes.

There was that potent punch in my gut again.

"Is he?" I managed to squeak out.

Abita didn't play coy. "Yes."

Jericho rolled to his feet and wrapped his arms around his mother's leg. "Mama, I'm cold. We go now?"

They couldn't leave.

Somehow I made my knees bend and I hunkered down beside him. "I'd like it if you stayed."

He hid his sweet face in his mother's skirt.

I tried again. "Would you and your mom like to come inside? Have a cup of hot chocolate and some cookies?"

He peeked out, clearly interested. Then his dark

head disappeared again.

Abita said, "You don't have to—"

"I want to." I forced my greedy gaze away from her son. My brother's son. "We've got things to talk about, don't you think, or you wouldn't have come here."

She nodded.

Before I stood, Jericho bravely inched closer to me. I didn't dare move.

His hazel eyes were on my hair. Like all impulsive little kids, when he saw something he wanted, he just reached out and touched it. "Pretty," he said softly.

My breath caught, startling him back to the safety of his mother's skirt.

"Sorry. He's kinda curious."

"It's okay," I said, thinking of Martinez's obsession with my hair. "I'm used to it." I offered my hand, using the ruse that worked with my seven-year old neighbor, Kiyah. "I have mini-marshmallows. I'll even let you put in as many as you want."

Jericho's head popped out like a prairie dog's. "Really?"

"Really."

He ignored my hand and tugged Abita toward the steps by her skirt. "Mama. Come on."

I breathed a slow sigh of relief. Once they were inside, I wouldn't let them leave until I had some damn answers.

Kevin was slumped in the recliner, drinking my

beer. He gave me a strange look, but ever the gentleman, he left his comfy spot and rose to his feet.

"Abita," I said, "this is my partner, Kevin Wells."

"Nice to meet you," Abita said.

"The pleasure is all mine." He smiled. "Who's this little guy?"

Jericho lifted his head and looked right at Kevin.

"Holy crap," Kevin said, easing some of my doubts that I'd imagined the resemblance between the boy and Ben.

"Sorry." Kevin sent Abita a sheepish smile. "He looks so much like . . ." His eyes connected with mine.

"Ben."

"You knew Ben too?" Abita asked.

"Yes." Kevin hadn't looked away from me.

"I'm fine."

"Where's the marshmallows?" Jericho demanded.

"In the kitchen." I said to Kevin, "I promised Jericho hot chocolate."

We marched into my little kitchen. Abita and Jericho sat at my chrome dinette.

I scrounged around in the back of the canned goods cabinet and snagged three boxes of Girl Scout Thin Mint cookies. Not my favorite, but I was a sucker for the neighborhood girls looking so official and proud in those ugly uniforms, I ended up with a dozen boxes every year.

On autopilot, I grabbed the bottle of Hershey's chocolate syrup and milk from the fridge. Kevin unhooked a saucepan from the hanging pan rack. We worked in tandem like an old married couple. He matched up the cups and saucers; I lined the spoons and marshmallows on the serving tray. It felt normal until I glanced over and saw a mini-Ben staring at me.

My hands shook. Kevin gently took the tray.

Jericho slid me a sly smile and proceeded to put eleven mini-marshmallows in his cup.

Cheeky little thing.

We didn't bother to fill the empty air with mindless chatter.

Once Jericho had slurped the last glob of chocolate and stuffed eight more marshmallows in his mouth, I decided I'd waited long enough. "Do you let him watch cartoons?"

"Sometimes. Why?"

"Because we need to talk and it might be easier if he was otherwise occupied."

"Mama, I wanna watch 'toons!"

Her nervous gaze flicked to the door.

"The TV's in the living room. You can put your chair in the doorway, so you can keep an eye on him if you'd like," I added as an incentive.

Kevin helped her get Jericho situated. I stayed in the kitchen, adding a healthy shot of peppermint schnapps to my hot chocolate. I fired up a smoke. For the briefest moment, the taste combo brought me back to high school.

Abita returned and primly sat in the same chair she'd vacated.

I'd cracked the kitchen window and wiggled my backside into the countertop. I was too restless to sit. Pacing irritated the shit out of me even when I did it.

"How long have you two been partners?" Abita asked.

"About seven months."

She frowned at Kevin. "But, you said he knew Ben. How, if you've only been together a short time?"

Kevin laughed. I choked on an exhale.

"Julie and I are business partners. But we've been friends since we were twelve, so I knew Ben."

"Oh." Abita blushed. "Sorry. When you said 'partners' I assumed . . ."

"Natural mistake," he assured her.

An assumption most people made. In years past we went out of our way to convince skeptics we really *were* just friends. But in the last few months, we'd stopped the denial. Kevin and I had a long-term intimacy that defies explanation. If our relationship confused the hell out of us, why should we bother to clarify it for others?

"What is your business?"

"We're private investigators."

She blinked. A garbled phrase, which sounded suspiciously like foreign cuss words, tumbled out of her mouth as she made a circle on her forehead.

"Excuse me? What did you say?"

"It's a Hopi saying. Loosely translated, it means, 'Coincidence is fate in disguise'."

I shivered.

"About six months ago I thought about hiring a PI to find you, Julie."

"Is that how you found her?" Kevin asked.

"No." She looked at me. "The casino explosion in South Dakota was big news in the Indian newspapers across the country, including Arizona. I recognized your name. Ben mentioned you often enough, but he'd said you lived in Minneapolis and I didn't know your married name. So it kinda threw me that you hadn't changed it."

I hadn't taken my ex-husband's name. Julie Tooley? Eww. No thanks.

Abita added. "So I convinced myself I wouldn't be able to find you even if I tried."

I sucked in a deep drag. Blew it out. Decided to push her a little to see if she'd wobble. "You could've gotten in touch with me through our father at any point. His name hasn't changed."

"I know." She glanced at her hands, tidily folded in her lap, and clammed up.

43

Shit.

Kevin said, "I know Julie has a million questions, so why don't we start with the most obvious one? How did you meet Ben?"

Thank God Kevin was here. He'd keep me focused and if things turned ugly, he'd stop me from doing something rash. He'd also hold me up without me having to ask.

"I met him in our village when he first visited my uncle." She cleared her throat. "I should explain that our village is open to tourists who want to come and have a real experience with the Hopi people. We're still primitive as far as most modern tribes go. Anyway, we've got crafting areas and a cultural center. But visitors are separated from our school, our houses, and the ceremonies aren't part of the tour."

"Did Ben live there?"

"Not at first, he lived on the Navajo reservation about 100 miles south. He'd come to Arizona specifically to see how the Navajo Casinos were run. But after a couple of months he tired of the politics and stuff and was interested in how our Hopi leaders are able to sustain our tribe's treasury without gaming. He moved in with my uncle."

My cigarette froze halfway to my mouth. "Without gaming? But I thought there were tons of Indian casinos in Arizona?"

Abita nodded. "There are. However, our tribe is not part of the other Arizona tribes who have a gambling compact with the state. We're a bit of an anomaly. Bit of a throwback to the 'old ways.' Some of our members don't even have electricity."

Working with the Navajo? Then living with the Hopi? Ben hadn't told me why he'd gone to Arizona. His lack of disclosure about that part of his life still hurt me.

I squeezed my eyes shut. Would I ever be able to think of Ben and not associate it with pain?

Metal chair legs screeched on the linoleum. I sensed Kevin in front of me. "You okay?"

I shook my head.

"Let me have this before you light yourself on fire." He removed the cigarette from between my fingers. I'd forgotten it was even there.

Abita said, "I didn't mean to upset you. I'll go. I'm sorry."

I opened my eyes and leaned sideways around Kevin's to look at her. "Don't go. I've tried for years to get *any* kind of information on Ben. Now you're here . . ." My voice cracked.

"I'll just go check on Jericho." Abita scooted from the kitchen.

"You're starting to hyperventilate, babe. Calm

down. She'll tell you what you want to know. But you won't learn a damn thing if you're passed out on the floor." He grabbed the bottle of Don Julio.

Whoo-yeah. Sanity in a jug.

Kevin poured a generous amount of silver liquid in my empty mug and handed it to me.

I knocked it back. Not the best way to drink $100 tequila. But the smooth fire blended surprisingly well with the chocolate.

Abita probably thought I was some kind of freak. But as long as she told me every detail about the last months of Ben's life, I honestly didn't care what she thought of me.

"Everything all right?" she asked, hovering in the doorway.

"Fine," Kevin answered. "Julie just needed a break. Go ahead and finish what you were telling us."

She returned to her chair. "I don't remember where I was."

A laugh track blared from the living room. She gave the wall a narrow-eyed look, as if she could see through the sheetrock.

"What Ben was doing in your village," Kevin prompted.

"Oh. He mostly tagged along with my Uncle Wendell. They were always going on about boring business stuff, mostly about what he'd been doing working in

46

some new casino outside Big Pine. That Navajo tribe has bingo and a Class 3 Gaming license, but it is a commute from our village."

From working with our biggest client, Greater Dakota Gaming, I knew Class 3 Gaming meant slot machines on the premises, as well as dog and horse betting.

"You know what I don't get?" Kevin looked as if he'd been mulling everything over. "Ben hadn't been involved with any of the tribal casinos around here. Seems a strange career direction for him."

"That's not entirely true," Abita said. "Some tribal organization back here had sent him to Arizona to learn the casino business from the inside; that's why he was working in the Navajo casino."

Another piece of news I hadn't known. "What tribal organization?"

"I don't know if he told me. At any rate, I really don't remember. When we were together, we didn't talk about casino stuff." She blushed.

"What did you talk about?"

She blushed harder. "Everything. Nothing. He'd come in and watch me weave. We started out friends. Although my tribe holds to the old traditions, no one thought anything of letting us spend time together."

"Why not?"

"I was—I am pretty shy. I've never had the type of

face or figure that men notice. Besides, Ben was in his late thirties, I was seventeen; he was old enough to be my father, so we were basically unchaperoned.

"We kept it our secret for months. Before he went back to South Dakota, he promised to come back. He promised we'd be together." Abita gazed at the wall, lost in the past. "A month went by and I hadn't heard from him. I was mad, especially when I found out I was pregnant a few weeks after he left.

"I didn't know who to call, what to do, and I didn't have any money, so I did nothing. When it got back to us he'd been murdered, then I was scared to death. Nothing like that had ever happened to me before, or to anyone I'd known."

Some might say death is death, but violent death opens up a whole different set of questions and problems.

"My family found out I was pregnant and sent me away. I'd intended to give the baby up for adoption, until I learned more Indian babies were up for adoption than there were Indian families who could adopt. After Jericho was born I knew I could never give him up."

Kevin set a box of Kleenex on the table between us. Abita dabbed her eyes.

I didn't know what to say. I'd figured she'd tell me a sob story about how my brother had done her wrong. Not once had she played the "poor me" card. She didn't seem to be living in sorrow and self-pity either.

"Abita, after keeping Jericho a secret for three years, why are you in South Dakota now?"

"Curiosity."

I blinked with confusion.

She added hastily, "Back to the 'coincidence is fate in disguise' school of thought. There's a master weaver from Norway who hosts classes every couple of years. I applied, but didn't count on getting in. It seemed like a sign when my application was selected."

The weaver she spoke of was highly sought after to teach seminars all over the world. Abita must be a talented weaver to be asked to study with a master at such a young age.

"How long will you be here?"

"A couple of weeks."

"Where are you staying?"

"In a dorm at the business college in Rapid City. There are other women in the program who also have children so there's even daycare."

Through the tightness in my throat I asked, "Have you contacted the Standing Elk family?"

"No."

"Do you plan to?"

"I don't know."

"You should. They have a right to know about Jericho."

Shy Abita disappeared beneath a shrewd gaze. "Does the right to know extend to your father?"

That floored me.

Abita unfolded from the chair. "I should go."

"Hang on." I rifled through my purse for a business card. I neatly wrote down my home and cell phone numbers on the back. "You will come back? Stay in touch?" I asked as I handed her the card. What I really meant was: you won't take the one link I've got to Ben and vanish?

"When I can. The schedule is tough and when I'm done with classes I've have to take care of my son. I'm not used to being away from him for so many hours at a time during the day. It's all very . . . strange."

"And I'll bet it makes for a long day," Kevin said.

She smiled at Kevin. "It does."

Jericho ran into the kitchen. "Can I have 'nother marshmallow?"

I crouched down. "Do you promise to come back and visit me if I give you one?"

He nodded warily.

"Okay. Open your mouth and close your eyes and you will get a big surprise."

He giggled and squeezed his eyes shut, only peeking once.

I popped two marshmallows in his mouth.

He chewed. Swallowed. Grinned. His sticky hands

slapped my cheeks. "You're funny."

Jericho turned and ran. Abita chased after him, tossing out, "Thank you for the hot chocolate. I'll call you soon."

My fingers gripped the counter. I needed something solid to hold onto because my whole world had just been tossed upside down.

CHAPTER 5

I don't know why I was crying. Bawling never solved a damn thing. Plus, I felt stupid because I should've been overwhelmed with joy that a part of Ben had lived on, not crying like a sissy girl.

Kevin steered me to the living room and plopped me on the couch. I wallowed in his concern for . . . oh, about one minute . . . before I surrounded myself with my own brand of comfort: several mouthfuls of Don Julio chased by the fizzy goodness of Coors.

My eyes watered when I knocked back shot #5.

"Maybe you oughta lay off the tequila," Kevin said. "I haven't seen you cry this much since the day you squared off with Leanne about Kiyah last spring."

His hand froze in the box of Triscuits. Our eyes met in remembrance of a steamy kiss that wasn't unwanted, just untimely.

He glanced away quickly and rammed a stack of crackers in his mouth.

We'd never discussed our lapse in judgment. It was pointless now.

I smoked until his discomfort evaporated and the booze loosened my tongue. "Does this day seem surreal to you? Or is it just me?"

"Abita showing up with Ben Junior? Or watching Lang Everett end up in the pit of despair?"

Kevin's sense of humor always made me smile. "Both, I guess. Maybe it's selfish, but I'm thinking more of Abita and Jericho. What was your impression of her?"

"Damn young. But, at the same time, she seems wise beyond her years." Kevin dusted cracker crumbs from his shirt. "However, I don't think it's coincidental she's here now. What was your gut feeling?"

"Besides that she didn't try very goddamn hard to find me to tell me I had a nephew?"

"Would that've made a difference, Jules?"

I hated that he had a point. "No. It just seems so . . . soap-opera-ish. A secret love child. The father dies under mysterious circumstances. The mother fears for her life, so she keeps the child hidden until it suits her purposes, whatever those nefarious purposes may be."

Kevin's eyes narrowed. "She didn't say anything like

that."

"She didn't have to."

"What if she opts not to contact Ben's family?"

I tipped my beer to him. "More power to her."

"Seriously? Then I take it you won't be running to Doug with the news he's a grandfather?"

"Fuck off."

Kevin grinned. "I'm just saying . . ."

"You're talking out your ass trying to piss me off so I'll stop bawling."

"Hate to tell you, babe, but it's working."

True. My eyes were dry, even when my head spun, a combination of tequila and a merry-go-round of what-ifs. I rested my head in the couch cushions and closed my eyes. "Thanks."

"Anytime."

I needed to stop fixating on Abita and Jericho. My mind wandered. Oh joy. The other disturbing events pushed to the forefront. "Kev, what do you think was in that hole at the Everett place?"

"Doesn't matter. Our main concern is getting the tape from Sheriff Richards and turning it over to Rush-more West so we can get paid."

"That's it? You're not the least bit curious?"

"Only in that it'll prove we weren't at fault for his death."

I lifted my head and stared at him. "You used to love to figure out shit like this. What happened?"

"Serious, real life, pay-the-bills shit happened." He sighed and dragged a hand through his hair. "I hate to bring this up. I know tomorrow is Saturday and we've both been putting in a ton of hours, but we need to clear our desks before next week. In the next ten days Greater Dakota Gaming is sending us a huge roster of potential employees for their California operation."

Ninety percent of our business involved finding information for companies on potential employees, partnerships, verifying employment histories. Boring as that might sound, it kept us busy as bees and in the black.

"I thought they had an investigative firm in LA who handled that end of things."

"Evidently we're considerably cheaper so they're outsourcing to us. Could be slim pickin's in the next few months so we need to hedge our bets and pad our bank account."

"They give you a timeframe?"

"As soon as possible."

No complaint from me. My salary as a fulltime PI more than paid my bills. It wasn't like I'd had much of a social life in the last two months anyway.

Kevin shrugged into his jacket. "I've got meetings with three new potential clients in the next week. I wanted to make sure we're caught up first."

"I'll hold down the fort while you're out schmoozing."

"You gonna be okay tonight?"

"Yeah. I'm wiped. Since we're working tomorrow I'll probably just go to bed." Alone. It'd be nice to have the distraction of a warm body next to me.

Kevin read my transparent thoughts. "Any idea when Martinez will be back?"

I shook my head.

"Call me if you need anything. See you in the morning."

I set my home alarm system and indulged in a long, hot shower. After self-medicating myself with more tequila, I crawled in bed and fell into a surprisingly dreamless sleep.

☠ ☠ ☠

The next morning line two rang, which meant Kevin was on line one.

"Wells/Collins Investigations. How may I help you?"

Cough cough. "I'm lookin' for Julie Collins," the female slurred.

I couldn't identify the voice. "This is Julie."

"Don't sound like you."

"Who's this?"

"June." I heard her exhale, or rather, hack up a lung. "June Everett."

God. I needed to quit smoking. June wasn't that much older than me. How long before my voice became that raspy wheeze?

"Hey, June. How are you doing?"

"Shitty." A couple of loud sniffs.

"What can I do for you?"

"Got to thinking and realized I never said thanks to you. For yesterday. When Lang . . ." A rumbling laugh. "Can't even make myself say it. You didn't feed me a buncha bullshit 'bout why you was really out here. I 'preciate it."

What the hell was I supposed to say? "You're welcome?"

Another gravelly laugh dragged into silence.

"June? Is there anything else?"

She sighed. "Yeah. I was feelin' guilty that I didn't tell the cops everything yesterday."

"Whoa. Stop right there. I'm obligated to report anything you tell me."

"I know."

A snick of a carbonated can echoed in my ear. My gaze traveled to the hand-painted saw blade clock on the wall—a birthday gift from my pawn shop owning, weapons dealing, half-psycho friend Jimmer. Was June sucking down a couple of cold ones? At 10:00 in the morning?

Granted, it was a Saturday. "June, are you drinking?"

"Wouldn't you be?"

No self-righteous answer tumbled from my mouth.

"I miss him," she said softly.

I *so* did not want to deal with this. "What is it you want to tell me?"

"It's 'bout the hole that killed Lang. Remember I said I didn't know why it was there? You looked at me funny, like you knew I was lyin'. And I was." *Slurp slurp.* "Lyin', that is."

Dealing with a drunken, grieving woman wasn't an auspicious start to my workday. Yet, something had bothered me about the sudden appearance of that hole and why Lang hadn't known it was there.

"Why did you lie?"

"Trying to cover our asses. Now that Lang is dead it don't seem so important." She coughed. "So despite my constant drunken state in the last twelve hours, I'm confused on why someone would go diggin' that up again."

I counted to ten. "Digging what up?"

"Them bones that was buried there."

"What?"

"Human bones were buried on that ridge. We didn't know what to do with 'em, so we sort of covered 'em back up and . . ." She sniffed. "Lang wanted to call the cops. None of the rest of us did. Thought we'd wait and see

58

what happened. And look what happened. My husband is dead."

My brain had gotten stuck on the word *bones*.

"Can you come out here? And I'll tell you everything before we go talk to the sheriff? You seemed to know him."

"I worked for him for three years," I said absentmindedly, thinking about bones and who she'd meant by the *rest of us*.

June made that chuckle-cough-growl sound again. "Well, your partner is a might easier on the eyes than Richards. Don't blame you for switchin' jobs."

A natural reaction to Kevin. Sometimes I forgot he was such a head-turner. I didn't see his face anymore as much as his soul. "June, I'm not sure about this." Might be selfish, but I did not want to spend my one day off with June Everett.

"It don't have to be today. Don't even have to be tomorrow. I gotta go to the funeral home later this afternoon. Probably won't be fit for company until Monday at least."

I didn't understand why she'd mourn a man who beat her, still I didn't envy her the task of picking out a casket. Selecting hymns. Writing an obituary. Choosing his burial clothes. Before I'd thought it through, I said, "You're not going alone, are you?"

"Nah. My brother Jeff said he'd go with me. He ain't exactly thrilled 'cause he thought Lang coulda treated me better . . . well, I know Lang wasn't perfect. We had our problems."

"Like?" fell from my mouth before I could stop it.

"Usual guy-type stuff. Same as every man I know—he had a thing for titty bars and porn. Stayed out too late and lied about where he'd been. Drank too much. But in some ways, he was the most honest man I'd ever known. He didn't hold back nothin'."

Including his flying fists.

Uncomfortable silence. "Guess that's a little too much information. Shit, someone's at the door. See you guys Monday afternoon." And she hung up.

Her phone call left me so frazzled I contemplated switching from coffee to tequila. But when I saw the towering stack of folders on the corner of my desk, I knew there'd be no numbing nip in my future.

Kevin strolled in. "You want to get a quick bite before the lunch crowd hits?"

"Where you thinking?"

"Tally's."

Tally's is an institution in downtown Rapid City —an old-fashioned café with a menu chockfull of home-made comfort foods. Kevin and I had eaten there a lot in the last few months.

"Tally's sounds great." I stood. "I can fill you in on my phone call from June Everett."

He groaned and helped me put on my leather coat. "I'm not going to like this, am I?"

"Probably not."

CHAPTER 6

EVEN DOG-TIRED, I SHOT AWAKE WHEN HE SLIPPED INTO my bed.

Glad I'd slept naked.

He layered his smooth, hard body to mine from calves to thighs. Warm lips brushed my bare shoulder, sending a spine-tingling shiver through me. He draped his arm over my waist and spread his large hand flat on my belly to pull me flush against him.

I attempted to roll over to steep myself in his scent. His heat. To make sure he really was here and not just another damn dream. He tightened his hold, keeping me close, but keeping me in place.

"I didn't mean to wake you." He nuzzled the back of my head. "Go back to sleep."

I scooted into him and floated away.

🕱 🕱 🕱

Callused fingertips danced up the outside of my thigh. Insistent kisses tracked the curve of my neck.

I sighed. Shivered. Stretched. Opened my eyes.

Ribbons of pale pink light streamed through the blinds.

And those clever, clever fingers moved higher.

My blood heated.

I turned my head and caught his mouth with mine. Kissed him until his soft, slow breathing became hard and fast.

We rolled. He ended up on top.

Impatient, he swept the pillows to the floor.

I kicked away the quilt, the sheet, the blankets and everything else.

He clasped our hands together and slid them across the flannel sheets and up above my head. He held them there. Watching my eyes, he lowered his face until I couldn't see anything but him. Couldn't feel anything but him. Then he covered my lips with his and I was lost.

My legs parted and hooked his hips.

He drove inside me.

I arched off the bed, breaking the kiss on a gasp. "Jesus, you're good at that, Martinez."

His low rumbling chuckle reverberated though us both. Warm breath teased my ear as he whispered, "Missed you," and proceeded to show me just how much.

☗ ☗ ☗

Coffee brewed while he showered. I gazed out the back door at the frost sparkling in the field behind my house. A flock of turkeys pecked the hard ground; tan and gray feathers flew as they fought for bits of nothing.

The weather had changed. Seemed like a lot had changed in the endless days Martinez had been gone.

Was he interested in what I'd been doing? Would he care about Jericho's appearance in my life? Would he tell me anything about the Hombres' meetings he'd had in Denver?

By unspoken agreement, we avoided business discussions. At times it made me crazy, the separation of our private lives from our public selves. It didn't seem to bother him. And I'd sound needy and desperate if I brought it up.

Screw that.

The kitchen floor behind me creaked. Martinez circled his arms low on my waist and shrouded his face with my hair. "You didn't have to get up."

"Someone had to make coffee."

"It can wait."

"Mmm." I leaned against him. "Why aren't you racing out of here like usual?"

He pushed aside my tangled mane, rubbing his freshly-shaven jaw against my cheek. "Because I've got nothing going on until this afternoon. *Late* this afternoon."

My stomach swooped. "You *did* miss me."

"Yeah." He delicately bit the skin where my neck curved into my shoulder. The magic spot that shut down my normal brain functions and literally made me weak-kneed.

Martinez untied the satin sash and loosened the lapels of my robe. Leisurely, he ran his hard-skinned palms up my belly, over each rib, and cupped my breasts. "Come back to bed, blondie."

"We making up for lost time?"

"Something like that."

My robe slithered to the floor.

Coffee was overrated anyway.

☠   ☠   ☠

"Uncle." Winded, I slumped forward on his damp chest.

He casually dragged his fingertips up and down my spine.

After we'd caught our breath, Martinez lightly pushed

my hair from my face. "You okay?"

No. Between him being gone, a front row seat to Lang Everett's death, and finding out about Jericho, I'd been off balance. I wasn't surprised he'd noticed, but I doubted he wanted the gory details.

So I said nothing. I just closed my eyes and listened to the steady beat of his heart beneath my ear while I breathed him in.

"Julie?"

"Hmm?"

"Tell me what's going on."

Was he picking a fight? Already? I rolled away and perched on the edge of the bed. "Nothing."

Next thing I knew, he'd spun me and pinned me to the mattress. "Get off me, Martinez. I need to take a shower."

"Answer the question," he said in that deadly, don't-fuck-with-me tone.

"I did. Now let me go."

"No."

He had me at a disadvantage, physically and mentally, which I hated, which he also knew.

"Fine. You were gone, what? Two weeks? Why didn't you call me?"

Martinez didn't move a muscle. "That's what's bugging you?"

"Yes."

Coolly, he said, "I could ask you the same."

Deflect. Another tactic he used. "Yeah. Well. I had a lot on my mind."

"A lot besides me, apparently."

"Don't do this, Martinez."

"What?"

"Act like an asshole and try to make me cry. I've cried enough lately, all right?"

His mouth hardened. "You'd rather take a punch than shed a tear."

"No shit."

"So, who hit you?"

"No one."

"Then why were you crying?"

"Jericho, among other things."

"Who the fuck is Jericho?"

Was that jealousy in his eyes? "My surprise nephew. Ben's son. I didn't know about him until his mother showed up here two days ago. Evidently she was pregnant with him when Ben was murdered."

"You sure he's Ben's kid?"

"Jericho looks exactly like him."

Martinez rested his forehead against mine. "Jesus Christ. I cannot fucking believe the shit that happens to you. What else?"

"I saw a man die right in front of me while Kevin and I were on surveillance."

He flinched. Subtly, but I felt it. In a show of reassurance I let my hands drift up and down the tensed muscles in his naked back.

"You should've called me."

"What could you have done?"

His body stiffened and he pushed himself away.

Maybe it'd been a smarmy response, but I couldn't help the annoyed, "What?" as I perversely scooted closer to him.

Martinez palmed my head and coiled a hank of hair around his index finger. "Sorry. I've been a little on edge lately."

"Do ya think?"

"Smart ass."

"Can I ask you something?"

"Sure. Doesn't mean I'll answer."

My, my, wasn't he paranoid today. "Why don't you talk about your kids?"

His eyes flashed.

I'd shocked him. Good.

"Where in the hell did that come from?"

"After Jericho showed up, I remembered the first time we met in Dusty's, you'd talked about your ex-wife bleeding you dry on child support." I locked my gaze to his. "Since we're . . . involved, I deserve to know if any Tony Juniors are running around."

He stared at me for the longest time. "Not kids. Kid. I've got a fourteen-year-old son."

"You ever see him?"

"Not since he was two."

"Why not?"

"His mother felt my lifestyle wasn't an appropriate environment to raise a child in."

A strange band of jealousy tightened my gut. "Didn't she know about the Hombres before you got married?"

"Yes."

Silence.

Jesus. He was gonna make me fucking drag this out of him. "*And?*"

Martinez sighed. "And, one night our house was raided by the cops because of my position in the club. She took the boy and left Colorado the next day. Now we only communicate through our attorneys."

"What's your son's name?"

"Alejandro."

"Do you ever wish—?"

"No," he said curtly, which meant end of discussion. A calculating look returned to his eyes. "Why the questions all of a sudden, blondie?"

"Trying to piss you off, naturally."

Then he gifted me with that lethal smile that made my insides do the cha-cha. He traced my lips with the pad of his thumb. "I can't believe I missed your smart mouth."

I angled my head to kiss the inside of his wrist. "Is that why you're pissed off? You didn't want to miss me?"

"Maybe." He sighed again. "Anything else you wanna talk about?"

"Nah. I'd rather try to take that edge off you instead." I trailed my mouth over his smooth chest and down his abdomen. Lingered on the scorpion tattoo below his belly button.

"You trying to distract me with sex?"

"Mmm-hmm. Makeup sex is always hot. Is it working?"

"For now."

"Good."

"Maybe you really did miss me," he murmured, and it was a long time before he said anything else.

💀 💀 💀

Another workweek dawned. Mondays were always busy and I welcomed the distraction from obsessing over Martinez returning to town. Or obsessing that I hadn't heard from Abita. Obsessing that I'd seen my seventh dead body in so many months.

I'd just cracked my mid-morning Diet Pepsi when

the door to my office opened and shut softly.

That gave me pause. Kim usually left it open, hoping the scent of Shalimar and her throaty southern laughter would draw Kevin in. It usually did. I closed the document file and revolved my office chair.

Holy shit. Instead of the totally put together woman I admired, Kim was a disaster. She wore ratty purple sweats that clashed something awful with her burgundy hair. Not a hint of blush or eyeliner on her waxy face. Usually her locks were impeccably coiffed. Today it looked like she'd combed her hair with a toilet brush.

"Oh, God, Jules, I have to talk to you."

My heart rate kicked up. Her good eye was puffy and red from crying, which accentuated the creepiness of the glass one.

Kim paced, chewing her unpainted lip.

I circled the desk and nudged her toward the two cloth wingbacks, kitty-corner from the window. I drew the line at letting her sob in my beloved buffalo skin chair. Besides, I suspected she'd sat on a bag of Cheetos, as her butt was an odd shade of orange. "What's wrong?"

Kim's tears fell in a steady stream. "I'm pregnant."

I didn't move. I didn't breathe. I didn't know what to say. So I sat there like a dumb ass and let her cry.

Her Kleenex was little more than tatters. I found my wits and reached for the box on my desk, handing

LORI ARMSTRONG

her two.

"Thank you."

She blew her nose, not like a honking duck, but a delicate sniff, her perfect southern breeding intact.

Kim's good eye met mine. The glass one focused on my shoulder. She snapped her lids shut, reopened them and got it back in alignment. Weird to think she had a tracking type device in her head. Very *Six Million Dollar Man*.

I said, "Who?"

"Who what?"

"We're not playing this, are we?"

She shook her head, bowed it, and began to cry again.

"Come on, Kim. You brought this up. Who?"

"I don't want to tell you who."

Only one reason she wouldn't want to tell me: if I was acquainted with the father. I automatically dismissed Martinez. Kim wouldn't poach, and Martinez had an obsessive thing about fidelity. And blondes. And me.

Every muscle in my body went rigid.

Kevin?

How would I react if Kevin was the father? He was my best friend, my business partner, *my* Kevin. Yet, Kim was an attractive, gregarious woman. Kevin was crazy about her. I couldn't pick a better match for her, or for him for that matter. Still, the idea of them together

72

made me . . . strangely jealous.

I braced myself, and repeated, "Who?"

She blurted, "Murray."

"Murray? As in Murray, our dentist, Murray? Murray who has offices on the second floor?"

Kim nodded.

A hysterical, relieved giggle escaped from me. "Hey, I know you don't have dental insurance, but isn't sex an extreme solution for getting a reduction on your teeth cleaning bill?"

Her hands came up, covered her face, and she sobbed.

Sometimes I amaze myself with my bad timing and smart mouth.

I knelt in front of her. "Okay. Bad joke. I'm sorry. It's just . . . I didn't know you and Murray . . ."

"I didn't want you to know."

"Why not?"

"Because you're sneaking around with sexy stud, alpha biker, Tony Martinez. Going out with Murray Fetzer, DDS, seems a little vanilla in comparison."

That absolutely floored me. Didn't she know I'd give anything for some of that vanilla in my relationship with Martinez? It made me mad that she thought so little of me. Hell, made me mad that I thought so little of myself.

"Jesus, Kim. Why would you give a shit what *I* think?

Especially about your choices in men?"

Startled by my vehemence, she scooted back.

"How long have you been seeing Murray?"

"That's the thing. We've gone out off and on for the last couple of months. It wasn't supposed to be a big deal. I mean, we never even talked about us not seeing other people."

"Are you seeing another guy?"

"No."

"Is he?"

"Seeing another guy? Gawd, I hope not."

Color me glad she'd calmed down enough to crack a joke.

"I can't believe it. We were so careful." Her good eye went wide. "Except for that one time, when we stopped into his office after hours and he showed me his new adjustable chair."

"You guys did it in his dentist's chair?"

Her cheeks flushed.

"Hate to tell you, hot mama, but there ain't nothin' vanilla about that."

Kim crumpled the Kleenex in her fist. "This is so screwed up. I can't believe this has happened to me."

"So, what are you, a couple of weeks along?"

"Six," she said and ducked her head.

Another bout of clumsy silence.

"Kim, do you want this baby?"

"I don't know." She raised wet eyes to mine. "I'm thirty-eight years old. I've been with more guys than is probably healthy and I've never gotten pregnant. Not once. What does that say? What if it's a sign? What if this is my last chance? What if it's my *only* chance?"

"Are you going to tell him?"

"Not if I . . ."

Not if she had an abortion. I was relieved she hadn't automatically discounted that option. "And if you decide to go through with the pregnancy?"

"I'd tell him for sure."

"Who else knows?"

"Just you."

"If he walks away, are you prepared to raise a child on your own?"

"I don't know." Kim looked up. "If you were me, what would you do?"

Figured she'd ask that. "Think about it before I made a decision either way. But not for too long."

"That's what I'm afraid of. Murray is such a great guy, and if I tell him I'm pregnant, he'll want to do the right thing."

"And that's bad because . . .?"

"Because I don't want him to feel obligated to me."

Neither of us said anything for a while.

I wanted to smoke. I didn't. I had a feeling I'd better get used to not smoking around her and the baby.

That sounded weird to say even in my own head.

Kim sailed to her feet. "I'll go. Thanks for not freaking out. I know swapping secrets isn't your favorite thing, but I just needed to talk to someone."

"Anytime, toots. And no matter what, I'll respect your decision. You know I'll be here for you, right?"

Her eye teared up. "Wow. We have made progress. You actually admitted you care about me and didn't choke on it. Now I'm really scared."

"If you tell anyone I'm getting soft I'll start telling people exactly how you let your dentist use his tool on you."

She smiled and blew me a kiss. "Later, shug."

I fired up a Marlboro the second she left.

It boggled my mind that she was pregnant. Thrilled as I was to be the first person she'd confided in, it bothered me how she viewed my relationship with Martinez. It wasn't vanilla, but it wasn't normal by any stretch of the imagination, either.

After my divorce I'd avoided normal relationships. I wanted hot sex and nothing else. Can't be disappointed by bad relationships if you've got no expectations in the first place.

Not a disappointing thing about Tony Martinez.

So, why did I want more with him? I didn't want

to change him. Yet, would it kill him to take me out to dinner once in a while? Or any place besides Fat Bob's and my house?

I inhaled. Exhaled and stared at the ceiling.

Three months ago, after I'd wrapped up the case that'd brought Martinez into my life, we'd taken a week-long vacation in Florida. It'd been idyllic. No bodyguards, no friends, no business, no ghosts, just us.

We spent hours strolling on the beach, talking if the mood struck us, discovering our common interests, lazing in bed. Martinez redefined the perfect lover; he was attentive, aggressive, inventive, sweet, demanding, and generous. After the intensity of our hook-up, I think we both expected that week would be a fling. We'd burn ourselves out with lots of steamy sex and move on.

It hadn't turned out that way and by mutual agreement we felt we were starting something instead of ending it.

After our return to South Dakota, things went back to the way they'd been. I hadn't seen him at all during the Sturgis Motorcycle Rally, which had been my choice. The minute the bikes roared out of town, I expected he'd relax his guard and we'd do normal "couple" things.

Wrong.

We never went anywhere together in public. It drove me apeshit, until I realized that *was* normal for us.

Didn't mean I liked it. Just meant I'd let it slide until he either changed, or I got sick of it.

The door hinges groaned as Kevin strolled in. "What was up with Kim? She looked like she was crying."

"She was."

"Why?"

"Bad hair day."

Kevin frowned. "She okay?"

"Yeah. Makes her feel better to see what a screwed up mess my hair is on a daily basis." I crushed my cigarette in the seashell ashtray. "What's up?"

"Wondering where you were on the employment checks."

"Halfway through. Why?"

"Want to take a break and grab lunch?"

The phone rang. Kevin was closer to my desk so he answered it. In a clipped tone he said, "It's Martinez."

"Thanks." I grabbed the receiver. "Hey. What's up?"

"I need you to come to Fat Bob's."

"When?"

"Right now. Hang on. I've got another call. I'll explain when you get here." *Click.*

I hung up. I hated when he did that. Why had I been so upset that he hadn't called me when our phone conversations usually ran along those curt lines?

"I take it you have a better lunch offer?"

"Not better. Different." I managed a smile. "Can I take a raincheck?"

"Sure. Without being a pain in the ass, I'll remind you we're supposed to go out to June's at 2:00, so keep your afternoon delight brief, okay?"

I doubted there'd be anything delightful about Martinez' summons.

CHAPTER 7

You'd think being the girlfriend of El Presidente I'd get special perks, but no; I was still forced to enter Fat Bob's through the back door.

Big Mike escorted me into Tony's private office suite. We weren't alone. I gave Jackal—the new Hombres enforcer—a feral smile.

He growled.

Since I didn't smell food I doubted the gig with Martinez included lunch. Jackal acted like he hadn't been fed. It didn't help my frame of mind he looked as if given the chance he'd chew me to pieces.

Jackal didn't like me. I didn't like him. Big fucking surprise.

From the second I'd met Jackal my distrust had kicked into overdrive. Beady blue eyes, long rat brown hair and rattier beard, shaggy Fu Manchu mustache. He strutted around like a rooster with a corncob shoved up his ass.

Bad looks and bad attitude aside, what bothered me the most was Jackal's lack of respect for Martinez. The rest of Martinez' Hombres brothers—be they bodyguards or employees or patched in members of the club—treated him with deference. After all, he was the Commander-in-Chief, the supreme badass of the biker universe. He held the highest office in the Hombres organization: National President. His word was law.

Jackal acted like a law unto himself. He treated Martinez' bodyguards like idiot employees. He treated me like a low class whore. Oftentimes, and this is what fried my circuits the most, he treated Martinez like he was doing him a favor by working for him.

But it was none of my business. I kept my mouth shut, a difficult feat for me in any situation, especially when it came to someone I cared about.

Martinez kept me waiting while he finished up a phone call.

Jackal glared at me.

I ignored him and smoked. I wished Big Mike would bring me a beer or even a crappy microwave Chuckwagon sandwich. Hell, I'd settle for a packet of BeerNuts or a red-hot Tijuana Mama pickled sausage.

Martinez left his cell phone on the desk and saun-tered over. Instead of sliding next to me on the comfy loveseat, he straddled the hard-backed chair opposite the coffee table.

In front of others, Martinez stayed a respectable distance away from me and never gave any indication anything was going on between us.

But when we were alone, I couldn't pry him from my side with a crowbar. It bothered me and I felt ridiculous that it did. We were adults. I didn't need him to hold my hand to prove he and I were an item. Not that anyone besides Kim and Kevin and Martinez' bodyguards knew we spent nights together.

The sense I was his dirty little secret persisted.

I ground out my smoke and glanced up to see both Martinez and Jackal studying me like a science experi-ment. "What?"

"You said anything to her yet?" This from Jackal.

Martinez shook his head.

"So she don't know nothing about it?"

Again, Martinez shook his head.

"When did you plan on talking to her?"

"Hey, Jack*ass*, I'm right here in the room. You can talk directly to me."

His eyes glowed the demented yellow of his namesake. "Tell your bitch to watch her mouth or I'll muzzle her."

At times like this I missed Harvey, the former enforcer. God. I was seriously screwed up if I looked back on his death threats and sneering stoicism with fondness.

"I don't have to put up with his shit, Martinez." I shouldered my purse. At the door I remembered someone had to unlock this fortress before I could escape.

When I spun around, Martinez had boxed Jackal in on the couch. He was speaking in the low menacing tone that sent shivers up my spine.

Without moving his gaze from Martinez's face, Jackal recited, "Sorry, Miz Collins."

Martinez glanced at me over his shoulder. "Stay."

With a resigned sigh, I traipsed back to my lonely little corner of the couch. "What's going on?"

He paced to the desk and picked up a half-empty bottle of water. "I need a favor."

"What kind of favor?"

He and Jackal exchanged a "How do we play this" look.

Another weird feeling rippled through me.

"Have you done any bartending?" Jackal asked.

"No. Why?"

"Because we need you to—"

"Let me handle this," Martinez said.

I lifted my brows. Did he mean handle this situation? Or handle me? Why hadn't he asked this *favor*

83

when we were alone last night?

He sighed. "Someone is ripping me off. Cash drawers are coming short. Started out small amounts, but we're down more than $500 some nights."

"Has someone been watching the employees?"

"Not with any success. If I hang out, the bartenders and the wait staff are on their best behavior."

No kidding. No one would be stupid enough to steal right in front of him. "What about surveillance systems?"

Martinez said, "Security cameras aren't an option."

I hated to think it was because he didn't want physical proof of the Hombres' illegal activities. "What do you want me to do?"

"Work for me."

"Come again?"

"If you went in as a new hire, no one would suspect you were a plant."

"But I've been in Fat Bob's plenty of times. Someone is bound to recognize me."

"He's not talking about Fat Bob's," Jackal said. "He's talking about Bare Assets."

My mouth dropped open. "You want me to go undercover in a strip club? *Your* strip club?"

Martinez didn't even blink.

Jackal retorted, "At least he didn't ask you to go undercover as a stripper. Not that you could pull it off."

"Shut up, Jack," Martinez said. "You're not helping."

Evidently they'd discussed this option in depth before I arrived. I sat there and gaped at him. I didn't know what to say. Well, besides a resounding *no*.

My continued silence increased Martinez' agitation. His expression hadn't changed, but I'd been around him enough in the last few months to gauge his different moods.

"Say I agree. When would I start?"

"Thursday. I'd need to tell Crystal today so she can fit you in the weekend shifts."

"Who's Crystal?"

"The club manager."

"Won't she be suspicious if *you* tell her you hired me?"

"She brought the shortages to my attention."

"I don't know if I trust her," Jackal said.

Did he mean Crystal? Or me? I faced Jackal. "What's your part in this?"

He grinned nastily. "What part of *enforcer* is unclear?"

Martinez didn't deny he'd let Jackal handle the punishment portion of the situation. Then again, I hadn't expected him to.

"One problem: I know a helluva lot more about sucking down drinks than making them."

"Big Mike volunteered to give you a crash course," Martinez said.

Great.

"Most guys who hang out in Bare Assets drink beer or mixed drinks."

Seemed he'd thought of everything.

"So. You in, or what?" Jackal asked impatiently.

I glanced at Martinez, leaning nonchalantly against the wall—Antonio Banderas and a flinty-eyed young Steve McQueen rolled into one. "Why me?"

He sipped his water. Either he was considering his answer or he didn't plan on giving me one.

Which he knew drove me crazy.

"Are you asking me this *favor* as an investigator, Martinez?" I'd promised Kevin I would keep my relationship with Martinez on a strictly personal level. I hadn't told Tony in so many words, but I suspected he knew.

When he didn't respond and continued studying me in that unnerving manner, I felt entitled to provoke him. "Or is this your subtle way of getting the chick you've been fucking to learn some new moves?"

Without breaking eye contact with me, Martinez said, "Get out," to Jackal.

Jackal's boots hardly touched the carpet as he hustled to the door.

I said, "Stay right there." If the question made Martinez uncomfortable, all the better. "You brought this up in front of him." I pointed to Jackal. "If it is Hombres business, he deserves to hear why you think I'm the best candidate for the job. So, answer the goddamn question, Martinez."

For once he didn't hedge. "Fine. You ran a restaurant in Minneapolis. You know the routine, how to handle customers, what kind of suspicious behavior to look for, which is one of the reasons I asked you."

"And the other reason?"

He grinned. "No male bartenders at Bare Assets. Guys are more inclined to buy drinks from a hot chick than from another guy."

If he thought that "hot chick" comment and sexy smile would win him points, he was sadly mistaken. My eyes narrowed.

"Ooh, watch out, boss. She's going all self-righteous and feminist on us now," Jackal jeered.

Then I knew if I continued to push and argue, Martinez would lose credibility with his new enforcer. I realized that's exactly what Jackal anticipated, so I let it drop.

"You honestly think I'll fit in?"

"Yeah."

Not exactly the ringing endorsement I'd hoped for, but the bottom line was I wanted to do it. If for no other reason than to hear what Martinez' (female) employees thought of him. Was he an asshole who made them cower in fear? Did he take special interest in the skills of his dancers? Or did he audition them personally?

Pathetic, my petty jealousy, but there it was. "Fine. I'll do it."

The lines around his eyes relaxed. "Good."

Something else popped into my head, something horrible. "Unless I have to wear a G-string and pasties. Then no fucking way."

Jackal snorted into his beard.

Martinez shot him a look. "Bartenders wear black. Skirts, pants, shirt, whatever, just as long as it's all black."

Probably so they blended into the background and wouldn't compete with the strippers. With my flat chest that wouldn't be a problem; I'd be wallpaper.

"How many days are we talking?"

"However many it takes."

"Not good enough. Need I remind you I already have a job? I can't just blow it off to do this favor for you, Martinez."

"I'll make sure Crystal schedules you to come in as late as possible. But I'd like to have you on shift Thursday, Friday, and Saturday nights this week. Tuesday next week."

"After that we'll see. No promises."

"I'm used to the *no promises* parameters with you, blondie."

What the hell? Was that a shot at our relationship?

Before I demanded an explanation, Jackal said, "Big Mike's ready for you." He flipped locks, swung the door open and waited.

Martinez said, "Hang on," and pushed away from the wall.

I scrambled away before he could grab me. The second that man put his hands on me I'd forget why it wasn't the best idea on the planet for him to put his hands on me.

Talk about pathetic.

"If this is about lunch, forget it. I've only got thirty minutes left to learn how to make a proper whiskey sour."

Martinez didn't even try to argue.

💀 💀 💀

I'd actually told Martinez a little white lie; I'd been a bartender for a semester in college. Since that's how I met my ex-husband, I'd completely blocked the unhappy memory and refused to talk about it. Period. To anyone.

Big Mike didn't say a word about me being such a quick study. To show my gratitude for his discretion, I schooled him on how to pull a perfect draft beer. Of course, we had to drink his mistakes.

"What do you know about the set up at Bare Assets? Employees, customers, and all that jazz."

He rested his lower back against the cooler. "Busier than we are, especially on weekends. Different clientele.

Four bartenders from 8:00 until close. Four to six cock-tail waitresses. Three to five strippers. Two to three bouncers and one deejay."

"Are Hombres members used as bouncers like they are here?"

"A few are. Mostly Bare Assets is a good training ground for Hombres pledges."

"Pledges?"

"Guys who've passed the first tests of the Hombres membership requirements."

Tests? Membership requirements? "Like a country club?"

Big Mike's eyebrows squished together as he frowned at me. "You really don't know anything about the Hom-bres club, do you?"

"No. Martinez doesn't talk to me about this kind of shit."

"That's standard procedure."

"But under the circumstances, don't you think I should know some of it?"

He shot a look at Martinez' office. "That's not—"

"Please. Just the basic rundown. That's all."

"The Hombres are fairly exclusive, we don't allow just anyone to join. First step for possible membership is the interested party needs a recommendation from an-other club member. Then background checks are done.

Followed by a probation period where we test them on several skills."

Hmm. I didn't ask for elaboration on those skills.

"If all goes smoothly, we have a pledge ceremony. For the next year, they're basically apprentices — they do whatever we tell them to."

In other words: free slave labor. "And if they don't do what you tell them?"

"Instant dismissal. They're permanently ostracized by the members who recommended them. Biggest obstacle to completing the pledge year is family interference. Most pledges wash out before the probation period is up."

"Do you get many pledges?"

He sighed. "Way more than we can keep up with." His gaze snapped to mine. "It's against the rules for me to tell you how many members are in the organization, so don't ask."

"I wasn't planning to. So, what happens after the year is up?"

"The candidate gets to wear the official Hombres patch and is a full-fledged, dues paying member with voting privileges and other . . . responsibilities to the club."

I chewed on that for a minute. "Let's say someone gets patched in and after a few years wants to quit?"

"Not an option. Membership is for life."

Yikes. I changed the subject. "So have you ever

worked at Bare Assets?"

"Not since I was a pledge eight years ago, and only if I've got no other choice. Most times I've been in recently have been because the bossman wanted to check up on things."

Pointless to ask how often Martinez showed up there. He owned it, he was a hands-on owner at Fat Bob's, logic dictated he'd be the same with Bare Assets.

"When I go work there, you really don't think anyone will know who I am?"

Big Mike smiled. "No. Bossman keeps you to himself."

I froze.

His smile disappeared. "Shit. That didn't come out right."

"Believe me, I've noticed how little he and I get out."

We drank our beer in the dead silence, the bodyguard and the secret girlfriend.

I crushed out my cigarette and ducked under the partition. "Let's keep my previous slinging drinks experience between us."

Suspicion lit his eyes. As Martinez's bodyguard he considered everything a threat. Even little ol' me.

"It doesn't have anything to do with Martinez. Just bad memories I'd rather not drown in, okay?"

After a second, he grudgingly said, "All right."

I went back to my real job. I didn't share my upcoming moonlighting gig with Kevin. I wasn't getting paid, so technically I wasn't violating our understanding.

But part of me felt like Martinez had violated my trust just by asking.

CHAPTER 8

As Kevin and I rolled up the Everett driveway, I said, "Seems like I should be bringing a meat tray or something."

"This is not exactly a social occasion. When did you turn into Miss Manners anyway?"

"I've always been Miss Manners—mine have just been bad."

Kevin reached for the volume control on the CD player. Foo Fighters' *Gimme Stitches* faded into the background. "I have a bad feeling about this, Jules."

I did too.

The mangy dog bounding down the steps looked half Border Collie/half wolf. A ferocious bark meant nothing when I noticed the long, swishy tail wagging in welcome.

"I hate dogs," I said.

"You and me both."

Neither Kevin nor I were pet people, something pet people don't understand, and was useless to try and explain. I'm not talking about PETA fanatics. I'm talking normal people who boast about "loving all animals."

It bothered me that animal lovers were willing to spend piles of money on pet food, pet grooming, pet toys, and pet medication, wouldn't cross the street to give a homeless person a sandwich. Sobering, to think dogs and cats and are treated better than some children in this country.

A beat-up Harley Davidson was parked next to the Cavalier.

The dog barked twice. The front door opened and June stuck her head out. "Rusty! Shut up!"

Rusty turned tail and slunk around the side of the house.

Kevin and I looked at each other again. He mouthed, "Rusty?"

I bit my lip to keep from laughing. "Rusty" didn't have a speck of red fur. Made me think of the dog in *Family Vacation*. I made a quick survey of the area. We could've stepped onto the set of a low budget Chevy Chase movie.

Then I spied the smashed up four-wheeler and remembered this was no laughing matter.

A tall, skeletal man with stringy black hair stopped and glared at us. He wore a faded black T-shirt with the words LED visible beneath a red jacket identical to the one Lang had died in. "Who're you?"

June came up behind him. "These are Lang's friends from Rapid City."

Her red-rimmed eyes pleaded for us to play along.

"What're they doin' here?"

"Payin' their respects. Ah, this is my brother, Jeff Colhoff."

"Kevin," he said, thrusting out his hand. "Sorry for your loss."

"Julie." I followed Kevin's first name only lead. "I'm sorry too."

June placed her hand on Jeff's shoulder. "Thanks for coming with me today, string bean. Don't think I could've done it by myself."

Jeff crushed her in a bear hug. "Don't need to tell me thanks, Junebug."

June began to bawl.

Kevin and I were helpless to do anything besides stand and watch June Everett fall apart in her brother's arms.

I had to look away. Despite the sad event, they had each other. It was more than a lot of people had.

Kevin's warm hand grabbed mine and squeezed.

I squeezed back.

Finally, Jeff released her. "You need anything, call me, all right? Don't matter what time it is, call me and I'll be right here."

"Will Jeannie let you out of her sight?"

"You don't worry none about Jeannie. I'll handle her."

Jeff gave us one last suspicious scowl before he climbed on the hog and roared off.

"Sorry 'bout that," June said, wiping the tears from her chalk white face. "I wanted to talk to you guys before I said anything to him. Poor bastard is so goddammed henpecked a trip to the funeral home is a mini-vacation from his responsibilities. That woman he married has sucked the life right out of him. You'd never guess just a few short years back, ol' Jeff used to be the best lookin' guy around."

"You're lucky you have him to help you through this," Kevin assured her.

She nodded. "You wanna come in? Bit nippy to be talkin' out here on the porch."

"That'd be great." We followed her inside.

The smell of cat urine assaulted us at the threshold. Another reason not to have pets. At least candles and air freshener masked the lingering odor of cigarette smoke.

The interior of the farmhouse wasn't any better than the exterior. Stacks of newspapers were piled by the door. Once we skirted them, we entered the tiny living room.

A burnt orange sofa decorated with gigantic yellow flowers abutted the front windows. Two slate blue La-Z-boy recliners book-ended the couch and faced the big screen TV, which sat on a piece of plywood stretched across two sawhorses. A small electric organ took up one corner. The bench seat was mounded with more newspapers. Cardboard boxes packed with magazines were stacked to the ceiling.

The particleboard coffee table sat smack dab in the middle of the room, leaving little space to maneuver. Empty Busch Light cans were heaped three high on one end of the table. On the other end a dozen pill bottles teetered on top of a carton of generic cigarettes. A ceramic ashtray overflowed in the midst of the rubble like a white-trash centerpiece. Dirty bunny slippers were discarded under the table. Crumpled Kleenex spilled out of a pizza box.

"Go ahead and grab a place to sit. Want a beer?"

"No thanks," I said.

"Suit yourself. I ain't gonna pretend I don't need another beer after what I just been through."

June's pink robe dangled off the arm of the closest recliner. I perched on one end of the couch. Kevin gingerly pushed aside a red and purple afghan, mimicking my posture on the other end.

I shook out a cigarette and lit up.

June returned with an unopened twelve pack of Busch Light.

How much of that was she planning to drink by herself?

As much as it took to numb the pain.

Like I had any business judging her.

She cracked a beer.

Kevin nodded at me. Guess I'd be asking the questions. I inhaled, held it in until I felt dizzy, then exhaled slowly.

My eyes met June's. "Tell us about the bones in that hole."

Kevin sighed.

"Get right to the point, doncha?"

"Don't see why we shouldn't."

She tipped the beer. "Fine. I ain't gonna beat around the bush either. Lang always had something up his sleeve. He was one of those get rich quick kinda guys." She gestured around the cluttered room. "We ain't exactly livin' high on the hog. There's been times we've had to do some things we ain't proud of jus' to make ends meet."

Like faking a workman's comp injury? "What kind of things?"

"No kinda handouts from the government or nothin'."

I nodded. Folks down on their luck always felt compelled to make it clear they weren't on the dole.

"Anyway, we started out takin' money from guys so they could hunt on our land. Didn't matter to us none if it was the right season or not, money's the same color year round. Course, we had to split the take with Jeff. The ranch belongs to both of us, we didn't divvy it up after my folks died."

Chauvinistic that I'd assumed the land belonged to Lang, not June.

"After my dad passed on, we kept our resources pooled with the rest of my family, like it's always been."

"Who's the rest of your family?"

"Me, Jeff, his mean as a snake wife, Jeannie, Uncle Charlie and Charlie's son, my cousin Willie, and his wife Lindy. Charlie and Willie's ranch borders ours."

Kevin's eyes had glazed over, a sign I needed to get her back on track. "June, what does that have to do with—"

"Grow some patience, girl. I'm getting to it." She drained her beer and popped the top on another.

"With Lang being injured and out of work, things have been a little tight. So, a few weeks ago, when a couple of guys wanted to hunt on our land, we let 'em."

"What were they hunting?"

"Does it matter?" She chortled. "As long as they paid cash up front and didn't do nothin' stupid to get caught, they could hunt bald eagles for all I cared."

June Everett's attitude wasn't unique although those politically incorrect comments were usually implied, not stated outright.

"But, the stupid out-of-state assholes tried to set up a deer blind on the top of that bluff."

Kevin and I exchanged a look. A deer blind? Out in the open? No wonder poachers got busted so often.

"Anyway, they couldn't get the thing level and they started diggin' and scrapin' away the dirt and that's when they saw part of a skull and hand bone pokin' outta the ground."

Chills went up my spine. "Did these hunters tell you right away what they'd found?"

"Yeah. Couldn't believe a buncha rednecks who loved killin' stuff would go ballistic 'bout an old pile of bones. Me and Lang rode up there on the four-wheelers. Sure enough. Weren't animal bones, but human bones." June shivered. "Weirded me out, if you wanna know the truth."

"How long do you think the bones have been there?"

She signaled for me to toss over her pack of menthol GPC smokes. "Couldn't tell. Might've been a year, might've been a hunnerd." She lit up. "We didn't know what to do. While we was arguing, Uncle Charlie, Willie, Lindy, and Jeannie showed up to put their two cents in.

"Jeannie, Willie, Lindy, me, and Uncle Charlie

wanted to rebury them bones and forget we ever saw them. Don't need no cops snoopin' around on our land. Plus, the bones was found in a section that we all but abandoned the last six years during the drought."

I frowned. "What about Lang?"

"He was stubborn as a mule 'bout us callin' the cops." She flicked an ash in a crumpled beer can. "His brother Clint went missing in Vietnam. Never found no trace of him. Lang thought he'd be easin' some family's mind, but we convinced him it'd be best to rebury them. So that's what we did."

"If that's the case, then how did the hole get there?"

Tears glistened in her eyes. "That's what I want to know. At first it hadn't been dug very deep. Not like it was when Lang hit it."

"Didn't Lang help fill it in?"

She shook her head. "He couldn't because of his back injury."

What was the point of continuing the charade about Lang's bogus workman's comp claim? I glanced at Kevin. He was frowning too.

A gust of wind rattled the windows so hard it stirred my hair. I shivered.

June disposed of the two empty beer cans next to the others. "Sure you don't want one?"

I stubbed out my cigarette. "I'm good."

"Why didn't you tell the sheriff about the bones when he was at the scene?" Kevin asked.

"I needed to get it straight in my head." She wouldn't look at either of us. Then she sighed wearily. "That ain't true. Might sound stupid, but it pissed me off that Lang was dead. I told him not to get on that four-wheeler in his condition. Dumb son of a bitch wasn't wearing his glasses, either."

That explained his erratic driving that day, and why he hadn't seen us. "Where was Lang going?"

"Beer run over to my uncle's place."

"How far is that on the four-wheeler?"

"About twenty minutes. Less time to get to my brother's place, but Jeff's wife don't let Jeff drink with our family very much. Jeannie don't let him do nothin'."

"How far to your cousin's place?"

"Fifteen minutes."

"Do you know if Lang had been out there sometime in the last few weeks after the bones had been reburied?"

"No. He'd've told me." Her chin wavered. "And he sure as hell would've avoided that hole if he'd known about it."

I looked longingly at the beer.

"Do you know if anyone else—your family members—went back?"

She shrugged. "If they did they didn't tell me."

Kevin said, "What about the hunters? You think they could've brought some buddies out to the site to show off their gruesome find? Dug it up again to prove it?"

Evidently that scenario hadn't occurred to her. "No, they packed up their guns and shit and lit out during our family argument. Don't know what you'd find out from them anyways. Damn out-of-staters probably didn't even give us their real names. And they paid in cash so there ain't no way to track 'em down."

My patience was wearing as thin as her robe. "Somebody went back there, June. Who?"

Silence.

Kevin's cell phone chirped. "Excuse me, I need to take this call." He practically sprinted from the house.

Way to leave me with the surly widow, Kev.

June snagged another beer, hunched into the chair, and deeper into herself. She closed her eyes.

Great. Be just my luck if she passed out. "June?"

"I keep thinkin' I'll wake up and he'll be layin' beside me, fartin' and snorin' like usual." Her voice was a hoarse whisper. "I'll wake up soon and realize these last coupla days have just a bad dream."

It'd take weeks for that surreal feeling to lessen. Maybe months. But sharing my grief experiences wouldn't help her, so I said nothing.

"I miss him. I'm sure you probably don't understand why after seein' him slap me. But it's not what you think."

My well of empathy was only so deep—and she'd run it bone dry. "No? Explain why it was any different from all the other fucked up situations just like it, where a woman stays with a man who beats her?"

Her eyes flew open.

"Lang hit you. Wasn't the first time, wouldn't have been the last." No point in masking my frustration. "Have you convinced yourself you deserved it? He'd been under stress. None of it was his fault, right?"

She didn't interject objections. Fat tears dripped down her nose, reddened from booze and bawling.

I felt like a total shithead for berating a grieving woman. "Sorry. Look, Lang isn't calling the shots any more. You are. You're doing the right thing by going to the sheriff's office today."

June looked away quickly.

What was she hiding? I counted to ten. "Isn't that the reason I'm here? To hold your hand when you talk to the sheriff? Or is there something else you aren't telling me?"

"No. It's jus' . . . I been thinking. I was shitfaced and kinda jumped the gun when I called you."

"How so?"

"It might be better to wait until after Lang's funeral before we go traipsing into the sheriff's department. That's only two days. Havin' all sorts of strangers out there diggin' around for them missing bones . . . that ain't what I want people gossiping about on a day I'm buryin' my husband. Be an insult to Lang's memory, that some old bones were more important than givin' him a proper send off."

For once, she made sense. And honestly, I'd agree to anything just to get the hell out of there. My senses were overloaded with too many hideous colors, too many rank odors, too many stacks of junk, too much misery. "Fine. But if I find out you're putting off this trip for another reason, you're on your own. I won't help you where the sheriff's concerned."

Her lower lip stuck out in a childish pout. "You ain't as nice as I thought you were."

"And I'm not as stupid either. Keep in touch."

Kevin slouched against the truckbox on the passenger side. He wasn't even pretending to talk on the phone. "Sorry. I'd had enough. What are we even doing out here?"

"Hell if I know. Let's go."

We hit the Westside McDonald's drive-thru when we returned to Rapid City, and congregated in the conference room with our double cheeseburger specials.

Kevin said, "What is your reaction about the bones the Everetts found?"

"Gut feeling? Those bones are part of an Indian burial ground."

"Why?"

"Because someone came back and dug a bigger hole. I'm betting they uncovered more than just bones. Maybe Sioux funeral objects. Those kind of artifacts bring huge cash on the black market." And were illegal for anyone besides museums and tribes to possess.

Artifact.

Crap. "Hang on a second." I chewed a fry as I rummaged in the right pocket of my jacket and unwound the braided rope I'd stumbled over the day Lang had died. I set in on the table. "With everything else that's happened, I totally forgotten I found this."

Kevin's index finger traced the rope, down to the beads. "What do you think it is?"

"Not sure. But it's not faded, so it was buried with whatever else was in that hole."

"We have to turn this and the information about those bones into the sheriff's department." He looked at me sternly. "You know that, right?"

I nodded.

In the last case I'd worked on, I'd made a judgment call Kevin hadn't agreed with. Since my involvement with Martinez, Kevin erred on the side of vigilance when it came to trusting me.

Did it piss me off? A little. But his suspicions were entirely justified, especially when that line between right and wrong wasn't so obvious to me.

"Can we wait, though?"

There was that suspicious look again. "Why?"

"Lang's funeral will be over soon. It's traumatic enough for June that she's burying him, without the added stress of having people digging around where he died."

"Okay. But we don't wait beyond that."

"I agree. But, thanks." I fingered the rope. "Besides, another day or so will give me time to contact a guy I know who works for an agency affiliated with the Native American Grave Reparation Act. I'll call him and see if he can tell me anything about this."

Kevin frowned. "Who's your contact?"

"Ben's friend, Darrell Pretty Horses. Remember him?"

"Vaguely. Where does he live?"

"Last I knew he divided his time between the state tribal offices in White Plain and the national offices in DC."

Sadness punched my gut like a steel spike on a railroad tie. I hadn't spoken to Darrell since Ben's memorial service, a Lakota tradition that marked a year since a loved one's passing. At that time, the deceased's earthly possessions are dispersed.

The ugly incident still made my cheeks burn with

shame. Ben's sister, Leticia, had barred me from the cere-mony. Darrell had been the only one to stand up for me.

I hadn't wanted to make a scene, because the day was supposed to be about Ben. I sure as hell hadn't wanted one of his high school cross country trophies as a memento of his life. But as I'd huddled alone in the corner of the community center, two things had be-come abundantly clear. One: the Standing Elk family had no intention of giving me anything. Two: The only tangible remembrance I'd cared about—the necklace I'd given Ben—wasn't up for grabs. Nor was the other necklace, the old one Ben hadn't taken off in more than twenty years.

I fingered the braided rope and was immediately thrust back in time, to a sweltering summer night as Ben and I stargazed in the back of Ben's piece of junk pickup, sharing dreams and telling stories. Somehow we'd seg-ued into the subject of inheritances and family heirlooms and I'd asked about his necklace.

The Sioux are incredible oral storytellers. So as Ben detailed how the necklace had ended up in his posses-sion, chills raced up my spine. The story haunts me to this day.

Ben had befriended a lonely old man, a Lakota elder named Mida, who'd been diagnosed with terminal can-cer. During Ben's frequent visits, Mida told Ben stories.

Some traditional, some personal remembrances of his life. The most fascinating tale involved Mida's necklace, given to Mida by an old Lakota medicine woman, a survivor of the 1890 Massacre at Wounded Knee. She swore wearing the necklace had spared her life, but warned it only wielded power on the living. If the necklace wasn't handed to a living soul before the wearer passed on, it would lose its protective power. Mida also insisted the necklace had saved his life during World War II.

Sadly, Mida's condition worsened. Because Mida couldn't count on his family to visit him before he journeyed to the Great Spirit, Mida had given Ben the necklace.

Ben had been torn: to refuse the gift was an insult; to take it meant denying the eldest male in Mida's family the right of ownership. But Mida insisted the *necklace* had chosen Ben as the next recipient, not Mida.

At the time, Ben hadn't believed in the mumbo jumbo about his Lakota Sioux spiritual heritage, but he said the minute the braided leather and horsehair necklace, decorated with ancient bones, beads, and animal teeth had circled his neck, he'd known it contained mystical properties.

Mida died the next day.

Ben had waited for angry family members to demand the valuable family heirloom be returned. But no one even noticed it was gone.

It bothered Ben that Mida's family had been so self-absorbed they hadn't realized the talisman, which hadn't left the old man's mortal flesh for seventy-eight years, had disappeared.

Right then Ben had vowed never to take off the necklace until it was his turn to pass it on.

Had history repeated itself with the Standing Elk family? They'd had no idea what the necklace had meant to Ben? The missing heirloom bothered me too, because I knew Ben hadn't been buried in it. For the hundredth time, I wondered what'd happened to it.

I hated to imagine the necklace had been cut along with his throat. Were the beads and bones tumbling around in the bottom of Bear Butte Creek? Or had Ben's killer taken it as some kind of sick trophy?

Kevin interrupted my musings. "Hey, now I remember that name. Isn't Darrell the guy who popped your cherry?"

I managed a small grin. "One and the same."

"Didn't Ben beat the hell out of him when he learned his buddy had deflowered his baby sis?"

"Yeah, but once the blood dried, they got over it. I've been meaning to call him anyway to tell him about Abita and Jericho."

"Anything new with that situation?"

"No. She called last night. When I mentioned contacting Ben's family, she changed the subject."

"Why is that?" Kevin asked around a mouthful of apple pie. "Seems weird."

"Yeah. Part of me wants to keep Jericho a secret from them. Seems I'm well versed in keeping a dirty little secret. Or should I say, in *being* a dirty little secret."

His head snapped up. "What?"

"Nothing."

"Come on Jules, that's crap." Kevin peered at me intently. "Trouble in paradise with Martinez?"

"Some. I doubt you want to hear about it."

"Try me." Kevin's expression remained neutral.

In the past I'd usually regaled him with tales of my sexual exploits, but what I shared with Martinez was too intimate to joke about. So my frustrations poured out like poison.

After I finished venting, Kevin sighed. "Not to be a dick, but why is this a problem? You've been, 'give me an orgasm then get the hell away from me' with every other man who's bounced in your bed in the last few years. This sounds like your ideal set up."

I broke eye contact.

The silence between us made my ears ring.

"You gotta be kidding. You want more from Martinez than just sex?"

"Sounds crazy, huh? It's like we . . . fit, you know?"

No response.

"What?"

Kevin twirled the striped straw in his McDonald's cup. "I'm not sure how to say this without pissing you off."

"Then just say it."

He looked straight at me. "You wouldn't put up with this shit from anyone else, relationship, perfect fit, or not."

Bingo. "So now you know why I'm so wigged out about why I'm willing to settle for the little he's willing to give me."

Rather than face more questions—his or my own—I escaped to my office.

CHAPTER 9

THE PHONE RANG FOR ABOUT THE MILLIONTH TIME. Damn sledgehammer was never around when I needed it.

"Wells/Collins Investigations. This is Julie."

"Ooh. You sound so official, that's so totally cool. Oh, umm, this is Brittney."

Why was my father's eleven-year old daughter calling me? "I knew it was you, smarty-pants. What's up?"

"Nothing much, except I was wondering if I could ask you if you'd do me a favor?"

What was it with people asking me for favors? "Depends on what it is."

"Well, our class is having career day and I hoped maybe you'd come in and talk about being a private eye."

"Really?" Not what I'd expected. "When?"

"In a couple of weeks. Mostly you'd tell us what you

like about your job."

Today my answer would be *nothing*, after being emotionally beat to shit by grief and half-truths.

Sensing my hesitation, sweet little Brittney initiated the hard sell. "I already made up a list of questions, so you really don't have to do anything but show up. I can even drop them by your house. It'll be easy cheesy, I swear."

Strangely enough, I was flattered. "Okay, kiddo, I'll do it."

"Really?" She squealed. "I can't wait to tell my friends my big sister is coming for career day!"

The other office line rang. "Look, Britt, I've got another call coming in. Keep me posted."

"Sure thing. Bye."

I clicked over to dead air. I hoped it wasn't important.

👹 👹 👹

Although it was late afternoon, I called the number in White Plain for the NAGRA tribal liaison office.

"Assistant Director's office."

"I'd like to speak with Darrell Pretty Horses."

"Is he expecting your call?"

"No." I didn't elaborate.

Her tone turned frosty. "If you'll give me your name and number, he'll—"

"This is Julie Collins from Wells/Collins Investigations in Rapid City, regarding an artifact recovered from a potential burial ground theft. I'm sure Mr. Pretty Horses is a busy man, but why don't you tell him I'm on the line? I'll wait."

Sure enough, about a minute later Darrell's voice cut off the snappy saxophone/clarinet version of *Livin' La Vida Loca*.

"Is this *the* Julie Collins?"

"The one and only, baby cakes."

He chuckled. "And to what do I owe this honor?"

"To a couple of really bizarre things that have showed up in my life recently."

"My secretary said something about a burial ground theft?"

"That's the first thing. The other day I found this long braided object, with beads on one end. It looks like an Indian artifact, a rope of some kind."

"Where'd you find it?"

"About fifty yards from where someone had recently dug a hole, filled the hole, then dug it out again."

"Private or public land?"

"Private."

He paused. "I don't mean to be condescending, but why would NAGRA be interested in this situation?"

"Because in addition to the artifact, there were also

bones nearby. Human bones that have since disappeared."

Utter silence. "Now you've got my attention."

"Good. Because there's a slight glitch. I told the landowner I wouldn't give the information about the bones to the sheriff's department for a day or two. But I'm curious to know what this thing is. So, if you can only get involved in an official capacity, then I'll move on to the second reason I called."

Darrell sighed. "I have some leeway with official agencies, but not much. But it'd be no problem for me just to take a look at it."

"Good enough for me."

"Where is the artifact now?"

"In my hot little hand."

Papers rustled in the background. I smoked and tried to imagine Darrell as a pencil pusher. Didn't work. He'd always been the hotshot stud with the fast car and faster hands.

"I can be in Rapid City day after tomorrow. Soon enough?"

"Yep."

"I'm almost afraid to ask about the second thing."

I extinguished my cigarette and swallowed a big drink of Diet Pepsi to moisten my dry mouth. "It's about Ben."

I sensed his exasperation through the phone lines. "Julie, how many times are we going to go through this?"

"Did you know Ben had a child?"

Dead air. Then, "*What?*"

"Ben left a pregnant girlfriend behind in Arizona."

"I-I had no idea. When did you find this out?"

"A couple of days ago. This woman showed up on my doorstep with a three-year-old boy."

He sighed. "I'm just going to say this straight out, Julie, so don't get mad. I know you'd do anything to have a little part of Ben back. But this is just too . . . unreal. Coincidental."

Coincidence is fate in disguise.

That weird *woo woo* shiver worked through me again.

"Why did she come forward now?" Darrell asked.

"I don't know. She's here taking a class."

"Did she ask you for money?"

"No."

"How can you be sure it's Ben's child?"

I closed my eyes. "Because he looks exactly like Ben. Not a little bit, *exactly.*"

Quiet on Darrell's end.

"The other thing is, Abita filled in some of the blanks on what Ben had been doing the last few months before he died. She claims Ben had been working for a tribal agency back here, but she wasn't sure which one. That came as a total shock, because in all the years I've been trying to find out anything, there wasn't a damn hint that he'd been sent to Arizona on official business. You don't know anything about that, do you?"

Silence.

A sickening realization pervaded every inch of my body.

"Goddamn you, Darrell."

"Julie, listen—"

"No. His murder eats at me every fucking day. Every. *Fucking*. Day. I was stonewalled at every turn by every goddamn official agency on the planet. I went to you for help because you were his friend and I thought at least *you* would care that somebody slit his fucking throat. And you were holding out on me?"

"Julie. Calm down. It's not what you think."

My blood pounded furiously in my heart, my head, yet my soul was peculiarly empty.

"You know what I think, Darrell?"

He waited.

"I think you're lucky you're not in the room with me right now." Unconsciously my voice had taken on that low, dangerous tone Martinez used.

"Give me a chance to explain. I can't talk about this now. Especially not here. When I see you I'll tell you everything I know."

Without another word I quietly hung up the phone.

Scars I'd believed long healed opened up and began

to bleed anew. I was breathless. Numb. Enraged.

In the background I heard Kevin conferring with our new clients in the conference room. There'd be no breakdown for me. No tears or rants. No throwing cups and glasses or beating my head and hands and heart into the wall.

On the outside I suffered in silence. But inside?

Inside, I was screaming.

CHAPTER 10

I DROVE HOME ON AUTOPILOT. IN MY HOUSING DEVEL-
opment, the Dubrowski's house and mine were the only
ones completely dark and unwelcoming.

I hadn't spoken to my neighbor girl Kiyah since last
spring. Once in a while I'd find a token from her on my
porch. A bundle of dandelions. A Dixie cup bursting
with sun-ripened chokecherries. A green willow stick
with my initials carved in it. But nothing lately.

After being in June's filthy house, I yielded to the rare
urge to disinfect my crappy sanctuary. I changed clothes,
dug out the cleaning supplies, and cranked up my CD
player. Audioslave thumped through the speakers.

By the time I finished the mindless chores of scrub-
bing and vacuuming, the day's distressing events had
faded somewhat. I admired my sparkling bathroom and

dust free coffee table before I slid between freshly laundered sheets.

☠ ☠ ☠

After my third cup of coffee the next morning, I wandered into Kevin's office. "What's on the agenda for today?"

"I'll write up the final report on the Lang Everett case and send it off. Then I'm meeting with National Loan Centers to pitch our services." Kevin shuffled through a stack of papers. "Did you call that Rosette guy and give him the weekend rates for us shadowing his wife for two days?"

"Yeah. He muttered something about highway robbery and hung up on me."

With no fault divorce laws, tailing an alleged cheating spouse was an expensive process, not much fun, and a bit risky for us. Contrary to my past experiences investigating in the field, I'd rather sit on my butt for nine mind-numbing hours than spend nine seconds with a gun shoved in my face.

"You want me to come along to National?"

"No, I can handle it." His loafers hit the floor. "Until we get the rest of the names from Dakota Gaming, there's not much for you to do."

"That mean I can go home?"

"You wish."

After he'd left the office, I forced myself to file back cases. I hated filing. It was gonna be a long-ass day.

That evening Martinez didn't bother to call or stop by. I went to bed alone for the second night in a row. I was beginning to get used to it.

☠   ☠   ☠

My phone rang at 5:30 the next morning.

I fumbled for the receiver and barked, "What? This had better be goddamn good."

"Julie?"

"Who's this?"

"Darrell Pretty Horses. Sorry about the early morning call, but I had a last minute schedule change and wondered if we could meet today?"

I scooted upright. "What time?"

He hesitated and then cleared his throat. "In about an hour?"

I groaned.

"Come on. A hot babe like you doesn't need much time to get ready. Bet you roll out of bed lookin' like a million bucks, eh?"

"Charm will get you nowhere at 5:30 in the morning, Darrell."

"What will?"

"Chocolate covered pastries and a gallon of coffee."

"Consider it done."

I yawned and rattled off my address.

"Will you still be in bed when I get there?"

The man was a shameless flirt. "You wish."

"*Shee.* You used to be more fun. See you in a bit."

☠ ☠ ☠

I fretted in front of my mirror, feeling ridiculous fussing over my appearance. But Darrell was an old lover. After I applied makeup to hide the luggage under my eyes, I dressed in my favorite pair of Levis and a black cashmere sweater. I threaded a jaunty leopard print scarf through my belt loops and tugged on my Justin boots.

I drifted into the spare bedroom and pushed aside my bow and portable targets. I popped the latches on the plastic gun case and lifted the Browning from the foam cutout. It fit my hand perfectly. The oily scent of Tri-Flo teased my lungs. God. I loved this gun.

Kevin and I deluded ourselves that our regularly scheduled target practice sessions were to keep our reflexes fresh. In actuality, we were competitive as hell. I've shot a bow for over twenty years; my hand/eye coordination is damn good. Kevin spent his formative years hunting and eight years in the military; his is better.

I never let that deter me from trash talking and whipping his ass a time or two. I eyed my holster. Damn. So much for my sassy belt. I looped the scarf around my neck instead and attached the holster. A Browning Hi Power made a much bigger fashion statement anyway.

Two solid raps echoed from my living room.

I opened the front door to a white bakery box.

"Chocolate-covered goodies as per milady's request."

I stepped aside and let him in, then shifted the box so I could check him out.

Darrell Pretty Horses was a pretty man; there was no other way to describe him. His facial features were sharply defined, yet ruggedly masculine. High cheekbones, a square jawline, full lips. Not a strand of gray tarnished his coal black ponytail. Thick dark eyebrows accentuated soft brown eyes. Even the crow's feet gave him a distinguished air.

He whistled. "Julie, my magnificent girl, I've been such a fool. Run away with me, eh?"

I kissed him square on the mouth. "You blew your chance years ago, buddy."

"Figured as much."

"This way. Coffee's on."

He lightly grabbed my arm but his gaze was on my belt. "When did you start wearing a gun?"

"When people started shooting at me. Now I shoot back."

His eyes widened and I didn't bother to hide my smile.

He tagged along to the kitchen, seating himself at the dinette table as I rounded up plates and cups.

Darrell tapped a teaspoon on the placemat. "You want to chew my ass first? Or have me check out the artifact?"

"Chew your ass. Tell me why someone who professes to have been my brother's friend purposely kept information about him from me?" I sipped my coffee. "Go ahead and justify it, Darrell, because I'm dying to hear your fucking excuses."

"If I didn't like you so much I'd walk out of here after that comment," he grumbled.

"Wrong. If you weren't feeling guilty as hell you would've stomped out."

Darrell frowned. "Glad I didn't marry you, *winyan.* You'd have made my life hell."

"Flattery will get you a big fat lip. Start talking."

"About a year before Ben died, he contacted me because he wanted my opinion on a job he was thinking about taking."

"What job?"

"Working for the Sihasapa Tribal Council."

"Obviously he didn't take it. Ben never worked for them."

126

"That's where you're wrong."

My stomach lurched. I calmly shook out a cigarette. Lit it and considered him through the smoke. The parallels weren't lost on me. I'd been subjected to smoke and mirrors for years. "What was the job?"

"Glad-handing, mostly, you know, like a lobbyist? Convincing general members of the tribe to vote for the initiative that would allow the Sihasapa Tribal Council to negotiate a gaming compact with the governor."

"Leticia's pet project."

"Yeah. I know you didn't live around here then, but the tribe had been seriously divided on the issue."

I inhaled and stared at him.

"Because of the threat of a state moratorium on all Indian gaming, the Sihasapa Tribal Council knew they'd have one shot with the general membership to convince them to act quickly on the proposal that gaming was the best solution to their financial problems."

"This is where Ben came in?"

He nodded. "Since Ben and his brother Owen were both so well-liked, Leticia recommended them to the Sihasapa Tribal Council. The tribal president agreed, with the stipulation that his cousin Roland Hawk also was hired to help out." Darrell scowled in his coffee cup. "Nepotism at its finest. Problem was, Owen couldn't stand Roland."

127

I hadn't liked Roland either. He'd always struck me as one of those guys who hid a violent personality beneath a crafty smile. Kind of like my father.

Kind of like Martinez.

Damn. I did not have time to stew about that.

"Leticia didn't object?"

"At first. But the rumor was it was a token protest because she and Roland were having lots of private closed door sessions."

My mouth dropped open. "No shit? Queen bitch was doing the nasty with a thug like Roland?" Like I had any room to talk about falling for a bad boy. *Dammit, Julie, concentrate.*

"It never was confirmed, but it'd sure explain why she overruled Owen's protests. Besides, in Leticia's eyes, Roland's pedigree as a direct descendent of Chief Hawk outweighed his . . . *unsavory* reputation."

That was another thing I'd never understood about tribal politics; it rarely mattered what a person did in the present, as much as what glorious feats their Lakota ancestors had done in the past. Plenty of current and past council members had spent time in jail.

I couldn't fathom any other governmental entity that would overlook such behavior. So, did it speak of the tribe's tolerance? Or their stupidity?

I refocused. "Okay. So he had a job. It doesn't seem

like such a big secret deal. Why couldn't you tell me? Especially after he died?"

Darrell watched me closely. "Because of confidentiality laws. No one suspected where the Sihasapa Tribal Council planned to build the gaming facility once they got the governor's blessing. They wanted to keep it that way, because if it were common knowledge, it would've caused an uproar."

I squirmed. I knew where this was going.

"The truth is, it was an unusual situation because we were called to do a study on disturbing potential burial grounds and holy areas *before* they'd even voted on passing the initiative. We both know if the general membership had an inkling that the proposed building site for the casino was *Mato Paha*, it never would've passed."

I ground out my smoke. "Ben knew the proposed site was Bear Butte?"

"I don't think so. But if *I* would have told you any of this, Julie, I would've lost my job. In all the years I've been working with NAGRA, I've never had to sign so many nondisclosure documents as I did with that one situation. Only a select few individuals had clearance. They could've easily traced the leak to me."

But if Ben had found out about the proposed site, he could've caused problems by telling other tribe members. Would the council have taken extreme action and silenced him? "Who was tribal president then?"

"Auggie Two Bulls."

The name didn't ring a bell. "Where's he now?"

"Dead. Car accident outside of Chadron."

Scratch asking him any questions. "You're sure Ben's involvement with the tribe didn't have anything to do with his murder?"

He looked me dead in the eye. "Positive."

"What about Roland Hawk? Could he have had anything to do with it?"

"Doubtful. But stay away from Roland anyway. He is psychotic."

I shrugged.

"Promise me Julie. He was bad news back then, and he's even more unstable now."

I trudged to the sink and reflected on this new information. "Why didn't Ben tell me any of this?"

"I imagine he had some of the same confidentiality issues." A heavy pause. "Ben didn't tell you anything?"

"The last time I talked to him he told me he'd had a falling out with his family about the ranch. He didn't give me specifics." I faced Darrell. "You know anything about that?"

"I swear, Julie, this time, I really have told you all I know."

"When I asked you yesterday about Ben working for

tribal interests while in Arizona, it wasn't the tribal interests part that tripped you up, was it?"

He shook his head.

"So what specifically did Ben, Owen, and Roland's glad-handing duties entail?"

"Attending community functions, ball games, taco feeds, powwows. They enlisted Myron Blue Legs to help with the veteran contingent. Convincing the general members was supposed to have been done subtly, but Roland Hawk was about as subtle as a jackhammer. He caused all sorts of problems. Eventually the council fired Roland, Ben, and Myron."

In the past few months I'd learned firsthand the high stakes and conflicting issues with tribal gaming. With this new information, no wonder I'd been stonewalled while investigating Ben's murder. The Sihasapa tribe had a reputation for being secretive—especially to outsiders, especially when money was on the line.

I sighed. "I don't know what to think. I've never even heard of this Myron Blue Legs guy. Could he have had something to do with it?"

Darrell angled back and folded his hands behind his head. "He's . . . hard to describe. He was some kind of Rambo-type hero in Vietnam; he won all sorts of medals. These days he's eccentric and keeps to himself, yet he's highly opinionated. Most folks consider him a Lakota Holy man."

"And *Ben* was friends with him?" That did not sound right.

"Ben had lots of different sides, Julie. You didn't see them all. He was far too trusting, which is why lots of people took advantage of him."

Or why someone killed him. "But evidently Ben didn't stick around after he got canned. What happened after Ben left?"

"The tribe let Owen finish the legwork. Within a year, not only had they gotten the initiative on the ballot, it'd passed."

I decided not to share my information about Ben staying with the Hopi tribe in Arizona. "This stuff is making me crazy, Darrell. It's made me crazy for the last few years. Sorry I jumped your shit."

His skepticism gave way to an insurance salesman grin. "Don't sweat it. So, where's this artifact?"

I unwrapped the object from the paper towel.

Darrell didn't pick it up. In fact, he didn't move at all. "Where did you find this?"

"A ranch up in the northern part of the county. Why?"

He ran a finger down the length of the braid from the leathery top to the beads on the bottom. He drew his hand back as if he'd been burned.

Whoa. "Darrell, you're scaring me. What the hell is this thing?"

"It's a segment of hair." He flicked the beads and they rattled. "I can see why you thought this might be rope because it's so tightly braided." He pointed to the top. "This is what clued me in—it's hair. This is dried skin, or more accurately, part of a scalp."

"Eww! I've been carrying a scalp in my purse?"

"Yep."

"How old is it?"

"Without running tests I don't know."

"But doesn't the fact it's got a chunk of skin attached to it mean it's probably really old?"

Darrell smirked. "Like when we used to scalp the white man kind of old?"

I batted my eyelashes. "Ooh. Did it take a PhD to hypothesize that possibility, Mr. NAGRA?"

"Smart aleck, but you're right. I'd sure like to get a look at the area where you found this. Any chance we could drive out there now?"

Most likely June was in bed, sleeping off a drunk and hiding from the world. I certainly didn't fault her. But I had told her I'd wait before bringing in the law. Might be fuzzy logic, but Darrell wasn't the law.

Darrell said, "I don't mean to pressure you, but I'm flying to DC in the morning and I'll be gone at least for a week. It's important to know if we're dealing with a burial ground before you contact the sheriff."

"And if it's not?"

"Then the sheriff has a problem."

I frowned. "Like what?"

"Like who was buried there in the first place and why all of a sudden those bones have vanished."

Excellent point.

"I'll get my keys."

CHAPTER 11

DARRELL TOSSED HIS SHOVELS IN MY TRUCKBED BEFORE we took off.

I let *The Punisher* soundtrack serenade us. My truck, my rules.

During a break in the music he asked, "So, what guy you got on the hook now?"

"What makes you think there's only one?"

"Because no man in his right mind would share you."

I shot him a glance. "Or he'd make damn sure no one even knew about me."

"What?"

"Never mind. We're here." I turned onto the gravel road leading to the Everett place.

Darrell opted to stay in the truck as I dashed out.

The dog wagged his stumpy tail upon seeing me

climb the steps. I pounded on the door.

June answered my summons, dressed in the ratty pink bathrobe again. Tangled hair sheltered her bloated face. "What?"

"June? It's Julie."

"Julie?" Her chin came up but I doubted she could see me through her alcohol stupor. "What're you doin' here?"

"I know we talked about waiting, but I brought a guy to check out the hole where the bones were found. Thought maybe he'd save some time when we contact the sheriff. Is it okay with you if we go out there and poke around?"

"Yeah, like you're givin' me a choice. Do I hafta come along?"

Whew. She reeked of booze. Her breath. Her hair. Her skin. "No. I'll stop in before we take off."

The minute I climbed in the truck, Darrell said, "Did the landowner give you explicit permission to access this area where the bones were found?"

"Yep. Why?"

"I've run into problems in the past. People see an Indian guy and they usually shoot first."

"I'll protect you, darlin'."

"That's what I'm afraid of."

I smiled.

The gate to the pasture was humble; rusted barbed

wire loosely wrapped around a gnarled gray tree trunk, worn smooth by the oil of hands and gloves.

Darrell sketched in the notebook teetering on his lap. Even with the truck bumping up and down, his drawing didn't look like the random lines of an Etch-a-Sketch.

With the sun shining, I didn't recognize the bluff. This chunk of earth had seemed austere the day Lang Everett died. Probably the bleak circumstances had discolored my perception.

Upon closer examination, the low-lying plants I'd dismissed as dead and brown reflected shades of russet. Glimpses of crimson rose hips were interspersed with the puffy white mountain balm shrubs, milkweed seedpods, sage, and the occasional tumbleweed.

Yellow leaves shimmered in the trees beyond the plateau. The Black Hills were a faint bruise on the horizon. Not a bad final resting place for whoever had been buried here.

I sat on the bumper while Darrell scoured the perimeter. He jotted notes and measurements, all the while talking to himself. Wasn't exactly *Indiana Jones* stuff.

"Need any help?"

"No. Without sounding like a jerk, I'd appreciate it if you'd stay out of my way."

The contrary part of me wanted to watch Darrell work. The lazy part wanted to curl up on my leather bench seat.

A nap won out. I crawled in the truck and dozed off.

Revving of several loud motors jolted me awake. I blinked the fuzziness from my brain and checked the time on my cell phone. Damn. I'd slept for an hour.

I peeked over the dashboard. Three ATVs had circled Darrell Old West wagon train style. Three guns were pointed at his head.

My pulse spiked.

The gun-toting off-roaders were an odd lot. A heavy-set older man who reminded me of creepy Uncle Fester. A younger black-haired guy with mutton chop sideburns, and a skinny woman with a bad dye job and a big revolver.

I removed my gun from the holster, and tried to slip from the truck as stealthily as possible. They cut their engines. I rounded the back end by the bumper and came up on the weakest leak: the old guy.

"—the hell you think you can jus' show up on private land?"

"We had permission," Darrell said calmly. Even with his hands up in the air he kept a tight hold on the clipboard.

"From who?"

"From the landowner."

"Wrong answer, bub. You one of those sick sumbitches that sees an obituary and decides to come out and scavenge?

"No."

"And who do you mean by 'we'?" This from the Elvis wannabe.

Good as time as any to show myself. "He meant me." I had my gun out and pointed at Uncle Fester. "Drop the guns."

They looked at one another. With confusion? Or malice?

"I said: Put. Down. The guns. Now."

"Why should we? Three of us, one of you, and you're trespassin' on our land."

"This is June Everett's land. Which we've got permission to be on. So drop the goddamn guns."

They did.

"Tell me who you are." With the barrel I gestured to the old guy. "You first."

"June's uncle, Charlie Colhoff."

Mr. Mutton Chops went next. "Willie Colhoff. June's cousin."

I waved the gun between them. "How're you related?"

"Charlie is my dad."

Bad Dye job chimed in: "Jeannie Colhoff. I'm married to June's brother Jeff, and I think you're full of shit. June wouldn't let no one out here where Lang died. It's disrespectful."

"Why isn't your husband out here with you?"

She shifted her stance. "He's home with the kids."

A white Cavalier zoomed into view. June Everett climbed out. The robe? Gone. The tiger-striped spandex pants and a bleach-stained off-the-shoulder black sweatshirt wasn't any better.

I lowered the gun by my thigh.

"What the hell is goin' on here?"

"We were tryin' to figure out who they are." Jeannie gestured to me and Darrell.

"She's here to find out who dug the damn hole that killed my Lang."

Whoa. That wasn't why I was here at all.

The air expanded with dramatic pause.

Jeannie said, "Jesus. Are you drunk? Again?"

"What's it matter to you? Least I ain't hidin' it." June's gaze wandered to the pit. "Where's Jeff?"

"Minding the kiddies," Jeannie said.

"Ain't he always?" June muttered. "Poor bastard."

Jeannie's glower could've torched the prairie grasses.

"She don't look like no expert to me," Uncle Charlie said.

Darrell stepped forward. "That's because I'm the expert. I'm checking specifics before we talk to the sheriff."

"You called it in?" Jeannie demanded. "We made the decision—"

"—to ignore it! Now Lang's dead and them damn

140

bones are missing and I wanna know why."

For several seconds the outburst hung over us.

Jeannie clambered off her ATV and moved in front of June. "Honey, I know you're hurtin', but this ain't gonna bring him back. It's only gonna hurt us."

Her comment intrigued me. "How can figuring out why those bones were here, and where they went, hurt you?"

She whirled on me. "We'll all be in a world of hurt if Game, Fish, and Parks finds out we was lettin' guys hunt off season. Fines. Jail time. Then they'll wanna know who else's been huntin' around here and there ain't no way we're gonna snitch on our friends.

"Next thing you know, they're sayin' we ain't cooperating, then they'll freeze our bank account and take our vehicles. With no money we can't make the house payment. Then they'll auction off the family land and we won't have nothin' left, all because of a goddamn pile of bones! We got kids to worry about."

Her chest rose and fell fast as a cornered rabbit's.

I didn't try to allay her fears. The outrageous picture she'd painted actually happened all the time out here in the wide-open spaces, where landowners constantly squared off against various government agencies.

Darrell, however, was used to dealing with hysterical responses. "I understand where you're coming from Mrs. Colhoff, but let's not put the cart before the horse.

There could be lots of explanations for the bones found on this property. If you'll let me do my job, we'll have a better idea on what we're dealing with."

Charlie motioned Jeannie and June over. Willie shot me a glare that said it was a family meeting and I wasn't invited.

I returned to my truck and swapped the gun for my smokes and hopped on the tailgate.

Darrell pursued me. "This brings back memories."

I blew a smoke ring. Watched the ghostly distortion float away.

"Remember that night we went to the ball game in Faith? And Leroy's car broke down halfway to White Plain?"

"Yeah." The memory surfaced. A hot summer night in July. The moon had been so full and bright it'd blocked out starlight. Cold hot dogs and warm beer. The dusty ride to the reservation with Ben's rowdy friends.

The best part of the night? When Ben drove me home and I'd had his undivided attention. We'd talked about everything. Laughed. Sang along with the tunes on the radio. He'd teased me and I hadn't minded a bit.

A cold fist clamped my heart. Someone had taken that from me.

Engines sputtered, followed by a high-pitched whine as the machines sped away.

June reappeared. "Sorry."

Darrell jumped down. "Not the first time it's happened, believe me."

"Didn't think they'd be out this early. If you need anything else I'll be up at the house." She drove off. I thought it a bit odd that June didn't want to stick around to hear Darrell's hypothesis.

"Come on. I'll give you my expert opinion."

We traipsed over to the hole. He crouched down. "At first I thought this might've been what's called a 'high' burial ground. Where fallen warriors and holy men were buried separate from the tribe, in a place closer to the Great Spirit."

Darrell's index finger traced the drawings on his clipboard. "But as I diagramed the area, I realized the elements up here are harsh. Not only does the wind blow—that alone causes serious erosion—any type of moisture, rain, snow, would run back this way, not down the bluff, but away from it. If this were an ancient burial ground, the bones would've been exposed long before now."

It didn't make any sense. "Okay. This isn't a burial ground."

"Ah ah. Doesn't mean someone else wasn't buried up here. A settler. A soldier. A lone Indian. A miner."

"But the problems with the natural elements wouldn't have changed."

Darrell smiled. "Forgot you had brains, too, gorgeous."

I ignored his flirting. Why would someone move the bones? If they'd gone to all the trouble to dig them up, wouldn't they have finished the job and also refilled in the hole?

A hole that size would leave a considerable pile of dirt. So where *was* the dirt?

I spun in a circle. No dirt piles were scattered on the ground. The wind blew hard in South Dakota, but not that hard.

I paced to the edge and peered over.

No big chunks of earth covered the weeds growing up the slope. I had an *X-Files* moment. Either aliens had sucked it up or it'd been scooped up and moved.

"When you find a burial site, what do you do with the dirt?"

"Pile it up. Then it gets sorted a shovelful at a time. Why?"

"It's missing."

"What's missing?"

"The dirt!" I pointed to the hole. "Somebody dug the hole. Where'd the dirt go?"

"I don't know." He hunkered down again. "The emergency vehicles and traffic out here erased any tracks."

"There weren't any."

Darrell looked up at me sharply. "What?"

144

"When Kevin and I were out here waiting for the ambulance, I noticed there weren't any tracks of any kind. I thought it was weird at the time."

He kept his attention on the ground. "Wrong. Someone was out here spinning cookies. There isn't any tire pattern more than six inches long. Anywhere."

The hair on the back of my neck lifted. "Do you think whoever took the bones came out here and purposely destroyed the tracks so no one could trace them?"

"Yes. But they would've needed a small front end loader or a Bobcat to dig a hole that size and then transfer the dirt."

"How did they get that much dirt past the Everett's?"

"They didn't." He shaded his eyes and scanned the horizon. "They'd have had to drive across the field. Let's check."

We walked the flattest part of the land, the most logical path for heavy equipment, and kept a distance of about ten feet between us. After what seemed like a two-mile trek in circles, we stopped.

Nothing.

I kicked a rock. "This sucks. Those bones and that dirt have to be around here some place."

"Why is this so important to you, Julie?"

"Because somebody thought the bones were important enough to move and I need to at least try and find them."

Darrell placed his hand on my shoulder. "For who?"

"For me. Because it's the right thing to do." I knocked away his false show of concern. "You don't have any fucking idea, do you, of what it's like not to know. To wonder, day in and day out, what happened. The not knowing ties your guts in knots and burns a small hole in your hope. That hole gets bigger and bigger until you've got nothing left inside you but cinders."

Darrell flinched like I'd slapped him.

I marched back to my pickup. Two Marlboro's negated the fresh air in my lungs. I wandered a few feet and watched half a dozen ducks land on the stock dam.

Weird to see water. Most dams were bone dry.

I froze. Maybe . . . "Darrell? What about using a hole that's already there?"

"I suppose that's logical, but I don't see any holes nearby."

"I do." I pointed to the brackish water.

We each grabbed a shovel.

Darrell paced the perimeter of the dam, studying the vanishing trail. "If the dirt was dumped in here, it was dumped on this side."

"Which means because of the steep angle, the dirt pile should be close to this edge."

"In theory, yes. But consider other factors. Environmental—"

"I don't want to consider other factors. I want to know if the bones are in there." I gripped the shovel below where the metal scoop met the handle. "Let's poke around. See what pops up."

"Bones aren't going to float to the surface like pieces of wood, they're too dense. They'll sink to the bottom."

"Even if they're old?"

"They'd be lighter, but it wouldn't make that much difference.

"So, if I nudged one, it wouldn't rise to the top?"

He shook his head.

I shrugged. "Worth a shot anyway."

I carefully picked my way down the slope and dipped the shovel tip in the water.

Darrell snatched it from me. "Don't go indiscriminately jabbing with that thing. If there are bones, they might break if you smack them too hard. Let me do it."

Secretly, I was relieved. Made me shudder, thinking about the muffled crunch of metal striking bone, and the vibration of it traveling up the handle, and ultimately settling in *my* bones.

He started with a small circle and made it progressively bigger. We slid five feet to the right and he began the process all over again.

When Darrell jerked the shovel back, I knew he'd hit pay dirt. He switched the angle and dug in. The chink of the metal hitting something solid made my skin crawl. It could've been a rock. Digging up rocks produced a noise like that.

Darrell heaved a shovelful of wet dirt on the embankment. He used the curved side of the shovel to scrape and spread the mud flat.

I looked back at the dam and wished I hadn't.

A skeletal hand had appeared where the water met land.

CHAPTER 12

IN THEORY I THOUGHT FINDING THE MISSING BONES would give me a sense of relief. The reality was I wanted to vomit.

Darrell smoothed out the mud until the arm bones were visible. He said, "Call the sheriff. Suggest he call the Pennington County Search and Rescue team. Non-emergency situation."

I scrambled up the embankment, away from the gruesome find. Luckily the sheriff was in the office. No big stunner he wasn't thrilled I was involved in another bizarre circumstance in Bear Butte County.

Then I called Kevin. He wasn't very happy with me either, but he was on his way out to run interference.

"Julie?" Darrell shouted.

I made myself approach the edge. Didn't mean I

had to look at the bones. "Yeah?"

"Will you help me for a second?"

Crap. "What do you need?"

"Find a stick so we can mark the initial starting place."

"No problem."

I roamed through disintegrating cowpies and compressed grasses. After circling several times, I stopped. "I can't find anything."

"Bring me a big rock, or anything to use as a marker."

Rocks were in abundant supply. I carried a couple of flat, crumbly ones down the slope, keeping my eyes on the back of Darrell's head.

Absentmindedly he said, "Thanks."

Since neither of us was in the mood to talk, I left him to his site marking and drifted away.

What would happen now? June would be in trouble for withholding information from the sheriff. Would that trouble extend to her uncle, brother, and sister-in-law? Would the inquiries bring the GF&P around?

Would identification of the bones fall to Bear Butte County? Or would the state take over? Jurisdictional issues between the various government entities made my head spin. Even when I'd worked for the county I'd never known who was in charge.

I strayed among the flat slopes and dormant yucca plants. Chunks of rocks stuck up everywhere so if I wasn't paying attention I tripped. The bluff and the stock dam were the only points of interest. Without trees or houses or telephone poles, once you were out in the middle of this land, it'd be easy to get lost.

If someone was hiding a body, it seemed foolish they'd pick such an obvious place.

Kevin arrived before the sheriff. His Jeep crawled to a stop and he parked next to my pickup. He bypassed me and headed for Darrell, still holding vigil by the bones. After he and Darrell shook hands, Kevin leaned over.

My throat closed and I looked away.

Two patrol cars and a Pennington County Dive Rescue van bumped across the terrain.

Sheriff Richards was the first one out, Deputy Peach Fuzz close on his heels, once again tapped for camera duty. Richards sauntered up to me. "Collins. Stay right there. After we're done here plan on spending some time in my office." He directed everyone to the stock dam.

I figured I'd be cooling my jets alone, but pretty quick, Kevin returned. He'd been kicked off scene too. Damn.

The dive team reconvened at the van. Three men and one woman donned dry suits and unrolled a finely woven net. A "drag and bag" operation. Might be fascinating to some, but it made me nauseous.

"You all right?" Kevin asked.

"No. I don't want to watch this."

"I don't think the sheriff will let you watch. He's pretty pissed off at you."

I headed toward my truck, climbed into the cab, cranked the heater and sank back into the leather seats.

Kevin followed me. "What did Darrell tell you about that thing you found?"

"Human hair. That piece at the top? Part of a scalp."

"Gross. What else did he say?"

I smoked. Everything Darrell had kept from me about Ben tumbled out. By my third cigarette, my earlier anger returned full force.

Kevin didn't say anything for quite a while.

"What? Please don't tell me you think Darrell did the right thing?"

He shook his head. "Knowing how destroyed you were after Ben's murder I couldn't have looked you in the eyes and lied."

"But?"

"But, I think he's probably telling the truth. You didn't live around here when the Sihasapa tribe started making noise about their lack of a gambling compact. Any type of gambling was under fire. Deadwood casino owners wanted high stakes betting, the state wanted a bigger chunk of video lottery money, and it seemed like every tribe in the state was building a new casino. State politicians and tribal councils wanted to put a moratorium on any additional gaming. And they had the clout to do it. Everything ground to a halt for about a year."

"I know you said you never saw Ben, but do you think he could've been involved with the gaming issues?"

Kevin scratched his chin and peered at the activity outside. "Yes. It would explain why his murder was brushed under the proverbial tipi."

"Darrell said the tribe didn't have anything to do with it."

"Darrell would say anything to save his own ass," Kevin muttered.

I frowned. "How do you know?"

No response.

"Come on, Kev, tell me."

"As I was leaving, Darrell told Sheriff Richards he hadn't wanted to come out here in an 'unofficial' capacity, especially after you showed him the section of human hair. He claimed he preferred to have proper paperwork at his disposal, but you browbeat him into it since he'd been friends with your brother. He said you wouldn't even let him out of the truck to verify with the landowner you had permission to be on the land."

"That lying piece of shit."

"Jules, I think there's way more going on here than either of us can fathom."

"With Ben's murder?"

"Among other things."

I didn't dispute his statement because I was secretly relieved. I nestled my head in the headrest. Kevin did the same. We both fell asleep. When Kevin woke me up, the patrol cars were still there as was the dive/rescue van.

Two hours passed before the sheriff knocked on my window. "Gonna need both of you to come to the office."

Kevin returned to his Jeep. I waited for Darrell. Instead of returning to my truck, he climbed in the van with the rescue workers.

What the hell? He just left without explanation? Why?

Because he wants to distance himself from you.

Story of my life.

🕱   🕱   🕱

June Everett wasn't at the sheriff's little soiree. Neither was Darrell Pretty Horses. Just me, Kevin, Sheriff Richards and the new Deputy, whose name I'd learned was Deputy White. I'd have to try not to slip up and call him peach fuzz. He wasn't seasoned enough to have a sense of humor.

Kevin and I were seated at a table in the small conference room B, right off the booking area. While I'd worked here we'd never called it an "interrogation" room because so rarely did Bear Butte County officers have the need to interrogate.

Styrofoam cups of coffee in hand, we waited for Sheriff Richards to begin.

He sighed. "I've watched the tape you made for your client. I know Lang Everett's death was an accident. What I don't understand is why you didn't disclose the information on the contents of the hole. Or turn in the object you found on the Everett property. Who wants to go first?"

Kevin nudged my foot under the table.

Jerk.

"In all fairness, Sheriff, I didn't know what had been in that hole until yesterday."

"How did you learn about the bones?"

"June Everett."

"She just called you out of the blue?"

"Yes. She called me—drunk as a skunk—to thank me for staying with her at the accident site. While she was up looking at the sinkhole, she freaked out and said something like 'Who dug that up again?' I questioned her on it at the time but she clammed up. So I dropped it."

"She say anything to you in the patrol car?"

"No. She called me Saturday to tell me what was in the hole." My gaze locked to his. "She wanted me to come with her when she told you. I figured since they were bones, it wouldn't matter if it waited until after she'd buried her husband."

The sheriff flinched. "What about the section of human hair you dug up? You didn't think that was worth reporting?"

"I didn't 'dig it up', it was just lying there. Never crossed my mind it was anything besides a piece of rope. I picked it up, put it in my pocket and completely forgot I had it. When I showed it to Kevin we decided it might be an Indian artifact. I knew Darrell was an expert so I called him to identify it."

"Did you also suspect the artifact was linked to an Indian burial ground?"

I nodded. "Another area of Darrell's expertise. I thought I would kill two birds with one stone."

He motioned for his deputy to refill our coffee cups. During the lull I ached for a cigarette.

"Anything else you want to add?"

"Yes, contrary to what Darrell has told you, he went out to the Everett place with me willingly. In fact, it was his idea. He said he could get a better idea if he saw the spot where I'd found the braid." I slanted forward. "You honestly think I wanted to find a pile of bones today?"

The sheriff didn't answer.

"So maybe after the idiot Colhoff family came around with guns ablazin' we poked around. When that skeletal hand appeared I called you right away. I've done nothing wrong. And I worked for you long enough that you think better of me anyway."

"Julie," Kevin warned.

Deputy White's face matched his name.

I fumed.

The sheriff fumed.

Kevin's face stayed blank.

Sheriff Richards barked, "White, go see if Deputy John needs any help."

White tiptoed from the room.

The sheriff laced his hands behind his head. He leaned back in the crappy conference chair and gazed at the discolored acoustic ceiling tiles.

He wouldn't be any worse on me if I just asked the questions burning my tongue. "Are you going to tell me anything about what you found in that stock dam today?"

"Damned if you do, damned if you don't? I wondered how long it would take you to come to that realization, Collins. The dive rescue team dragged the dam. Four times. Came up with human remains and a blue tarp."

Kevin said, "That rules out any kind of burial ground, doesn't it?"

"Yes. The remains have gone to the state crime lab in Pierre."

"Any chance they can be identified?"

"A good chance. They have a list of missing persons from West River. They'll try for a match with the cases they've already got dental records on file. If they don't get a match, they'll expand to other open cases statewide."

The ugliness of the situation spread.

"There can't be that many unsolved cases from around here."

The sheriff sat up and dropped his elbows to the conference table. "More than you think."

"Got a ballpark?" Kevin asked.

Wish I would've thought of that question.

"I know of ten missing persons cases off the top of my head. Some a few years old, some as far back as twenty."

"Do you have any idea who?"

"Yes, I do. Before you ask, Collins, no, I don't have any intention of telling you."

Huge surprise there.

On his face was weariness, not anger. I wished Deputy Peach Fuzz was here to see the toll the damn job took on the most dedicated men.

"I'd also appreciate it if neither of you said anything to anyone about this. Don't know how long we can keep it under wraps; I'm hoping until the DCI can identify the remains."

Kevin said, "No problem."

"Are you bringing June Everett in for questioning?" I asked.

"In about an hour, why?"

"Because I promised her I'd be with her when she talked to you."

"At the risk of sounding like an ingrate, you don't want to be around. We're also bringing in the rest of her family. Separately, of course."

Three knocks at the door. Missy popped her head in. "Sheriff? Al and John are here for shift change."

"Tell them I'll be there in a minute."

She fluttered her fingers at me and shut the door.

Kevin stood. So did I. "Anything else?" I oozed saccharine.

"No, you're both done. And no offense, Collins, but I hope it's a really long time before I see you again. Trouble follows you like a lovesick dog."

"I don't try to get in trouble. It seems to find me."

"Then it's not your goal to make my job hell?"

"I wish it would've been anyone else who would've found those bones. But you know what? Maybe now a family who's been living in limbo can have some closure."

"Nice rationalization. Truth is, that body didn't wrap itself up in the tarp, nor did it dig its own grave. Foul play opens up a whole other can of worms. Trust me, there will be plenty of people fishing for answers."

He lumbered from the room.

Kevin and I looked at each other. The sheriff was absolutely right. Finding those bones was a beginning, not an end.

CHAPTER 13

AT HOME I SPLASHED BAILEY'S IRISH CRÈME IN MY MUG and downed it like milk.

Between the booze, my flannel robe and my star quilt, I still hadn't gotten warm. No luck blocking the vision of those discarded bones from my mind, either. Not only the who, but the why. Add in the shitty way Darrell had acted, the ass chewing from the sheriff, and no phone messages from Kim, Abita, or Martinez, and my mood darkened.

The combination of alcohol and lack of food hit me all at once.

I scrounged up a can of Campbell's Chunky Sirloin Burger soup and a package of stale crackers. Talk about gourmet. As I huddled at my tiny dinette set, alone, I decided the only way my life could be more pathetic was if I was confessing my woes to a cat or ten, while watching *Wheel of Fortune*.

My lone dish done, I shuffled into the living room and curled up on the sofa. TV didn't interest me. News shows returned my focus to the day's harrowing events I'd been trying to avoid.

I half-dozed. My front door opened. I didn't get up; I knew my visitor was Martinez.

When Martinez started staying overnight with me frequently, his bodyguards had insisted on installing a security system. I thought it was a bunch of bullshit, but I knew better than to argue with four 250 pound armed gorillas.

My alternative was to have his security team parked in my house every time Martinez showed up. Restricting our amorous activities to the bedroom would put a serious crimp in our sex life. Plus, I didn't know if I could even *have* an orgasm with No-neck in the next room.

Beep beep echoed as he reset the alarm.

Leather creaked as he removed his jacket and his vest. His boots hit the floor. A jangle of chains chinked on the coffee table. He'd divested himself of his wallet and his keys. *Thud.* His knife. Louder thud. His gun. Another series of beeps and he'd shut off both his cell phones.

He yanked back the blanket and crawled on top of me.

"Hey!"

"Scoot over. It's damn cold out there." Martinez burrowed in behind me until his back molded into the cushions. After covering us up with the quilt, he twined his arms and legs around me and kissed the top of my head.

It surprised me tough guy Martinez was so . . . dare I say, cuddly? Personal space wasn't an issue when we were together because I had none.

I didn't have the energy to be churlish. I was glad he'd shown up. "You okay?" I murmured.

"Tired. Can't believe how fucking tired I am today."

It was unusual for him to acknowledge the smallest fallacy to me. I kissed his chin. "So take a nap."

"Maybe just a short one."

He fell asleep right after the words left his mouth.

I closed my eyes, curled into him, and let the events of the day disappear.

💀 💀 💀

Martinez woke up a couple hours later feeling refreshed. *Very* refreshed. While I picked up my scattered clothes and put them back on, he rattled around in the kitchen.

After he finished his snack, he didn't look very relaxed and was staring at me oddly.

"What?"

"What did you do today?"

I blinked. What the hell? Martinez and I never swapped "How-was-your-day-today-dear?" stories. Something was definitely up with him. I doubted he'd tell me so I played it cool. "Worked on a case."

"Anything interesting?"

By the way his black eyes bored into me I knew his wasn't a casual question. But I'd promised the sheriff I'd keep the bone discovery confidential and frankly, I had no desire to rehash that nasty business anyway.

"Nah. Same old, same old." I studied his face. "What about you? What did *you* do today?"

Pause. "Same shit, different day."

The way emotion bled from his eyes indicated he was either hiding something or flat-out lying.

"Yeah? Things working with Jackal? He was an asshole the other day."

"Jackal is Jackal."

I counted to ten. Twenty. He stayed mute. "I'm going to bed."

He scowled at me. "Now? It's early."

"Maybe in the bar business 11:00 is early. I have to be to work by eight."

"You'd better get used to the late hours. You're bartending at Bare Assets tomorrow night, remember?"

I'd completely forgotten. "What time?"

"Crystal needs you there at six."

"Fine. I'm still going to bed."

After a short pit stop in the bathroom, I wandered to my bedroom. I stripped. Peeled the quilt back and saw Martinez lounging against the doorjamb. "What?"

"That felt like a dismissal, blondie."

"It was if you plan on leaving."

"And if I want to stay?"

"You won't. You fuck and run. And since we're done with the first one . . ."

"I thought that's what you wanted."

Darkness hid the blush staining my cheeks. I crept between the sheets and willed sleep to come quickly.

The bed shifted. The covers lifted. Then his hot, naked body rocked against mine.

I scooted to the far edge of the bed.

Martinez chuckled confidently in my ear. Then he put his hands and his mouth and his sexual whammy on me and I was putty.

Pathetic.

Later, as I drifted to sleep, I murmured, "Stay with me tonight, Tony. Don't leave."

But I woke early the next morning alone.

I rarely asked Martinez for anything. Whenever he'd asked me to stay with him, I had, every time, without questions, without parameters, because I knew if he'd asked, then he'd needed me.

It stung my pride to find out my needs weren't important to him. But mostly, it hurt.

So instead of my usual method of lashing out, I reversed course and pulled inward—a turtle retreating to the safety of that hard shell. And I'd be damned if Martinez would get a chance to crack it again.

💀 💀 💀

An hour later, after I'd parked in the office parking lot, a rusty green extended cab van pulled up next to me, blocking me in. The driver's side door opened and a big Indian guy/Sumo wrestler scrambled for my truck and rapped on the window.

Fear lanced me like a spear. I said, "Yes?" through the glass.

The Lakota giant grinned. "He wants to speak to you."

I scanned his bare arms. No bloody dagger tattoo, so the summons wasn't from Martinez. "He who?"

"Marlon."

Yikes. "Where is he?"

"In the van. Come on. I'll take you to him."

I hit the door lock button.

Lakota/Sumo guy laughed. "A little paranoid, eh?"

"Do you really think I'm stupid enough to get in a

van with two strange men?"

His jocularity fled. "Marlon Blue Legs is a Lakota Holy man. An honored member of the Sihasapa tribe and a decorated Vietnam veteran."

"Yeah, well, bully for him. But I've only got your word that it's actually him chilling in the Mystery Machine."

"Don't you know Marlon?"

"No. Just his name."

He frowned and muttered, *"Ah-chay?"* Then it dawned on him and he grinned again. "Hang on. I will get him."

Lakota/Sumo guy lumbered to the sliding van door. A mechanized flat silver platform swung out from the side and dropped parallel to the open door.

Then a man in a wheelchair slowly rolled onto the platform.

My jaw dropped. Marlon Blue Legs had *no* legs. Now I felt like a complete heel. I waited until his wheelchair was on the ground before I exited my truck.

Marlon offered his hand. "Julie Collins?"

"Yes." I clasped his cool dry hand in both of mine. "Sorry about making you get out. But I've had some run-ins in the past with guys who weren't so nice. And 'talk to you' is a euphemism for 'beat you up'."

"Ah. I have no intention of beating you up. But I would like to speak to you, if you've got time."

"I'll make time."

His smile landed squarely between charming and threatening. Something inside me screamed a warning.

"Shall we have this discussion over pigs-in-a-blanket at Tally's?"

I nodded.

Lakota/Sumo guy wheeled Marlon down the sidewalk and I trooped along behind.

Once we were seated at a handicapped accessible table in the back room, and we'd ordered our breakfast, I studied the mysterious Marlon Blue Legs.

I guessed his age to be middle-sixties. He could've been sent from a Hollywood casting agent. From the waist up his appearance gelled perfectly with my mental depiction of an Indian Holy man. Burnished red skin. The lines on his thin face were jagged and deeply grooved beside his high cheekbones. Those lines continued up across his narrow forehead. Long gray hair was plaited into two braids, which hung to his sternum.

He gazed at me with clear wise eyes the color of shale.

Yeah, I blushed. Big time. I'd been flat-out sizing him up. It didn't seem to bother him because he flashed me his mostly toothless grin again.

"Is good to know the face of your enemies as well as your friends, eh?"

I wouldn't want this guy for an enemy. I sensed

aggression beneath the benign smile. "I suppose. So, which are you?"

He didn't answer, merely gawked at me.

"I'll warn you, I've got plenty of enemies. So, I'm hoping we're friends since in the last couple of days I learned you were friends with my brother, Ben Standing Elk."

"Yes, Ben was a friend of mine. And a pupil."

Pupil? "You're a teacher?"

"Among other things."

Great. Another round of secret bullshit. "I heard you met Ben when you worked together for the tribe?"

"My friendship with Ben went beyond a working relationship. But, yes, that's initially why the tribe hired me. I'm afraid I didn't last long as an employee."

"Why not?"

"Oh, several reasons."

God. This was like pulling teeth—if he had any. "Such as?"

"Because I lost respect for the tribal council who sold our souls for games of chance and nickel slot machines."

"But didn't you know what you were supposed to be doing when you took the job?"

Our food arrived. Steaming plates of fluffy pancakes, drenched in butter, wrapped around a thick link of buffalo sausage. Lakota/Sumo guy dumped his whole pitcher of syrup on his stack. And then he grabbed mine. And Marlon's. The poor waitress should've just brought the maple tree.

Breakfast was a silent, serious affair.

After I forced myself to eat, my nicotine habit made me jittery. I hoped Marlon would get to the point so I could satisfy my Marlboro craving, because so far, this visit was totally pointless.

Fresh coffee, full bellies. What was he waiting for?

I sighed.

Marlon gave me a tolerant smile, which set my teeth on edge.

"You have questions."

"Well, yeah. This pupil-student-working friend situation might've happened years ago for you, but it's news to me. Okay, so you hated the tribal council, but liked my brother. Where did Roland Hawk fit in?"

An expression of distaste flitted across his craggy face. "As much as I didn't like Roland or his tactics, his attitude served my purpose as well."

"Which was?"

"To know the face of my enemy."

Snap. I'd hit the end of my patience. I set my elbows on the sticky table. "I'm tired of the cryptic Lakota wise man crap, Marlon. Tell me something new about my brother, and what he was doing with you, or I'm out of here."

Lakota/Sumo guy growled. I growled back.

"Spirituality is a private thing, Julie. I owed Ben his privacy even in death."

"What the hell does that have to do with anything?"

"Ben and I stayed in contact after we were fired. When Ben was in Arizona, the Hopi people showed him a better, simpler way of living. He returned here brimming with plans and ideas on how to keep Bear Butte a Holy place, where all people could find themselves and not lose an arm and a leg to the addition of gambling— pardon the pun. As expected, he met with resistance from the tribe, his friends, and his family. It was a frustrating time for him.

"He had no place to go so I took him in. With my help, Ben reconnected to the spiritual course he'd begun in Arizona. But in order to thrive, he cut himself off from everyone."

"And somebody cut his throat."

Marlon flinched.

Time to go on the offensive. "Why was he killed?"

He didn't have a wiseass answer for that.

"Do you know who killed him?"

"No."

"Got any good guesses?"

He shook his head. "Even if I did, I wouldn't tell you. Revenge is never as sweet as people claim it is."

Wrong. "Then why did you track me down, Marlon?"

"Because Darrell Pretty Horses asked me to."

"Out of guilt for Ben?"

"No. I'm not here for Ben, *kola*, I'm here for you."

Again that *woo woo* shiver trickled down my spine. I had a flashback to another Lakota Holy man who'd temporarily soothed my soul . . . only to wind up dead. "Are you trying to convert me?"

Marlon chuckled. "I would if I could, but by the skeptical look in your eye it'd be a waste of my breath. So, I'm here to give you some free advice."

I tapped my fingers on the paper placemat. "Which is?"

"Let it go. Drop this crusade to find out the 'why' that ended Ben's life, and be content with the knowledge that the last few months of your brother's life were happy."

Happy? Maybe that's what burned my ass; I hadn't been part of Ben's life at all for those happy months. "Was part of Ben's newfound happiness because of Abita?"

That shocked ol' Marlon. "He told you about her?"

I smiled. Meanly. Two could play his game. "Thanks for the advice, but on this matter, I will keep my own counsel, as I have done for the last few years."

"It will end badly for you."

Another round of icy fingers danced up my spine.

This guy could give Stephen King a run for his money for the spookiness factor. "Believe it or not, Marlon, I'm used to everything in my life ending badly."

He circled his hand around my wrist. "I'm not joking. If you pursue this, you'll lose something important."

"Your advice sounds suspiciously like a threat."

"No, but it is a warning."

"Ah. So, in addition to your holiness status, you also have the gift of second sight? Did you have a vision about me or something?"

Marlon's toothless grin suddenly wasn't so charming. "You ain't as nice as Darrell said you were."

"And yet, I don't take that as an insult." I jerked my wrist from his hold. "Tell me. If you were so chummy with Ben, why don't you want me looking for justice for him?"

"Because what's done is done." His fingers fiddled with a strand of tiny beads, like an Indian rosary, which rested below the silver star bolo, tied at the hollow of his throat.

Which reminded me . . . "One other thing I need to know. Did Ben wear an unusual necklace when he stayed with you?"

Marlon nodded.

"The last time you saw him, he had it on?"

"Ben never took it off." Marlon's eyes turned shrewd. "He wasn't buried with it?"

I shook my head. "Nor was it given away during the mourning ceremony."

"All the more reason for you to tread lightly, Julie. Bad forces are at work here, and you can't afford to lose anymore of yourself to this crusade. Let it go."

I craved a smoke so bad my lungs were twitching. "Umm. Let me think about that. *No.*" I pushed away from the table. "Thanks"—*for nothing*—"but I have to get to work now. It was interesting meeting you Marlon."

Yeah, I left him with the check. If he was connected to a higher plane, he should've seen it coming.

CHAPTER 14

I KEPT MY DISTURBING CONVERSATION WITH MARLON to myself. I buried myself in paperwork and phone calls.

After a long day of office drudgery, I reluctantly headed for my moonlighting gig.

Although I'd driven by Bare Assets damn near every day, I'd never been inside. The building was off the main drag in an old three-story brick warehouse wedged between the railroad tracks and a newly constructed strip mall.

The irony wasn't lost on me.

The front entrance was tastefully done. Besides the requisite blacked out windows, there wasn't a neon sign flashing:

!LIVE NAKED WOMEN!

or any of the tawdry signage associated with the lewd

acts that commenced inside. A black awning stretched to the curb, with a red carpet beneath it.

Classy.

A bouncer was parked in the middle of the doorway leading into the club. He wasn't as big as the muscle at Fat Bob's, nor did he wear an Hombres jacket, but his wiry carriage was that of a man well versed in knocking heads together. One of those mysterious pledges?

"ID," he said without a smile.

"I'm here to see Crystal."

"About?"

"A job. I start work at six tonight."

His contemptuous eyes raked over me.

I'd purposely dressed down in loose black pants, a long sleeved black tuxedo shirt buttoned to the neck, and flats. My hair was in a high ponytail. I'd donned a pair of trendy "smart girl" glasses with clear lenses. Even my makeup was understated. I'd blend. Or attract the type of men who liked nerdy girls, and I'd bet my last buck they didn't hang out in strip clubs.

He crossed his arms over his chest. I caught sight of the bloody tip of a dagger beneath the cuff of his shirt. This guy was Hombres muscle all right. "What's your name, sweetheart?"

"Julie. Who are you?"

"Dave. You have experience tending bar? It'll be

hoppin' from 'bout 9:00 on tonight."

"Guess we'll see if I can keep up."

Dave unclipped a walkie-talkie and mumbled into it. "Crystal will be right up."

The plastic curtain separating the bouncer's station from the main part of the bar parted, and techno dance music blasted out behind a tiny woman.

Crystal wasn't what I expected. Around forty-five, petite, and curvy, she had straight, shiny blue-black hair hanging past her ass like a sheet of marble. She was a cross between Angelica Huston and Elvira, Mistress of the Dark—in miniature form. Except for her breasts: those were super-sized. Even in high-heeled boots she barely reached my shoulder, which made me feel like an Amazon.

A flat-chested, clunky Amazon wearing ugly orthopedic shoes, geek glasses, and Johnny Cash's castoffs.

Martinez owed me big time.

"Hi, Julie," she said in a voice thick with years worth of cigarette abuse. "Follow me."

The bar was enormous, the stage dead center. Three poles were evenly spaced, and a kaleidoscope of spotlights swirled on the empty floor. Chairs and tables were positioned for viewing. A long counter-like table—an extension of the dance floor—wrapped from wall to wall.

It wasn't as dark as I'd imagined. Clear rope lights twinkled around the ceiling. Away from the stage were a couple of conversation areas with real furniture. For lap dances?

The deejay booth was in the corner by the front door. Drumbeats echoed. A strobe light flashed.

I lagged behind Crystal through a swinging door at the rear of the main bar. In the Manager's office, she skirted the desk and motioned for me to sit. "Smoke 'em if you've got 'em; when we get busy no one gets a smoke break."

I took my Marlboro Lights and lighter out of my pocket. I'd purposely left my purse in my truck. Didn't want anyone snooping through my things.

Crystal gave me a blatant once-over. "What's your full name and who do you work for again?"

"Julie Collins. I'm a partner in Wells/Collins Investigations."

Her penciled-in eyebrows disappeared into her hairline. "You were there when that Indian casino blew up."

God. I'd never live that down. "Yeah."

"Do I need to worry about anyone recognizing you?"

"Probably not."

"What about you setting off an explosion in this club?"

Ooh. Bitchy. "Not unless you've got a propane leak, a member of a Lakota Holy Group protesting the desecration of sacred ground, and a disgruntled employee from the New Jersey mob holding the match."

"You're a real smart ass. Tony warned me about you.

How well do you know Martinez?"

I bit my tongue against asking her to clarify if she meant in the biblical sense. "I've done some work for him in the past. Why?"

She tapped her front tooth with her red fingernail and continued to study me. "He must trust you, because he's never brought in an outsider to handle our problems."

"Maybe that's why you have problems. Some situations become incestuous." I smiled cagily. "Why don't you tell me what's been going on?"

"He didn't tell you?"

"Yes, but one source of information is always skewed. I like to draw my own conclusions. From multiple viewpoints."

A husky laugh tumbled out on a cloud of smoke. "Martinez know you're second guessing him?"

"Yep. Not the first time; won't be the last."

"A few months ago our tills started coming up short 100 bucks or more damn near every night. It bugs the shit out of me because I trust everyone who's worked the nights money is missing."

"Who has access to the tills?"

"Cocktail waitresses, bartenders, bouncers. In case the bartender is busy, the cocktail waitresses have to make change in a hurry, as well as security."

There was the first mistake. Not every employee should

be allowed to have a hand in the cookie jar. Too tempting to take extra cookies. "You haven't had any luck pinpointing and cross-referencing who might be responsible?"

"You want a list of who *I* think could be doing it?"

Crystal had bristled up, so I backed off. "I'd rather draw my own conclusions than go in with preconceived ideas. Give me a rundown on the pecking order. Obviously Martinez is on top of the heap. Then you?"

She nodded.

"Who's next?"

"Dave, the security guy you met out front."

"Where do the strippers"—I caught myself and amended—"dancers come in?"

"They're our draw, so we've got to keep them happy. Bartenders come next, then the cocktail waitresses."

"How do they feel about being at the bottom of the heap?"

"Most are okay with it. A couple of them have dreams of moving up the pole, so to speak." Crystal pointed with her cigarette. "One thing. If you run into any problems, take it to a bouncer. Do not try and handle it yourself."

"We talking customers or employees?"

"Customers. You're on your own with the employees."

Great.

"Last chance to ask questions before we head out."

I shook my head.

"Well, I've got a question for you."

"Shoot."

"You think you can catch whoever is doing this in a few nights?"

"I hope so."

She stood. "I hope so too, because the thing the boss hates worse than mistakes is failure." She grinned. "But, hey, no pressure."

CHAPTER 15

CRYSTAL HANDED ME THE PAR SHEET, WHICH LISTED what should be stocked at my station.

Hard liquor was kept locked up in a separate room. If a bartender ran low on Wild Turkey, Crystal had to replenish that stock. It didn't make sense to lock up the booze and allow unlimited access to the cash. Didn't seem like something Martinez would overlook.

I peeked in the employee break room; a chipped yellow Formica counter, covered with ashtrays brimming with lipstick stained butts. The counter faced a blank wall, with a coat rack on the left, a cube of stacked metal lockers on the right.

"Is this where all the employees keep their stuff during their shift?"

"Everyone except the dancers." She indicated a silver beaded curtain by the rear exit. "The dancers have a separate dressing room."

"Is that the only exit?" The door was identical to the one at Fat Bob's, minus the locks.

She nodded. "It's used for deliveries."

Another steel door, naturally, covered in locks, naturally, loomed at the end of the corridor. "Where does that go?"

"Upstairs to Tony's private offices."

"How long have you worked for Martinez?"

"Almost ten years. I bartended after I retired from stripping. When he opened this club, he asked me to manage it."

"Does he let you?"

Crystal looked confused. "Does he let me what?"

"Does Martinez actually let you manage? Or is he constantly underfoot telling you what to do?"

"I'm in charge of everything from the vendor orders to the weekly schedules to hiring the dancers."

I didn't have to feign surprise. "Isn't hiring the dancers a task he'd rather do himself?"

Her answering laugh sounded like the low rumble of a jet. "No. He spends most of his time at Fat Bob's." Crystal winked. "I think he's got a girlfriend over there."

"Wouldn't surprise me. Martinez seems the type who'd always have a chick hanging on his arm."

"I've hardly ever seen him with one." She confided, "Ain't for lack of candidates. Every woman who works here would kill for a chance at him."

I wanted to demand, "Including you?" but managed a bored, "Yeah? Any of them succeed?"

"Not as far as I know. Banging Tony Martinez would score serious bragging rights. Makes you wonder if all that mystery would live up to the hype?"

Oh, yeah, he lived up to the hype and then some. I couldn't share that juicy morsel with her, so I merely smiled.

We returned to the main bar through the swinging doors. Crystal showed me my station, farthest from the stage.

"Thought it might be best if you started in the back. Better to get your feet wet than drown the first night. The most important thing is to keep the liquor flowing."

"Good luck," Crystal said and ambled over to the DJ booth and left me alone to supply my station.

I situated lowball glasses and beer mugs in the mini dishwasher and figured out how to make the machine work. Then I lugged eight cases of beer to my seedy corner. Good thing I had a strong back and arms from shooting my bow. I felt superior about the fact this physical labor would've killed a lesser woman. Felt even more superior I wasn't a bit intimidated working in strip club.

While restocking bar napkins, an overpowering

stench of Elizabeth Arden's Red Door perfume assaulted me. I looked up.

A malodorous bimbo with raccoon eyes and skunk hair snatched a maraschino cherry. She popped it between her frosted purple lips and sucked off the fruit, then spit the stem on the floor. "Here's the deal. I'm the cocktail waitress for this section. If you get my orders right and up on time, we'll get along just great."

"And if I don't?"

"We'll have a serious problem."

Barely twenty seconds passed and I already had a serious problem with her. "I didn't catch your name."

"Charity. Trust me, I don't give nothing away for free." Her malicious gaze sized me up. "Can't see you'd have aspirations to be on that stage."

I wanted to lie and confess my only goal in life was to dance naked for strange, drunken men. "Me? God no." I paused. "How about you?"

"Of course. Look at me. I'm a natural."

What precisely on her was natural? Miss Clairol blond #33. Sprayed on tan. A set of implants that'd sent some plastic surgeon on a nice vacation. Fake claws and false eyelashes that reminded me of poisonous spiders.

"Wow." I couldn't think of anything else to say.

"And I'm classically trained as a ballet dancer. I can dance circles around the amateurs who bump and grind here."

So why don't you? Ooh. Meow. "Does Crystal know you'd like to be a dancer?"

Charity looked at me like I was a total idiot. "God. Do you *think*?"

My violent thoughts went from whacking her clown face with the tray to bruising her lips permanently purple with my fist. I wrung out a bar towel, pretending it was her neck.

The bar began to fill with customers. Charity was as lazy a waitress as I'd ever seen. She spent most of her time gazing longingly at the empty stage and chomping ice.

So far I hadn't seen anything suspicious, however, the show hadn't started. I figured whoever was ripping off the tills waited until all eyes were on the stage.

The deejay announced the first dancer. Named Candy. Bow Wow Wow's song, *I Want Candy* blasted. A statuesque brunette promenaded on stage decked out like a life-sized candy cane in red-and-white striped spandex.

She gyrated, hands above her head; six-inch red stilettos made her tall enough to dangle from the poles, conveniently running above the stage. She performed a pull-up and straddled her legs midair, flashing a white g-string before landing soft as a cat.

Around the stage, bills began to appear.

My gaze slid to the Bare Assets patrons. The place could've been hit by a scud missile and these guys wouldn't have known, so rapt was their attention on Candy.

Smiling, swinging her gleaming hair, Candy dropped to her knees and gyrated like a slinky to customer #1. She flicked the money to the back wall, spun and backed her ass right into the guy's face.

Whoa. Was that . . . legal? I watched raptly as she did it again.

"What the fuck is wrong with you? Why are you staring? You've never been in a strip club before?"

My eyes met Charity's. I refused to blush. Or to answer. "Did you need something?"

"Yes," she hissed. "I've asked you *twice* for a gin and tonic. Get your eyes off Candy's tits and do your job."

"Coming right up." *You miserable little bitch.* I glanced at the clock. Only two hours had passed. At this rate I'd have no tongue left, or I'd be in jail for assault.

The song, *Lollipop* blared from the speakers. Candy ripped off the spandex, grabbed a prop—a big dildo thinly disguised as a colorful sucker—opened her mouth and thrust it down her throat.

Money flew on stage.

Another cocktail waitress came on shift. A young blond waif who weighed about 100 pounds soaking wet and was high as a kite. She said, "I'm Trina. Ignore Charity-case. She's just pissed she's not up there flashing her ass for cash."

"Does Crystal know you're stoned?" Charity oozed false sweetness to Trina.

"Yep. I told her I'd have to be high if I was working with you." Trina smiled at me and sashayed back to her section.

I was loading the dishwasher when I heard the cash register beep. I whipped around. Charity's hand was in the drawer. "What the hell do you think you're doing?"

"What the hell does it look like?" She smirked, jamming a stack of one dollar bills in the slot and pocketing a twenty.

"Like you're stealing."

She slammed the drawer shut. "Piss off."

I grabbed her shoulder. "Keep your hands out of my till."

For a second, she appeared startled, then she laughed. "Or what?"

"Or I'll break your fucking fingers."

"Ooh, little mouse does more than squeak." Pointedly, Charity pushed my hand away and said, "Touch me again, and I'll tell Crystal your slimy hand was on my ass. You'll be fired so fast your pea-sized brain will wonder what happened." Charity ambled away.

I wanted to kill her.

Two more strippers came and went. After a short break, the star performer was announced. A long line formed from the front of the stage and wound through the tables. For what?

I said to Trina, "Who's next?"

Trina cocked a hip against the bar, empty tray clasped across her flat chest. "Mistress Dominique. She's a big draw from Denver. She plays here about once a month."

The lights dimmed. Smoke swirled. A strobe flashed. Mistress Dominique leapt on stage to the strains of *Dr. Feelgood* by Motley Crue.

Her name should have been Mistress Dominatrix, as she was all legs, tits and platinum hair. She wore black vinyl boots that ended an inch above her knee. The matching black vinyl skirt molded to her hips, showing two inches of her ass cheeks. The bustier, a tangle of metal chains and leather straps crisscrossing breasts, had to be at least a size 44D. Shimmery lace gloves extended to her elbows. Clutched in her right hand was a cat o' nine tails.

She smacked the crop on her leg.

The crowd of men went nuts.

Mistress Dominique plunged to her knees in front of a lucky patron. She whacked the whip on the stage, twirled around and backed up, grinding her booty into his face. Her spine arched, she set the crown of her head on the floor between her elbows and plucked the paper bill from his mouth with a flex of her butt cheeks.

I squinted. No way. It had to be an illusion. A sleight of hand or ass or something. No one was that flexible. I leaned forward. "Did she just . . .?"

"Yep," Trina said. "Keep watching. It gets better."

When the second song, Puddle of Mudd's *You and Me* began, she peeled off the gloves, whipped off the bustier and strutted to the procession of drooling men. Reaching for the overhead brass bars, she tiptoed the four-inch stiletto boots up customer #1's torso. She hooked her knees over his shoulders and shimmied toward his grinning face until it disappeared between her thighs.

I honestly couldn't believe this. I couldn't believe my fucking *boyfriend* owned this place. Shit. So much for my earlier false confidence. I was totally out of my element. I snuck a shot of Jack Daniels and knocked it back. Didn't help.

The DeVinyl's *Touch Myself* was the final tune. Mistress Dominique unzipped the skirt and kicked it off. Spread her legs wide and rubbed the whip over the scrap of leather masquerading as a thong.

Trina spoke in my ear, "See those circles below her hipbones? They're tattoos."

"Of what?"

"Eyeballs."

"She has eyeballs tattooed above her groin?"

"If you were closer, you could see the eyeballs are

looking down at her crotch."

My own eyes widened.

Trina laughed. "Funny, huh?"

As Mistress Dominique jiggled her ass at the crowd, I noticed she had another tattoo in the small of her back. "What's that tattoo above her butt? It looks like a barcode or something."

Trina spun, her stoned face confused. "You've never seen one?"

A bad feeling churned in my gut. "No. What is it?"

"It's a brand."

"What kind of brand?"

"It says, *Property of the Hombres*."

The shot of Jack threatened to crawl back up. "Property?" My voice rose. "As in the Hombres think they *own* her?"

"Ssh," Trina said, looking around wildly. "Not think they own her, they *do* own her. She's under their protection. But the tattoo announces that she belongs to the club and to the club members and they can do whatever they want to her, whenever they want."

"Is that the way it is with all the strippers in here?"

"No. Just a few." She frowned. "Hey, you *do* know who owns this place, don't you?"

"Yeah."

Martinez. I'd fucking kill him.

CHAPTER 16

WE WERE SLAMMED AFTER MISTRESS DOMINQUE'S PER-
formance.

The strippers were mingling with the customers before the second set. Trina told me the dancers' main
job was to get guys to buy them shots—the real money
maker in the bar business.

In that hour, I'll bet I poured 100 shots. It was hard
not to feel sorry for the guys who were blowing all their
money on women who'd never blow them, no matter
how much booze they bought.

Cynical and crude? Yep. No point in sugar coating it.

The bar was busier for the second set. I'd positioned
myself to watch the other bartenders, but so far no activity from unauthorized persons in either cash drawer.

An off night? Maybe. The only way I'd know for sure was when Crystal counted the take. I wished this shift would speed by so I could go home. Hell, I wished I'd never agreed to do this favor.

Charity bustled up. Yanked down her shirt so her nipples practically popped out and smeared on a fresh coat of gooey purple lipstick. She fluffed up her carpet of teased hair.

Tempting to ask if she was spiffing up because her parole officer had snuck in, but I kept a bland expression.

However, Trina wasn't going to let it pass. "What's up with the excessive primping, Charity-case?"

"Did you see who came in? Mr. Martinez and his posse."

I went absolutely still. Was he was here checking up on me? Jerk. I slammed a screwdriver on the counter with more force than I'd intended, drawing Charity's attention.

Her eyes glittered. "What's your problem?"

"Nothing."

"That's what I thought." A smug smile. "I'll bet you don't even know who we're talking about."

I drew my eyebrows together as if in deep thought. "Crystal mentioned a Martinez. He's the guy who owns this place?"

Trina angled her head his direction. "That's him.

At the center table, surrounded by all those big guys."

"The dark haired one?"

"Uh huh. Isn't he a total yummy, naughty package?" Trina added.

I shrugged. "If you go for that bad boy type."

"You don't like bad boys?"

"Not really," I lied.

"He won't go for you anyway," Charity said snottily. "A mouse like you couldn't handle a tiger like him."

Ugly, thick, black jealousy arose. Why did I have a burning need to prove to this sow I could handle Tony Martinez just fine? "But I'm sure you think *you* could handle him?"

"*Think*? Watch and learn." She thrust out her chest, flipped her hair, and sauntered away like she had a stripper's pole jammed up her butt.

Trina said, "Ignore her. She's like that to everybody."

"Everybody?"

"No. She'd be nice to you if you had a dick."

I laughed.

"Or if you were a dancer or had the power to make *her* a dancer."

Charity prowled to Martinez' table. "Think she's got a chance with him?" I said.

"No one who works in here has got a chance with him. He doesn't date his employees."

I affected surprise. "Really? Not even the dancers?"

"Especially not the dancers."

"Why not?"

"Rumor has it his ex-wife was a stripper."

That rat bastard. I was absolutely going to kick his ass.

I glared as Charity smiled, tried to flirt, tried to get his attention. Tony gave her a brief nod and continued his conversation with Big Mike.

Our eyes met for a heartbeat. I ignored the flash of sexual heat and let him read YOU BIG JERK in mine before I ripped my gaze away.

"So? When's the big date?" I asked Charity when she deigned to return to her section.

"Nothing firm yet, but he's definitely interested."

You wish.

Ana Lucia was on stage. I was wiping down the sticky condiment tray, when I heard a familiar male voice. "Can I get a Bud Light?"

I glanced into Big Mike's amused eyes. "Sure. In a bottle or on tap?"

"On tap."

"Coming right up."

"Nice specs. I almost didn't recognize you."

"Glad my disguise is working."

Since no one was around as I poured, Big Mike leaned over the bar. "How's it going?"

"It sucks. Big time. Thanks for asking."

"That bad?"

I think I growled.

He grinned.

I placed the frosty mug on a cocktail napkin and slid it across the bar. "That'll be four bucks."

"Put it on Martinez' tab." He slurped the thin layer of foam. "He recognized you right off the bat."

"Bully for him."

"He knows you're pissed."

"So?"

"So. He wants to talk to you about it."

"Tough shit. Tell him I'm busy."

"He thought you might say that."

I folded my arms over my chest and waited.

Big Mike sighed. "Come on, Julie. You know how he gets."

"I'm finding it hard to be sympathetic to 'how he gets' when I'm doing this because *he* asked me. He's also made it abundantly clear we are to pretend we don't know each other in public. So if he bitches about my behavior, tell him I'm acting exactly like he does."

"Hey, I understand why you're upset. But can't you give him five minutes?"

"No."

"What would it hurt?"

196

My pride. "Might hurt his chances of finding out who's ripping him off if we're seen together. It's a chance I'm not willing to take."

"Is this really about your professional reputation?"

"Partially."

"And what's the other part?"

"Woman's prerogative."

He shook his head. "This ain't gonna make him happy. He's already been on edge since he got back from Denver."

"Yeah? It'll get worse when you tell him I don't want to see him *at all* until this is over."

"At all?"

"Nope. Not here. Not at my office. Not at Fat Bob's. And definitely not at my house. That about covers everywhere he allows us to spend time together, doncha think?"

"Fuck." Big Mike slammed his beer. "Think your night sucks? At least you don't have to tell your boss he ain't getting any anytime soon."

I turned away and hid my smile. Score one for me.

The next time I glanced over to the other section, Martinez and company were gone.

CHAPTER 17

FRIDAY MORNING I HUNCHED OVER MY DESK BLOT-
ter and brooded. About Martinez. About how ticked off
Kevin would be if he found out I was bartending at Bare Assets. About why I was always the last to know everything.

I thought about Ben. Why hadn't law enforcement
talked to Roland Hawk?

Because everything was a big fucking secret.

I logged into the online database. Typed in my password, Roland's name, his pertinent details, and kicked
back, letting the search engine do its thing.

The little bar gradually filled the middle of the screen
and the information was complete. The screen split and
the data appeared.

God. I loved technology. In the old days I would've
had to pound the pavement for days for this information.

I scrolled past the first entry. Roland had two felony convictions for assault. Fourteen calls (in the past three years) for suspected domestic violence, all charges dropped. Five years back he spent a few months in the county jail on a domestic charge. Under suspicion for gang activity on the White Plain Reservation. Under suspicion for drug distribution. Under suspicion for industrial theft.

Shit. Roland Hawk was a bad dude. Question was: Is he a killer? Specifically, my brother's killer?

Only one way to find out.

💀 💀 💀

Although it'd been years since I'd spent time in White Plain things hadn't changed. A new hospital complex had been built, a new high school, a few fast food joints. Two miles north of town, a housing development had been platted and the builders announced lots for phase two were for sale.

Still, poverty ran rampant.

Like other South Dakota reservations, White Plain had no street names or addresses. All mail—personal, business and government—had to be picked up at the post office.

I parked at the convenience store on the corner of

the intersection of County Road 12 and State Highway 9. The store, named Too-Tall's, was more than just a place to buy overpriced candy bars and frozen burritos. Too-Tall's was a community center, a hotspot for activities and gossip. I noticed a gang of teenagers lurking in the back parking lot.

My plan was to hang out, see if anyone talked to me. Sometimes the natives were friendly, sometimes not. As a blonde I stuck out like a white thumb, and ideally someone would strike up a conversation with me. Then I'd work in Roland's name and see the reaction it received.

In addition to the usual c-store fare, Two-Tall's had a cafeteria-style restaurant, specializing in starchy, fat-laden foods: a pizzeria, a sub shop, and jammed in a tiny corner, an authentic Indian taco stand.

Coolers of soda and sports drinks lined an entire wall. Conspicuously absent in the beverage section: beer, wine, or spirits. It was illegal to sell or consume alcohol of any kind on the reservation, a provision of some treaty from the late 1800s, a policy that didn't work then, or 120 years later, since the rate of alcoholism on reservations neared 70%.

Keeping liquor stores from operating on the reservation hadn't curbed the temptation to drink; it'd just made the business owners who were smart enough to set up stores close to the reservation border, very, very rich.

At least if the tribe were allowed to operate liquor stores, they'd have financial benefits. Maybe they'd even lower the drunk driving fatalities because residents wouldn't have to get in their cars and drive to find a bottle of ripple.

I snagged a copy of *Indian Country Today* and bought a cup of *wojapi* before I settled in the far back corner.

A pudgy girl stoned to the gills slipped into the booth and slurred, "Wanna buy some real Lakota beaded earrings, eh? Only ten bucks."

"Nope. I wanna buy some information. Pass that along to your friends hanging out by the back door." Sioux kids ran in packs. For most of them having a circle of friends was the only way to deal with their shitty home lives.

She scowled and slunk away.

I'd just sparked a Marlboro when a young Indian male stood next to the booth. He was clean-shaven. An enormous Denver Nuggets jersey flapped around his hips. A black do-rag covered his head. Crude black and blue tattoos created from Bic pens dotted his knuckles.

He slid into the booth and grinned. Not a particularly friendly smile, a bit charming, a bit hopeful, a lot challenging.

"*Hoka hey, wigopa,*" he said.

This punk had a lot to learn about intimidation.

"Hoka hey, kola."

His smile faltered. "You know Lakota?"

"Some. Enough to know you called me a pretty woman instead of a *wasicu*. So, what's the scam today? You here to offer me a gen-u-wine Indian experience with a real, live Indian? A private *inipi* in your uncle's ceremonial sweat lodge, perhaps?"

He slouched back and said, "Shee-it."

"I must've looked like a pretty good mark, huh?"

"Yeah."

Locals took advantage of tourist's fascination with the Indian culture. As long as they didn't inflict pain—besides on the tourist's wallet—I didn't begrudge the natives their entrepreneurial spirit. "What's your name?"

He grabbed my pack of smokes. Lit one. Got a bit surly as he measured me through the haze. "Why?"

"Your day's take might not be totally lost. I'm looking for some information. Might be willing to pay for it if it's good enough."

"You don't look like no cop."

"See? I knew you were smart. That's because I'm not a cop. What's your name?"

"Denny Bird." He exhaled. "What kinda information?"

"I'm trying to hook up with an old friend of my brother's."

202

"Who are ya lookin' for?"

I moved the paper aside, positioning the ashtray between us. "Man by the name of Roland Hawk. Know him?"

"*Shee.*" His gaze shifted to the gas pumps outside the window. "Everybody knows Roland. He's one bad motherfucker. Whatchu want with him?"

I rolled the cherry of my cigarette in the bottom of the metal ashtray, wondering how to play this. "I've got a couple of questions to ask him, that's all."

Denny laughed. "'That's all', she says. Think you can jus' roll upta his place and knock on the fuckin' door?"

"That's what I was thinking."

"You thought wrong."

"Help me out then, Denny."

Still skeptical. "Who's your brother?"

"He's dead."

"Still gotta name, don't he?"

"His name was Ben Standing Elk."

"*Shee.* No wonder you know some Lakota. You related to that bitch Leticia?"

I shook my head. "Ben and I shared the same white father. Only blood between me and Leticia is bad blood."

"Hear ya there, sister." He held his fist over the table. In a split second I realized he wanted to smack his knuckles with mine in a gang type show of solidarity. I did it. Much cooler than the high fives of my teenage years.

"You don't like her either?"

"Bitch fired my uncle Leon for no reason. He'd been workin' on the ranch for her brother Reese, not her."

We smoked. The silence wasn't alarming, just obvious.

Finally, I said, "What about the rest of your family, Denny?"

"My dad is dead. Been livin' with my Uncle Leon on and off. Sometimes I stay with my dad's mom, my *Unci* Bird if she's feelin' okay. Don't get along with my mother's boyfriend."

I didn't comment. Being shuffled from one relative to another was the norm here.

"What's your name?"

"Julie. You gonna help me out, Denny?"

"Depends."

"On?"

"How much you payin' me?"

"Twenty?"

He didn't so much as twitch.

"Thirty?"

"You can do better."

"Fifty?"

Denny grinned. "Done." He held out his hand.

I dangled the bill out of his reach. "Tell me the truth, Denny boy, about where Roland lives, or I will track you down and demand my money back."

He tucked the money in the outside pocket of his backpack. Then his gaze swept the perimeter. It encompassed the restaurant area and convenience store. Satisfied, he angled over the table. "Follow County Road 9 until you're almost outta town."

I snatched a napkin and rooted around my purse for a pen.

Denny slapped his hand over mine. "Fuck. Don't write it *down*."

"How am I supposed to remember?"

"Ain't that hard. Listen okay? On the left side there's a turquoise buildin' with a Red's Repair Shop sign. Turn there. Keep goin'; you'll come to a hill. Down the other side there's an old horse barn. Behind that's a trailer. That's where Roland's old lady lives."

"What's her name?"

"Bonita."

"Bonita what?"

"Bonita Dove."

I rolled my eyes. "You fucking with me, Denny? Roland *Hawk* and Bonita *Dove*? Come on."

His confusion was real.

"Never mind." He kept staring at me until I snapped, "What?"

"You ain't bullshittin' me. You know Roland, right?"

"Been a long time, but, yeah, I sort of knew him."

"Then I guess I don't gotta tell you you'd better bring along protection."

As I formulated a response, he vanished out the side door like a vapor trail.

👹 👹 👹

Before I went looking for Roland, I reached under the seat for my gun case. I flipped the latches, eased my gun from the foam cutout and popped in the loaded clip.

I unlocked the glove box and grabbed my stun gun, stowing it in my left coat pocket. Like Jimmer always said: better to be armed than sorry.

Denny's directions proved accurate. I crested the hill and coasted down the other side.

I rounded the corner of the barn. Three vehicles were parked at varying distances. An avocado green El Camino missing the back window. A bronze Monte Carlo circa 1970-something, the rusted left rear rim propped on cement blocks. A scratched up, mud-covered red Dodge Durango.

Stuffing burst from a stained mattress thrown next to the trailer's front door. Loose papers, broken bottles, rusty cans, and plastic grocery bags were strewn across the ground.

After I secured the Browning in my right pocket, I

climbed out.

Two snarling, snapping dogs came at me.

I nearly jumped on the roof of my truck.

A clank of chains hauled the mutts up short. They barked, growled, and lunged, slavering to tear me limb from limb. Damn near every rib on their scrawny frames stuck out.

The front door flew open. A woman with a shotgun shouted, "Get outta here. You's trespassin' on private property."

Shit. Nothing like staring up a shotgun barrel to make pee run down your leg. I swallowed and held up my hands. "For Christsake don't shoot! I'm looking for a friend of my brother's."

"He ain't here," she said. "Now go on. Git." She yelled at the barking dogs, "Cujo! Killer! Shut the fuck up!"

The woman had greasy black hair, dirty bare feet, and wore an ugly housedress covered in peacocks. The Roland I'd remembered had a disturbing thing for attractive young girls.

I hollered over the staccato barks, "You sure Roland won't talk to me?"

"Cujo! I said SHUT UP!"

The dog whimpered.

She kept the gun trained on me. "Who's Roland?"

I laughed. Yeah, it was nervous laughter. "If Roland's

in there, let him know this is about Ben Standing Elk."

She didn't move. Nor did she lower the shotgun.

Behind her a man sauntered into view. A chicken drumstick in one hand, a Keystone beer can in the other. His sunken chest was bare, scarred, and covered in prison tattoos. Filthy, baggy jeans hung off his scrawny hips. He leaned a shoulder against the warped metal doorjamb and gnawed on the chicken.

The dogs went nuts.

He sucked the last of the meat and threw the chicken bone at the dogs, laughing as they tried to rip out each other's throats for the measly scrap.

Yep. This sadistic fucker was Roland.

He drained the remaining beer and belched. I didn't hear it over the snarling dogs, but I saw it. He tossed the can to the ground.

"Why you wanna know about Ben Standing Elk? He's been dead for years." He squinted at me. "Who the fuck are you anyway?"

Before I could answer, he shouted, "Bonita, either shut them fuckin' mutts up or give me the goddamn shotgun and I'll do it!"

"Killer! Cujo! SHUT UP!"

Wasn't exactly the horse whisperer, but it worked. The dogs cowered in the garbage with a final whimper.

I eased my hands in my pockets and wrapped them

around my weapons.

Roland said, "You that skinny white kid sister of Ben's?"

"Yeah."

"What's your name again?"

"Julie Collins."

He cocked his head like he'd recognized it. I braced myself for the inevitable casino explosion question. None came.

"Why you here, Julie Collins?"

"To ask you some questions."

"What makes you think I'll talk to you, eh?"

This was going about the way I'd imagined. Did I have the balls to push him? Ben's face swam into view and brought my rage to the surface.

"I came across some information I'd like to ask you about."

"Why would I give a shit about your information?"

"If you won't talk, that proves you've got something to hide about Ben's murder." I cocked my head the same way he did. "Interesting, that you weren't questioned about it back then."

"Ain't interestin' to me."

"Yeah? Might be interesting to the Bear Butte County Sheriff's Department, the FBI, the Native American Gaming Commission, and the BIA, don't you think?"

Roland stormed through the garbage.

I stayed put. I wouldn't show this piece of shit fear, even when I felt it. I'd look into his eyes and demand to know if he'd killed my brother.

And if he had? What then?

He stopped about three feet from me, close enough to hear my heart slamming.

"You fuckin' cunt. Who you think you are, eh? Comin' here, askin' me questions."

"I'm someone who knows way more than you want me to, Roland."

He laughed. "Like?"

"Like does Bonita know you were playing hide the sausage with Leticia Standing Elk when you were 'working' for the tribe?"

"Last chance to get outta here. I ain't got nothin' to say."

Thoughts of revenge made me reckless. "That's because you are nothing, Roland. Nothing but a big fuckin' blowhard." I angled my head in Bonita's direction. "Gonna have her shoot me? Rumor has it she's got you by the short hairs, but I didn't realize she'd taken control of your balls too."

I'd actually shocked him.

"Shut the fuck up."

"No. You listen up. If I find out you had anything to do with Ben's murder I'll kill you. I will chop off your head, gut you like a deer, and wrap your innards around your dead body like a strand of Christmas lights. Then I'll cut off your tiny dick and balls and feed them to your fucking dogs."

A flash of movement and Roland jerked me by the hair and spun me around. A knife appeared by the corner of my eye; cold steel pressed into my throat. Then he slowly dragged the blade down my neck.

I bled.

He laughed. He dragged the knife through the cut again. "Big tough talk only gets you in big trouble."

Jesus. It burned so badly I stopped breathing. But I wouldn't give this vicious motherfucker the satisfaction of seeing a reaction. I didn't utter a peep.

"Shouldn't have come here, bitch." He jockeyed himself so he stood in front of me, holding the knife close to my carotid, keeping a death grip on my hair.

Were Roland's crazy eyes the last thing Ben had seen? If Roland planned to kill me, I had nothing to lose by asking the question that'd defined my pitiful life the last few years.

"Did you use that knife to kill my brother, you piece of shit?"

"Wouldn't you like to know? You won't either. When I'm through cuttin' and carvin' you inside and out, you'll wish I'd have slashed your fuckin' throat." He waved the blade in front of my eye. "See this? The tip is hooked. Really fuckin' sharp too. Lemme show you."

Roland pushed the tip above my right breast and turned it like a screwdriver. He backed up to watch me bleed.

The immediate burst of pain spurred me into action.

I pulled out the stun gun, rammed it into his bare stomach and zapped him.

Roland fell back, his hold on my hair tightening, jerking me with him for a second before he let go. I queued up the gun and nailed him again.

He twitched and flopped in the dirt and garbage.

The Browning came out of my other pocket, I aimed at his head and screamed at Bonita, "Put down the goddamn shotgun. Now!"

She hesitated a beat too long.

I swung the gun and shot a series of bullets in the trailer, less than two feet from where she stood.

The dogs went crazy.

My ears rang. I hollered, "Put the fucking shotgun on the ground NOW!"

She did.

"Get back in the trailer."

Bonita backed up. Over the cacophony of howling dogs she shrieked, "Roland will kill you for this."

I picked up his knife. Ignored the queasy sensation

that I might be holding the instrument of Ben's death.

Bonita hovered in the doorway of the trailer. I pointed the gun at her as I inched sideways to my truck. "Stay there until I'm gone."

The knife clunked as I whipped it in the truckbed.

I'd purposely left my keys in the ignition. I slammed the gearshift into reverse and hit the gas. Just about nailed the Durango with my backward arc. Driving up that steep hill in reverse wasn't an option.

I threw the truck into drive, ducked, and stepped on it. I'd made it to the barn when I heard a loud clank. In the rearview mirror I saw Bonita holding the shotgun, taking aim.

Shit. I sped up and nearly caught air when I hit the crest of the hill and barreled down the other side.

I didn't slow until I'd screeched up to the highway.

At the stop sign, I took a second to regain my bearings. My heart was pumping like mad. When I looked down, I saw blood. Lots of blood.

I backed up and parked in Roy's Repair Shop lot between a semi-cab and a Chrysler mini-van. With any luck I could hide until my wounds quit oozing.

With the Browning on my lap, I let my head fall back to the headrest. Feeding my nicotine habit wasn't as pressing as the need to close my eyes. Just for a minute.

I'd slowed my breathing when the *chink chink* on

the glass had my eyes flying open and my gun aiming at the window.

Denny's hands went up. "Jesus! Don't shoot! It's me. Denny. Remember?" Wide black eyes gaped at my bloody shirt. "Holy shit! You're bleedin'. Did he cut you?"

"Just a flesh wound. You'd better get out of here before someone sees you."

He disappeared. Smart kid.

About two seconds later *chink chink* echoed from the passenger's side.

Denny's head popped up. "Let me in. I got some stuff that'll stop the bleedin'."

Persistent bugger. Why I trusted him was a mystery, but I did. I punched the door unlock button and he scrambled in.

He unzipped his backpack and unrolled a white T-shirt. "Here. Press down with it and try to stop the blood flow."

"I'll wreck your shirt."

"So? Ain't like it's Armani."

I held the shirt to my neck with both hands. "Thanks."

"He cut ya?"

"Yeah." The impromptu piercing Roland delivered to my chest hurt like a bitch too.

Denny rummaged in his backpack, unearthing a baby food jar filled with what resembled green gelatinous snot. "An ointment my *unci* makes. Best stuff in the world for cuts, burns, and bruises."

"You use it on the bruise on your jaw?"

He froze. "*Shee.* You noticed that?"

"Yep. How old is it?"

"Five, six days."

"Really? Stuff must work. But you gotta tell me what's in it before I smear it on my delicate white-girl skin."

He snorted. "Sage and some other junk." His gaze narrowed on the front of my body.

Embarrassed by his scrutiny, I shifted sideways.

"I ain't lookin' at your tits. I jus' wanna see how deep he cut you."

I lowered the T-shirt.

He sucked in a harsh breath. "I hate that fucker."

I angled the mirror to see the gash. Not deep, but it was wide. I swirled my index finger inside the jar and dabbed on a thick layer of greenish goo that felt like Vaseline. It smelled like burnt sage, horse sweat, and oranges. A weird combination, but not unpleasant. I gave Denny my back, unbuttoned my shirt and checked out the puncture wound.

A line of blood ran down my belly. The skin around the entry point was red. Puffy. I buttoned up and snagged my smokes. Tossed the pack to Denny and rolled down the windows.

"Why'd you follow me? You work for Roland?"

"Hell, no." He flicked his cigarette ash out the window. "I felt guilty. Never shoulda tole ya where he lived. Did he answer your questions?"

The abrupt subject change didn't surprise me. "No."

"He never does. He don't answer to nobody."

"How do you know Roland so well if you don't work for him?"

"His old lady, Bonita? She's my mother."

CHAPTER 18

"BONITA IS YOUR MOTHER?"

"If you can call her that."

My stomach pitched at the idea of this kid being around Roland on a regular basis. The hair on the back of my neck stood up. What were the chances I'd run into Bonita's kid? At the first place I stopped?

Better than average, since White Plain Reservation is so small. But still . . . there was some *woo woo*, Indian shaman-magic-fate-destiny stuff about the situation.

Coincidence is fate in disguise.

Unexplainable things had happened to me too many times, for too many years, and in too many different situations, for me not to believe meeting Denny was some kind of divine intervention. Too early to tell if it was a good or a bad cosmic sign.

"How long have Bonita and Roland been together?"

He twisted the black nylon backpack cord around his palm. Unwound it and repeated the process. "On and off for most of my life."

"How old are you?"

"I'll be eighteen next month."

I exhaled slowly. "Got big plans?"

Denny's gaze caught mine to see if I was teasing him. Deciding I wasn't, he said, "I used to think I could get her away from him. Then just me'n her would move in with my *unci*. Ain't worked out that way. She'd rather be beat to shit by Roland than be without him. And my *unci* Dove washed her hands of both of us years ago."

"Your grandma, Bonita's mother, doesn't take care of you?"

"No. She says Roland has influenced me. **She thinks** I'm violent just like him. I'll *never* be like him. So screw her. Don't need her shit anyway."

What kind of woman would turn her back on her abused daughter and her grandson? I purposely looked at Denny's bruise. "He beat you too?"

His face flushed and he snapped, "This one ain't from him," even when we both knew it was.

Christ. I'd cry if I didn't suck it up and act the tough chick. My tears would make him bolt for sure. Quietly, I offered, "My dad used to smack me around. I

218

even found the guts to hit him back once. Always made it worse."

Denny wouldn't look at me. "I was ten the first time I hit Roland back. He broke my arm. Second time was a coupla years later when I tried to get him to stop punchin' my mom in the face. He hit me once. Said for every punch I landed on him, he'd hit her twice. She never did nothin' to defend me or herself so I stopped interferin'."

"At least you can go to your other grandmother and uncle's house. Anyone else watching out for you?"

"Nope. Got a small family as far as Indians go. My mom's sister, Maria, run off a few years back, which is part of the reason my *Unci* Dove don't want nothin' to do with us. She blames Roland. My uncle Phil got kilt durin' Desert Storm. Uncle Leon ain't married, and my mom didn't have no more kids."

Good thing. "Look, Denny, I hate to bail, but I need to drive back to Rapid City. Can I drop you off at your *unci's* house?"

His thick eyebrows drew together. "Nah. Don't worry 'bout it. I kin take care of myself."

"I'm sure you can. But before I go, I want to know if there's a safe place you can stay tonight."

The surly boy reared his proud head. "Why you bein' so nice to me, huh? What's in it for you?"

I could've told him to get his ungrateful self right

219

out of my truck. Instead, I brandished the bottle of ointment and mimicked, "Why you bein' so nice to me, huh?
What's in it for you?"

A boyish half-smile appeared. "You're a smart ass."

"So I've been told. I've also been told I'm a pain in
the ass, so you'd better answer 'cause I ain't leaving until
we're straight."

Shame burned his cheeks again. "I got a place to go."

"Good." I dug out a business card. Scribbled my
cell number on the back and pressed it in Denny's palm.
"Thanks for helping me out today. If you need anything,
call me, day or night, okay, *kola*?"

He nodded and left.

💀 💀 💀

My wounds stung. I didn't want to go home.

I called Kim. I'd been so wrapped up in my own
fucked up life I hadn't been a very supportive friend.

After the shock of seeing me in a bloody shirt wore
off, Kim lectured me on my risky behavior. Once I'd
been sufficiently chastised, she let me shower and lent me
some clothes. I dabbed on Denny's grandma's miracle
goo. The cuts weren't bad enough to need stitches. Or
so I told myself.

Wearing a pair of Kim's yoga pants and an old T-shirt, I cozied into her fluffy pink couch. Kim was wound tight as the balls of yarn in her craft basket. She fussed with pouring us each a cup of perfumy smelling herbal tea, rearranged the silver teaspoons, the frosted butter cookies, and embroidered napkins.

My gaze fastened on buttery yellow yarn, soft as down, peeking from a white wicker basket on the end table. Bet if I checked I'd see an itty-bitty pair of baby booties dangling from the knitting needles.

I looked at her. "Appears you've made your decision."

She nodded.

"Does Murray know?"

"I'm going to tell him tomorrow night."

"You scared?"

"Terrified." Her hands were shaking so hard the gold-rimmed teacup rattled in the saucer.

Gently, I removed the cup and placed it on the teak serving tray. I clasped her icy hand in mine, which startled her. "What can I do?"

"Tell me I'm not making a mistake."

"You're not making a mistake."

"Tell me I'll be a good mother."

"Kim, you'll be a great mother."

"Tell me if he walks away I'm better off without him."

"He's an idiot if he walks away."

"Tell me if he isn't around you'll be my childbirth

coach."

"I'll be in the delivery room, cursing men, and helping you breathe every painful step of the way."

"Tell me you won't abandon me when my life revolves around dirty diapers, bottles, and baby stuff."

"That I can't do."

Stricken, Kim gaped at me. "What?"

"I draw the line at changing diapers, my friend."

She burst into tears. "Oh, you. 'Bout gave me heart failure, Jules."

I handed her a Kleenex. "Congratulations, Kim. I'm happy for you. But for the record? I'm serious about the diaper thing."

CHAPTER 19

I CALLED CRYSTAL AND TOLD HER I'D BE LATE. SHE WASN'T happy, but what could she do? Fire me?

I scooted home to slither into my bar wench clothes and knock back some painkillers. Aspirin with codeine helped my mood. A black turtleneck concealed the gash on my neck.

The parking lot behind the club was full. The service entrance door was unlocked. With the paranoia Martinez' security team had about safety measures? Somebody had dropped the ball. Big time.

I dumped my stuff in the last open locker in the employee break room. Knocked on Crystal's door.

No answer.

"Crystal?" I eased the door open and slipped inside.

Dave straightened up from the safe tucked in the

corner of the room, a wad of bills in his hand. "What the hell do you think you're doin' barging in here? This is a private office."

Question was: What was *Dave* doing in here? Unattended? "I'm looking for Crystal."

"She ain't here. Now, get out."

"But—"

"But what?" Crystal said behind me. She skirted me and scooted behind her desk. The glow from the computer screen turned her black hair electric blue. "Is there a problem?"

My gaze flitted between Dave and Crystal. Why wasn't she demanding to know why Dave was loitering in front of an open safe with a mitt full of cash?

Maybe Crystal was involved with the employee theft. Bringing the shortages to Martinez' attention would throw suspicion to the waitstaff and away from her. But that wouldn't be smart. So why wasn't she freaking out about Dave?

"She's waitin' for your answer," Dave snapped.

The smarmy fucker didn't bother to hide the money clutched in his grubby hand. "No. I just wanted to tell you I'm sorry I'm late."

"No biggie. You're in the back section."

"Fine." I'd made it to the storage areas, when a hand clapped on my shoulder. I wheeled around, resisting the urge to lead with my fists.

Dave sneered. "Don't know what hard luck story you told Crystal, but you pull this shit again and you're out the door."

"Fine. Whatever."

His grip tightened. Made my skin crawl.

"I'm watchin' you."

Little did he know I was watching him too. Closer than ever. Maybe Crystal thought the shortages were from the tills when they were really from the safe after she counted both at the end of the night.

A niggling feeling persisted. Something was . . . off here. This favor seemed too easy. Too obvious.

Out in the club, Trina slapped her tray on the counter. "Surprised to see you. Charity said you quit."

"She wishes. Whatcha need?"

"Two Jack and Cokes and Miller Lite in a bottle." Trina was twitchy, shifting from side to side, scouring her section, tapping her fingers on the counter.

Her actions bothered me enough I decided to keep a close eye on her.

Trina flitted between a bald guy nestled in the corner and a punk wasting air by the bathrooms. As the young tough sucked down the beer, she hotfooted it back to the cue ball. Another short verbal exchange between them and he nodded.

She picked up the empty lowball glass with a crumpled cocktail napkin stuck in the top from the bald guy's table and sashayed back to the seedy-looking kid.

I almost missed it. Trina set the empty, dirty lowball glass on the punk's table. He dropped an undisclosed amount of cash on her tray. She then revisited bald guy, gave him the other Jack and Coke on her tray and the money.

For all intents and purposes, it appeared she'd given the baldie a fresh drink and his change. My gaze swung back to the punk. Whatever had been in that glass, including the napkin, was gone.

Trina was stupid enough to sell drugs right under Tony's nose? Unless . . . Martinez knew exactly what Trina was doing. Shit. Maybe this was her job. Acting ditzy and performing a slight of hand that'd make Criss Angel jealous.

The dirtball kid vanished. An equally scraggly guy slid into the booth. The process started all over again.

A different cocktail waitress, another blonde (what was it with Martinez and blondes?) sidled up to the bar. Her breasts were perky, her grin toothy, her hair shampoo commercial glossy. She looked about thirteen. "You're new. I'm Megan."

"Julie."

Megan squinted at me. "Have we met? You seem

awfully familiar."

I tamped down panic. "I get that a lot. What do you need, Megan?"

"Four Coors Light on tap for the bachelor party whooping it up in the back."

While I poured, I asked, "How long have you been working here?"

"A little over a year. Good money. Which is probably why I haven't punched Charity in the face."

"You guys don't hang out after hours?"

"Please. The only reason she's still here is because she's screwing . . ." Her gaze zoomed to the DJ booth. "Never mind."

A smidge of trepidation roiled in my belly. "Come on, Megan. You can't dangle that hook and jerk the lure back before it even hits the water."

Megan smiled coyly. "Okay. She's bouncing on Dave's pole."

"Really? This been going on a long time?"

"As long as I've been here." Megan snitched a stack of bar napkins. "Charity-case thinks banging him will get her closer to dancing around that real pole."

"Will it?"

"Hasn't so far."

The guys surrounding this bar drank heavily while keeping their eyes glued to the stage. When my gaze swept the bar as a whole, I had a hard time believing anyone outside of employees could get a hand in the cash drawers. The missing cash had to be an inside job.

I suspected Martinez already knew that. He wasn't stupid. So why had he really hired me?

I loaded glasses in the dishwasher. Out of the corner of my eye I saw Dave's paws in my cash register. I slammed the drawer shut so fast I nearly chopped off his fingers. "Keep your hand out of my till, Dave. I'm in charge of this station."

"Who do you think you're talking to?"

"I'd say a trained monkey, but I'm guessing that's his job." I jerked my thumb toward a bruiser with the banana yellow crew cut, eyeing me, ready to acquaint me with his fists.

Dave glared and he and monkey boy returned up front.

I breathed a sigh of relief, which lasted all of sixty seconds until Charity barreled over.

"What'd you say to Dave that pissed him off?"

"None of your business."

She angled closer and her eyes glittered with malice. "You dumb bitch."

My body hurt and I'd had enough verbal abuse today.

"Who do you think—" The rest of her sentence disappeared on a gasp because I stretched the hose on the soda dispenser and sprayed her chest with Coke.

228

Charity shrieked like a teen scream queen.

I tugged the striped tubing and pointed the nozzle at her head. "Back off. The next thing I aim for is your bouffant."

She hissed, "This'll be your last shift. I'll make sure of it."

"I wish," I muttered to her back.

Seemed I'd scared away not only Charity, but also the other cocktail waitresses from my station. I used the time to study the clientele.

My gaze landed on two men at the end of the bar. Something about those guys clicked in my memory. I'd seen them someplace recently . . . but, where?

The one on the left had stringy hair, a slight frame. His companion had thick black sideburns, the envy of Elvis impersonators everywhere.

When stringy hair guy twirled his barstool to ogle the strippers, I saw the back of his red jacket, identical to the one Lang Everett had worn. Whoa.

This guy was June Everett's brother. So much for my undercover work.

Then again, would he remember me after our brief meeting at June's place? Probably not. My sense of relief was short-lived when I realized the other guy was his cousin. Shit. Chances were much better Cousin Willie *would* recognize me since I'd aimed a gun at his father's head.

Crystal made a beeline for me, blocking me from view, ending any chance of analyzing their behavior. Her eyes raked me up and down. "Julie. You're off the floor. Now."

Inside her office, Crystal let loose. "What the hell are you doing? Mouthing off to Dave? Spraying down my cocktail waitress? You're supposed to be—"

"I'm doing exactly what I was hired to do."

Crystal lit a cigarette.

I snagged one from her pack and did the same. Yuck. Menthol.

"Okay, wise ass, you've been on shift two nights. Who do you suspect?"

"Everyone. Interesting, that Dave and Charity are involved after hours. Kinda makes you wonder what they're up to during working hours, doesn't it?"

The glare Crystal shot me rivaled the club's spotlights.

"So, yeah, Dave is on top of the list. Why does he have access to the safe?"

"Because he's head of security and sometimes he needs to make change for the different stations."

Not a valid reason. "Who else?"

"Just me. Dave doesn't have the combination to the safe, the only time he's allowed in the safe is when I'm here."

I stayed mum.

"What? Dave has worked here for three years and he's a valued member of the Hombres."

"Which is why no one would suspect him, that whole code of honor bullshit, right?" I inhaled. Let it out slowly. "Before you ask, I don't have proof. But Dave having unfettered access to the safe and the cash drawers might be too big a temptation to resist. Did the tills come up short last night?"

"A hundred bucks."

"Who knows about the shortage?"

She squirmed. "I told Dave."

Great. "Think Dave blabbed to Charity?"

"Maybe."

"What about that other bouncer?"

"Beau? Nah. Beau's muscles are in his arms, not his head. He practically has to drop his pants to give customers back change from a twenty."

I hid my smile.

"What are you going to put in your little report to Martinez?"

My humor disappeared. Crystal didn't like me tattling on her. Too fucking bad. "First: stricter enforcement on who can be in the tills and the safe. Second: Dave needs a Hombres refresher course on security measures because his suck."

"You don't know—"

"—know how I got in tonight? The service entrance. I waltzed right in. Your door wasn't locked. Oh, and you *weren't* in the office when I caught Dave with his hands in the safe before I came on shift."

The color drained from her face.

"Where were you?"

"In the goddamn bathroom. I was gone for, like, two minutes, max."

"But you left him in here? Alone?"

"Yeah. Shit."

"As manager, the lax security measures are gonna come down on you." I finished my cigarette before she spoke again.

"Anything else I need to fix before Tony pays me a visit?"

"Not that I can think of right now."

"Good, cause I'm sick of dealing with you. Get out of here."

My body throbbed from my run-in with Roland. Even hurt to put my damn coat on. The cold night air sent a shiver though me. Other night noises were noticeably absent.

I'd nearly made it to my truck when an ominous silhouette glided along the backside of the Dumpster.

My fight instinct spiked.

Had Roland Hawk followed me from White Plain?

Or maybe Martinez had sent one of his goons for me. Or maybe it was just a run of the mill creep hanging out in the parking lot of a strip bar trolling for easy prey. Fuck. I was so whipped Jericho could take me in a fight.

The shadow materialized into none other than Bo-Bo the security brute.

I wasn't exactly relieved. "What the hell are you doing out here?"

"Waiting for you. I've got a message from Dave."

Huddled in my coat, it probably looked like I cowered in fear. But when I jammed my hand in my pocket, I realized I'd forgotten to take out the stun gun. Bo-Bo would get a shocking surprise if he came one step closer.

"I'm supposed to warn you that if you ever question his authority again, he'll make sure your bartending days are over."

I merely blinked at him, without visibly shrinking away, which confused poor Bo-Bo.

Another menacing step. "Do you understand?"

"Yep. Give Dave a message. If he ever threatens me again, I'll use this on *him*, not you." I whipped out the stunner and placed it on the largest target—Bo-Bo's chest—and pressed the button.

He hit the ground like a felled pine tree.

Huh. Since I'd used the stun gun twice in one day, maybe the damn thing was starting to pay for itself.

After what I'd been through with bullies today, I felt no guilt whatsoever as I stepped over his twitching form, scrambled in my truck and roared off.

CHAPTER 20

Sheriff Richard's phone call yanked me out of a deep sleep early the following morning. He asked me to meet him at The Road Kill Café.

I slid into the last booth in the back and tossed my cigarettes on the table, just so he knew he wasn't sitting in the nonsmoking section.

Misty waddled over with a pot of sludge, a Road Kill specialty. I'd already set my cup at the edge of the table. She didn't bring a menu since I always ate the same thing.

"Hey, Julie. How's it going?"

"Good."

"Your partner joining you today?"

"No. Sheriff Richards is. Might as well pour him a cup while you're here."

Misty peered at me, debating on questioning me

further. She probably wanted to ask why the sexy Mexican guy hadn't been in with me recently. Martinez was a hard man to forget. I fumbled with my cigarettes. The situation with Martinez was making me crazy.

"I'll wait 'til the sheriff gets here before I put your order in."

The place was surprisingly quiet for Saturday morning. A couple of ranchers sat at the counter, chrome stools separating them as they scoured *The Rapid City Journal.*

A tinny bell above the door jangled. The sheriff strode over in civilian clothes: jeans, a green and black plaid western shirt with pearl snap buttons, scuffed cowboy boots, black Stetson, and a black Carhartt coat. I'd bet my tips from last night he had his gun on beneath that beat-up coat.

He folded his large frame into the booth, bumping my knees. I scooted closer to the wall to give him more room. He scowled at my cigarette but said nothing as he removed his hat and set it on the seat beside him.

"This mine?" He pointed at the coffee.

"Yep."

Misty appeared. "You guys want me to put your orders in now?"

The sheriff was a regular so he didn't need a menu either. He nodded. Misty's ample hips swayed as she walked away, rattling the silverware on the tables.

"So, what's up?" I didn't bother with the, weather's-been-nice-but-we-need-the-moisture chitchat.

"I need to ask you a favor."

My back snapped straight. The last favor requested of me involved working in a joint with naked women. "Is this an official favor?"

"Yeah."

"That mean I'm getting paid?"

He lifted his mug. "Depends on if you give law enforcement a discounted rate." He grimaced at the taste of the coffee. "We don't have extra money in the budget this time of year."

"I'm listening."

"We got an ID on those bones you found."

My eyebrows shot up. "Wow. That was like *CSI* fast."

"I called in a couple of favors. Mostly the reason they came up with a match so promptly is because they had dental records on file."

"Who?"

He sighed. "A young Indian woman. Missing for five years. She was from White Plain."

I repeated, "Who?"

"Maria Dove."

The coffee in my stomach churned into acid. "Shit."

His brown eyes narrowed. "You know her?"

"No. But there is a connection I'll share after you tell me why you need my help."

"The case is five years old. Maria's mother won't care, because to her, it's a new case. If I don't have someone looking into it, she's gonna start screaming racial discrimination."

"And because I basically did the same thing with Ben's case you think I'm the logical candidate to deal with her?"

"Listen—"

"You want me to share my crappy experiences in trying and failing to find answers about who murdered my brother?"

The flat, cool cop's eyes stared back at me. "Back off, Collins. Don't go jumping to conclusions. Yes, I asked you partially because you might have better luck explaining she might *never* get answers. That's not the reason I'm asking for your help."

"Then why are you asking me?"

"Right now I don't have the extra manpower to handle the stuff that happens in my county on a daily basis, say nothing of investing taxpayers' money to investigate a cold case." He sipped his coffee. "You are a good investigator. Better than anyone on my payroll right now."

His comment, while flattering, didn't ease my sense of unease. "And?"

"And, although you are tough as nails, you've developed a soft spot for situations like this. It'll bug you enough you won't stop until you figure out what happened."

"Because she's Indian?"

"No. Because you found her remains." He braced his elbows on the table. "I know you, Collins. You'll keep poking around whether I want you to or not. I'm offering a little compensation for the time you'll spend."

I smiled meanly. "How little compensation we talking here, sheriff?"

His answering smile was just as ornery. "A pittance."

"I'm used to it, since that describes my salary for the three years I worked for you."

"I haven't had a pay hike in five years, so you'll get no sympathy from me."

"Why do you keep doing it? Is it the gun? The title? The snappy, hip uniform?"

"Been asking myself the same question lately." He spun circles with his spoon. "Too stupid to quit, I guess. It's all I know how to do. Hell, it's all I've ever *wanted* to do."

Compliments weren't my forte, but if he could toss one out, so could I. "Tom. You're a great cop. Money isn't everything."

"Tell that to Bernice."

"Your wife been ragging on you about it?"

"Some. Her best friend just got back from Hawaii. She's been dropping some heavy duty hints she'd like to go."

"So take her."

"Can't do that on a cop's salary."

I mock whispered, "That's why there's Visa."

His brows knit above his tiny crooked nose. "Even if I did charge a couple of tickets, when would I have time to go? We're short-staffed, I'm training a rookie—"

"The Bear Butte County Sheriff's Department will survive fine without you for one lousy week. How long has it been since you took a vacation? Two, three years? You need a break as much as Bernice."

"Probably."

"Definitely. Schedule the time off and set it up. It'll shock the hell out of her. Plus, Bernice will think it's romantic."

The sheriff looked at me strangely.

"What?"

"Since when do you give a crap about romance, Collins?"

Heat flashed in my cheeks. Dammit. Since I didn't have any in my life. "We're talking about you, not me."

Misty brought our food. She had a knack for impeccable timing.

We ate quickly and got down to business.

"Did you bring a copy of the file?"

"No. Damn copier jammed again. I'll fax the info to you as soon as I get back to the office."

"Why don't you give me a rundown?"

He angled back, buffing his hand over his nearly bald pate. "Late spring five years ago, Maria Dove disappeared. Clothing and personal affects were gone from her apartment. Rumor was she'd been talking about taking off for greener pastures, so at first no one seemed too concerned."

"Except for the Dove family," I said.

"Exactly. Maria's mother swore her daughter wouldn't just pack up without saying good-bye, or without telling them where she was going. Hard to prove foul play without a body, so she's been listed as missing."

"Seems kind of morbid Maria's family would have her dental records on file with the state, just in case."

"Not when you consider some Indian shaman told the family a couple of months after Maria disappeared that she was dead."

A family adhering to traditional Native ways wouldn't question the vision of a Lakota Holy man.

"They hoped if an unidentified body turned up— which as we both know is a rarity in South Dakota—it'd help the investigators process it faster and give them the positive ID. I drove out to the Dove's yesterday."

241

"What was their reaction?"

"It's just Sharon now. Her husband Clem died a year after Maria disappeared. Sharon was relieved at first, then angry." His gaze cut into me. "You gonna tell me about the connection?"

"I uncovered a lead on Ben's case in the last week." As dispassionately as possible, I relayed the visit from Abita and Jericho. What I'd learned from Darrell Pretty Horses. I left out the assault portion of my visit to Roland Hawk, but I connected the dots to him and Marlon Blue Legs.

Sheriff Richards' mouth was a hard line. "Burns my ass, Collins, that no one came forward with this information. I won't pretend to understand the Sihasapa tribe's habit of keeping to themselves, but we might've been able to solve your brother's murder."

"I will solve it." I smashed my cigarette in the ashtray. "You, or any of the other investigators really didn't have this information?"

"No. I would have told you."

Our eyes met. "Don't bullshit me."

"I'm not."

He studied me so intently I wondered if I had egg on my face. "What?" I said with annoyance.

"Roland Hawk is on the list of suspects who murdered Maria Dove."

My blood ran cold. "You gotta be shitting me."

"Nope. According to Sharon Dove, five and a half years ago, Maria tried to stop Roland from beating on Bonita, and Maria ended up on the receiving end of Hawk's fists. She called the tribal police and had him arrested. Unlike Bonita, Maria wouldn't drop the charges. Roland did six months in jail on a domestic charge. Sharon Dove swears he threatened to make Maria pay for humiliating him."

"Wasn't he under suspicion after Maria disappeared?"

"Some. But at the time Bonita swore Maria bragged that she had a new boyfriend. Bonita says they took off together before Roland was released from jail."

I frowned. "Who was Maria Dove seeing?"

He drained his coffee. "Sharon didn't know. She claims Bonita made up the story about the mysterious boyfriend to cover for Roland." He sighed. "It's a pretty screwed up situation. I ain't expecting miracles on a cold case. Just find out what you can. No rush on this."

I already had plenty on my proverbial plate. "Who else was on the list of suspects?"

"The mysterious boyfriend. Bonita Dove. That's about it."

"Will Sharon Dove talk to me? I'm not exactly Miss Popularity on the White Plain Reservation."

"Sharon is good people. She'll talk to you, Julie.

Maria didn't have many friends, so that list is short."

Good, because chasing down five-year old employment records would suck. "Where'd she work?"

"Some restaurant in Rapid City. There is one other name you should know that wasn't on the initial list."

"Who?"

"William Colhoff. Sound familiar?"

I shrugged. "Yeah. Why?"

"He's a registered sex offender in our little county. He's also June Everett's cousin."

My gaze whipped back to his.

"That's what I thought. Interesting, the remains of a pretty young girl happened to show up on his cousin's piece of land, isn't it?"

I'd have said creepy, not interesting. "I'll check him out. Don't think I'll pay him a personal visit, though."

"Good plan."

Misty swung by for a refill. I was coffeed out; my bladder was protesting. The sheriff and I were adrift in our own thoughts, but the silence wasn't stifling.

After a time he said, "Does your father know about Jericho?"

"No."

"Don't you think you oughta tell him?"

"Not my business to tell him. Probably piss him off more than anything."

"Maybe not." He watched me with pensive eyes. "Why don't you spend any time with his and Trish's kids?"

I hadn't expected that question. Then again, Sheriff Richards didn't reckon any topic was taboo. "Because even though we share the same blood, we don't share the same father."

"What's that mean?

"Trish would never let him beat on DJ and Brittney the way he did on me. I don't resent them; I resent *him*."

"You telling me you'd like them better if they were being abused? You'd stand by and let it happen?"

"No. But since it's not happening, it's a moot point."

He wiggled his hat on his head; his ears stuck out like Yoda's. "You might not need them, but they might need you in the same way you needed Ben, Julie. Think about it, okay?"

I couldn't mouth platitudes.

"Talk over the case with your partner and let me know if he has any problems. Especially when he sees the lousy pay rate."

"Will do."

"Kevin doin' all right since his girlfriend died?"

"He takes it day by day. Keeping busy maintains his sanity."

"I know how that goes. You two gonna quit playin' around one of these days and make it official?"

My stomach tumbled my biscuits and gravy into a thick mass heavy as wallpaper paste. "Make what official?"

The bench seat squeaked as he scooted from the booth. "For a smart woman, Collins, sometimes you are one dim bulb."

"It's not what you think."

"Keep telling yourself that. You might start to believe it." He snagged the bill and ambled to the register.

Guess the all powerful Oz hadn't heard I was the old lady of an outlaw biker.

For the first time I was glad it wasn't common knowledge.

CHAPTER 21

ABITA FINALLY CALLED. SHE AND JERICHO WERE COMING over.

Despite a pounding headache from my conversation with the sheriff, and the lingering effects from my run-in with Roland, I smiled when Jericho burst through my front door.

"Guess what?"

"Chicken butt," I said.

He giggled.

That childish laughter should've filled the void inside me, but it made a wider chasm.

"Know why?" he said, playing along.

"Cow pie," I answered.

He giggled again.

The crack expanded.

"Wanna see it?" he demanded.

"A cow pie? Eww. No way."

He wrinkled his nose. "Not that."

"Good, because that would be totally gross. What-cha got?"

"A dinosaur!" He wiggled a plastic green T-Rex; the jaw was wide open, the eyes glowed red, and a long, spiked killer tail swished back and forth. "It bites stuff." He clamped the mouth on the edge of the table and growled chomping noises.

"Cool. Where'd you get it?"

Abita said, "Dinosaur Park, in the gift shop. All those life-size concrete dinosaurs are a little boy's dream come true."

Jericho threw a handful of Matchbox cars on the floor and flopped on his belly. T-Rex stomped on the cars like *Godzilla*.

Boys.

Abita twisted a turquoise ring on her thumb. "Thanks for letting us come over at the last minute."

"I meant it when I said you could call me at any time."

"Good. Umm. I need to ask you a favor."

My defenses kicked in. Pathetic, but true. "What?"

"Will you come with me to meet Ben's mother?"

At my look of shock, she blushed.

"I got to thinking about what you said, and I realized

you were right. So I called Ben's mother this morning."

"What did Yvette say?"

"Not much. I don't know if she believed me or not about Jericho, but she's willing to meet me."

"When?"

"Umm. In about an hour." She cringed. "Sorry for the short notice. I thought it was something I should do on my own. Now I'm not so sure."

If Yvette came alone, Abita would do fine. But if Leticia showed up, she'd rip Abita to shreds like a rabid coyote with a deer carcass.

"We're meeting at a restaurant outside of the reservation. She gave me directions but I'm not sure if I can find it."

Crossing paths with Yvette Standing Elk made me realize my headache was about to get much, much worse.

Abita insisted I drive. She divided her time between gazing out the window and entertaining Jericho in his car seat.

"It's so different here. Everything is so . . ."

Ugly. Late fall is the ugliest time of year. Trees look half dead; washed out leaves dangle on the ends of bare branches. During the peak of summer, prairie pastures were a dazzling spectrum in shades of green and gold. At this time of year the silky strands and fat seedpods were long gone. Nothing remained but dried, faded stalks, and stubbly brown ground cover, sporadic dots of interest spread across ginger-colored dirt.

"Pretty barren, isn't it?"

"Nothing is as barren as miles of desert. How much farther?"

"About twenty miles. Are you nervous?" I passed a tractor hauling round bales of hay. The rancher waved a gloved hand. I waved back.

"Yes."

"If my presence causes problems, Abita, promise me you'll stay. Don't allow how Yvette feels about me to interfere with Jericho connecting with his family."

The fallow fields and empty grazing land held her interest for several minutes. Finally she said, "Ben hated it, you know. How his family treated you."

A lump rose in my throat.

The restaurant, Pete's Pantry, was out in the middle of nowhere. No clue how it stayed in business. I parked next to a silver Chrysler Le Baron with '71 county license plates.

Jericho drummed his feet and hands. Abita unbuckled him, settled him on her hip and scooted to the door.

I trudged behind like a reluctant dog.

Inside, standard red-checked plastic tablecloths covered the tables. Skinny clear glass vases crammed with artificial purple daisies were centered between bottles of ketchup and taco sauce. An empty salad bar curled around one corner.

Yvette wasn't hard to spot since she was the only customer in the joint.

She didn't wave us over. Maybe it was shock at seeing me that kept her back rigid against the brick wall.

Abita gracefully wended through the empty tables, stopping in front of Yvette. "Mrs. Standing Elk? I'm Abita Kahlen. We spoke on the phone."

Jericho hid his face in his mother's neck.

I stood there like a dumb ass.

Yvette wasn't paying attention to Abita, but to Jericho, or rather, the back of Jericho's head.

Ben's mother hadn't changed much in the years since I'd seen her. Same shoulder length black hair. Square glasses on a round face. She was short and squat with a heavy upper body. Yvette wasn't a particularly pretty woman. Nor did she have a dynamic personality. I hadn't pegged her as strong-willed either, so she'd always been a bit of an anomaly to me.

Ben didn't resemble her a bit. He'd been tall and gangly, like our father. Like me. That's where the similarities ended; Ben hadn't looked any more white than I looked Indian.

Yvette finally acknowledged my presence when I lit a Marlboro. "Thought you might've had somethin' to do with this."

"Julie didn't have anything to do with me contacting you."

Her attention returned to Abita. "Why did you contact me?"

Abita blushed and lowered her chin slightly to kiss Jericho's head. "Curiosity, mostly."

I frowned. Abita had hedged that question with me too.

An older waitress chatted with Yvette, jotted down our drink orders and left us alone in prickly silence.

Abita whispered to Jericho, and unwrapped his arms from her neck. She set three cars on the table and unzipped his coat.

Jericho faced Yvette for the first time.

I watched her shamelessly, preparing myself for her gasp of recognition. Or tears of joy.

But I was doomed to disappointment. Yvette remained statue-like.

Once Abita had situated Jericho in a high chair between us, she jammed a straw in her Sprite. "You don't have any questions?"

"Of course I have questions."

"Are you questioning whether Jericho is Ben's son?"

"All's I hafta do is look at him to know he's Ben's kid."

I choked on my Diet Pepsi. That comment shocked

the shit out of me. I'd expected her to demand a paternity test, and then whip out a test kit.

"You Hopi then?"

"Yes."

"Both sides?"

"Yes, except for a great-great grandmother who was Mexican."

"I'm a third generation descendant of Chief War Bonnet. The Standing Elk family is descended from Red Cloud."

But Ben's heritage was mixed; half white, half Sioux. Jericho's heritage took him further away from the Sioux purity they were so proud of. Was that part of the reason Yvette hadn't welcomed Jericho with open arms?

Politely, Abita said, "Family history fascinates me." Several agonizing minutes passed as they made inane conversation about family trees.

Another weighty silence hung over the table like lead.

Yvette squinted at Jericho and cocked her head at Abita. "Ben told me about you. Not much, but I recognized your name when you called. It's very unusual."

The casualness of her statement nearly knocked me out of my chair. Ben had told his mother about Abita? She'd known about her?

"Did Ben know you were pregnant?"

Abita shook her head. "I kept it from my family and

everybody in the village until it was obvious I wasn't just getting fat."

"How old were you?"

"Seventeen."

"I had Ben at seventeen."

I shot Yvette a sideways glance.

She was looking at Jericho, and for just a minute her mouth softened. When she caught me scrutinizing her, her lips drew back into a line as tight as a drum skin.

I should've taken a deep breath, given myself a moment to get myself together. But I was so goddamn mad I blurted, "Why didn't you tell me you knew about Abita?"

Yvette showed not a lick of emotion. "Maybe you should be wondering why *Ben* didn't tell you, eh?"

Bulls-eye.

Jericho reached for a blue crayon. I rolled it closer to his chubby little hand. He smiled at me with Ben's eyes.

My world spun with the depth of Ben's duplicity.

Satisfied she'd put me in my place, Yvette refocused her interest on Abita. "Why are you here now?"

"I'm taking a weaving seminar at National College." Abita blathered nervously about various classes and classmates, then her enthusiasm tapered off and we were back to quiet.

"Them kinda classes are expensive, especially comin' here all the way from Arizona."

"I know. I couldn't have afforded it if the tribe wasn't paying my tuition."

Feminine laughter trilled in the kitchen, beneath the sounds of an ice machine dumping cubes into a metal bin.

The air at the table became chilly.

"Sounds like you don't have much money. So, if you're here to ask *us* for money, you're wasting your time. Our family ranch passes to the eldest Standing Elk male, making Jericho ineligible to inherit. Ever. And my daughter is a lawyer and she'll make sure he don't get nothin'."

Sweet, bumbling Abita vanished. She slapped her hands on the table hard enough it wobbled.

Yvette, Jericho, and I jumped.

"You happy now you've insulted me? You've insulted my child, your son's *only* child. You think the reason I've come here is to hit you up for money?"

Jericho began to whimper.

"This is why I didn't contact you when I had my baby alone. This is why I hesitated to contact you at all. Because I knew it would be a mistake.

"I want nothing from your family. I've never wanted anything, especially not compensation. Having *my* son is more than enough compensation for the short time I spent with *your* son." Tears glittered on her dark lashes. "I was

255

taught to respect my elders, and I have. But I'm done. Forget we ever came here, because we won't be back."

Abita straddled Jericho on her hip and stormed out the door.

Unhurriedly, I picked up Jericho's cars and rolled up the picture he'd scribbled. Then I leaned over so Yvette had no choice but to hear what I had to say.

"Did Leticia give you pointers on the cold bitch act?"

"You've no right to talk to me that way."

"Yeah? I never would have guessed such a heartless woman raised such a warm, loving person as my brother."

She flinched slightly at the phrase "my brother."

"Yes, I said my *brother*. Ben belonged to me too. That child is the last link we have to him. Maybe it doesn't matter to you, but it sure as hell matters to me.

"Who cares if your heritage can be traced back several generations? I doubt those all-important ancestors would've been proud of the way you acted today.

"Maybe you got a secret thrill, keeping the information about Abita from me. I've spent the last three and a half years chasing every lead, no matter how small, because I am driven to find out what happened to my brother. I cannot fathom why, as a mother, as *Ben's* mother, you wouldn't want the same thing.

"So go home and gloat with Leticia and Owen and Reese about how you put Abita in her place. But be warned: your little secret reinforces my suspicions there are plenty more secrets left to uncover. And you bet your ass I will find out every goddamn one."

I managed a dignified exit.

Outside, Abita and Jericho were sitting on the concrete parking blocks, digging in the gravel. Crap. I'd forgotten her car keys were in my pocket.

Jericho's head whipped around at the *chirp chirp* of the doors unlocking. He ran to me, hand outstretched. "Look! A pink rock!"

"Cool." If I kept talking I'd feel less like crying.

Abita's entire posture was glum. "Sorry."

"Don't be. You ready to go?"

"Yes." She stopped. "Oh no. I left his c-a-r-s inside."

I smiled despite the bad taste in my mouth from the conversation with Yvette. "I have them."

After Jericho nodded off, I said, "That didn't take long."

"I'm sorry I asked you to come along."

That made two of us.

Low clouds of fog created an eerie mysticism. The tires made a soothing *clack-clack clack-clack* in the quiet of the car. I was dying to smoke, not only out of nerves, but nicotine helped my focus. Something was out of synch here. But I'd be damned if I could put my finger on it. Seemed like everything in my life was out of synch.

"What are your plans now that you've met Ben's

mother and she didn't give you a T-shirt emblazoned with the family crest?"

"I don't know."

"You could always hang out with me. That ought to really piss them off."

Abita smiled serenely, appearing far older than she was. Truthfully, it spooked me a little. "You're exactly like Ben described you."

"How's that?"

"Tough, smart, and funny. Sweet."

My jaw dropped. "Ben said I was *sweet*?"

"Why does that surprise you?"

"Because no one has ever called me 'sweet'."

"Ben recognized qualities in others they didn't recognize in themselves." She stroked her braid in long, continuous movements. "Even though that was a fiasco, I wish I knew . . ."

"Knew what?" I swerved to avoid a dead raccoon in the middle of the road. Made me think of Charity. Should've run the damn thing over. "Something else going on?"

"No. Forget I said anything, I'm just babbling because I'm tired." Her head fell back into the headrest and she closed her eyes.

She'd neatly sidestepped another question. Why?

Every so often I'd glance in the rearview mirror and

watch Jericho's sweet face, deep in sleep, and wonder if he was just another male who'd eventually break my heart.

CHAPTER 22

With multiple projects pulling me different directions, after Abita and Jericho left, I headed into the office to catch up on cases that paid the bills. After a couple of hours, I took a short break and popped in Kim's hair salon on the bottom level to wish her luck with the evening's conversation with Murray.

When I returned, a woman waited in the reception area. Her back was to me.

"May I help you?"

She spun around.

Leticia Standing Elk. Her usual superior expression distorted her blocky, hatchet face.

"Tell me, what gives you the right to call my mother a cold-hearted bitch?"

Did the Standing Elk family use smoke signals? Because barely three hours had passed since Abita and I parted ways with Yvette.

"Correction. I didn't call her a cold-hearted bitch, Leticia. I called *you* a cold-hearted bitch. Big difference."

My response jarred her. I hadn't been the fawning teenage girl who craved a connection with her for a long damn time.

"Did I clear that up for you, or was there some other reason you're here?"

"You think you're pretty clever, don't you? Big difference between being smart and a smart ass."

"You would know." I purposely glanced at the clock. "Nothing else? Show yourself out. I've got things to do." I turned on my bootheel and made tracks for my office.

My hands trembled as I lit a cigarette. By the third drag, Leticia had wandered in.

"I don't know who you think you are, but no one talks to me that way."

"Pity," I said. "Continual reverence seems to have given you an over-inflated sense of self-worth." I indicated the chair with a quick thrust of my chin. "Either sit down or get out."

Her thin upper lip curled. "And if I don't? You going to call security?"

"No, I'll throw your ass out myself." I angled across my desk. "I've looked forward to this moment for years,

261

Letty, so give me a goddamned reason, because I'd do it in a fucking heartbeat."

No snappy come back from her as she seethed.

Leticia resembled her mother, not the beautiful, glowing fictional version of an Indian woman like Pocahontas or Sacajewa. She was stout as a whiskey barrel. Her small black eyes were deeply set in her chubby face, her reddish-brown skin pock-marked from acne. A mass of thick, unruly black hair curled past her shoulders. Expensive clothes hid her figure flaws. Nothing hid her disdain for me, not that she'd tried.

Her mannish fingers pinched the creases in her navy suit pants before she perched her big butt on the chair edge.

"What brings you by?"

"As if you don't know."

"Let's pretend I don't." I smiled, blew smoke in her face.

"What did you hope to accomplish by bringing that Hopi tramp here?"

I didn't rise to the bait. "Unlike some members of the Standing Elk family, I didn't know about Abita until she and Jericho showed up on my doorstep last week."

An ugly frown flared her nostrils. "You're lying. No members of my family knew about her."

Well, well, wasn't this interesting. Mommy Dearest kept the information from the princess too. "Gosh,

Letty, I wish I was. But when we met with Yvette today, she already knew about Abita. Evidently Ben had told her years ago." I let an expression of shock cross my face. "It was news to me, but your mother didn't tell *you*? Wow. That's harsh."

"Regardless. Ask yourself what this girl has to gain by coming forward now?"

I shrugged. "Maybe nothing more than knowing her son's heritage."

Leticia sneered. "I think the word you're searching for is *inheritance*, not heritage."

"We both know the Standing Elk family has more pride and prejudice than cash. Same can be said for me, so I'm thinking there's another reason she's here."

"The great detective has a theory? Need a magnifying glass, a pipe, and a trench coat?"

"Just a notebook." I reached for the legal pad on the corner of my desk. Ashes from my ashtray floated over her plus-size Ann Taylor suit. "Sorry. Okay. Now, where were we? Oh, right, my brilliant theory. I'm actually beginning to think you're right. There has to be another reason Abita showed up after . . . what? Four years since she'd seen Ben? I think she knows something about who killed him."

Silence. Then Leticia cackled. "That ought to be fascinating, since she was about twelve? When Ben knocked her up. Maybe she thinks it was Santa Claus. Sorry to burst your little bubble, but I wouldn't believe a word she said."

I smiled, though seething inside. "It'd take a lot more than that to destroy my hope."

"What has she said to you?"

"Nothing concrete. Not yet anyway." I crushed out my cigarette. "You don't believe Jericho is Ben's son?"

"My mother is convinced this boy is Ben's child. I'm reserving judgment. Especially if she wants to enroll Jericho in the Sihasapa tribe."

"Why would she want to? Jericho has more Hopi blood than Lakota." Here was the opening I'd been waiting for. "Speaking of the Sihasapa tribe, I was surprised to find out the tribe had hired Ben at your urging to schmooze the tribal members about getting behind the proposed gambling compact a year before he was murdered."

Leticia was utterly flabbergasted.

"Is there a reason you didn't tell me? Mainly, just to be contrary, I'm sure. But I don't know if the cops and the FBI would see it that way. I'm assuming you didn't give them the truth either when the authorities deigned to sniff around?"

Her eyes became mean slits. "How did you get that information?"

"I can't divulge my source, as it would violate client confidentiality laws. As a lawyer, you know how that goes."

She fumed.

I pressed on. "I really don't understand why you kept it from me. What's the big deal? Ben only worked for them for a couple of months. Owen took all the credit, despite the fact Roland Hawk and Marlon Blue Legs initially helped. You got the initiative passed, Owen got a seat on the Sihasapa Tribal Council." I frowned. "What did Roland get again?"

"He got paid," she snapped.

"What is Roland up to these days?"

"Do I look like his social secretary?"

"Temper, temper. I was just wondering. Since he and Ben had always been friendly . . . then again, I heard *you* and Roland were particularly cozy for a while."

"You have a sick, perverted mind."

"Better than a small mind."

Leticia's laugh hung in the air like sour milk. "Let's get this straight; I've *never* liked Roland. He has a history of violence and aggressive behavior dating back to juvenile. Not just simple childhood bullying; he's a nasty piece of work."

"Why did you hire him?" I knew she hadn't, but I wanted to see if I could catch her in a lie.

"I didn't. The tribal council did. I knew it was a mistake, and when we tried to rectify that mistake, Ben became livid and threatened to quit."

Ben? Livid? That didn't sound like him. But it was easy to blame a dead guy.

"Despite his lineage, rumors have floated around the reservation for years that Roland killed people who crossed him. None of it could be proven, but a few people just disappeared."

Like Maria Dove?

If Roland had such a bad reputation, wouldn't the cops and FBI have checked him out as a potential suspect? From memorizing Ben's case file I knew he'd never been interviewed.

"Why didn't they investigate Roland for Ben's murder?"

"I don't know. They did a half-assed job on every aspect of his case."

It almost sounded like she cared. *Not.* "You going to get to the reason you're here?"

"Yes." She fussed with the slim band on her gold Timex before she glowered at me. "Stay away from my family. It's bad enough we've all had to suffer through your obsession with Ben's case. He's dead. He's a dead *Indian.* The bottom line is no one cares. No one has *ever* cared. My family has tried to move on from the tragedy, but you won't let it go."

That sinking sensation tickled my stomach again.

"Personally, I find you beyond pathetic. Ben made

no bones about the fact you've never had a relationship with your father. Why do you keep punishing my family? Because you don't have a family of your own to destroy with your bitterness? Spending your life mourning and glorifying the dead is pitiful. Ben certainly wouldn't have wanted to be on the pedestal you've created for him."

She gestured to the paintings on my walls, the vibrant watercolors and sedate charcoals, created by local Native American artists. "You aren't Indian. You'll never be Indian. Doesn't matter how much artwork you buy, or how many powwows you attend, or if you've got a dead half-brother who had Sioux blood. Nothing will make you like us. And nothing will bring him back."

By the mean glint in her eye I think she expected me to break down. Tearfully demand she leave my office.

Leticia didn't know me very well. She never had.

I took my time lighting a cigarette and let it bob in the corner of my mouth as I clapped four times. Slowly. Sarcastically. "Great performance, Leticia. Would've been better if you could've worked up a few tears." I drew the cigarette from my lips and blew smoke at her. "But I highly doubt you even cried one fucking tear for Ben."

"You have no right—"

"You've always craved the spotlight, but you've been forced into the shadows—Ben's shadow. Must suck, to have to prove yourself all the time, eh?"

"I don't have to prove anything. To you or anyone else."

"Isn't that why you're here? To prove I'm nothing? To prove Abita and Jericho are nothing?"

"No. I'm here to tell you my family, every single member, is off limits to you."

"Good thing that's a short list." I cocked my head. "Remind me again how many children you have?" I paused, flicked an ash. "Oh, that's right. None. Reese? Is he still pretending he's not gay? Owen? Does he still have a thing for white girls? Interesting, don't you think, that my dead half-*white* brother is the only one who's contributed an heir to that all important Standing Elk *family* line?"

"That's enough," the angry male voice intoned from the doorway.

I focused on the tall Indian glaring at me. "Owen. Long time no see. Nice suit. You here to defend Leticia's honor?"

He stalked in and squeezed the back of the buffalo skin chair with a slender hand. "Her honor doesn't need defending. It's yours that's in question."

"Right."

Leticia hefted her girth upright.

"Leaving so soon? Does that mean I'm not invited to the 'Welcome to the family' celebration in honor of Jericho? Or are you expecting me to entertain Abita since neither she nor I are *Mitakuye Oyasin*?"

Ticked them off I used the Lakota phrase for 'All My Relations.'

"Not even close," Leticia snarled.

"We're here to demand you stay away from our mother."

I granted Owen a once-over. He'd plumped out a bit, but it didn't look bad on him. His black hair was crewcut short. The wire rim glasses perched on his broad nose added interest to an otherwise bland face.

"Well?" he demanded.

"Done," I said. "Anything else?"

Confused by my quick agreement, they left without another word to me.

Pompous fuckers. I'd take Ben off that pedestal when I found out who killed him.

🐾 🐾 🐾

Slamming tequila shooters wasn't an option for a distraction from my piss-poor mood. I propped my feet on my desk and sorted through the papers Sheriff Richards faxed over during my tête-à-tête with Leticia.

Page one was a missing persons report on Maria Dove, filed in Pennington County. The officer noted no foul play was suspected.

The black-and-white picture of Maria verified she'd been a knockout. An ethnic beauty with exotic almond-shaped eyes, prominent cheekbones, a regally thin nose, and a generous mouth curled into a come-hither smile.

I skimmed the information until I found the page with Maria's last place of employment. Casa Del Rey. Well, that idea was bust. The restaurant had filed for bankruptcy and the building was bulldozed to make room for another Walgreen's. I missed those tasty margaritas.

I flipped to the interview with Maria's former co-worker, Jackie Ryland. I checked the local phone book. No listing. Jackie could've gotten married and divorced a couple of times in five years. I booted up my computer and ran a reverse trace.

Noises echoed from the street below. I brooded out the window about my shitty day. Wisps of white clouds were a stark contrast against a sky the color of smudged steel.

The computer beeped, announcing the end of my search.

Jackie Ryland, now Jackie Moorcroft, lived in Sioux Falls. I checked the time. Most of eastern South Dakota was an hour ahead. It was the weekend. Maybe I'd get lucky and find her at home. I dialed the number.

A female voice answered on the second ring. "Hello?"

"Jackie Ryland Moorcroft?"

"I ain't buying whatever you're selling so just—"

"Jackie, I'm not a telemarketer. I'm calling for information on a friend of yours from a few years ago."

"Who is this?"

"Julie Collins. I'm working with the Bear Butte County Sheriff's Department on the case involving Maria Dove."

"Oh, shit. Hang on." The receiver clattered. "I read in the *Argus Leader* today that her remains had been found."

"You sound surprised."

"Yeah. Well, I was stunned, actually. I thought she'd taken off for Denver. She'd talked about it enough . . . getting the hell out of Rapid City. Makes me sick she's been dead and buried the whole time."

"How long did you work with Maria at Casa Del Rey?"

Pause. "Eight months, probably. But we'd known each other since high school."

"Then you knew her pretty well?"

"I thought I did."

No elaboration.

"Jackie, I'll be honest. Anything you can tell me about her, or her frame of mind before she disappeared will be a big help."

"The truth is, when we were girls I knew Maria really well, but we stopped being friends our first year of high school."

"Why?"

"I don't mean to speak ill of the dead, but I discovered a side of Maria I'd never would have believed if I hadn't seen it firsthand . . . She lied to everyone, and stole from her friends, and she absolutely lived to pit one person against another. She was one of those cruel, beautiful women, know what kind I mean?"

I knew exactly what she meant. "So you didn't hit the bars and stuff after work at Casa?"

"No. At first she wanted to hang out, like all the time, but then she hooked up with that loser guy and quit asking me, thank God."

My ears perked up. Ah, the mysterious boyfriend. "What loser guy? There wasn't a boyfriend listed on any of the interview paperwork."

Another round of sticky silence.

"Jackie?"

"Yeah. All that stuff seems like it happened a lifetime ago."

"I'm sure it does. But anything you remember could be important to helping us find the person responsible for killing her." Damn. Talk about sounding like bad dialogue from an old TV cop show. "Tell me this boyfriend's name."

"Maria never told me the guy's real name. She called him by his nickname, Beaner or something stupid like that. But she did let it slip he was married."

I wrote that down. Not a smart move for Maria, screwing around with a married man. "What else about him?"

Jackie snorted. "Guess he was really good looking, or so she said. This bozo had given her that same old tired line about leaving his wife for her. Right. Then the two of them would ride off into the sunset on his motorcycle."

"Motorcycle? He was a biker?"

"Biker wannabe. She acted like Beaner being in a biker gang was the coolest thing in the world."

We were getting somewhere, but I had a sneaking suspicion this information would lead me to a place I did not want to go. "How did she meet him?"

"At her other job."

The pen in my hand froze above my notes. "What other job?"

"Shit. You don't know? It ain't in any of those reports?"

"No. Casa Del Rey was listed as her last, and only, place of employment."

"I'm not surprised she'd hide it, or lie about it. Probably her mom didn't even know what she'd been doing."

I counted to ten. "Hide what, Jackie?"

"Hide that she was working in a strip club downtown."

Blood whooshed in my ears. "You're shitting me."

"Nope."

"Which strip club?"

"Bare Asses or whatever it's called. Anyway, Maria

had only worked there about two weeks and she hooked up with Beaner. The psycho followed her to her apartment. Since Maria didn't have no car, she walked everywhere. Instead of freaking out about him basically stalking her, she was flattered."

If Mr. Mysterious was a stalker before he'd met Maria . . . and if she'd tried to break it off with him, he might've killed her in a fit of rage.

"What did Beaner do at the strip club?"

"He was a bouncer, working as security, because he wasn't a full member of the gang yet. He had to pass his pledge initiation first."

"She told you all this, and yet you never met this guy?"

"No. Like I said, we weren't friends; Maria didn't have friends. The only reason she spilled this shit to me was because we worked together. No one else at Casa could stand her. So, yeah, at times I felt kinda sorry for her."

"Did you tell the cop who interviewed you any of this?"

"No. He was goin' through the motions, you know? Big fuckin' deal, another missing Indian. I'm sure he thought she'd show up at detox or the women's shelter. Didn't much care one way or another. And I really thought Maria had just packed up and left town and that's what I told him."

The conversational break was awkward.

A high-pitched scream pierced my eardrum through

the phone lines.

"Look. My daughter is having a temper tantrum. I gotta go."

"I appreciate your time, Jackie. You were a big help. If you think of anything else, call me." I rattled off the number and hung up.

The words I'd written plowed me over like a gravel truck.

The dead woman had worked for Tony Martinez.

CHAPTER 23

JUNE EVERETT SAT ON THE EDGE OF THE BLUFF, WATCHING the sunset; the sky was a swirl of red, pink and orange.

She tossed the empty beer can, listening for the hollow ping as it bounced off rocks, then hit bottom.

Probably Lang had made a much louder thump when he'd landed.

She shivered.

She reached over and pulled another can of Busch Light from the twelve pack. Popped the top. Drank like she was dying of thirst. Eight down; four to go.

It'd be dark soon. Nights were the worst, when she was alone. She missed Lang. God. She missed him something fierce.

And now? Now she knew why them goddamn bones had been moved. As soon as she'd seen the paper today, she'd recognized the girl's name. Poor thing.

What should she do?

Lang's gruff voice drifted on the chilly breeze. *"Call the sheriff."*

Shivers skittered down her spine and she went motionless. Shit. Maybe she was drunker than she thought if she was hearing her dead husband's advice out in the middle of nowhere. Where he died.

June drank steadily. But as the cold beer coated the hot lump in her throat, she realized Lang's ghost, or whatever the hell it was, was right: She *had* to make that call. She was a big girl, not a chickenshit. June Everett didn't need no one to hold her hand. She'd really do it, not just talk about it . . . just as soon as she finished her beer.

She flipped open her cell phone and dug the crumpled card from her pocket. On the backside she'd written the number for the sheriff's department. She turned the card over and over, running her ragged thumb across the raised black letters. Wells/Collins Investigations. On impulse she dialed the number.

The answering service picked up.

She took that as another sign that calling the sheriff really was something she had to do on her own, and hung up without leaving a message. She set the cell phone on the ground beside her and threw the business card alongside the twelve-pack.

Lost in her own thoughts, June didn't hear the footsteps. By the time she registered the hands on her head and chin, she knew nothing beyond the quick sound of her neck breaking.

Her dead body tumbled down and rested motionless at the bottom of the bluff, a mere foot from where Lang's had landed.

The cell phone was slipped in a pocket. The wadded up business card caught air like a paper snowflake and disappeared on the wind.

CHAPTER 24

WHAT WERE THE ODDS THAT SEPARATE PATHS IN MY life—a last minute job with the sheriff, and an undercover gig with my lover—would intersect with a five-year-old missing persons case? A case in which I'd inadvertently discovered the remains of the victim? True, South Dakota was a small state, and there were only so many missing persons cases in West River, as well as only so many bars, restaurants, and nightclubs in Rapid City, but still.

Coincidence is fate in disguise.

Jesus. I flipped back to the page listing Maria's basic stats. The initial report listed her age as twenty-two.

Maybe she hadn't been a cocktail waitress. Maybe she'd been stripping. Maybe that's why Maria's mother hadn't known about her extra nocturnal activities.

Maybe after seeing her naked Mr. Mysterious had

fallen madly in lust with her. I had to get my hands on her employment records from Bare Assets.

Yeah, right. I wasn't exactly Crystal's favorite person after my diatribe about the security infractions. Then again . . . maybe I could use that to my advantage.

☠ ☠ ☠

Bo-Bo and Dave shot daggers at me when I moseyed in. Before I ditched my coat and smokes, I barged in Crystal's office.

Crystal wasn't surprised to see me, but her eyes were chips of ice. "You better have left that stun gun elsewhere. If I wasn't under orders to keep you on, your ass would be hitting the fucking pavement."

"I'm making no apology to you, Martinez, or that ape Bo-Bo for zapping him last night. He's goddamn lucky I didn't tell Martinez about Dave's threat to me. We both know the stun gun is the lesser of two evils."

"Martinez got a soft spot for you, Collins?"

I shrugged. Let her draw her own conclusions.

"You're here early for a change. Gonna criticize me some more about my piss-poor management skills?"

"No. I have some non-security related questions to ask you about your staff."

"Thank God for small favors."

Should I build up to the question? Flatter her to get on her good side?

"You planning on asking the question today?"

So much for my ability to suck up. "Do you go through a lot of employees?"

"Tons. Why?"

"Where's the biggest employee turnover?"

"Cocktail waitresses, by a mile."

"But didn't you tell me most of the current cocktail waitresses have worked here awhile?"

"Yeah, all of them a year or more, which is like a club record. It's also why I'm having a hard time buying they're suddenly ripping off the cash registers." Her gaze narrowed. "Did you see something last night you're not telling me?"

Trina's shell game came to mind, but I opted to keep my mouth shut. "No. Actually, my questions are about a woman who used to work here. She's connected to another case I'm investigating."

Seeming relieved, Crystal lifted her hair off her neck and it swung behind her like a black curtain. "Who?"

"Maria Dove. This would've been about five years ago. In the spring. Do you remember her?"

"Vaguely."

"Was she a dancer or a waitress?"

"Uh uh. Confidential information."

I offered my best pitch. "Which is why I need to get a look at her personnel records. Please. It's really important."

Her jaw fell. "Are you out of your fucking mind? I can't let you do that."

"I know. I'm hoping you'll make an exception. I'm backtracking this case and it's hard enough getting old information."

She concentrated on stubbing out her cigarette. "I told Tony I'd cooperate with you on the employee theft thing. But that's it. I'm already on his shit list about the security infractions."

I waited a beat. "I haven't told him."

Crystal's head snapped up. "What?"

"I had other commitments today and I haven't had a chance to type up the report and give it to him yet."

My intentions hung in the smoky air between us.

"You sneaky bitch. You suggesting you'll overlook the issues with the security problems for another day or so if I let you snoop in those records?"

"That pretty much sums it up."

Crystal considered it for all of ten seconds before a crafty smile appeared. "Deal." She walked to a bank of dingy gray filing cabinets surrounding the safe. Drawers slammed as she rooted around, muttering to herself. She turned around, clutching a folder.

"That's weird." She tipped the folder upside down. Not a single piece of paper dropped out. "No copies of her W-4 or I-9 or driver's license or social security card. No application. Nothing."

"Who else has access to the files?"

"No one. Besides, it's mostly junk in there anyway. All the important paperwork is kept at the accountant's office." She slapped the folder on her palm. "So, tell me what's going on and why this is so important."

"Maria Dove was listed as a missing person five years ago. Her remains were found earlier this week."

"Holy shit. I hadn't heard nothing about it. What the hell happened?"

"Her family filed a report, but somehow Bare Assets wasn't listed as one of her places of employment. No one came here and asked you questions about her?"

"No. I'd've remembered that."

I didn't get the feeling she was lying. "Was she a stripper?"

Crystal shook her head. "Cocktail waitress. She only worked here about three months or so. One night she didn't show up for her shift."

"And you didn't think anything of it?"

She gave me an are-you-kidding look. "It happens all the time for any number of reasons."

"Like?"

"Like the girls only want to earn a certain amount of

cash and when they've made it, they stop working. Or they get too old. Or they get pregnant. Or their boyfriends or husbands make them quit and we never hear from them again. There's always another woman ready to step in."

My anger surfaced. "Cocktail waitresses are disposable then?"

"No. They're interchangeable. And I don't need a goddamn lecture on morality and feminism from you, okay?"

"Fine." I don't know why I'd directed my frustration at her anyway. Not her fault I'd hit a dead end. "Do you know anything about the guy she'd met here? An Hombres pledge working security? Evidently they were an item."

"Pledges come and go. I ain't got time to keep track of them, nor do I care who's banging who. You know rumors fly in the bar and restaurant biz and they usually don't mean dick. As long as my employees are doin' their job, I stay out of their personal shit."

Maybe she should pay closer attention. Case in point: Charity and Dave. And Trina. I picked up my coat instead of picking at her some more. "I'm in the back section tonight?"

"Yep." Crystal opened the safe and removed a cash drawer.

"Were the tills short last night?"

"About $500 between all the registers."

I whistled. "Did you tell Dave?"

"Yeah. He blamed you."

"I figured he might." I'd keep an eagle eye on him to see if he'd make creative change from other stations. "Anything else?"

"Watch your back. Charity, Dave, and Beau are pissed off I didn't fire you." She shook her finger in my face. "Don't take matters into your own hands again."

I smiled nastily. "No guarantees."

It was a long ass night.

CHAPTER 25

KEVIN PICKED ME UP THE NEXT MORNING AFTER HE found my note about Sheriff Richards hiring us. He wasn't happy I'd already tentatively agreed to investigate the Dove case. He was even unhappier when I confessed my undercover work at Bare Assets.

I girded my butt cheeks for an ass chewing that never came.

Finally, I couldn't stand it any longer and demanded, "Aren't you going to rail on me?"

"No. It sucks that he put you in such a bad position. Damned if you do, damned if you don't. Just finish this favor for Martinez as soon as possible, because it's seriously fucked up. Sounds to me like there's more going on there than he's telling you."

True. I batted my eyelashes and cooed, "You could

help me. If you watched one of the other sections, maybe you'd see something I'm missing that would wrap this case up."

Kevin's grin was predatory. "Hate to tell you this, babe, but I wouldn't be watching the bartenders if I went undercover in a strip joint. But I'll think about it. Take one for the team, so to speak. When's your next shift?"

"Tuesday."

We were cruising through rugged ranch land. In early fall, bushes and trees scattered across the horizon were a tapestry of color, nature's own crazy quilt. The landscape's natural dips and crevasses, striped with multi-colored layers of sediment, broke up the startling visual impact of vastness. Dirty clouds reigned over the sky.

The gloomy day, my scattered thoughts and the reality of what we were about to do— interview a grieving mother—gave me a serious case of déjà vu.

Not déjà vu. Kevin and I had been in this situation seven months ago when we interviewed Shelley Friel about the murder of her daughter, Samantha. That'd been the beginning of a string of dead bodies.

I hoped this wasn't another case of history repeating itself.

The Dove house was nice, probably built in the 1940s after WWII. Two stories with a front porch that'd recently been modified with a 'three-season' room. Two barns, an old red wooden one and a metal monstrosity twice the size of the house and barn combined. Next to it was a machine shed with a door propped open.

My gaze swept the pasture. Beyond the metal fence, Hereford cattle drank at the stock tank. A carport angled to the right side of the house, close to the front door. Beneath the canopy was a silver Buick and a white Dodge 250 diesel truck.

Didn't appear the drought had affected the Dove family.

"Do you know how you're going to approach this?" Kevin asked.

"Nah. I'll wing it." I wanted to size up Sharon Dove before I brought up Maria's moonlighting gig, mostly to see if she'd offer it up first. Then maybe that'd give me a better indication on why she'd abandoned her other daughter and her grandson.

A woman, maybe early sixties, met us at the front door. She was part Native American/part Mexican, stalwart, her short dark hair tamed into a sleek bob. Easy to see where Maria had inherited her looks. A pair of red reading glasses dangled from a beaded chain around her neck.

"Mrs. Dove? We're the investigators Sheriff Richards sent. I'm Julie Collins, and this is my partner, Kevin Wells."

"Call me Sharon. Please. Come in."

We traipsed behind her into the sun porch, decorated in the typical Midwestern version of a tropical theme: white wicker furniture precisely arranged around a glass-topped coffee table. The cushions were tastefully understated pseudo-Hawaiian prints done in pastel shades. Kevin spread out on the settee. I opted for a chair next to the windows.

"Coffee?" Sharon asked.

"That'd be great, thanks."

While she brought out the sugarcane-shaped serving tray and fiddled with cups resembling coconut shells, I had that oh-my-god-I-have-to-get-out-of-here-right-fucking-*now* urge to run to the closest Tiki bar and gorge on rum. And to top off my claustrophobia, I was in the throes of an epic nicotine fit.

Kevin sensed my distracted state and helped matters by glaring at me.

Sharon sat in the wicker rocking chair, pouring coffee from a French press. "I suppose the sheriff has filled you in?"

"Some. You reported Maria missing, although she wasn't living here at the time of her disappearance. How did you find out she was gone?"

"We were on vacation in Hawaii for two weeks prior to that. When we returned I kept calling her and getting no answer. I knew something was wrong."

A spoon rattled. Kevin loaded his cup with sugar cubes. He was as bad as Martinez.

"How often did you talk to Maria?" This from Kevin.

"Not as often as I liked after she rented the apartment in Rapid City. She didn't have a car, so I didn't see much of her either."

"Did you ever stop in to see her at work?"

"If we were in town."

I'd posed the question innocuously, but it didn't trip her up. Sharon hadn't known about Maria's other job.

"Didn't you have a key to her apartment?"

"No. I promised I'd give her space. And look what happened." Her voice cracked, she clapped her hands over her trembling mouth, but gut-wrenching sobs poured out anyway

Her grief pounded at me like a tidal wave.

In that second I hated Sheriff Richards for putting me in this position. Mostly I hated myself for being a sucker and not saying *no* when I had the chance.

I battened down my emotional hatches. When her storm of grief subsided, I felt I'd weathered it pretty good, considering I hadn't given into my desire to run like hell.

Kevin handed Sharon a lace hankie from a stack on the end table and murmured soothingly to her.

Sharon sagged in the rocker. "Sorry. It probably seems silly to you, because Maria has been dead for years."

"The sheriff mentioned you'd talked to a Lakota Holy man a few months after Maria's disappearance, and the holy man indicated Maria was dead."

"Yes."

"And yet you still held out hope she was alive?"

She nodded. "Hiring a holy man to spiritually search for answers was my late husband's idea, not mine. I went along with it because it eased his mind."

"Who was the holy man?"

"Myron Blue Legs."

Shit. A shiver of foreboding tracked my spine along with the reminder of Abita's prophetic phrase, *coincidence is fate in disguise.* Why did I feel the universe—or fate, or karma, or kismet or whatever the hell it was called, conspiring against me to make my life one big ball of chaos? And the dangling strands of that mass were nothing more than dead-end cosmic threads that offered no hope of finding a common connection? The deeper I looked, the more *I* unraveled.

Sharon kept talking. "He and Clem had been friends since they served in Vietnam. I didn't put much stock in what Myron told us. He's a bit of a shyster. I can't believe he was right." Sharon wiped her nose. "Anyway, I thought finding out what had happened to her couldn't possibly be worse than not knowing." Her gaze locked to mine. "I was wrong."

Oh no, she wasn't going to drag me into a confession about my situation with Ben. By the look in her eye, the sheriff had already given her an earful. I had to toe the professional line, more for my own sanity than anything else.

"The reports gave us the basics, so why don't you tell us about the Maria you knew."

"My Maria was a nice, sweet woman. She'd always been such a good girl. Sure, she had some problems, like most kids. Nothing major, physically harmful or illegal, unlike her—"

She caught herself, frowned at her coffee and didn't finish the thought. At least, not aloud.

"So, you never believed she'd gone to Denver?"

"No. I'm aware that's what her co-workers told the cops, but it wasn't true. Maria would've told us. I mean, I can understand her keeping it to herself until she'd actually left and settled in, because she would've known her father and I would be upset about her moving. But to purposely cut herself off from us? Permanently?" Her hair brushed her square jawline as she shook her head. "No. Makes me angry the police never looked beyond that."

"We've heard from more than one source that Maria had a boyfriend," Kevin said. "Was she seeing anyone in particular?"

"She was a beautiful girl; she always had men chasing after her." She shifted and tapped her fingernail on the coffee table. "That's another dead-end. I know her friend Jackie claimed she was hot and heavy with some unknown man, but I don't buy it."

I prodded her a little. "Why not? Do you think you know everything about your daughter's life in those last few months? Especially when you've already told us she'd been keeping to herself?"

"No." The polite veneer vanished. "I think she was in the wrong place at the wrong time. I'm sure those reports have given you the lowdown on her sister, my oldest daughter, Bonita, and the situation with the horrible man she's been living with. Maria had been helping Bonita, trying to get her away from him, even when she knew how dangerous it was. How dangerous *he* was."

Sharon calmed herself. Poured everyone another round of coffee. My cup was still full and had gone cold.

Too bad I hadn't brought my hip flask. Strangely enough, not for me, for her.

"You're talking about Roland Hawk, right?" Kevin said.

"What a miserable man. For years Roland has controlled my daughter like a puppet. It frustrated our whole family, Maria most of all, because at one time, during

Maria's teen years, she and Bonita had been close. Every time Roland beat up Bonita, Maria was there for her."

A lesser professional would've demanded, "What about you? Why weren't you there for her? Or Denny?" but luckily I'd left smarmy girl at the office. I listened, wondering how Sharon Dove could act so . . . righteous when she'd been so clueless about her daughter Maria's life, and so apathetic about Bonita's.

"The last time Maria stepped in to save her poor stupid sister, *Maria* wound up in the hospital, not Bonita. She filed charges against Roland. And they stuck. For the first time."

Her furious gaze locked to mine. "So, you see, I know who killed her. I've always known. Proving it without her body has been the problem."

"Who do you think killed her?"

"Roland Hawk."

"You sound certain."

"I am. Roland was livid. He swore he'd get even with Maria for humiliating him. I've no doubt he tracked her down, strong-armed her into going with him, hacked her to bits and buried her in a hole in the middle of nowhere. It wasn't the first time he'd done it, either."

I froze. "What?"

"An old friend of mine is a youth counselor with the worst juvenile offenders on the reservations. Years ago when he got wind Bonita was involved with Roland, he called me in a panic. Seems when Roland was in the juvenile system he kept getting caught with shanks and knives. They had to isolate him from the other kids because he literally lashed out with them.

"So the counselors, in their infinite wisdom, put his anger to good use, assigning him to work in the kitchen. Yes, they gave him a meat cleaver and it didn't set off warning bells that Roland could hack a chicken to pieces in no time flat."

I swallowed hard.

"Evidently, one borderline retarded boy, who scrubbed dishes, really got on Roland's nerves. This kid mooned around Roland like newly weaned calf. Roland tried to bully him to get him to leave him alone, like he did everyone else, but this boy didn't understand why Roland didn't want to be pals with him. When Roland hit him to get his point across, the poor confused kid hit back. And since the kid was considerably bigger, he pounded the living tar out of Roland before the counselors broke it up. After Roland healed up, the kid disappeared. They never found any trace of him, but I'm betting Roland honed his hacking skills on him first." Another choked sob.

My mind had gotten stuck on *hacked to pieces*. A vision of the Maria's remains flashed in my mind. I'd compartmentalized the bones and dehumanized her. Sharon had blown the lid completely off my pathetic rationalization.

Sharon's cup clattered in her saucer. "So please, don't waste your time searching for some mystery man. Find proof Roland did this to Maria and let him get the punishment he's had coming to him."

An ugly, thick silence hung like a dirty mop.

Kevin nestled his empty cup on the tray next to mine and unfolded from the settee. "Thank you for your time today, Sharon. It's hard, dredging all this up again. We'll be in touch."

Ever the gentlemen, Kevin held the door for me. I had a Marlboro between my lips before my foot hit the bottom step. My feet itched to sprint to the safety of his Jeep. I mentally urged Kevin to hurry, to leave black tire tracks on the driveway in my haste to escape.

We zipped down the gravel road. I'd the sucked my cigarette to the filter so fast I felt nauseous. I said, "Kevin, pull over." As soon as he did, I jumped out and threw up coffee and the bitter taste of my sheer stupidity.

My gut clenched again when I remembered cruising to the rez—alone—tracking down Roland, again,—alone—rolling up to his house—alone—like some bulletproof fucking superhero. Mouthing off, tossing around threats, zapping him with my stun gun, shooting up his trailer.

Jesus Christ on a crutch. I was the dumbest person on the planet. I was goddamn lucky I wasn't dead, hacked to bits, stuffed in a hole some place on the White Plain Reservation.

Roland wasn't the type to forget my bravado. I'd have to be looking over my shoulder for the foreseeable future. I had no one to blame for this predicament but myself.

My face burned hot with shame and fear. I stared down the gravel road, seeing nothing, feeling lost and alone in yet another set of bad choices I'd made.

A door slammed. Kevin came up behind me. He kept his distance, never sure if I'd shrug off his support.

"Julie? You all right?"

"Yeah." I blinked the tears blurring my vision and wheeled around.

His green eyes went completely cold. "Bullshit. Fool yourself, but you can't fool me. What haven't you told me?"

"You know how you're always warning me not to go off half-cocked? Well, I did something bad, Kev, real bad. And I'm scared."

CHAPTER 26

I BLURTED OUT EVERY DETAIL ABOUT MY TRIP TO THE rez, and showed Kevin the slash mark on my neck from Roland.

Kevin peered out the window of his Jeep, his hands in fists on his lap. "Does Martinez know this?"

"No."

"Is there a reason he doesn't?"

I almost told him I was afraid Tony would kill Roland, but I didn't know if that fell under a 'lover's secret' category. "I haven't seen Martinez since it happened."

Kevin faced me. "Doesn't he show up in Bare Assets?"

"Only once, the first night I worked. Evidently his priority is Fat Bob's. I told him I didn't want to see him at all until the problems at Bare Assets were solved."

"Is it over between you two?"

"I don't know."

"So the guy with the army of bodyguards isn't around to protect you when you actually need it?"

"No."

"I absolutely do not believe your bad luck. You're gonna have to watch your back at all times, which is a near impossibility for you, isn't it?"

"Yeah. I guess that means I'd better brush up on my shooting skills, huh? Wanna cap off a couple hundred rounds?"

"Sure, tough girl. Let's see what you've got."

Kevin and I target shot for over an hour. The Browning was lighter than his H&K P7, so it took a few clips for him to adjust. The guy was a serious dead-eye. Yeah, kind of humiliating to get bested on my own gun.

When I returned home there were two messages. One from Kim, one from Brittney. Man, that kid was becoming a serious pest.

Maybe she needs you like you needed Ben.

Was that a possibility? Was I short-changing us both by not developing a relationship with her?

Yet another phone call interrupted my strange musings.

"Hi, Julie, it's Abita. Are you busy?"

She'd called me two days in a row? Something was up. "Nope. What's going on?"

"We have a free afternoon. Jericho's acting cooped

up and he needs to run. Got any ideas?"

"How about Canyon Lake Park?"

"Is it easy to find?"

"Yeah." I distractedly rattled off directions.

"Umm. If you're not super busy do you want to come and hang out with us?"

It amazed me this shy, unsure girl and my brother had been intimate enough to create a child. "That'd be great. In an hour? By the duck feeding station?"

"Good. I'll see you then."

It'd give me enough time to stop at *Toys "R" Us*. Not that I was trying to buy Jericho's affection . . . Well, maybe a little. I wanted to give him something tangible to remember me by.

Naturally, I went overboard, buying a midsize Tonka truck, a backhoe, and a couple of bitchin' Hot Wheels cars. A squishy ball made of soft gel-like plastic that resembled an alien life form with tentacles. A book on dinosaurs and one on trucks. A dinosaur with red glowing eyes that made the most godawful roar when the massive jaws opened.

I left my window rolled down on the drive through Rapid City to the park. Amber sunshine had burned off the chill in the air, leaving one of those perfect crisp fall days, tranquil and cool with no breeze.

A carpet of brown leaves crunched beneath our feet.

Feeding the ducks didn't fascinate Jericho as much as chasing the red squirrels flitting from tree to tree, packing away pine nuts for the winter. His attention span was as fleeting as the squirrels'.

I pushed him on the swings. Played follow-the-leader through the playground stations. We tossed the ball around. When he got bored, we had a rousing game of tag. He caught me and I let him bury me in a pile of leaves.

I was absolutely in heaven.

While I released my inner child, Abita sat at a picnic table, eyes closed, basking in the sun, but I knew she was aware of everything that went on.

Jericho carted the trucks to the sandpit area. Abita and I plopped on the cold ground and watched him dig holes. Neither of us spoke for the longest time.

"Without seeming like a pain, can I talk to you about a couple of things?"

"Sure."

She blurted, "Yvette tracked me down at the college last night after our fun-filled meeting yesterday afternoon."

"Really? Why?"

"To apologize." Abita plucked the dead clumps of grass. She'd rip out a few blades, twirl them between her fingers and toss them aside, then begin again. "Now I don't know what to think."

Was her constant fiddling from nerves? Or because

as a weaver she was used to constantly doing something with her hands? "Think about what?"

"About her. She was really nice. She brought Ben's baby picture so I could see how much he and Jericho looked alike. Then she told me what a great kid Ben had been, how he'd been the joy of her life. And how her family had pressured her to give Ben up for adoption too."

Whoa. First time I'd ever heard that. Had my father been involved in that coercion? Is that why he was so bitter Yvette had kept Ben?

I sensed Abita's hesitation. "What?"

"It was strange to think we're in the same situation."

I frowned.

"Then she started asking stuff. But the questions she asked me about Ben were sorta strange."

"Like?"

"Like, was he happy in Arizona? Did he talk about his family? Did he have plans to return to the ranch? Or would he and I have stayed in Arizona with my tribe?"

"Did you answer any of her questions?"

"Some."

Such as? was on the tip of my tongue, but Jericho interrupted, bounding over like an eager puppy. "Mama, I'm hungry."

"Me too," Abita said.

"I'm afraid I don't have much to offer in the way of food. Why don't you grab a bite to eat and then come out to my house?" I caught Abita's gaze. "I'd like to finish this discussion, okay?"

She nodded.

I pointed to the trucks Jericho had abandoned in the sand pit. "Forgetting something, sport?"

"Uh uh. Them aren't mine."

"Yes, they are. They are a present from me, remember?"

His somber eyes lit up. He gave me a calculating smile so much like Ben's my heart stopped. A double pat to my face with his sandy hands and he declared, "You're nice," before he raced off to collect his booty.

Jesus. The kid owned me. I'd never be able to deny him a damn thing. I needed to leave before I offered him the world if he'd only stay in mine.

💀 💀 💀

Jericho noticed the other *Toys "R" Us* bag on my coffee table first thing. "Is that for me?"

"You'll see soon enough, Curious George."

"My name isn't George."

I tousled his soft hair. "My mistake, curious Jericho."

"Mama, look! Books." Then he saw the dinosaur and the books were forgotten.

"Julie, you didn't have to do this."

"I know, that's why it was so fun."

"I hope you don't mind. I brought some homework with me."

"Not at all. I'd love to see what you're making."

Abita spread out her goodies at the kitchen table. First, she set out a small wooden loom, then unwrapped colorful skeins of yarn from a plastic bag. She didn't chatter as she meticulously wove the stands through the taut strings. She used a wooden stick-like thing to push the thread flush with the others.

I smoked, put off by the uneasy silence.

Normally, I'm not at a loss for words, but I didn't know how to broach the subject of additional information on the months Ben had spent in Arizona. Because I didn't know what questions to ask.

Abita had covered the basics. How much would delving into the intimate details of their relationship tell me about Ben's fame of mind before he was murdered?

Maybe she considered that time with Ben uniquely hers and sharing the memory would somehow taint it.

That made me think of Martinez. Our time together was exactly that: ours alone.

Finally Abita spoke. "After the conversation I had with Yvette last night, I wasn't expecting any more visits from members of the Standing Elk family."

My body went rigid. Had Leticia harassed her too?

"But I had another weird thing happen this morning." She snipped a vibrant red piece and left the ends dangling. "Jericho and I were leaving the campus cafeteria and a man approached us. He said he was Ben's brother, Reese. He kinda looked like Yvette and Owen." Pause "Do you know Reese?"

"Not very well. What did he want?"

"To see Jericho. Then, out of the blue, just like Yvette, he asked me the oddest question."

"What?"

"If Ben had left anything in Arizona."

I inhaled. Exhaled. "Did he?"

Abita rearranged the loops of yarn on the table according to color. "Just a small box he'd made in the shop with my uncle. He'd put a couple of things in it. Nothing substantial or worth any money."

"Did you tell Reese about the box?"

"No."

What was she hiding? "Why not?"

Her black eyes met mine and snapped defiance. "That's one of the few things I have of Ben's. As far as I'm concerned it belongs to Jericho. I'll give it to him when he's old enough to understand."

"Understand what?"

Jericho skipped into the kitchen and crawled on his

mother's lap, cuddling into her.

Abita didn't answer. I whisked my cigarette under the faucet and threw the soggy butt in the trash.

Had Reese been searching for something in particular? He should've gotten his share of Ben's earthly treasures after the mourning ceremony.

"I think somebody's sleepy," Abita murmured. She kissed Jericho's crown. "How about if Julie reads those new books to you?"

My breath stalled. *Please don't say no.*

"Okay." He scrambled down and out of the room.

I exhaled a sigh of relief. "Thank you."

"He likes you." She gathered her weaving odds and ends and arranged them in an oversized canvas bag. Without looking at me, she said softly, "I hate to impose, but is it all right if I use your phone? I need to call home. It's long distance, but I can pay you."

"Don't worry about it." I dug my cell phone out of my back pocket. "Use this. Free long distance on weekends. Talk as long as you want."

"Thanks. I'll be in the backyard if you need me."

Jericho snuggled into me. He was warm, and soft, and smelled like I imagined little boys did, earthy, like dirt and sweat with an underlying hint of soap and French fries. He asked a million questions. But by the time we'd read the second page of the second book, he was sweetly asleep.

It was unbelievably peaceful, having my brother's son dozing on my lap. I shut my eyes and basked in the moment.

☠ ☠ ☠

Tapping on the metal screen door woke me from a light sleep. I slipped a pillow beneath Jericho's head.

Brittney grinned at me from my front porch. "Hi. We were out running errands and I wanted to drop off the questions for career day."

I peered over her shoulder, half-afraid to see my dad's Dodge truck. But Trish's navy blue Buick was idling in the driveway.

Brittney had grown since the last time I'd seen her, yet she was still at that gangly stage. Her teeth were a snaggle-toothed mess beneath her crooked smile. I smiled back until I noticed hers fading as she stared behind me.

Shit.

On cue, Jericho stood. Rubbed his eyes with confusion and wailed, "Mama? Where's my mama?"

Abita tore into the living room the same time my father stepped through the front door.

Everyone froze.

Jesus Christ. Could nothing in my life go smoothly?

Abita gaped at Doug Collins. My father's gaze narrowed on Jericho and didn't waver.

"Now that he's awake we'd better go," Abita said.

"No, you can stay. This'll just take a minute."

"Mama, wanna go now!" Jericho clutched the books to his chest and blinked at Doug Collins.

Abita scooped up her bag and jostled him on her hip. "Thanks for everything today. I'll call you soon, okay?"

My protest fell on deaf ears as she scurried out.

With any luck my father would assume Abita and Jericho were just friends of mine and leave it at that.

But I took one look at him and knew that wouldn't be the case.

My dad said, "Who were those people, Julie?"

I could lie. I could be petulant. Guess which one I picked? "Why do you care?"

"Because that boy was the spitting image of Ben. Is that his kid?"

Our gazes clashed.

"It doesn't matter. You didn't give a rat's ass about Ben, so don't you dare pretend you care about his spawn. Isn't that what you called him once? Unwanted spawn?"

"You always got a smart answer, don't you?"

"Daddy? What's going on?" Brittney asked.

He scowled at her. "Head on back to the car, Britt.

I'll be right there."

"But Dad—"

"Go. Now."

Brittney's confused, frightened gaze darted between us and she ran out the door.

I needed a minute to think, to breathe, to get away from him. I wheeled around and stomped to the kitchen.

My damn hands shook as I lit a cigarette. I poured a shot of tequila in my coffee mug. I didn't really taste it as it slithered down my throat.

I'd taken a healthy drag when I sensed him in the doorway. "I'm asking one more time, girlie. Is that kid Ben's?"

I exhaled. "Yes. Ben left a young, pregnant girl-friend behind in Arizona no one knew about. She's here because she's curious about Ben's family."

"Didja plan on tellin' me about this boy?"

"Not my place."

"But I suppose the injun family knows."

"Yep."

"But I ain't got a right to know?"

"Why? You have a hankering to be a grandpa, *Doug*?"

"You got a smart mouth."

"Like that's a big surprise."

He snorted. "The injuns throwing him a big 'wel-come to the tribe' powwow?"

Stay calm. Don't react. "No, so I can see where Abita wouldn't want a repeat performance with you after her meeting with Yvette and Ben's other siblings. Did you forget you washed your hands of Ben and anything associated with him years ago? So your 'rights' are non-existent, Dad."

He gave me a fiery look of hatred. "You don't get to decide that, and I ain't done with this. You tell that girl to call me at the house. If she don't, it's gonna come down on you."

I didn't move for the longest time.

Yeah. My life was a tangled mess. Jerk a loose thread and it wouldn't pull free but was guaranteed to become another knot.

☠ ☠ ☠

I stole into bed for a few hours. I deserved a nap.

The insistent ringing of the phone woke me. I blinked at the clock, as the time registered early evening, not the middle of the night. The caller ID read: *rural pay phone.* "Hello?"

"Julie?" a garbled male voice said.

"Who's this?"

"Denny Bird."

"Hey, what's up, Denny?"

"Umm. Nothin'."

That didn't sound convincing.

"Okay, something came up. Remember when you tole me to call you if I needed anything?"

I jackknifed in my bed. "Yeah. What's going on?"

"I kinda did a dumb thing. I hitched a ride off the rez, you know, to clear my head? And I got no way to get back, no one to call, so I wondered if you could pick me up and give me a ride back there?"

"Where are you now?"

Pause. Traffic noises droned in the background.

Dread swirled in my system. "Denny? You still there?"

"I'm in the Save-Mart parking lot. Know where that is?"

Denny was in Sturgis? "Yeah. Give me twenty minutes."

"Thanks." *Click.*

I flopped back in my pillows. What the hell had I just agreed to? Hadn't I suffered enough self-recrimination about my stupid choices today?

But I *had* told Denny to call me if he needed anything, not that I'd expected him to take me up on it. I couldn't rescind the offer now, as much as I was beginning to regret it.

Both the clips in my gun were empty from shooting with Kevin. I reloaded and set the gun on the seat beside me in my truck. With the way my luck had gone lately, I wasn't taking any chances. I slid my stun gun into my right jacket pocket.

I hadn't spent much time in Sturgis recently. It shocked me the Save-Mart had closed its big red doors. A 'For Sale' sign decorated the front windows. The parking lot was empty.

Where was Denny?

My feeling of dread mushroomed.

I spied the pay phone and a form huddled on the ground on the far left corner of the building.

Shit. Was Denny hurt?

I hit the gas. Threw the truck in Park and jumped out.

The second I got within three feet of Denny, I realized my mistake.

Roland Hawk oozed from the shadowed corner of the brick building.

My gaze whipped to Denny. His face was a mass of bruises, cuts, and scrapes. His left eye was swollen shut, the skin surrounding it a mottled red. Some abrasions were lightly scabbed over, some were fresh. The right side of his face bore the imprint of knuckles: purple bruises scattered like ink spots.

I choked on a stream of bile snaking up my throat.

Roland got right in my face. "Nice you could join us, bitch. See, I've already started this little fucker's punishment for helping you."

Started? Jesus.

"But then I realized I needed him to get to you, so I couldn't finish until you joined my party."

I flinched at his stench of brutality. Automatically, my right hand dropped to my weapon.

Not quickly enough. Roland grabbed my wrist, twirled me around and twisted my arm. "Whatcha got in your jacket?" His free hand dove inside my pocket with enough force the seams ripped. He didn't release my arm as he waved the compact black box in front of my face.

"I was hopin' you'd bring this. Oh, look, and it ain't got no safety pin." Roland ran the prongs down the side of my neck in the same path his knife had taken. "Know how it feels to get zapped like a fuckin' bug? I'll bet not. Wanna see the fuckin' burn marks you left on me? How about if I demonstrate on you?"

"No," Denny warbled. "You said you weren't gonna do nothin' to hurt her. Leave her alone."

"Aw. Ain't that sweet? Little fucker has a crush on you. Just to prove I'm a standup guy, I'm gonna do what you asked, Denny Birdbrain. I'm gonna use it on you."

I was so scared I couldn't find my voice.

Roland shoved me forward. "Watch this neat trick." He dialed it to the highest setting.

Denny whimpered.

"Quit fuckin' bawlin'. Be a fuckin' man. Spread your legs, dickless wonder. I'm gonna zap you where you should've been born with balls."

"No. Please, Roland, don't."

"Shut the fuck up, and spread your fuckin' legs or I'll change my mind about usin' this on her right now."

Denny slowly parted his thighs. Tears leaked down his battered face. His knuckles were white beneath the bruises and scrapes as he clenched his hands into fists.

Horrified, I couldn't breathe as Roland bent down and placed the prongs on the crotch of Denny's jeans. He grinned at me and depressed the button.

Denny's immediate shriek of pain was lost to the motions of his body twitching and writhing on the pavement.

My vision blurred from the tears and lack of oxygen to my brain. I swayed briefly, only to be jerked upright again.

"Remember when you did that to *me* you fuckin' cunt? Huh? 'Cept if I recall, you used this clever fuckin' thing on me *twice*. So, what goes around comes around, and guess who gets to feel the sting the second time?"

My lips moved but no sound emerged.

Roland bent my wrist until the tendons popped. "Answer the fuckin' question."

I swallowed. "Me. You're gonna use it on me."

"Knew you weren't as dumb as you look." He pushed me and I landed on the ground. Cement scraped my palms and burned my knees though my jeans. Immediately I pivoted and crab-crawled away.

"None of this shit would've happened if you wouldn't have come sniffin' around my place, threatenin' me 'bout something that happened years ago. Why the fuck you tryin' to dig up shit on Ben now? Don't fuckin' matter. He's still dead."

"It matters to me. Did you kill him?"

Denny moaned.

"Fuck, no. I had no beef with him."

"Did you have a beef with Maria Dove? Did you kill her?"

"What the fuck you talkin' 'bout?"

"Maria had you arrested. Did you kill her after you got out of jail?"

"No. Christ. I wish I would've. That little sister of Bonita's was a first-class liar. And a two-bit whore. She chased after me from the time she was twelve. So, yeah, if tight, young pussy is flashed in my face, I ain't about to say no. But the night she went cryin' to the cops that I'd supposedly beat her up? *Shee.* Bonita done that."

I sat there like a lump, soaking it in, yet scared to make another peep.

"Everybody in her family 'cept her mother fuckin' hated that bitch. We didn't give a shit when she disappeared, but I sure as fuck didn't have nothin' to do with it."

"So, it was Bonita's fault you sat in jail on a domestic charge?"

His eyes glittered with rage. "Yeah, but she paid for it. Trust me. Now it's time for you to pay."

My mind registered the steel prongs digging into my belly and every muscle in my body spasmed. Then nothing else registered but debilitating, excruciating pain.

An eternity later I quit jerking and twitching. My face was ground into the cement and dirt coated my mouth as I panted, trying to force my lungs to work. My whole body spasmed involuntarily. I was caked in sweat, from fear, from the toll of 300,000 volts on my body. I was half-afraid I'd wet myself.

"Take this as a fuckin' warning, which is better than I give most people who fuck with me. Stay the fuck out of White Plain. I catch you there again and I'll kill you."

Bootsteps thumped and faded. A car engine started and I dragged myself out of the way in case Roland decided to run me over. My back hit a solid object.

I slumped against the building and passed out.

CHAPTER 27

A CHILL BURROWED UNDER MY SKIN. MY EYES OPENED slowly and I didn't know where I was.

The crackle of a neon sign across the road reminded me.

Right. Going off half-cocked again. I was pretty sure I was close to the end of my nine lives.

I shivered. Rolled to my knees—shit that hurt— and wobbled to my feet. I pressed my forehead into the brick and regained my bearings.

I turned around and saw Denny. He'd positioned himself against one of the cement posts. His arm dangled between his knees, my gun clasped in his hand. And he'd found the knife I'd taken from Roland.

"After you passed out I took these out of your truck in case that cocksucker came back."

I swallowed, trying to get moisture in my mouth so I

could speak. "And if he would have come back?"

"I'd've killed him."

I didn't doubt that a bit. I wouldn't have shed a single goddamn tear, either. I might even have pumped in a round or two myself. "You okay?"

"No. Motherfucker fried my nuts."

A hysterical giggle slipped out and I clapped my hand over my mouth.

"It's all right. Though, I'm hopin' if I ever have kids they'll have some kinda super powers from my balls getting electro-charged."

Tears prickled my eyes from Denny's pseudo-blasé attitude. What a tough kid. He reminded me of . . . me, actually.

"Let's get out of here."

He stiffened.

"Denny, come home with me, then we'll figure out a place for you to stay tonight. I've got your *unci's* ointment. That oughta help with the hamburger that's your face."

"Don't it make you nervous, bringin' an injun into your house after what Roland done to you?"

"Should I be nervous?"

Denny shook his head.

"Didn't think so. Besides, I'd planned on calling my friend Kevin to help us out. He's a cool guy."

"He your boyfriend?"

"No, business partner."

"Don't you got a boyfriend?"

Question of the month. "Sort of. It's complicated. Look. I'm dying to get the hell out of here. You coming or not?"

"I'm coming." He heaved himself up and shambled to the passenger side.

We lit up and lit out.

After a bit, I switched off Gretchen Wilson's *Skoal Ring* and said, "You okay?"

"I didn't think it'd hurt that bad."

"No shit." I felt a tiny bit remorseful about using it so callously on Bo-Bo Saturday night.

"Didja notice he took it?"

"Yeah."

"Sure hope he don't use it on my mom, even though I'm really pissed off at her." He ground out his cigarette in the ashtray. "She called my cell and told me my *Unci* Bird was in the hospital. I got there and they was waitin' for me. Somebody had seen you and me together in Too Tall's and ratted us out. Roland made me call you. Sorry."

"My own stupid fault. I never should've gone to his house in the first place. Think he'll come after me again?"

"Wish I could say no, but I ain't sure about nothin' as far as to how Roland's warped mind works."

❧ ❧ ❧

Kevin showed up in record time. Between the two of us we patched Denny up and fed him.

I quizzed Denny on the truth of Roland's claim about Bonita's sister. He admitted Roland hadn't been lying about Maria. She'd been causing family problems for years and had her mother completely snowed. That piece of information added a new wrinkle to the case. Not a judgment on Maria's character; rather maybe there were others she'd crossed who might want to see her dead. Far fetched? Stranger things had happened.

Denny shuffled off to the guest bedroom to crash.

Kevin and I sat in the kitchen and drank beer, more out of habit than need. "What can we do about Denny? He can't go back to White Plain. Although I can't fathom why Sharon Dove wouldn't take him in."

Kevin finished his beer. "He can stay with me."

My cigarette stopped halfway to my mouth.

"What? You're the only one who's allowed to have a social conscience? I have an extra bedroom, and frankly the company would be nice." He cracked a fresh Coors. "I couldn't live with myself if I let him go back to that shitty life. I hated being so . . . fucking powerless when you were in that situation."

Shame made the tips of my ears fiery red. Good

thing they were hidden beneath my hair. I coughed. "You knew?"

"Yeah. You weren't a very good liar." He studied me with that unnerving intensity he was so good at. "You're still not very good."

"What?"

"Call Martinez. Not only does he need to know what that piece of shit Roland has done to you, *twice*, but also this personal problem with him is eating you alive, Jules. Call him."

Kevin sacked out on the couch.

I didn't call Martinez. What would I say? *Hey, come take care of me because I've been making bad decisions? I can't think rationally when you aren't around?*

Screw that.

I'd get by fine on my own, just as I always had.

CHAPTER 28

DENNY AGREED TO STAY AT KEVIN'S PLACE TEMPORARILY.

I was an emotional and physical wreck, so when Kevin suggested we take the day off, I didn't argue. I curled up in bed, burrowed to the safe place deep inside myself and didn't stir until the phone rang late afternoon.

Ugh. Crystal asked me to fill in for Megan. I think she forgot I wasn't an actual employee.

Which reminded me: I was almost officially done with my favor for Martinez. Maybe I should buck up and report in. I scrolled through my phone book until TM was highlighted. Impulsively I hit Dial. My heart raced as I waited for him to pick up, but the busy signal buzzed in my ear.

At least I tried.

Yippee. My heart heaved with joy to see Charity

and Dave when I slunk into Bare Assets. I grabbed my cash tray and opened the bar by the front entrance. First time I'd worked this section. Had Crystal put me there because she suspected my suspicions about Dave might hold truth?

All in all it was a shitty night, made worse when Jimmer strolled in and plopped front and center at the main stage. Stupid me. I'd known he was a regular and I should've had a plan in place for when our paths crossed. The best one I came up with on the fly? Avoidance. I kept my back to him, hoping the mousy posture and the fake glasses would throw him off.

No such luck.

Jimmer approached when no other employees lurked nearby. His massive chest shadowed the width of the counter.

"What the fuck you doin' workin' in here, little missy?" His brows drew together. "That son of a bitch Wells payin' you shit wages so you gotta schlep drinks in a hole like this?"

"No, Kevin is paying me plenty."

He gave me 'the look' and I cracked like ice.

"Okay, I'm working undercover for Martinez as a favor."

"That don't make me any happier, Jules. In fact, it pisses me off even more. That dickhead has no right to use you or expect you to do shit for him for free. You deserve better than that."

I was ridiculously touched by Jimmer's loyalty. It made me a little misty-eyed. "Thanks. But this is a temporary gig."

"No matter. If Martinez cared about you, he wouldn't have even asked."

Pathetic, and humbling, to realize Jimmer had a better understanding of my situation with Martinez than Martinez did.

"Don't worry, little missy. I'll take care of it."

My immediate panic stirred visions of Jimmer using Martinez for target practice. "Umm. What are you gonna do?"

"Have a very personal, very detailed chat with Tony. Be seeing ya." He chucked me under the chin and ambled away before I could protest.

And so it went. The 'B' team was stripping and even the customers couldn't muster enthusiasm for the performances.

I returned from the cooler to see Charity had littered the bartop with every dirty glass and empty bottle from her section.

I'd had it. With this place, with her, with Martinez. I stormed up to her at a table and towed her back to the bar. "What the fuck is this? I am not your goddamn busboy. Get this shit off my bar right now."

Her glossy mouth drew into a flat line. "Dave made me clean up the back booth because the big b—"

"I don't care. Your mess; you clean it up."

"Or what?" she sneered. "Little mouse gonna go cryin' to Crystal?" Charity pressed her nose to mine. "I see your mouth moving but all I hear are little tiny squeaks. Clean it up yourself."

She flounced away.

I could've let it go. I should've let it go.

I didn't.

I seized her hair in my fist, twisted one arm behind her back and sent her tray flying like a Frisbee. Then I rammed the side of her face into a sticky pool of maraschino cherry juice on the bartop.

"Crazy bitch! Let me go!"

"Not until you understand you *will* clean up that mess."

"Ow. You're hurting me."

"That's the point."

Charity tried to kick me with her stilettos. I stomped on her toes.

"Last chance. Clean it up or I'll keep your ugly face pinned to the bar until your beak breaks."

"Okay, okay, I'll clean it up. Now lemme go."

I straightened her up before I released the death grip on her tacky mane. I retreated but not fast enough.

Charity swung and her haymaker connected with

my jaw.

Fuck. That stung. My pride more than anything.

In warfare mode, I lunged and knocked her on her ass. She screamed as I pinned her spineless body to the tiled floor.

Bar patrons came running from every direction.

Wasn't twenty seconds later, after I'd landed a good hard blow to her empty head, that I was airborne, a meaty fist clutching the back of my shirt.

But the bouncer wasn't smart enough to secure my hands. I landed two solid punches to a soft head. He dropped me like a stone. I whirled and saw Dave holding his ears.

I didn't have time to feel smug because my arms were jerked behind my back. I recognized the mouth breather right off: Bo-Bo. He buckled my wrists until my shoulders nearly popped from the sockets.

Breathing hard, I managed, "Get your fucking hands off me."

"You're in no position to be makin' demands."

"You're starting to piss me off."

He whispered, "Not so tough without that stun gun, are ya?"

Bo-Bo detained me as Dave shuffled closer. I had a nightmare flashback to another time when one bouncer immobilized me while Dick Friel punched me in the stomach. No one jumped in to save me that time either.

Never again. I threw my head back and connected with Bo-Bo's chin. My fake glasses slid down my nose. I kicked, distorting my body to break his hold.

I heard, "Jesus Christ, Julie, stop struggling."

Couldn't be. I froze.

"Let her go right fucking now."

My arms were released so fast I stumbled. Then strong hands gripped my biceps and I was hauled to my tiptoes.

"Look at me."

I slowly lifted my head.

Martinez was as mad as I'd ever seen him.

I blurted, "She started it."

"Save it."

"But—"

"Not another fucking word. I hate these things." He plucked my glasses from my face and hurled them on the floor.

"Hey—"

"My office, blondie. Right now."

Shit.

"Can't we—?"

"No." He circled one hand around the back of my neck and squeezed a warning.

The crowd of customers and employees, including

327

Crystal, parted as Martinez marched me through the bar. The macho jerk even stomped on my glasses. He unlocked the door near the storage areas, revealing a narrow staircase. I trudged behind him up the stairs.

The second Martinez unlocked the door to a dark room I blew past him. Keys jangled behind me and I heard the locks click.

Damn security measures; I was sick of them.

My heart thumped, my body was flushed, and perspiration coated my skin. I didn't know where we were. He'd said his office. I'd be pissed if he'd dragged me to a private room used for lap dances.

Impatient, I waited in the darkness.

For what?

Footfalls sounded to my left. A click, then light from a small banker's lamp glowed green across plush white carpet.

I crossed my arms over my chest and sucked in a quick breath at the sharp pain. Damn. I'd forgotten Bo-Bo had twisted my arms into a pretzel.

"Does your jaw hurt?"

My fingers poked the spot where Charity had hit me. I couldn't believe she'd actually made contact with that wild girly swing. "Not too bad. She can't hit for shit."

"Lucky for you."

"No, lucky for her."

"Yeah? How do you figure?"

"Because if she'd tried to inflict any real damage on me I'd still be down there beating on her dumb ass."

No comment from Martinez.

I was strung tight as a new barbed wire fence; he was a master at the silent treatment.

The adrenaline rush from fighting hadn't faded. But when that feeling of power waned I wanted to crash alone. Breaking down in front of him wasn't an option.

"What were you thinking taking after her like that?"

"Gee, Martinez, I guess I wanted her to shut her stupid mouth and do her job."

"You should've let it go. You are supposed to be working undercover, remember?"

"Are you actually taking her side?"

"No."

"Good, because she asked for it."

"That's not the point."

"Then what is the point?"

"Your goddamn temper, Julie!"

"*My* temper? You're the one who practically dragged me away by my hair in front of the whole fucking bar, Martinez!"

His leather vest creaked. I figured he'd probably thrown up his hands in frustration. He did that a lot around me.

"What was I supposed to do? Stand there and let you beat the shit out of my employees?"

"Your goon Bo-Bo got a shot in before you jumped in the fray."

"Is it true you zapped him with your stun gun a couple of nights ago?"

I was surprised Bo-Bo admitted I'd won that little contest. "Yes. It was his own damn fault since he was hiding out by the Dumpster. He scared the crap out of me."

"You're a fucking menace with that thing," he snapped. "Tonight Beau was doing his job. You should have been doing yours."

"So fire me for screwing up."

"Not a chance."

"Then I quit."

"Nice try, but not an option."

"Here's where I remind you that you aren't paying me."

His pause cooled the air in the room. "Do. Not. Go. There."

"Why not?"

"Because you don't understand what's really going on."

"Then tell me."

Another one of his tough guy silent moments.

Jesus. The man made me want to scream. "Fine. Let me tell *you* something. I went against not only my better judgment in taking on this assignment, but against my

330

partner's express instructions."

"Wells knows about this? I thought I told you—"

"Kevin is my partner, so yeah, I told him about this *favor*. He's not happy since he'd made me promise my relationship with you would be strictly personal." I laughed cynically. "Relationship. What a fucking joke."

"Explain that bullshit *joke* remark."

"No. I shouldn't have to spell out the obvious."

"Do it anyway."

"We don't *have* a relationship, Martinez. I did this favor to help you out. End of story. And I'm done."

"No, you're not. I've never known you to do a half-assed job; that's why I hired you. I'm counting on you to finish it."

"Tough. I hadn't counted on having to put up with every nasty, half-naked chick on your payroll who wants to be in your bed."

"Jealous?"

"Yes. I mean, no. Shit." *Just breathe. In. Out.* "Goddammit, the bottom line is Charity has been baiting me for the last three shifts, and I lost it. Beau threatened me on Dave's behalf, so I zapped him. I'm pretty sure Dave is the one who's been ripping off the tills, but Crystal doesn't want to believe it because he's been such a model employee.

"One of the cocktail waitresses is selling drugs on

the floor right out in the open. As a sideline? Or is that part of her job? I don't even want to get into how fucked up that would be. So, with everything else that's been going on in my life, I'd had enough. I overreacted. I do that sometimes."

I lifted my chin and glared at where I suspected he lurked in the shadows. "I'm not the model of detachment that you are."

Martinez' immediate dangerous laugh sent chills up my spine. "Detached, huh? That's what you think of me?"

I held my ground even when I heard his muffled footsteps edging closer. "Yes."

Then there were no shadows between us, no darkness to hide in as he materialized and I could see his face.

My stomach clenched at the hard glint in his eyes.

"Wanna know a secret?" he whispered.

His lethal tone scared the crap out of me. I managed to make my head nod one time.

"Detached is the *last* thing I am when it comes to you." His ragged breath drifted across my cheek.

Baiting a caged tiger, when I was also in the cage? Not a good plan. Naturally, that's the one I chose.

"Yeah? How do you figure?" I tossed his words back at him. "I don't see you outside my house, or outside of Fat Bob's. When I do see you away from a room without a bed, you act like you don't know who the hell I am.

Seems pretty goddamned detached to me, Martinez."

The air between us became so heavy I doubted an axe could've cut through it.

Every cell in my body went on high alert.

Instead of denying it, he grabbed me and crushed his mouth to mine. Hard.

The kiss was angry. Hungry.

It was hot as hell.

My adrenaline spiked higher.

Martinez' hands were everywhere; squeezing my ass, my hips, my breasts. One hand tugged the hair tie from my ponytail. When my hair was free, he gathered a fistful, angled my head to his liking and ate at my mouth with zeal bordering on brutality. Fingertips roved my face; his thumb tested the pulse pounding in my throat, stopping at the collar of my shirt.

Buttons flew as he ripped my blouse open.

This was absolute insanity. One minute we were tearing into one another; the next we were tearing off each other's clothes.

Welcome to sexual obsession.

My back hit the door. I bit his bottom lip, but it didn't faze him. Not even when we shared the taste of blood.

Neither of us had an ounce of restraint.

Someone had to show some sense.

Not me. I'd been low on common sense my whole

life and my ability to protest was buried in Martinez' demanding mouth.

He kneed my thighs apart, sliding his muscular leg between mine until I was riding his thigh.

Ah, man, that felt so goddamn good. I squeezed my legs together and ground against him, aching for that perfect amount of hard friction that would send me off like a rocket.

My shoulders scraped the door as he wrenched my shirt off. When he realized I wasn't wearing a bra, he groaned.

I arched into his greedy hands, letting him take what he wanted, giving me what I needed. I craved this side of him; completely out of control, completely focused on me. On us. Sex leveled the playing field. Sex was the sphere where we were in perfect synchronicity.

His thumbs stroked my nipples. Chills raced through me. My belly swooped when that invisible cord connecting my breasts to my sex hummed, electrified by his touch.

My hands traced the hard contours of his jaw, the rigid muscles in his neck until I reached his skin hidden beneath leather. I jerked the snaps on his vest. *Pop pop pop.*

The vest thunked to the floor.

A tight T-shirt kept me from all that warm, smooth

flesh. I tugged the tail free from his jeans, rattling the tangle of chains dangling from his belt loops.

With one hand Martinez grabbed the back of his shirt and yanked it over his head.

Hot skin. God. I nearly purred when his bare chest touched mine. I nearly cried when he removed his thigh and set me back on my feet.

Then his teeth nipped a path down my neck and his hands were on the waistband of my pants. While he tore at the zipper, his mouth latched onto my right nipple.

Primal heat like I'd never known burned through me; I swore blisters formed on my skin in the wake of his scorching mouth.

My pants slithered down my legs. He lifted that busy, skillful mouth long enough to say, "Shoes," then dragged hot, wet suckling kisses to the other breast.

I kicked my shoes off, my pants away.

Martinez dropped to his knees.

My heart beat faster. Sweat tracked my spine. I threaded my fingers through his soft hair as he kissed my belly. His tongue slipped inside the waistband of my thong and my head fell back as I lost myself in mindless urgency.

Strong hands gripped my hips so tightly I knew he'd leave finger-shaped bruises.

I didn't care.

"Tell me no. Tell me this isn't what you want."

I couldn't. He knew it.

His hot breath fanned over the center of me. He brushed his mouth back and forth where I was hot. Wet. Aching.

He tugged and the seams on my little scrap of panties tore like rice paper.

Martinez bent his head and tasted me. Teased me, proving the mastery he had over my body. Pleased himself as he made me thrash and whimper and shake as he purposely kept me hanging on the ragged edge.

It'd been too damn long. God. Why had it been so long? My body trembled like a junkie desperate for a fix.

I was at his mercy.

He lifted his face and looked up at me. I almost came right then.

Warm, rough-skinned palms skimmed the outside of my legs from ankles to hipbones. Back on his feet, he kissed me, an unhurried, deep, thorough swamping of my senses. I heard him unhook his belt. Heard the zipper slide down. His damp lips grazed my ear and he said, "Turn around."

I expected he'd throw me up against the wall and fuck me senseless. Countless times we hadn't made it to a bedroom and had improvised on any nearby flat surface. Vertical. Horizontal. Didn't matter.

Evidently he had something else in mind.

"Do it," he hissed.

I did it without question.

Anger had spiked his primal instincts to dangerous levels. Yet, Martinez wouldn't hurt me. He wouldn't go beyond the parameters we'd established. There was a marked difference between forced violence during sex and mutual intentional roughness.

I liked him rough, raw, and as needy as I was.

Erotic sensations bombarded me, the cold door pressing my cheek, the warmth of his chest firm against my back, the labored sounds of our breathing. The cruel possessiveness of his hands.

And his scent. Oh, God, the way he smelled seeped into my lungs. An elixir that made me dizzy, crazy, and stupid. Made me forget everything besides gorging myself on everything that *was* him.

Denim scratched the back of my thighs and his jeans fell to his knees.

"Tell me no," he whispered in my hair.

I still couldn't. *Wouldn't.* I wanted this and he knew it.

He widened his stance. "Put your feet on my boots." His hands tracked my hips, the sensitive bend in my waist, detouring over my breasts, across my collarbones and shoulders, to caress the underside of my arms.

I shivered with elemental need.

337

He flattened my palms on the door and reversed the sequence down my back, digging his thumbs into my spine while his maddeningly slow caresses intensified the tremors racking me inside and out.

Martinez bent his knees and leaned back until I felt the hard tip of his sex nudging between my thighs. He pushed aside my hair and placed his soft lips in the curve of my shoulder.

His rough fingertips pressed on my lower back, a lover's signal for me to raise my hips. Soon as I did, he slid inside me to the hilt.

My eyes rolled back in my head and I whimpered.

In his position when he began to thrust every inch of him hit that sweet spot. Every. Damn. Time. Over and over until I gasped for breath. For control. For *something*.

His lips, teeth, and tongue created a hot, wet, sensual onslaught on my flesh as he slammed into me. His thickly whispered Spanish phrases burned my skin like a brand. Then he sank his mouth into that magic spot on my neck and it was over.

I came so hard I forgot to breathe. I came so hard I saw stars. I came so hard Martinez didn't stand a chance at holding off and followed right behind me into oblivion.

When the roaring in my head stopped, I realized the room had cooled and was strangely silent.

My tangled hair hung in my face. My legs and arms shook. He seemed to be in the same stunned shape.

"Jesus Christ," I panted. "What the hell was that?"

Martinez kissed the spot below my ear and whispered, "Detachment."

CHAPTER 29

THE SEX HIGH WORE OFF IMMEDIATELY. I CRASHED.

Something inside me broke. I started to cry. Not delicate, controlled little sniffles. Huge, ugly sobs rippled through my body.

Martinez slowly pulled out of me. He set me back on my feet and stepped away from the train wreck.

Using the door for support, I lowered myself to my knees and crumpled to the floor. I curled into a ball and wept.

He didn't touch me for the longest time. Finally, I felt his gentle hands on my head as he tried to brush the hair from my face.

I flinched.

His hands snapped back like he'd been burned.

I cried harder.

His reaction didn't register until the worst of my sob fest had abated. I pushed up from the floor, wrapped my arms around my skinned knees and peered at him through my veil of hair.

He'd plunked down next to me, jeans refastened, purposely not touching me, his muscled forearms resting on his knees, his face pointed at the carpet.

And then I knew. He thought he'd hurt me. He thought my tears were because the sex had been so rough and raw.

My eyes filled again. My low, scratchy voice didn't sound like my voice at all. "You didn't hurt me, Tony."

He raised his head. "Then why the tears?"

"I don't know! I just feel so . . . so lost. I haven't seen you. And when I do see you alone it's a big explosion of sex that's hot and sweet and so goddamn perfect, and then it's awful because we fight and I know it won't last. Nothing ever lasts for me. You act so cool and don't seem to care that things are falling apart. Goddammit, *I'm* falling apart."

More tears fell.

Martinez swore. Next thing I knew, he'd scooped me into his arms. He carried me to a couch, cradled me on his lap and covered my bare skin with a soft blanket. I continued to cry. He squeezed me so tightly his belt buckle dug into my hip and I could hardly breathe. I

341

didn't care. I clung to him even when the tough girl inside me sneered and urged me to flee.

I burrowed my face in his warm neck and slipped my lips across his hot skin, tasting salt from his sweat mixed with my tears. I inhaled his familiar scent and let it calm me.

He swept the hair from my tear-dampened face and tilted my head back. Our eyes met and we measured each other.

I broke first. I always did. "What?"

"You are amazingly beautiful."

A funny tickle started low in my belly. Martinez never said things like that. Was he gearing up for the "It's been fun but it's not really working out" speech?

"I don't ever tell you, do I?"

I shook my head.

"It's not because I'm not thinking it." He twisted a section of my hair around his finger. "Every time I look at you, blondie, I wonder what the hell you're doing with me."

This couldn't be good. The damn tears came back.

Martinez cupped my face between his hands. "Jesus. Don't cry."

"If you're dumping me, you bastard, I think I'm entitled to cry."

A brilliant smile lit his face. "See? That smart ass

answer is why I'm so crazy about you." His thumb skated across my cheekbone, wiping away the tears. "I'm not dumping you, Julie."

"You're not?"

"No. You should dump me. Why you've put up with my shit in the last month . . ." His grip on my head tightened. "You should be pissed off about the way I've treated you."

"I am." I didn't look away even when his sudden ferocity scared me. "Do I embarrass you? Am I just your dirty little secret?"

"No."

"Then why don't you want anyone to see us together?"

"Don't you think I want to take you out? Show you off? You're beautiful and bright and the toughest goddamn woman I've ever known. I want every man to know you're *mine*."

Silence.

Normally such macho posturing would make my ears bleed, but it was a strange confession coming from Martinez. And as I watched that fierce, yet unsure glint return to his eyes, I knew it'd been hard as hell for him to admit.

"Well, good, but don't expect me to tattoo your name on my ass or anything."

He laughed. "I love this smart mouth." Then he settled his lips on mine and if I'd had any doubt his words were complete and total bullshit, they vanished in the way he kissed me.

I relaxed my forehead to his. "So, what do we do now?"

"I explain what's been going on."

A little too ominous for my liking.

His hands slid down my neck. He slapped my ass and jerked away the blanket. "Put some clothes on. I can't concentrate when you're naked."

"What am I supposed to wear? You ruined my shirt and my underwear, remember?"

"Vividly. And I'm not apologizing." He strode to where our clothes were strewn on the carpet like a yard sale.

He tossed me his T-shirt and my pants. With nothing on beneath his vest besides muscles and a colorful network of tattoos, he epitomized tough and dangerous.

Be still, my heart.

I dressed and curled in the corner of the couch and wished I had a cigarette. And a shot of tequila. I didn't see a bar cart in here. Fat Bob's was a more hospitable place.

Martinez didn't turn on more lights. Nor did he sit down. He leaned against the wall and stared across the dark room.

How long before he told me what was eating him?

"Remember when I went to Omaha?"

344

Not long at all. "Yeah."

"You have any idea why?"

"You said routine Hombres business?"

He made a disgruntled noise. "That's what I thought. I got down there and had seven chapter presidents waiting to jump my shit."

"Why? What happened?"

"Things have gone to hell in the last few months. Shipments intercepted. Arrests of our distributors. Problems we've never had before. They think we've got someone on the inside feeding the cops or the Feds or whoever information."

"Are you sure?"

"I'm not. They are. That's why we had another meeting in Denver. They've accused me of knowing about it and ignoring the problem."

I shivered. "How long do they think you've known?"

"Since before Harvey died." He closed his eyes. "They had the balls to question Harvey's loyalty. *Harvey*. Fuckers. Harvey had been with me longer than anyone. He was with me when I took the presidency."

Took the presidency. Not "was elected" or "won." I really did not want to know what that coup entailed.

Yet, this was the most Martinez had ever talked to me about Hombres politics. It'd be easy to say the wrong thing. Easy for him to clam up. So I listened.

345

For the first time since Harvey's death, I wondered who he had to talk to about this motorcycle gang stuff. He hadn't been confiding in me. He and Jackal barely tolerated each other. Big Mike? Maybe. I glanced at him, noticing the fine lines at the corners of his eyes and the furrowed ridge between his brows. The tense set to his shoulders. Some attentive lover I'd been. Too concerned with my own problems to consider he had problems of his own.

My face flamed. I felt like the most self-centered woman on the planet. "What did you do?"

"Knocked some heads together."

"Fighting always makes me feel better."

"Might be perverted, but damn, I've got a thing for watching you fight, blondie."

"Next time you should put Charity and me on the main stage and sell tickets. I'll make sure she bleeds."

He smiled slightly.

"Has anything changed since you came back?"

"Oh, yeah. Jackal thinks he's figured out who it is."

"Who?"

Martinez's laser gaze burned into me. "He thinks it's you."

"Me?" My heart rate kicked up. "Why the hell would he think that?"

"Because you used to work for the sheriff. Because

you're still around law enforcement all the time. Have you been meeting with Sheriff Richards recently?"

"Yes. Between Lang Everett's accident and me discovering those bones in that stock dam, yeah, I've had no choice but to spend time in the sheriff's office. But it hasn't been me breezing in there just to chat and create nefarious plans."

"Bones? When the hell did you find bones?"

"Last week. Sheriff's orders I had to keep it under wraps until the DCI identified the remains."

"No wonder you acted so weird that last night we were—"

"Yeah, I know, you left."

"You think I wanted to leave?"

"You sure as hell didn't act like you wanted to stay."

The vein in his neck throbbed. "I can't fucking believe the shit you get into."

"Is that why I'm under suspicion?"

"Partially. Jackal thinks you're the ideal plant because you're so obvious."

My cheeks grew hot. "That slimy little fucker. Where does he get off accusing me? He doesn't even know me. And I don't have a clue about the Hombres organization, Martinez, you know that. You don't believe him, do you?"

He stared at me.

"For Christsake! It makes more sense the problem is Jackal. He gets voted in chief enforcer and suddenly everything goes to shit? He knows everything that goes on. *He's* around you all the time, not me. Except for when you have to go to those out-of-town meetings, leaving him in charge, right?"

Martinez nodded.

"Blame someone else. Right. Smart move, throw suspicion on the secret girlfriend."

"Julie . . ."

I felt absolutely ill. "I don't believe this."

The chains on his jeans rattled as he switched positions. "I don't believe it either. Any of it."

My gaze caught his. "That's a big fucking relief."

Again he watched me. I fought the urge to babble.

"See? Him accusing you? That's where Jackal made his mistake."

"How so?"

"Like you said: He doesn't know you. He doesn't know me, and he sure as hell doesn't have a clue of what we went through last summer."

Martinez and I had seen lots of death up close and personal. We'd been forced to trust each other, and within that trust we'd forged a bond most people couldn't understand. They certainly couldn't see it, although it was there. And that bond—one I've never experienced with another lover—is why I hadn't walked away from him. What pulls us together is not just physical. It's deeper than lust and scares me like nothing else.

"That relief might be short lived when I tell you what I'm up against."

Everything inside me filled with dread again.

"I've given Jackal and every other Hombres member who knows about you the impression it's strictly sex between us. Know why?"

I shook my head.

"Because if they thought differently, they'd use you as leverage with me. They'd expect you to show up at the club parties. Those parties are free for all sex, drugs, and booze."

"Do you go to the parties?"

"I avoid them whenever possible. If I brought you to the clubhouse as my old lady, you'd consider the treatment of the club's female groupies . . . barbaric and get pissed off. Then you'd voice your opinion. Which is bad for you because women's opinions aren't welcome. It'd also be bad for me because I'd look pussy-whipped.

"But if I didn't bring you and people knew we were together, it's an insult to my brothers. To put it in the crudest terms: They wouldn't make *me* pay for the insult, they'd make you pay. They'd track you down outside of the clubhouse and consider you fair game."

"Fair game?"

"If you're good enough for me, but I'm not willing to put you under my protection, you're good enough for them. All of them. They'd pass you around like a blow-up toy. A gang bang is only the beginning."

I swallowed hard.

"On the other hand, if you're officially with me, you would in effect become the property of the Hombres. If you didn't do whatever the members asked, told you, or demanded of you, you'd be subject to punishment. Torture. Rape. And there isn't a goddamn thing I can do about it."

I looked at him like it was the first time I'd truly seen him.

He began to pace. "I don't agree with the shit they do. I didn't even before I was president. I don't encourage it, discourage it, or participate. So, if all of a sudden I started wigging out about any of them putting a single fucking finger on you, it'll just confirm Jackal's suspicions that I'm protecting you for some bigger reason."

"This is insane. I don't understand why you—"

"That's another thing I can't explain, Julie. It's who I am. The Hombres are *what* I am. We don't live by anyone's rules but our own. Sometimes those rules suck."

"So, you're telling me you've been treating me like this for my own good?"

"I know it sounds harsh—"

"It sounds like complete and total bullshit!" I leapt to my feet. "I can't do this, Martinez. You'll either own up to what this is between us, not only to me, but to everyone, including your archaic 'brothers', or you're gonna have to walk. You can't have it both ways."

I made a beeline for the door and tripped over my shoes. I heard, "Fuck!" then a hard thump.

I turned and watched Tony put his fist through the wall a second time.

"Own up to what's between us? You drive me absolutely fucking crazy." He was by my side in the blink of an eye. "I should let you walk out that door. I've tried to stay away from you, but it's pretty obvious I can't. I don't *want* to. Goddammit, I've given up enough for this goddamn organization and I'm not giving you up too."

I was as dumbfounded by his unexpected declaration as I was pissed off by it. I pushed him. He didn't budge. "*This* is how you tell me you care about me and want more than a casual relationship? By including it in another 'you drive me crazy' rant and swearing at me?"

"Surprised?"

"By your boorish behavior? No. That you actually admitted I'm not a casual fling? Yes."

He cradled my face in my hands and wouldn't let me look away. "This hasn't been casual since the day we met."

"It'd be easier if it was." *Breathe. Think this through before you do something rash.* "Okay, I'm just talking off the top of my head here. It's obvious I don't know anything about club protocol, but it seems to me if you're the president, you should get to make the rules. Or break them. Or change them. What's the point of being the Grand Pooh-bah if you're not afforded special privileges and can pull rank whenever you feel like it? You might as well be a lowly pledge."

Martinez studied me so thoroughly I thought I'd said the wrong thing again.

"What?"

He sighed. "How is it that you know exactly how to cut to the chase?"

"Yeah, the tact gene sort of skipped me."

"But the solution was so goddamn obvious I didn't see it."

I traced the frown line between his eyes. "You might have seen it if you would've talked to me about this sooner."

"True, but I haven't been talking to anyone. I don't know who to trust. Been a rough go with the Hombres these last few months. I haven't gotten my bearings back since Harvey . . . and if I'm not focused on club business all the time I'm accused of letting things slide."

One guess for the most vocal accuser: Jackal. "*Have*

you been letting things slide?"

"No. Appears I've been a fucking figurehead who lets lesser members dictate how I run things. No more."

"What are you gonna do?"

"Come out fighting."

"Might be perverted, but I can't wait to watch you kick some ass, El Presidente."

Martinez rested his forehead to mine. "Last chance to walk out that door, blondie."

"Tony, I'm not going anywhere."

"Thank God."

The lingering pause was as perfect a moment as I'd ever experienced.

He stepped back and frowned as his gaze traveled down the V-neck T-shirt and the exposed line of my throat. "Where'd you get that cut?"

Crap. I thought it'd healed. Evidently in the heat of passion he hadn't noticed the puncture wound above my breast. So much for the short lived perfect moment. "Umm. It's a long story."

Martinez lifted a brow. "Some place you gotta be that you can't tell me now?"

"Downstairs to finish my shift?"

"You're fired. Start talking."

I sagged on the couch and told him everything. The deeper I detailed the fucked up events, the more surreal it sounded even to me, and I'd lived it.

Martinez hadn't said a word. Silent rage poured from him, until the air in the room pulsed with it. After I finished speaking, he stalked to the wall and smashed his fist through it three more times.

Christ. I needed a drink. Then he loomed over me. I became shrink-wrap against the sofa in the heat of his anger.

"You should've called me. No matter how pissed off you were at me, I had a right to know. Since I've 'owned up' to what's between us, understand this: no one gets away with laying a fucking hand on you. *Ever*. May be archaic, but if they mess with you, they mess with me. That's how I operate. If you can't live with it, then there's the door."

"But—"

"This is a non-negotiable point, Julie."

"Fine."

"However, there is a line. If you go out and start causing trouble, invoking my name as protection, we will have problems."

"I can get into trouble just fine on my own, Martinez."

"I know that only too well."

We stared at each other. Had anything changed?

He clasped my hand and helped me to my feet. "Let's get out of here and I'll take you home."

"Why don't we go to your place?" When he didn't respond I said, "You don't live at Fat Bob's, do you?"

"Seems like it." He shut off the lights and locked the doors as I slipped on my shoes.

I followed him to a steel door covered in locks at the end of the hallway. "What's in there?"

"My private suite."

"Do you live *here*?"

Martinez spun around. "What's up with the interest in where I live?"

"Because I've never been there. And honestly, I'd like a chance to snoop through your personal stuff. See if you secretly listen to show tunes. If you collect Hummel figurines. If you wear pastel pajamas covered with dancing cats, that sort of thing."

He gave me a wicked smile. "You know I don't wear pajamas."

"Not good enough. I need to judge for myself if you've got any quirks I should be concerned about."

"Just the territorial instinct you bring out in me," he muttered.

I tapped my foot. "Funny. But I'm serious, Martinez."

"Fine. I built a house, way out in the Hills. It's secluded, next to Forest Service land. I end up staying here or at Fat Bob's way more than I'd like." He smoothed a strand of hair from my cheek. "Or I've been crashing at your place."

"Not lately."

"Will you quit pouting if I promise to take you to my house soon?"

"Maybe." I scowled at the door to the staircase.

Martinez sighed. "What now?"

"Do we have to go down there? I don't want to see anyone else." *Take a chance and tell him the truth.* "God, Martinez, it's been a hellish week and I don't want to be with anyone else. I don't want to share you with anyone else. I just want it to be . . . you and me."

His soft gaze swept over my face. "Jesus Christ, I can't believe how much I missed you. I'll grab your stuff and be right back. We'll bunk here tonight, okay?"

For the rest of the night, and into the wee hours of the morning, our world was a pair of reunited lovers, and it was more than enough.

CHAPTER 30

In the morning I zipped home and changed clothes before I went to the office. I was exhausted, but things had changed between Martinez and me in a positive way last night, and sacrificing sleep was a small price to pay.

I scrolled down my to-do list. I might as well get all the phone calls out of the way. I tracked down the Dove's number and dialed.

"Hi, Sharon, it's Julie Collins."

"Hello." Her voice was decidedly cool. "I hope you have good news with Maria's case?"

"Some. I've uncovered new information."

The phone was quiet for so long I wondered if my handset had died. "Sharon?"

"Yes, I'm here. I'm a little out of it. What new information?"

No way to easy way to say it except straight out. "Did you know Maria was moonlighting as a cocktail waitress at Bare Assets for three months before she disappeared?"

"What? No, you're mistaken, Maria would never—"

"—she did, I've verified it with the club manager. It also appears she had hooked up with a biker guy who worked security at the club, who went by the nickname, Beaner. Ring any bells?"

Silence.

"Sharon?"

"No, this is all news to me. Go on and tell me everything."

"This has to come as a shock, and I'm not trying to be difficult, but are you sure you've told me everything about what Maria was doing in the months prior to her disappearance?"

"Yes. And like I told you when you were here, the discovery of her surprising place of employment, the mysterious biker she was seeing on the sly; none of it's relevant."

I practiced patience. "Why not?"

"Because Roland Hawk killed Maria. You should be concentrating on finding proof."

Roland Hawk, Roland Hawk. Squawk squawk; she sounded like a parrot. "I talked to Roland. While he is a piece of garbage, he denies he had anything to do with Maria's disappearance. And I've gotten confirmation from a couple of other sources that she had been head over heels in love with this Beaner guy, despite the fact he was married."

"I see. And you're taking Roland's word for it?"

"No. I'm looking for other reasons and motives and suspects. The process of elimination is just part of the process."

"Have you ruled out Roland completely?"

"No."

"Good. Sorry, but I've got to run, we're planning Maria's memorial service. Keep me informed." She hung up.

I dropped my head on my desk. "That went well."

"What went well?" Kevin asked from the doorway.

"The phone call to Sharon Dove." I sat back in my chair. "She acted pissy when I mentioned the mystery man in Maria's life again. Do you think she knew about the scummy guy her daughter was seeing and disapproved?" I chewed on that for a second. "Nah, Sharon wouldn't keep that information to herself because she wants Maria's case resolved."

Kevin blew on his coffee. "You're learning the power of deductive reasoning, young Jedi."

"Speaking of . . . how is Denny today?"

"He looks better. He's applying for a cook's job at the new sports bar down the road from me. Within walking distance so he can get there on his own. I managed to get him to borrow some of my clothes, since he has nothing but the clothes on his back, his cell phone, and his iPod."

"If I haven't told you how unbelievably cool it is that you've taken him in, Kev—"

"It's just as good for me, Jules, as it is for him." He squinted at me. "You've got that High Pro Glow. You and Martinez finally kiss and makeup?"

Hoo-boy, did we ever. I smiled. "Yeah."

"Back to normal?"

"Better than it was."

His gaze narrowed. "Did you tell him everything that's gone on?"

I nodded. I couldn't disclose the Hombres problems to Kevin, even if it involved me to some degree. "What's on the agenda for today, boss?"

"Last batch of Greater Dakota Gaming employee lists came Fed Ex yesterday afternoon. I'll take half; you take half."

We worked in our individual offices all morning and ordered pizza for lunch. I'd returned to my desk when my cell phone rang. Hoping for Martinez, I frowned when I didn't recognize the caller ID.

"Hello?"

"Abita?"

"No. How did you get this number?"

"Umm . . . Abita called me from this number a couple of days ago. I'm trying to get a hold of her."

"Who is this?"

"Her fiancé, John Hooper."

Fiancé? Abita hadn't mentioned a fiancé. "I haven't seen or talked to her for a couple of days. Have you tried calling the dorm?"

"Yes, but no one ever answers. Its really important I get in touch with her as soon as possible."

"Has something happened to someone in her family?"

"No, nothing like that." The receiver shifted. "Our attorney hit a snag in the adoption paperwork for Jericho and Abita needs to call her to get it straightened out."

My vision dimmed. Adoption? What the fuck? "I'd planned on seeing Abita today so I can pass on the message. Does she have the lawyer's number?"

"She should. Just have her call me if she needs it. Please tell her to call me anyway."

"Will do."

"Thanks."

I shoved my phone and cigarettes in my purse, knocked on Kevin's door and poked my head in. "Look, something just came up I need to take care of."

"Something with Martinez?"

"No. With Abita. I'll explain it later, okay?"

During the short drive to the college I flashed back to my conversations with Abita and the suspicion she was keeping secrets.

I paced outside the closed classroom. Seemed like thirty hours rather than thirty minutes before the door opened.

Abita was the last student out. She froze when she saw me. "Julie? Why are you here?"

"I hadn't heard from you so I thought I'd drop by and see if everything was all right."

"I'm fine." She glanced over her shoulder. "I've only got a short break—"

"You've got half an hour, which will give you plenty of time to explain about your fiancé John, and why your attorney wants to talk to you about a problem with the adoption process."

Abita's eyes flared panic. "How did you find out?"

"John called my cell phone looking for you."

"I-I wanted a little more time before I brought this up with you."

"Wrong. I suspect you wanted to wait until the last possible minute to spring this on me because you probably knew I wouldn't react rationally."

"Can you honestly blame me?"

"No, but you'd better come clean about everything. I've been dealing with enough secrets and shit in my life and I'm sick of it." I spied a pair of wingback chairs in an alcove at the end of the hallway and pointed at them. "Sit and start talking."

Abita's fingers bunched the pleated folds of her broomstick skirt. She wouldn't meet my gaze.

"Tell me about John."

"I met him a year and a half ago. He's a member of a neighboring tribe. I-I didn't date after Ben . . . and John is the first person who showed a serious interest in me and my work. He talked to his elders about me coming to his reservation and teaching weaving classes. So, I've been working with his tribe. They're paying for this seminar."

"Why isn't your tribe paying?"

Her long braid coiled on her thigh like a snake. "Weaving has been a big part of my life since I was a little girl. It's all I've ever wanted to do. I'm pretty good, but my tribe already has a master weaver. Even if there wasn't one, I'm a single parent, not a good example for the young girls in our community.

"John's tribe welcomed my skills and didn't shun me. He helped me find a place to live with an older woman who needed domestic help in exchange for room and board. She doesn't even mind rambunctious little boys."

I held my breath because I knew what was coming.

"John and I fell in love. We're getting married next month and he is adopting Jericho."

A punch in the gut couldn't have produced more nausea. "Why didn't you tell me this right away?"

"I don't know."

"Does Jericho know Ben Standing Elk is his father?"

"No. Jericho's last name is Kahlen. I didn't list Ben's name on the birth certificate."

"Do you plan on telling Jericho?"

"When he's old enough to understand."

I remembered the day Ben had shown up on our doorstep. Looking for his birth father. Didn't Abita realize history was repeating itself? Didn't she understand how much the lie had tilted Ben's world upside down when he'd discovered the truth?

"Understand what? Ben is Jericho's father."

"No, John is his father, Julie, in every sense of the word. He has been for the last year. The only thing we're waiting for is the legal documentation."

I pictured Jericho's sweet face. My heart stopped at the idea of not watching him grow up and change, or seeing if he'd turn out to be a carbon copy of Ben.

I thought I'd suffered every imaginable pain in my life, but nothing prepared me for the visceral sense of loss of something I'd never really had.

Time stretched in a brutal stillness.

"Why did you bring Jericho into my life if you had no intention of letting me be part of his?"

Her gaze met mine. "Would you rather I hadn't?"

"I don't know. I didn't think—"

"That I'd ever get married?" she demanded angrily. "Come on. I had to grow up fast, but I've still got my whole life ahead of me. There have been times in the last four years I wondered if I'd ever stop being 'that poor girl who got knocked up and abandoned' and have any man look at me either without pity or like I'm some kind of easy slut. I can't survive on memories of Ben. I didn't want to then, or now. I deserve more and so does my son."

"But he's also—"

"No, he's *mine* and you have no right to expect *anything*. Especially after you sent your father after me."

A chill snaked up my spine. "What did you say?"

"Your father tracked me down. He told me I was a fool for coming to South Dakota and expecting anything but grief from the Standing Elk family about Jericho. Then he said with Leticia being a lawyer they'd get it in their heads they deserve visitation rights."

"What?"

Abita's eyes burned with fury. "Doug also warned me if they didn't pursue the visitation issue you would. Is that true?"

I was dumbfounded. "No. What other lies did my dad spew?"

"He demanded to know if I talked to Ben after he'd returned to South Dakota and what he said. When I refused to answer, he said if I was smart, and if I wanted to keep the boy safe, I'd return to Arizona as soon as possible and never come back."

Jesus. This was a nightmare.

Abita's cruel laugh made me cringe. "You know the funny thing? If I wouldn't have met Doug, I wouldn't have realized how much you are like him, nor would I have believed he's the only one making sense."

My mouth opened to deny, *I'm not like him at all!* But Abita didn't give me the chance.

She stood abruptly. "Just leave us alone. I-I can't handle you or anyone else right now." She hustled away from me, her skirt swishing as loud as pine trees in a windstorm.

I was too numb to do anything but let her go.

💀 💀 💀

On the way back to Bear Butte County, I detoured the long way to the Standing Elk Ranch. I parked in a gravel turn-around directly across from the gate.

Like most western South Dakota ranches, two tall

posts marked the main entrance. A wooden sign hung between the posts, with the Standing Elk name and their cattle brand burned into the wood.

The Standing Elk ranch wasn't huge, 10,000 acres, big enough to support a hundred head of cattle. The land had been in the family since the US Government had put the Sihasapa and other tribes on reservations in the late 1800s.

As I peered down the dirt road leading to the humble ranch house where my brother had grown up, I wondered who would take over the ranch once Verlin Standing Elk died. Reese, probably. If not, surely either Leticia or Owen would have married by then and it'd pass into the hands of another member of the Standing Elk lineage.

A beat-up International pickup slowed down at the entrance, then spun a U-turn and pulled up alongside me. I glanced at the driver. Reese Standing Elk. Great. Like I needed another confrontation in my life today.

He rolled down the window. Mine was already down since I was enjoying yet another fine tobacco product from the RJ Reynolds company.

"What're you doin' out here, Julie?"

Reese looked enough like Owen they could've been twins. Instead of a snappy suit, Reese wore denim overalls and a battered straw cowboy hat. Not a good look, especially not for a cowboy; a gay Indian cowboy.

"I was in the neighborhood."

"Slummin', are you?" His eyes were masked behind dark sunglasses. "If you're thinkin' about headin' to the house to harass my mother, think again."

"No. Actually, I was hoping to talk to you."

"What for?"

"To find out what you, Ben, and your dad fought about before Ben went to work for the Sihasapa Tribal Council."

"Why you think you've got the right to be askin' questions? You ain't our family."

"Ben was my family, so I do have a right to know what shitty things your family did to him before he was killed."

"Wrong. Go on. We don't want you here. We never have."

My mean girl surfaced. "How is it you defend them? I know how your precious family treats you, Reese. Ben told me."

"Shut up."

"Leticia and Owen make fun of you. Snicker behind your back. Made rude comments to your face. Does your father join in? What does your mother do? Defend you, like she did when they treated Ben the same way?"

Reese didn't rise to the bait.

I'd try a different tack. "Why did Leticia fire Leon

Bird? I thought you were in charge of running the ranch?"

"Not as long as she's payin' the bills."

"Come on Reese, that's crap. There's more to it."

Reese adjusted his hat. "You know what, I'm sick of actin' like this is some big fuckin' secret. It's not. Before Ben ran off to Arizona my dad told him he'd better pick another career because he'd give this ranch back to the government before he'd ever let Ben own it. Then he told Ben he oughta talk to Doug Collins, maybe he'd let Ben sponge offa him for the next thirty-five years because he was sick of Ben sponging off him. No wonder Ben took off. Sometimes I wish I coulda gone with him."

My heart lurched. Poor Ben. Neither Verlin nor my dad wanted him. No wonder he'd connected with Marlon Blue Legs.

Reese said, "I didn't agree with how Dad handled it. I don't agree with most things that go on around here. Here's something I guarantee you *don't* know: The ranch has been teetering on the edge of foreclosure for years. Leticia supports it, she supports us, which means she runs the show."

No bitterness. Just fact. "What about Owen?"

"Owen's about one step up from me on the totem pole. He knows how to toe the line just like the rest of us do."

"Reese, I'm sorry."

"Now you know all our dirty laundry. Now you got no reason to cause no more problems. Leave this be. Leave Ben's memory be. Diggin' 'round ain't gonna help nobody."

"Digging around is gonna help me," I said to the dented tailgate of his pickup. His tires spewed gravel as he shot across the faded blacktop road and through the open gate.

💀 💀 💀

Maybe it was masochistic, but instead of going home, I switched direction toward my dad's place. The dusty backroads, which boasted my beloved familiar vista of hills and plains and buttes, didn't calm me.

At the ranch, I pulled up next to the machine shed and jumped out.

Trish hustled down the porch steps, a checkered dishtowel dangling from her soapy right hand. "Julie? What's wrong?"

"I want to talk to him. Now."

"Come on in, he's in the kitchen helping Brittney with her homework."

"No. Send him out."

She didn't argue and disappeared back inside the house.

Several minutes later, my dad moseyed onto the porch. He leaned his shoulder against the wooden support post and studied me from beneath the brim of his John Deere ball cap. "What's the special occasion?"

"It's National Ass Chewing Day. And I want to know where you get off telling Abita some goddamn bald-faced lie that I would *ever* sue for visitation rights for Jericho."

He snorted. "Actin' pretty self-righteous, ain't you? Like you hadn't considered the possibility."

"I hadn't."

"Right. Like you ain't been obsessed with everything surrounding Ben for the last few years?"

My immediate denial stuck on the tip of my tongue.

"I just thought that young gal oughta be aware of what lengths you'll go to keep a flesh and blood link to your treasured half-brother."

Ignore the sarcasm, he's trying to lure you another direction. "How did you find her?"

"You ain't the only one with investigative skills, girlie."

"Oh, do tell. Maybe I can pick up some tips from you."

Dad flashed his typical cruel smile. "Her car with Arizona plates was parked at your house. After I left your place, I noticed that car had stopped at the convenience mart."

I stomped up the walkway. "So you just gave her the what-for right there in the parking lot? In front of Jericho and Brittney?"

"Yeah. I figured you wouldn't do nothin' 'bout tellin' her I wanted to talk to her, so I took the opportunity that was offered."

"An opportunity to see if Ben had talked to her after he returned here?" My gaze swept his weathered, non-committal face for a hint of emotion. "Why would you care? It wasn't like you kept in contact with Ben."

Immediately his body rivaled the porch post for rigidity.

And I realized the Standing Elk family wasn't the only one keeping secrets. Fuck. My hatred for him expanded. "You mean, smug bastard. Something happened between you and Ben, didn't it? Reese told me Verlin Standing Elk had informed Ben he couldn't inherit, or even work on their ranch in the months before he was murdered. Did Ben take Verlin's advice and come to you?"

The wait for his answer was excruciating.

"Yes, Ben came here, demandin' I finally acknowledge his birthright," he sneered. "I don't know what he expected. Me to welcome him with open arms after forty years? When the injuns don't want him no more he shows up actin' like he's entitled to somethin'? Ticks me off his mother didn't do like she'd promised and kept my name off the birth record. No one was ever s'posed to know about my mistake."

Oh, Jesus. Dad hadn't actually called Ben a mistake to his face, had he?

"I'd put that incident behind me, hid my shame, moved on with my life, and then lo and behold, Ben showed up like a bad Indianhead penny. Your mother didn't know nothin' about him, you decided he was the end-all and wouldn't just let him fade back into the background where he belonged. And suddenly my shame had a name and a face. And everyone knew."

He scrubbed his knuckles along his stubbled jaw. "I lived with the embarrassment all those years, not that you cared. Does it make me a bastard 'cause I didn't have no magical attachment to him because I poked his mother one night when I was drunk? Or did it just make *him* stupid to believe I'd ever treat him like a son, when for his whole life I'd made it clear I din't want nothin' to do with him?"

I stared at him, dumbfounded.

"After harassin' me for a couple of weeks, when he figured out I wasn't gonna give him squat, *ever*, he said when I kicked the bucket he'd sue for his share of the ranch."

"You're lying." That did not sound like my gentle, laid back brother.

"No, I'm not. I'm sure since you've put him on a pedestal you think he was above such behavior. He ain't.

No one is. Come right down to it, I was happy to see the ass end of him. I told him the next time he set foot on my property, I'd have him arrested for trespassin'."

My vision wavered from the blood pulsing behind my eyeballs.

Doug Collins eased away from the post. From his perch on the porch he looked down his nose at me. "I told that girl to forget any designs she might have on that boy inheritin' anything from me. She'd be better off to take the kid and go back to the desert where she belonged." He cocked his head. "I'll bet she's hit you up for money, huh?"

Although Abita hadn't asked me for a dime, I said sweetly, "It's *my* money, Dad. I can do whatever the hell I want with it."

The curtain in the living room twitched, temporarily distracting me. Who was skulking in the shadows watching? Probably that snot-nosed DJ, taking notes on how to turn into a first class asshole like our father.

"I raised you better than that, Julie Ann, to fall for every sob story that comes down the pike."

"Well, I guess since beating it into me didn't work, you've got no one to blame but yourself for *my* failings."

His posture challenged me. His gaze dropped to my hands, curled into fists at my sides and he smirked. "Still actin' the tough girl?"

Take a swing. Just haul off and hit him and let your knuckles wipe that fucking, self-righteous smirk right from his face. See how he likes to bleed.

Slowly, I unclenched my hands. I wouldn't give him the satisfaction. "You're a pathetic, shallow man and I truly hate you." I turned on my heel, returned to my truck and didn't look back.

CHAPTER 31

My jumbled thoughts jumped track to track: Abita, Jericho, The Standing Elk family, my father, Maria Dove, Sharon Dove, Roland Hawk, Bonita, Denny Bird, Martinez, the identity of the biker. I needed information on that pledge.

Could anything else in my life be more fucked up? When I had drama, I had it in spades. It never spaced itself out. No, everything piled on top of me at once to see how quickly I'd topple under the weight.

One dead body. A secret nephew. A friend's unexpected pregnancy. Two bar fights. Unearthing human remains. Working for the sheriff again. Working in a strip club. Two run-ins with a knife and stun gun wielding psycho. Multiple run-ins with Ben's family. A nasty revelation from my father. Under suspicion as a possible snitch for a motorcycle gang . . . Gee, was I forgetting anything?

Yep. I'd totally forgotten to talk to Martinez about Trina's drug deals at Bare Assets. Oh, joy, I could hardly wait to broach that subject.

A shower, a shot, and two hours worth of *Highlander* reruns hadn't kept my problems bobbing in the background.

I left Martinez a message about my trip to talk to Crystal and spent more time than usual on my hair and makeup. I'd show that bimbette Charity mousy.

In my truck the Dixie Chicks sang about not being ready to make nice. I had no choice.

A pledge I'd never seen was stationed at Bare Asset's front entrance. I bypassed him without incident, slipped into the back and knocked on Crystal's door.

She didn't beat around the bush. "So you're the one making time with Tony."

I smiled, a little cockily.

"I wondered the minute you walked in here."

"Why?"

"Because you didn't quiver in your boots at the mention of his name. And he stopped coming around when you were working."

"Might've been because he trusted me to do the job without having to keep an eye on me."

"He can't keep his eyes off you, *that's* the problem."

She exhaled. "How long?"

I shrugged. "A few months. Not exactly common knowledge."

"It is now. You here to gloat?"

"No. I've got another employee type question."

"Shoot."

"Do the Hombres' pledges get paid while they're working security here?"

"No."

"Then there's no record of who worked here, when they started, and for how long?"

"Nope. The Hombres send them over, I send them out front, and they're supervised by one of the patched-in Hombres members. Did you ask Tony if the club historian keeps records about stuff like that?"

The Hombres had a club historian? "Not yet." It appeared now I'd have no choice but to ask Martinez. And in light of his enforcer's suspicions about me . . . Yeah. This was gonna go over great.

"Thanks, by the way, for figuring out Dave was ripping us off. Fucker. He had excuses up the wazoo. He tried to blame Charity."

"You really had no clue about him?"

"No. Like you said, I even trusted him alone with a goddamn unlocked safe, fucking-head-of-security-piece-of-shit-asshole. I'd like to kick that cocksucker's ass."

Whoa. Her creative vernacular rivaled mine. "Well, I had to tell Martinez about the other security problems. His A-team would have a fit if they knew this building wasn't secured."

"I know. Tony talked to me about it today. He wasn't happy, but he's not sending Jackal in to chat with me, so I ain't complaining."

Smart move.

"As long as we're coming clean about everything . . ." Crystal's Cheshire grin unnerved me. "I told Tony that you'd asked to see some personnel records."

Tit for tat? Great. Be even harder now to chat with him about Trina's sideline. "Gee, thanks."

"Share the shit, that's my motto."

I'd have to remember that one.

While I skulked along the back wall of the club, avoiding Charity, Trina, and Bo-Bo, I noticed a guy sitting alone at a table near the stage. His ugly red jacket stuck out like a stop sign. Had to be June's brother, Jeff Colhoff.

Again? He'd been in here Thursday night with his freaky looking cousin Willie, who gave me the willies. Seemed Jeff had slipped the old ball and chain twice in a week. Wonder how little wifey felt about that?

I froze.

A mental whack. Then another. Yeah, I'd had a lot on my mind recently, but why hadn't I connected the dots when I'd seen the Colhoff boys in here last week? Maria Dove's remains had been discovered on June Colhoff Everett's land. Jeff and Willie were both married. And they'd argued with Lang on what to do about the bones.

Who had they been trying to protect? Each other? Or someone else? The implications made my head hurt. I'd have to talk to Jeff, but I couldn't stomach another confrontation tonight when I still had one to get through.

Speaking of . . . I looked up as Martinez and company—the Trifecta of Terror, Big Mike, No-neck and Buzz—blew in.

My heart pounded in synchronicity with the sultry salsa beat as he sauntered across the room toward me like I was the only one in the universe. I wondered if I'd ever get used to him looking at me like that.

Martinez didn't lay a big, long, wet kiss on me, but he offered me a devastating smile, which was good enough.

"I hoped to catch you. Hold on for a minute? We've gotta do a security check."

Martinez motioned No-neck, Big Mike, and Buzz to go ahead. He placed his hand in the small of my back and guided me through the swinging doors.

"So, you hungry, blondie? Wanna get something to eat when I'm done here?"

"Together? In public?"

"As opposed to separately in private? Yeah."

"Okay. But speaking of, there are a couple of things I need to talk to you about first. In private."

Martinez' teasing mood fled. He said, "Hey, Mike," and Big Mike rematerialized immediately.

Talk about being at the bossman's beck and call.

"Yeah?" Big Mike said.

"We'll be upstairs."

"You want Cal to stick around here?"

"For a little while."

While he locked and unlocked a billion doors, I searched for professional distance.

The soundproofing in the suite above Bare Assets equaled that inside the bowels of Fat Bob's. The space was laid out apartment style: a small kitchenette abutted a decent sized bathroom, which connected to the bedroom. The walls, the carpet, the furniture, everything was bachelor bland. The only décor I remembered from the bedroom was the bed. Big, soft, and sturdy.

I flopped on the velvet sectional while Martinez rummaged in the cabinets in the kitchen. I couldn't even gaze out the living room windows at the lights of Rapid City, as the windows were completely blacked out.

Martinez returned with a bottle of Parrot Bay rum. He sat across from me and filled the shot glasses, passed me one and chinked his glass to mine.

The sweet aftertaste was worth the initial sting. I licked my lips and jiggled my glass for more. After the second blast, I recited the scant facts on the Maria Dove case.

He shrugged. "Employees come and go. I don't remember her."

"It doesn't matter; it's not actually her I'm interested in. It's the guy she was seeing. An Hombres pledge."

"Who?"

"I don't know. That's what I'm hoping you'll tell me."

His protective shields dropped and my lover morphed into the hard, tough, biker badass everyone else saw.

"I know Crystal told you I convinced her to let me look at Maria's employment file. I know Jackal suspects I'm some kind of spy for whoever the hell he thinks I'm spying for. And just when you've decided I'm trustworthy, here I am, asking you about confidential Hombres club shit."

Martinez' unyielding stare continued.

"So, I'll phrase it as . . . vaguely as I can. Suppose a guy was a pledge, say, five and a half years ago. Say he hadn't passed the initiation and was still working security at Bare Assets. Let's also assume he never made it to the Hombres patched-in status as a full-fledged member. Would there be a record of him someplace?"

No answer.

Crap. I snagged the rum and helped myself to two

more shots. When I reached for additional courage, he curled his hand over mine and took the bottle for himself.

"Yes, there are records. That doesn't mean shit because I can't tell you anything."

"Can't? Or won't?"

"Even if I knew every single fucking name of every pledge, which I don't, we've got some high profile members on the list, and there's a serious trust factor I won't breach. And yes, those records include guys who've washed out for some reason or another. We keep tabs on the dropouts, purely a business decision, to make sure they're not out causing problems, bragging about being an Hombres member when they're not."

Martinez had matched me shot for shot, then upped the ante with two more.

From past experience I knew he could guzzle the whole damn bottle and still act totally sober.

He handed the rum back to me. "You said there were a couple of things you needed to tell me. What else?"

"I thought I'd give you a head's up that Trina, the airhead blond cocktail waitress who's always stuck in the back section? Not only does she come to work high, she's selling drugs or something on the floor during the show." This time I didn't bother to use a glass; I swigged straight from the bottle.

As usual, he waited for me to elaborate.

"So, I've had to ask myself. Is she running her own scam? Or is she running yours?"

Martinez' shark-like smile appeared. "Why didn't you call the cops and let them sort it out?"

"Because busting your cocktail waitress for intent to distribute wasn't part of the deal. I did the favor you asked. But I'd be remiss in my duties as a professional investigator if I didn't share my incredible powers of observation with you." I batted my eyelashes. Smiled cheekily.

He let the pause linger.

My inner tough girl said *fuck it* and lashed out. "Know what I don't get, Martinez? Why you hired me to tell you something you already knew." I swallowed another mouthful of truth serum. "Regardless of what Jackal says, you don't let things slide. You aren't dumb. Only two people could've taken the money. Crystal or Dave. And we both know Crystal never was suspected. So what was I really doing there?"

A tiny muscle under his left eye twitched. "You aren't dumb either. Don't you think *I* know how goddamn good your powers of observation are?"

"Yes. So I didn't have to prove anything to you."

Thorny silence.

The truth smacked me hard. I might not have to prove anything to Martinez, but I did have to prove my trustworthiness to Jackal.

Fuck. I'd been played.

I sailed to my feet. "You sent me to Bare Assets so I could catch *Trina* doing her shit."

"Yes."

"Why?"

"It was a test."

"A test?" I aped. "Why would *I* need a *test*?"

"To see if all of a sudden Bare Assets was besieged by cops after you saw drug deals going down in my club."

The booze and the fury mixed into a toxic cocktail and I spewed venom. "You bastard. Not only don't you trust me, you used me."

"You're a fine one to talk about trust."

My mouth fell open.

"Sit down."

"No. I can't believe—"

"I said: Sit. Down."

"I am not a fucking dog, Martinez."

Irritation flared in his eyes. "Losing my patience with you, blondie."

"*You're* losing patience with *me*?" I was so incensed I grabbed the rum bottle and whizzed it at the wall behind his head. Stupid thing didn't make a very loud crash as it shattered and Martinez didn't even blink.

Coolly, he said, "You done?"

"No. Yes." I had to get out of there. I stalked to

the door, my flight instinct in full gear. Nothing clicked as I twisted the surplus of locks. I resisted the urge to throw a complete temper tantrum and beat my fists into the steel.

"Give it up. You won't get out unless I let you out."

"Great." I pressed my forehead to the cool metal door and willed my world to quit spinning for about the millionth time in the last week.

The couch squeaked. His quiet footsteps grew louder and stopped right behind me.

"Unlock the goddamn door, Martinez."

"No."

He'd shifted close enough I felt his body heat. "Don't touch me."

Martinez sighed.

"God. I don't believe we're going through this again."

"Will you let me explain?"

"Explain what? Why you used me in your little Hombres political games?"

"You think I had a choice?"

Yes.

"I told you the shit I'm up against. It wasn't my idea, okay? Jackal wanted to prove that if you saw drugs floating around you'd go running to the cops."

"I didn't. I wouldn't have. Not without talking to you first. You should know that." *Breathe. In. Out.*

"I did. I do."

"Then why did you listen to him?"

"Because I wanted to ram it in that devious fucker's face that he was wrong about you. Jackal doesn't know a thing about loyalty. And it sucks I had to use you to prove what loyalty is. Christ. I'm not perfect, Julie. And I sure as shit haven't had my head on straight about club business since Harvey shot himself . . ." His voice wavered.

Don't cry, don't break down, don't even fucking bend.

Martinez said, "I had no idea how much I relied on him until he wasn't there."

I hated he was still hurting. I hated my anger was waning.

"And Trina? What was her part?"

"She didn't have a clue what was going down. She just does what she's told."

My mind flashed to my conversation with Trina about Mistress Dominique's tattoo. No wonder Trina knew what the tattoo meant; she had one. "Because the Hombres own her." Jesus. I felt stupid just using the word *own*.

"Yes."

"And if the cops would've come calling, she was the fall guy? You would've disavowed any knowledge of her sideline and let her go to jail?"

No answer.

"I hate this."

"I know."

An eternity passed as we stayed silent, separate, angry.

I released a slow breath.

He said, "Talk to me."

"Are we ever going to figure this out?" If I had to clarify "this" we were in even bigger trouble than I feared.

"We already are." Martinez latched onto my hips and rubbed his face in my hair. "I wish I could say I made a mistake. But the truth is, even if I had a chance to do it over again, I'd probably handle it exactly the same way."

I bit my tongue against a smart ass response.

"I've got a couple of bottles of tequila and whiskey if you want to hurl some more shit at me," he offered.

"I'm not sorry. You deserved it."

"Probably. I'm glad it wasn't the good stuff."

He gently turned me around, probably expecting me to melt into his arms.

Man, was he surprised by my hard ass expression.

"What?"

"Here's the deal. I'll forget all about your lack of trust, the shitty hours I worked for *free* in your titty bar, being lied to and used and tested . . . if you do one thing for me."

His eyes narrowed. "Give you the names of the pledges."

"Yep. And it's a nonnegotiable point, Martinez."

He leveled that gut-wrenching stare at me, expecting me to crack. And for once I didn't. I gave him a haughty stare right back.

"Fine. I'll have to talk to some people, but I'll get you those names. In the next day or so, okay?"

I resisted doing a victory lap around the room. "Thank you."

Martinez smoothed my hair from my face. "We done now?" He bent forward and kissed the hollow of my throat. His breath was a warm, sweet promise of seduction.

"Stop pawing me. Didn't you say something about food?"

"After."

"After what?"

"After I have dessert." His teeth sank into the arc of my neck. Then he soothed the love bite with a flick of his tongue.

My knees dipped and it wasn't from too much rum. "Are you trying to distract me with sex?"

"Mmm hmm." His hot kisses zigzagged down the center of my body and nearly torched my clothes. "Makeup sex is always hot. Is it working?"

"For now."

"Good."

It was a long time before I said anything else. He

had a lot to atone for.

We never did make it to a restaurant.

CHAPTER 32

I DECIDED I'D PAY JEFF COLHOFF A VISIT BEFORE I WENT to work the next morning. I called June. No answer. I looked up the address, knowing it had to be close to June's place, and I drove there to spread my special brand of morning sunshine.

Jeff and his wife lived in a trailer. Not a nice modular home on a slab or with a basement, but a circa 1970s tin shack, rusted out siding, tires on the roof, plastic kids' play sets scattered around like the scratch n' dent toy department at Kmart had exploded.

Huddled in my coat, I knocked on the door. Just when I thought no one would answer, the door swung open and nearly knocked me off the buckled steps.

"What?" Jeannie had a fat baby perched on her bony hip, and a younger kid about two, clinging to her skinny leg. Another boy, around five, peeked from the opposite side of the doorframe.

"Hi, Jeannie. Julie Collins, remember me? I wondered if I could talk to Jeff."

A cigarette bobbed in the corner of her mouth. She squinted one eye against the cigarette smoke and peered at me through the haze. "He ain't here."

"Do you know when he'll be back?"

"You're that PI June hired and was calling all the time, blabbin' about our family business."

"She didn't—"

"I don't appreciate the fact you shoved a goddamn gun in my face, when I was tryin' to protect what's mine. Don't think I've forgotten about that. Don't know what lies that screwed up woman told you about us—"

"Hold on. June didn't hire me; the sheriff did. And while I appreciate your concern, I need to talk to Jeff in private—"

"Then maybe you can catch him at the sheriff's office, since that's where he's at." She pinched the cigarette butt from her mouth and flicked it to the ground.

"What's he doing there?"

"Givin' a statement about June."

I frowned. "June? What about her?"

Jeannie sneered, "She's dead."

"Dead? Since when?"

"Jeff found her yesterday afternoon, her neck broke, at the bottom of the bluff where Lang got kilt."

My guts twisted into a knot. "What happened?"

"Looks like she got drunk and jumped over the ledge in the last coupla days, I guess. After Lang's funeral she told everyone to leave her alone. Jeff couldn't get a hold of her on Sunday or Monday so he went lookin' yesterday and found her."

Then he went to Bare Assets to comfort himself with nubile young naked flesh after finding his dead sister? Talk about stone cold. I'd bet a month's worth of cover charges little wifey hadn't known where her husband had been drowning his sorrows last night.

"Didn't he talk to the sheriff after they found June?"

"Yeah. Jeff didn't get home until late, but he still had to go back first thing this morning."

So Jeff *had* lied to his wife about his whereabouts. Why?

And why hadn't Sheriff Richards called me with this disturbing news about June Everett? It directly affected the case he'd passed off to me.

Then again, I hadn't been home last night and when I had stumbled in, checking my phone messages hadn't exactly been on the top of my agenda.

Jeannie glowered at me like I was a bill collector. "Anything else?"

"No." I couldn't muster a smile. "Thanks. I'll try to catch him there."

"Don't keep him too long. He's got responsibilities to tend to here." She didn't gift her children with a loving look; she continued to glare at me like I was responsible for keeping her beloved husband from home and hearth.

Weird. I left before I said something I'd regret, which might've been a first for me lately.

As I drove to the sheriff's office, I realized Jeannie hadn't seemed particularly broken up about her sister-in-law's passing, or worried about her husband's frame of mind. Just . . . territorial.

I cooled my heels in the parking lot next to a dirty red Dodge truck. It shouldn't take too long. The quiet gave me time to sort out truth from conjecture.

Was June's death being ruled a suicide? I had my doubts on whether June purposely pitched herself over the edge in a fit of grief.

Unless . . . when the identity of the remains was made public, maybe June had recognized the name of the victim and realized the connection. Realized it wasn't bad or random luck the bones had been discovered on their land.

But where was the connection? To who? Lang?

Not Lang. If he'd had something to do with initially burying the body five years ago I doubted he'd be insistent on bringing the cops in.

Another reason I didn't see June killing herself: I remembered from our previous investigation of Lang's workman's comp claim he had a decent life insurance policy, around 150K. The claim would pay out quickly. With Lang's demise on tape there'd be no suspicion of foul play. Out from under the thumb of a man who beat her, and a cash windfall? I didn't see June throwing it all away.

Maybe I was looking too deep. With all the shit that'd gone on in my life, I had a tendency not to focus on the obvious. Could be June wanted to feel close to Lang, headed out to the bluff and had fallen. Accidents did happen. Lang Everett was the perfect example.

Before I could ponder other scenarios, Jeff shuffled out.

"Hey, Jeff."

He faced me with a frown. "Umm. Hi."

"Julie, remember? Sorry about June. I just heard."

"Thanks." He shot a glance over his shoulder, then back at me. "Why are you here?"

"Instead of working at Bare Assets?" I countered.

Jeff's doughy face paled further. "I-I thought June said you were a friend of Lang's?"

"No. I'm a private investigator. Sheriff Richards hired me and I've been investigating a case at Bare Assets in the last week. Imagine my surprise when I saw you there. Twice."

"Have you been following me?"

My immediate response was why? But I amended it to, "No."

"Then how did you find me?"

"Jeannie. I stopped at your house first."

"You didn't tell her about the strip club, did you?"

I lifted both brows. "And if I did?"

Jeff turned on his heel. Paced. Came back. "Because I'd be in deep shit, okay? Jeannie don't know I still go to them once in awhile. She don't understand."

"Why don't you explain it to me?"

"Right. So you can judge me? Look down your nose at me?"

"Not my concern or the reason I'm here." Since my boyfriend owned the joint I'd be the last one to pass judgment.

"Then why are you here? To make me feel guilty about having a fantasy? For a few hours I can forget my lousy life and pretend a beautiful woman is dancing just for me."

"Again, your fantasy life isn't my concern. The reality is the dead girl found on your land used to work at the club you, your cousin, and Lang have been known to frequent. The chance that's merely a coincidence is getting smaller and smaller."

Jeff shoved a hand through his stringy hair.

"Now June has had an accident?"

His whole body seemed to shrink within itself.

"Jeff, tell me what's going on. Let me help you."

No response.

"Why is your sister dead?"

When he looked at me, his red-rimmed eyes were small and hard as stones. "What's goin' on is I ain't thinkin' straight. You sayin' my sister's dead, fast and mean like that? Is that supposed to bring the reality of her being gone home to me?

"Don't you think I know she's dead? I found her for Christsake. My sister . . ." His voice broke. "What gives you the goddamn right to chase me down and ask me a bunch of questions at a time like this?"

Every muscle in his body was rigid with rage. I automatically stepped back.

"You got no respect for grief. You went around June's express wishes, dragging a buncha strangers out to the place her husband died, on the day before she buried him. She asked you to wait. Did you? No. You did what you wanted, not what was right or decent."

Spittle flew from his mouth. "Do you even know what it feels like to lose someone close to you? Or several someones? To have your whole world turned upside down? Your heart ripped out? Do you?"

His animosity toward me seared my vocal cords shut. "Back off. Leave me alone."

I remained motionless as he peeled out of the parking lot. Smoke from Jeff's burning rubber hung in the air. I didn't smell it; I couldn't take a breath. I was suffocating in my own self-righteousness.

The legitimacy of his words slapped me. Who the hell did I think I was? Charging after him like I had a right to find justice, no matter what, no matter how, no matter who I steamrolled to get it.

When had I become an automaton in the pursuit of truth? When had I lost my empathy and respect for those souls plunged into the black pit of grief?

Disgusted with myself, I didn't go in and talk to the sheriff about the new developments. I drove straight to work.

CHAPTER 33

Kevin had meetings scheduled with prospective clients so I dug into the employment checks I'd left unfinished. I didn't glance up at the clock until I closed the last folder.

Two o'clock. Time flies. My stomach growled.

I scrounged up a package of peanut butter crackers and a Diet Pepsi from the conference room. The phone rang as I trudged back to my desk.

"Wells/Collins Investigations."

"Julie?"

"Yes. Who's this?"

"Leticia. And before you hang up, or we start swapping insults, hear me out and give me a chance to explain why I called you."

"I'm listening."

"Look. We've never pretended to like each other. I don't even remember how this whole rivalry between us started." She sighed. "It's gone on long enough. It should've ended when we buried Ben. I'm not suggesting you and I will ever be the best of friends, but I'd like to come to some kind of understanding."

Bullshit. I didn't trust her as far as I could throw her. But that stupid voice in my head— the one that'd pointed out my single-mindedness to the exclusion of my humanity earlier today— asserted itself again and urged, "Go on."

"Since our last run-in I've spent a lot of time talking to my mother. She thinks I'm wrong in believing Abita has ulterior motives for bringing Jericho here. My mother wants to have a relationship with her only grandson, and she feels the friction between you and I will keep that from happening."

I bit my tongue against blurting out that she'd been right, Abita did have a motive and it was much worse than hitting us up for money; she was giving us a living reminder of Ben, then yanking him away.

But it wasn't my place to tell Leticia or Yvette of Abita's plan to have Jericho adopted by her fiancé. If I brought it up, I'd come across as petty, especially in light of Leticia taking the first step toward some kind of reconciliation.

"I wouldn't do that, Leticia, keep Yvette from Jericho. At least not on purpose."

She sighed again. "I have a free hour right now. Could we meet for a cup of coffee or something and hash this out face to face?"

"Sure. You could come here." Then I'd have home field advantage. Plus I could smoke.

Leticia laughed. "Parking downtown sucks during the day. How about the coffee shop at Mostly Chocolates? It should be pretty quiet."

"That'll work. I'll be there in fifteen." I slowly hung up the receiver, not sure what to make of this strange turn of events.

☠ ☠ ☠

Leticia held court in a corner table.

I salivated over the display cases packed with truffles of every flavor. The heady, almost orgasmic aroma of chocolate permeated every air molecule. I ordered an extra large, no frills coffee, and a hunk of milk chocolate macadamia nut fudge the size of my palm.

Leticia didn't smile. In fact, I don't know if I'd ever seen a real smile from her. She moved her cup and made room for my enormous indulgence.

We didn't bother with small talk.

"Would you have made this overture if it weren't for the appearance of Jericho?" I asked.

"No. It shocked me my mother had known Ben was seeing a girl in Arizona. It's strange, how you think you know someone and then something happens and you realize you don't know them at all. Everyone keeps secrets."

"True." I tore off a chunk of fudge. Sipped my coffee and the decadent goodness melted down my throat like an elixir of the gods.

She prompted, "You didn't know about Abita either?"

"No. Ben and I had lost contact for a few months."

"Why?"

I shrugged. "I was separated from my husband. Hated my job. Shit like that."

Leticia went to the counter for a coffee refill and returned with a portion of fudge a quarter the size of mine. "Yours looked good. I couldn't resist."

When her mouth was full I asked, "Although I wasn't responsible, why haven't you ragged on me about the explosion that leveled the casino? You spent what, four years planning it? And now it's dead?"

"Ah ah ah. Not dead. Merely derailed. Momentarily." There was the cunning smile I'd expected from her. "Don't count the casino out. I will get that sucker built. Eventually."

"Even if the tribe doesn't want it?

"*Shee.* The tribal members or council don't know nothin' 'bout what they want, eh? Hey, man, ennit cool 'bout getting my cuzin Leroy in office? He a righteous dude, he'll make shit happen, eh?"

She'd shed the cultured speech and slipped into the Lakota dialect so quickly it freaked me out.

"They're waiting for a sign from the Great Spirit. I just have to convince them *Wakan Tanka* are speaking through me and we need that goddamn casino." Her hand froze on the candy as if she were surprised she'd admitted that aloud.

"Is that what Ben was supposed to do when he was working for the tribe? Convince members that building a casino would be the best way to honor the Great Spirit?"

"At first. Then he wouldn't even do that. He was too damn busy—" Leticia caught herself. Smiled. "You remember, Ben could charm and cajole *anyone* when he put his mind to it. We wanted to utilize those skills.

"But Auggie insisted Roland Hawk be included in the project, and the next thing I knew, Marlon Blue Legs was involved." She scowled. "I entrusted my vision to a thug, a cripple, and a slacker, which is why all three of them were fired. Owen had to run interference with the locals and do damage control."

Silence descended. We drank coffee and pretended we weren't mentally loading up snappy comebacks.

"If Ben was a slacker, then I'm surprised he had the initiative to travel to Arizona on his own."

"He didn't. The tribe decided to send him down there to work within the Navajo casino system. We'd need experienced managers, surveillance crews, dealers, money handlers when the Sihasapa casino was finished. I wanted to get a jump on it."

A considerable jump. When they dispatched Ben to Arizona, the tribe hadn't even voted on the gambling compact issue.

"Ben was supposed to learn the management ropes from a Navajo guy I'd met through the National Indian Gaming Association. At the time, his tribe had successfully finished everything we were struggling with, and he offered to help us."

"Did he help?"

"He would have, had Ben done his part."

"What? Why didn't he?"

Leticia's nostrils flared. "When Ben first went down there, he reported in to his tribal contact regularly. Then he just . . . stopped going to work. He didn't last more than four months with a *real* job. Just goes to show you not to hire relatives. After the tribe quit sending Ben checks, he slunk back home."

Harsh. "What happened when Ben came back home?"

"I don't know. I had about four projects going during that time; I saw him maybe twice. He wasn't staying with Mom and Dad so I didn't know what he was up to before he died."

I almost snapped *before he was murdered*, but a group of red-hatted ladies came in, chattering like magpies. I shoveled in another bite of chocolate and decided I'd had enough of this "aren't we civilized" conversation.

"Why didn't you tell me any of this years ago?"

Leticia's eyes shrank to black pinpoints. "Because it was tribal business, Julie, and none of your business. There are nondisclosure contracts and legal lines I can't cross, nor can the tribal council. Regardless if you thought you deserved to know certain things about what Ben had been doing, tribal members wouldn't share information with anyone, especially with a white girl, even if they could, because they would've been thrown in jail."

My cheeks flushed.

"Back to thinking I'm a cold-hearted bitch, eh?"

I picked at my fudge. "No, Leticia, I'm thinking if you would've just explained this to me, rationally, years ago, I mightn't have thought you were a bitch at all."

Her brow furrowed. "Anyway, doesn't matter now. What does matter is my mother can glean a little happiness out of this bizarre situation."

End of topic #1. "I agree."

"I think that's a first for us."

No sarcasm. Wow. Was it possible she'd changed? We'd changed?

She slid her finger under the lace collar of her blouse and patted her chest. "Whew. Is it hot in here? Or is it just me?"

I curled my cold fingers into my palms. "Must just be you."

"I'm too damn young for hot flashes." She sighed. "Well, I'm on my way back to the rez. But I'm really glad we met and sorted this out."

"I am too."

Leticia gave me a sheepish smile. "I know this might sound strange, but would you want to get together sometime, and . . . swap stories about Ben? I'm sure you have some I haven't heard and vice versa."

It was the unsure smile, surprisingly like our brother's, that suckered me in. "Yeah." I focused on the Mylar balloons swaying beneath the heating duct. "To tell you the truth, I made a tobacco pouch a while back and I've been waiting for the right time to take it up to Bear Butte and hang it in memory of Ben. Kinda been dragging my feet because I don't want to go alone."

Take a chance, Julie, just ask. "Umm. Would you want to go with me?"

She didn't say anything. Just blinked rapidly.

Jesus. Was she crying?

Leticia cleared her throat. "I'd like that. A lot. I'll be waiting for your call. Soon, I hope."

Maybe I hadn't lost my empathy after all.

I ate every last bit of fudge without shame.

💀 💀 💀

Kevin called and asked if I'd seen Denny. When I told him I hadn't, he opted to go looking for him instead of returning to the office.

I shut off my computer and marveled at my clean desk. I couldn't wait to go home, linger under a long hot shower and indulge in a whole night of bad TV.

My cell phone rang. Martinez? Calling before 5:00?

"Hello?"

"Hey, blondie. You still at work?"

"Just leaving. Why?"

"Will you be ready if I swing by your house about 8:00?"

"Ready for what?"

"We're going out."

I froze. "Tonight? Where?"

"I'm taking you to the clubhouse after Lodge."

"What the hell is *Lodge*, Martinez?"

"The Hombres have a meeting on Wednesday

nights. In keeping with the spirit of the fraternal brotherhood of other dedicated men's service groups, we call ours *Lodge*."

"Ha ha."

"You up for it?"

No. "Sure. Any special dress code for Lodge?"

"No weapons."

"That's it?"

"Yep. One other thing: a guy who was head of security at Bare Assets and supervised the pledges during the time frame you mentioned will be there tonight."

Like I could refuse now. I heard Big Mike say, "Rum or vodka?"

Martinez said, "Rum. Look, I need to start the meeting. See you in a bit." He hung up.

Hard to believe I'd wanted this.

CHAPTER 34

THE HOMBRES SECRET CLUBHOUSE DISAPPOINTED ME.

I expected a door with a peephole. No secret knock or password like in a speakeasy. However, there was a guy obstructing the entrance, sort of a bouncer . . . if bouncers were allowed to carry a Desert Eagle, a twelve-inch knife, an anti-riot telescoping baton, and a crowbar.

The heavily-armed guy scrambled to his feet when we walked in. "Mr. Martinez. We wasn't expecting you tonight." Worried El Presidente might take it as an insult, he quickly added, "But it's always a pleasure to have you here, sir."

"Thanks, PT. Clear the main booth. We'll wait."

"Right away." He whistled. Another guy appeared, much shorter, much younger, and wearing a plain black T-shirt with the word PLEDGE emblazoned across the front, instead of the Hombres leather vest. The skittish kid shot Martinez a wide-eyed look and he disappeared as if the devil nipped at his heels.

The devil beside me chuckled.

Big Mike, No-neck, and Bucket crowded in behind us. I was glad Jackal wasn't in our little party. No one said a word. Sometimes, when I'm nervous, I babble. Not tonight. I sidled closer to Martinez, stopping short of reaching for his hand.

I checked out the surroundings. In a former life, circa 1973, I imagined this boxy warehouse had been a restaurant/nightclub, with one side for dining, the other for dancing and drinking. Now it was . . . exactly the same.

The pledge returned and mumbled to PT. He kept his gaze aimed at the scarred concrete floor.

PT smiled. "Go on in, sir."

Martinez nodded. He draped his arm over my shoulder and leaned in to whisper, "You sure you're ready for this, blondie?"

"No."

"Smart girl."

We headed into the lion's den.

The scents of smoke, sour beer, and restaurant grease wafted over me. The jukebox was playing some 70s southern rock crap. I tuned it out. Every single person in the place was staring at us. Well, not at me, specifically, but at Martinez.

Guess he really didn't put in an appearance at the clubhouse very often.

He didn't pay attention to the fear and awe he evoked. He steered me to a gigantic half-circular booth, blood red leather spattered with dark black splotches that'd probably been actual blood at one time. Martinez dropped his hand and motioned for me to slide in first.

I did. He scooted in right next to me. His bodyguards aligned themselves: Big Mike on my left, No-neck on Martinez's right, and Bucket looming off to the side.

The room began to buzz again. I soaked up the atmosphere. It seemed like the usual bar, with the exception of couches and chairs lined against the walls, in addition to tables. In fact, ours was the *only* booth. Raised on a platform against a paneled wall that overlooked all the action. No wonder Martinez preferred this spot; it was kind of like a throne.

Lotta people milled about. Guys wearing Hombres colors doing the white man shuffle on the improvised dance floor. Other older guys shot pool and played darts. Painfully young, flashy, trashy women, decked out in skimpy outfits, hung on the Hombres members like groupies on rock stars. I noticed there were other guys wearing pledge T-shirts racing around delivering drinks or whatever was demanded.

I tossed my cigarettes and lighter on the table. Big Mike snagged the ashtray and pulled it within flicking distance.

"Thanks."

Martinez said: "Feel like tequila or beer tonight?"

"Coors. In a bottle."

He ordered the same; Big Mike and No-neck opted for Budweiser.

When I felt Martinez's rough hand gliding high up my thigh, I jumped.

"Nervous?"

"Yes."

"Why?"

"Not only am I on your turf, I'm not used to you feeling me up in public, Martinez."

"I'm a new man."

I snorted.

His warm breath tickled my ear. "If you think this is too much, take a look at the action across the room. Don't say I didn't warn you."

I let my gaze drift until it focused on a once-white couch. Several people were crowded around and I couldn't see what was going on. When I leaned over to ask Martinez what the big fuss was about, the mob parted and I saw it firsthand.

Holy shit.

A barrel-shaped, bare chested man wiggled in the middle of the couch; a blond woman was on her knees in front of him. With the way her head was bobbing between his thighs I knew she wasn't down there shining his shoes.

Unbelievable.

I couldn't see his face. Hell, I didn't *want* to see his face. Or hers. Or the big finish.

Thankfully, a moment later a man resembling a gray grizzly approached the booth, garnering Martinez's attention and blocking the view. Our drinks appeared. I lit a cigarette. Since the guy talking to Martinez had edged closer, he planned on being there for a while.

I sucked in a deep drag and directed my curiosity elsewhere. After living in the vicinity of Sturgis, I'd gotten used to seeing wannabe biker rebels, those guys who'd let their hair and beards grow for a couple of weeks before the Sturgis Bike Rally, poseurs who were doctors, lawyers, stockbrokers, and investment bankers. These guys? They were the real deal.

I tried not to dissect why I felt like I was trying on someone else's skin, or why I'd ever expected Martinez should've included me in this part of his life. I shot him a sideways glance. He looked far more comfortable with the bowing and scraping than I imagined he would.

After a weird shuck-and-jive handshake, gray grizzly

lumbered off. A tiny guy who resembled a garden gnome crept up and Martinez motioned to Big Mike to exit the booth. Suddenly, I was sitting next to Grumpy, the dwarf, who conjured up a great evil eye and aimed it at my sternum.

Martinez said, "Julie, this is Tricks. Tricks, Julie."

"Hi, umm, Tricks."

He grunted.

"Tricks used to head up my security team at Bare Assets a few years back."

This little shrimp was a bouncer? What did he do? Bite guys on the knee? Rack them with a headbutt? Trip them?

As I was visualizing additional amusing scenarios with Mini-Me, Tricks said, "I ain't got all night. Mitzi's giving blow jobs in the back room and I don't wanna miss out because I hafta talk to her,"—he jerked his chin toward me but didn't make eye contact—"not that I think any of this shit's her business anyway."

Martinez warned, "Need a refresher on protocol, Tricks?"

Tricks squirmed and rubbed a long white scar carved on the back of his hand. "Ah, no. Sorry, Mr. Martinez."

"Go ahead, Julie."

It seemed as if I'd stumbled onto the set of a David Lynch movie. "I have some questions about a former pledge."

Tricks deigned to look me in the eye. "When we talking about and what's the pledge's name?"

"Around five and a half years ago. Near as I've been able to figure out, it was Beaner. Does that ring a bell?"

"No. What'd he look like?"

"I don't have a clue. Rumor was he was banging a cocktail waitress named Maria."

"What'd she look like?"

"Part Native American, part Mexican. Kind of exotic, I guess, according to her picture anyway."

Tricks' tiny hand slapped the table. "I remember her. Yeah. She was a stone cold fox. Man. I'd forgotten all about her. A nice piece, that one. But she had hooked up with . . . shit, what was his name? Not Beaner, but . . ."

I swigged my beer and waited.

Another smack on the table. "String bean, that was his name. Lucky fucker. He had it bad for her. Any of the customers put a hand on her ass or anyplace else and he'd practically rip it off. He was one tough mother. Good with his hands, if I remember. I was sorry to see him wash out. Hombres coulda used a guy like him."

String bean. Where had I heard that before? Recently? Something tickled my memory, just out of reach. "Do you remember his real name?"

"Hang on." Tricks stroked his mustache. "I something. Jerry? Jack? John? No, Jeff. That's it. Jeff. Don't recall his last name."

My hand froze on my beer bottle. Jeff Colhoff. Shit. Pieces clicked together; all but one. Was Jeff a murderer? Why had he killed Maria? In a fit of jealous rage? How the hell did I share this information with the sheriff? Was I even allowed to? Or was that breaking some Hombres "never talk to cops about club business" unwritten rule?

Martinez murmured in my ear, "You okay, blondie?"

"Uh. Yeah." I smiled at Tricks. "Thanks for your help."

"Anything else?" he said to Martinez.

"No. Keep your mouth shut on this and we won't have a problem, understand?"

Tricks nodded vigorously and zipped out of the booth.

I looked at Tony. His eyes were flat black as his gaze encompassed the room and he absentmindedly sifted my hair through his fingers.

Before either of us spoke, yet another Hombres member bent El Presidente's ear.

Big Mike nudged me as he slid back in the booth.

"What?"

"Nothin'. Sorry."

I sighed. Sipped my beer. Tried like hell to ignore the conversation Martinez was having.

"Fun, ain't it?" Big Mike spoke in low tone and

tipped his bottle of Bud and drank.

"You telling me this isn't your bag?"

"Not a bit."

"What would you rather be doing? Making sure Martinez is safe from all the dollar bills flying on the stage at Bare Assets? Or cracking skulls at Fat Bob's?"

"Neither."

"But isn't this what the Hombres lifestyle is all about? Why you've got so many pledges? Booze, babes and brawling? Brotherhood and good times? Lettin' it all hang loose?"

"Maybe it used to be; at times it still is. But bossman runs it like a business these days. That's why he's so successful. That's why he ain't seen the inside of a jail cell."

I flicked an ash. The idea of Martinez in jail made me queasy, but it could potentially happen. I'd worry about that when and if it did. "What don't you like about him being here?"

"First off; too many people. Don't know most of 'em. Hard to keep an eye on them all and him too."

"Isn't this about the safest place Martinez can be?"

"You'd think so. But nights like this when there are lots of nonmembers roaming around, his security team gets twitchy." He didn't elaborate, just took another swig of beer.

"He lets you drink on duty?"

Big Mike shrugged his massive shoulders. "Since 99% of the time we're in a bar, it'd be pretty hard not to drink. We all stop at one."

Good thing I didn't have to. I ground out my smoke, drained my beer and signaled for another. It appeared in record time.

Tony's hand squeezed my thigh.

The short, squat guy with a face like a pug moved out.

A pogo stick with boobs moved in. She angled across the table and grinned at Martinez. "Haven't seen you around here in a while."

Was it my imagination or did Martinez skooch closer to me?

"Been busy," he said to her face, not her breasts. Point for him.

I shook out a cigarette.

Martinez snagged my lighter, and brought the cigarette to the flame. Once the cancer stick smoked between my fingers, he draped his arm over my shoulder and continued winding his fingers in my hair. My, my, wasn't he proprietary tonight?

"Ain't ya gonna introduce us?" the pogo stick asked.

"Julie, this is Nyla. Nyla, Julie."

She rubbed the heel of her hand under her nose.

Eww. *So* not shaking hands with her. Nyla stared at me without blinking. Creeped me out. But I didn't look away.

Neither did she. Weren't we the height of maturity?

"She the reason you changed the rules?"

Heavy pause from Martinez. "My new rules were enacted barely two hours ago. How did you hear about them?"

"Yeah, well." She straightened up and itched her elbow. Her shoulder. Then her head. "News travels fast around here."

"Apparently."

Nyla shifted her stance, practically dancing on the balls of her feet. What was she on? Meth?

"What else did you hear?" Martinez didn't move. His voice had dropped to that lethal growl that made my hair stand on end and everyone within hearing distance take notice. "Every. Single. Word. Right. Now."

"We heard you were going soft. Not listening to other brothers' concerns who've been around a long time. Heard some things about her too," Nyla said to Martinez. "That she's a manipulative bitch who's leading you around by your dick. No offense, but she don't look all that tough."

My gaze narrowed and I lowered my cigarette.

Big Mike jeered, "I hope you don't have to find out how untrue that is, Nyla. Now get the fuck out of here before you really piss me off."

419

Whoa. Big Mike used his mouth and his muscles?

He didn't have to tell her twice. She bounced out of sight.

Martinez pressed his back to the booth and spoke to Big Mike behind me, so my head blocked their conversation from everyone in the bar. "Find out who's talking about club business to outsiders. Have Jackal handle it."

Big Mike hesitated a beat too long.

"What?" Martinez asked impatiently.

"And if Jackal is the one talking out of turn?"

"Then I'll handle it."

Chills raced down my spine.

Big Mike slid out to do bossman's bidding. No-neck became a bookend to Bucket on my side of the booth. Martinez and I were alone. Sort of. No one stared at us, but everyone watched. I put my hand on top of his on my leg and he let me.

More guys came by to pay their respects. I didn't say a whole lot. Didn't learn much besides it was boring as shit sitting there minding my manners and keeping my mouth shut.

Another round awaited me at the table when I returned from the bathroom. Martinez' arm automatically hooked my shoulder. He didn't miss a beat of his conversation with PT. Soon as the goofy bouncer left, Big Mike returned.

He loomed, putting us in shadow.

"What'd you find out?" Martinez asked.

"Just as I thought. The chief enforcer has a big mouth."

Pause. Thick. Deadly.

"Fetch him. Now."

"Gladly."

The little cocksucker deserved every bit of Tony's wrath.

Jackal ambled over, acting as if he was doing Martinez a favor. He perched on the bench seat next to Martinez, giving him most of his back. A sign he didn't see Tony as a threat? Stupid, stupid man.

Jackal ignored me. I think I pulled off nonchalance.

"Hey, Jack," Tony said. "Got a minute?"

"Sure. I was surprised to hear you graced us with your presence after the meeting," Jackal said. "What's the special occasion?"

Martinez removed his arm from my shoulder and reached for his beer. "I need a reason to mark time in my club?"

"No, but lately you have other *things*"—Jackal shot me a dark look—"demanding your time."

"Same could be said for you."

Jackal angled sideways in the booth and faced Martinez completely. "What's that supposed to mean?"

"You ain't dumb enough to play dumb, Jack. You've

been talking to nonmembers about *things* that don't concern them. Tonight, in fact. We both know that's against the rules."

Then Jackal said a foolish thing: "Maybe we should change those rules. Seems you did to suit your purposes."

Next thing I knew, Martinez had smacked Jackal in the forehead hard enough the beer bottle shattered. He grabbed Jackal by the back of the head and slammed his face into the table. A sickening crunch, then blood spurted out of Jackal's busted nose.

Wham wham wham. The remaining beer bottles wobbled and crashed to the floor. The ashtray jumped. Ash rose in the air like ghostly remnants from a volcano eruption.

I froze, apathetic, yet unable to look away.

Martinez ground Jackal's bloody face into the table. Jackal's breath whistled through his sinus cavity. He didn't fight Martinez, but he turned in my direction so he could breathe through his bruised lips.

He was a fucking mess.

Blood matted his beard. Covered his cheeks. A huge knot stuck out on his forehead. His eyes were squeezed shut. Martinez had chicken-winged Jackal's arm up his back. He steadily applied pressure until Jackal's arm popped from his shoulder socket; the cracking sound echoed like a gunshot.

Jackal grunted from the pain.

Someone had cut the jukebox. People in the club stayed silent and watchful.

I couldn't work up the tiniest bit of revulsion.

Martinez bent toward Jackal's ear. "Still think I'm soft?"

He didn't speak loudly; he didn't have to. His words were clear as a bell in the collective pause in the bar.

Jackal didn't move.

"My fucking club, Jack. My fucking rules, understand?"

Still, Jackal didn't move. Didn't so much as twitch.

"Answer me," Martinez demanded as he wedged the side of Jackal's face into the table, mashing his engorged nose into his swollen cheek. Jackal's fleshy lips were so distended I didn't know if he could speak.

"Yes," he finally panted. "I understand."

Drool and blood dripped from his mouth and pooled on the table next to the beer foam.

"For the record? She passed your little test. You failed mine. Remember, *hombre*, if you're not with me, you're against me. Don't take me on because you *will* lose."

Martinez jerked him upright by his hair. He released his hold on Jackal's arm. PT slid into view. "Take him out of here. Get him checked out and cleaned up so he can be in my office at Fat Bob's first thing tomorrow morning."

"Yessir." PT hauled Jackal up by his shirtfront and marched him from the room.

No one had taken a single step. Or a breath.

Martinez pointed to a goggle-eyed pledge, white-knuckling a barstool by the bar. "You. Clean this up. Now."

"Yessir. Right away, sir." He hustled over, wet towel in hand, gaze firmly on his boots.

No-neck slid the table out of the way so I didn't have to crawl through blood to get out.

When Martinez looped his arm over my shoulder, I realized he didn't have a speck of blood on him. Anywhere. His hands were perfectly clean. No one said a word as Big Mike, No-neck, and Bucket followed us out of the club.

💀 💀 💀

Martinez dismissed his bodyguards and drove his Escalade to my house. Took me ten minutes to work up the guts to speak to him.

"What was that about?"

He didn't answer right away. Finally he turned down Aerosmith's *Jaded*. "Reminding Jackal of his place. Reminding everyone else of mine."

Shit. "It wasn't just a show of testosterone for my benefit?"

"Partially." He parked beside my truck and switched off the ignition. "A refresher in case you've forgotten who—and what—I am."

"What's the other part?"

"A warning that my new rules shouldn't be questioned by *anyone*."

I didn't know how to respond or if he even wanted me to.

My grip tightened on my purse. "You coming in?"

"Aren't you repulsed by my archaic behavior?"

I thought of my father's violent streak and ignored the comparison. "No."

"Scared of me?"

"Yes. But not for the reasons you might think."

He lifted a brow but didn't ask for clarification and I'd be damned if I'd offer it up if I didn't have to.

💀 💀 💀

I dreamed of blood.

A body lay sprawled in the dirt. Fog and shadows swirled around me as I inched closer. My palms sweated, making the shovel handle slippery. I put my boot on the hip and kicked the corpse over.

Jackal. His throat sliced ear to ear. Just like Ben's. His eyes were wide open. Even in death he looked spiteful. I saw Martinez grinning crazily, a big, shiny knife clamped between his bright white teeth.

I stumbled as I ran from him. Right into another body sprawled in the dirt. Sunshine blinded me as I trudged closer. My palms sweated, slicking up the broom handle I used as a blind man's cane. I put my boot on the hip and kicked the corpse over.

Roland Hawk. His throat sliced ear to ear. Just like Ben's. Black puddles congealed beneath his head. Even the earth didn't want his tainted blood. I glanced at Denny flipping a straight-razor high in the air, then catching it by the blade. With each rotation, Denny lobbed off a finger. He lunged for me with blood-coated stumps.

I fell down as I ran. Darkness descended. I crawled in the dirt, lost, scared, and alone, until I hit the next body. Hands free, I patted the form until I connected with a small hand. With something clenched in a tiny fist. Light began to spill out of the palm like a magic trick. I knew who this sticky hand belonged to.

Jericho.

I dragged my gaze to his face. His neck was small and smooth, whole, not slit ear to ear. Not like Ben's. He wasn't moving, but he wasn't dead. I still had a chance to save him.

The *swish swish* of a scythe cutting through the forest got louder and louder. I tried to pick Jericho up, run with him, but he seemed to be rooted in the ground.

You can't keep him. You can't save him.

Frantically I dug around him with my bare hands. I kept digging, uncovering layer upon layer, but I couldn't budge him as his body sank deeper into the dirt.

A shadow fell across us. I made myself look up.

Abita was swinging the blade in a circle above her head like a helicopter rotator.

Jericho sat up like a horror movie zombie and morphed into a fire-breathing dinosaur with red eyes.

Kill her, I screamed, pointing at his mother.

But Jericho focused his attention on me. Snapping jaws, glowing eyes, sharp claws. The tip of one claw sliced my neck. Ear to ear. Just like Ben's. Just like all the others. Blood poured out. The dinosaur roared victoriously as I died.

I shot straight up in bed. Jesus Christ. Like I needed that fucking nightmare. I eased back the covers and shuffled to the living room. I fired up a Marlboro and aimed my unfocused gaze out the front window into the moonless night and tried to piece it together. Or dissect what the hell it meant. Another exercise in futility.

When I crawled back in bed, Martinez didn't stir. I envied him and his dreamless sleep. I wrapped myself around him and willed his body heat to warm me from the outside in.

CHAPTER 35

Somebody was beating on the front door. The alarm system began a series of annoying beeps.

Martinez groaned.

Whoa. 7:30 and he was still in my bed? I slipped away and grabbed my robe.

Yawning, I remembered to check the peephole before I disengaged the alarm. Probably Big Mike wondering where the hell Martinez was.

Brittney waited on the porch. *Brittney?*

I decoded the alarm and swung open the door.

She jumped back and bumped the porch railing.

"Brittney? Did something happen at home?"

"Umm. No."

"Oh. Well, it's a little early for a social call, isn't it?"

Her freckles stood out on her face like mud spots on

a palomino. "Probably. I-I just wanted to talk to you."

Her panicked gaze started at my wild hair. I was pretty sure she realized I was totally naked under my robe. As her wide eyes followed the curve of my neck, I wondered if Martinez had gifted me with hickeys. Her perusal stopped where the robe gapped between my breasts and she blushed. I glanced down and saw red streaks across my chest, courtesy of the razor stubble that covered Tony's face. Last night before the nightmare had overtaken me, Martinez reminded me of his place in my life. Numerous times.

She stammered, "I-I'm sorry. I didn't mean to wake you up."

"That's okay. Come in." I peered over her shoulder to the empty street. "How did you get here?"

Her pink flip-flops shuffled. "Got on the bus early and told my driver I left my backpack here. He dropped me off. I can ride to school from this bus stop."

Enterprising kid. "Does this have to do with the career day thing?"

"No. It has to do with Dad." Brittney raised her troubled eyes to mine. "I deserve to know the truth about why you hate him so much."

My stomach fluttered. Too goddamn early in the morning for this conversation, especially without caffeine. Or nicotine.

429

"You gonna send me away without talking to me?"

"No. But you need to give me a minute, all right?"

I puffed on a cigarette while the coffee beans whirred in the grinder, then I methodically readied the coffee pot for the brewing process. Nothing could've readied me for this discussion.

"You didn't deny you hate him," she said from the doorway.

"No, I didn't."

"Why? What did he do?"

Her innocent face had such a stubborn look of determination I would've laughed if it were any other subject matter. "You sure you want to hear this, Britt? Because it doesn't have a pretty ending."

She nodded.

"After my mom died . . . Dad went off the deep end. He took out his grief and frustration over her death on me. With his fists."

No response.

I could've left it there. I didn't. "He hit me a lot. Not spankings or the occasional slap on the face. He beat me."

"What did you do?"

"Bled. Cried. Hid my bruises." *And the shame.*

She scowled. "Did he ever hit you before your mom died?"

Why had she asked that? For justification that my mother's tragic accident had somehow triggered a cruel side in him? "Yes, he did, but it'd never been that severe."

"What did your mom do?"

"Nothing."

"Why not?"

"Because I hid it from her. Early on I realized he *liked* hitting me." I ground out my cigarette. "I took what he dished out and hated him. I didn't try to hide it, then or now. I've never gotten over it. I don't know if I can."

"I'm sorry. He's not like that now." She sniffled. "I-I don't understand how he . . . I'm just so . . . sorry."

The silence between us was brutal.

I tried for brevity. Levity. "Let's talk about something else. You want breakfast or something? Pop Tarts or toast?"

"Do we have any eggs?" Martinez sauntered in the kitchen. He headed straight for the cupboard and grabbed a coffee mug. He poured the thick brew, snagged the milk from the fridge, and dumped about a cup of sugar in as he stirred.

Brittney's hazel eyes grew big as pie plates at the muscled, tattooed, shirtless man, completely at home in my kitchen.

Martinez smiled at her. Thank God he hadn't done

the big-bad-wolf-growl-stare thing. Then again, that sexy smile of his was nearly as dangerous.

"Brittney, this is Tony. Tony, this is . . . my sister."

Her eyes cut to me and filled with shock before she dropped her gaze to the linoleum.

"You want me to cook you some eggs?" I asked Martinez.

"Actually, I'm not hungry after all. Coffee's fine."

"I'll go," Brittney said.

"No. Stay. I need a quick shower anyway." He pushed away from the counter. "Nice to meet you, Brittney." On his way out, he stopped in front of me and traced my cheek with his warm, rough fingertips, slowly brushing his mouth across mine. Twice.

A public display in front of a family member? I could scarcely wrap my head around this side of him.

After he'd left the room, Brittney blurted, "I thought Kevin was your boyfriend."

"Nope. Kevin is my business partner."

"Oh. So, is Tony your boyfriend?"

"Yeah. Why?"

" 'Cause he's kinda scary."

True.

"But he seems really nice," she added politely. "Is he?"

"What?"

"Nice or scary?"

432

"Both."

She expelled a girlish sigh. "Wow. You're so lucky. You can tell he really likes you and he's . . . a total hottie."

My answering smile wasn't faked. "Yes, he is."

"Look, I hafta catch the bus. Thanks, uh, sis," Brittney said and bolted out the door, leaving me staring after her.

No one had called me *sis* since Ben. Strange how it didn't sound wrong coming from her.

She was a sweet girl. I cursed my stupidity for telling her the truth.

"You all right?"

I didn't turn around. "You heard everything?"

"Yeah."

"Did I do the right thing?"

"Yes, she needs to know what he did to you." His arms engulfed me and he feathered kisses through my hair and on the back of my head. "I can't stomach the thought of anyone hurting you, blondie. Then or now. Makes me crazy. Makes me want to do crazy bad things." He nuzzled the side of my neck. "I've got to go. I'll call you later." And he was gone.

I hadn't made it into the shower when my phone rang. Caller ID said *Kevin*. Probably wondering if planned on working today. I answered, "I'm running late."

"Actually I hoped to catch you before you left."

"What's up?"

"Denny didn't come back here last night."

"What? Why? Did you talk to him?"

"Briefly. He said something about Maria's service and his grandmother. I think he headed back to White Plain. I don't even know what time." Kevin sighed. "He's almost an adult, and it might be stupid, but I'm worried."

"Me too." I had a bad, bad feeling.

"You know your way around the rez; maybe you could track him down."

"Okay."

"Call me and leave a message on my cell. I'll be in meetings with clients most of the morning but I want to know what's going on."

"Will do."

"And, Jules, be careful."

💀 💀 💀

I savored the scenic drive. Rising and falling stony hills yielded to flat prairie. This landscape was stark. Unforgiving. Distances were deceiving in the great wide open, when the horizon stretched for miles.

The poison ivy and sumac had long ago burned scarlet and withered away. Tumbleweeds dotted the barbed wire fences. Chalky white patches of alkaline soil stood out like pools of spilled milk against ground the color of melted caramel. It was stunningly beautiful to me.

As I drove I formulated a plan. I'd stop by the White Plain funeral home first. As a last resort, I'd go to Roland and Bonita's place.

Funeral homes gave me the creeps. There's something inherently wrong with people making money off death. With having a showroom dedicated to glossy coated, satin-lined coffins and fake-gilded urns. The sickly sweet scent of air freshener that never quite masked the antiseptic smell of embalming chemicals or the stench of death.

I didn't remember my mother's casket. Or the flowers. Only the surrealism of sitting in the front pew between my father and my mother's mother. I remembered my Grandmother Inga's cold, dry hand holding mine. Her confusion. She'd flown over alone from Norway and she hadn't spoken much English.

Mostly I remembered her sadness beneath the stoicism. I'd only met her once before. And the day we buried my mother was the last time I ever saw her. Strange, it was almost as if she'd washed her hands of me the same way Sharon Dove had with Denny.

Cool, rose-scented air assaulted me as I trudged into the entryway of the funeral home. I'd barely choked down the panic and nausea when Ichabod Crane skulked around the corner with—dare I say—a hopeful gleam in his eye.

"May I help you?"

I couldn't muster a smile. "Maybe. Have the services already been held for Maria Dove?"

His attitude cooled. He had no reason to be nice now; I wasn't a potential customer. "Just finished an hour ago."

"Was it held here or a church?" My gaze zoomed to the chapel area. Empty.

"Over at Saint Isaacs."

I'd try to catch Denny at the church while he was eating finger sandwiches, frosted cake, and making small talk.

Took me two spins around the ostentatious building before I found the mettle to park. I'd nearly made it to the steps leading into the vestibule when I heard, "Hey, over here."

I spun. Denny was hunched against a life-sized statue of the Virgin Mary. His hair was slicked back and he wore an ill-fitting plaid sports coat that made him look like Herb Tarlek from *WKRP in Cincinnati*. He smoked the tail end of a cigarette.

"Everything okay?"

"Nah. It sucks, you know?"

"Is your mom with your grandma?"

Denny snorted. "Right. Roland beat her up bad

again. She swears this time she's left him for good."

Ah, hell. "Where is she?"

"My Grandma Sharon wouldn't take her in, so she's sleeping it off at my Grandma Bird's house."

What the hell was wrong with Sharon Dove? "Didn't your mom come to the service?"

"No. Her face is swollen and she can't see nothin'. Don't matter cause she can't hardly walk anyway."

Stupid question but I had to ask. "Did Roland show up for Maria's service?"

Denny gaped at me as if I'd lost my mind.

"Sorry."

"S'okay." He flicked the spent butt and it bounced off a concrete angel. "Weird fuckin' day."

"You staying with your *unci* again?"

"Nah. I jus' wanna get outta here, know what I mean? You headin' back to Rapid City?"

"Yeah. You need a ride?"

"If it ain't too much trouble." He glanced at his grimy tennis shoes.

"No trouble. I gotta swing by Kevin's anyway."

"Cool. Let me run in and tell 'em I'm leavin'."

He trotted off. I considered the statue of Mary, beaming at the baby cradled in her arms. It amazed me, the serenity and contentment attributed to her.

Would Kim have that awe and air of accomplishment

when she held her child? Would I once again become an outsider?

Denny trundled back, frown creasing his face. "My *unci* wants me to pick up some stuff at Mom's place before I leave."

"From Roland's?"

"Yeah. And I ain't got no choice. But if you gotta get goin' that's okay. I'll catch a ride with someone else later."

"That's fine. I'm in no rush. Just hope you don't mind if I hide in the truck."

"*Shee.* Maybe we both oughta hide in the truck, eh?"

My insides tumbled as we coasted down the steep hill to Roland and Bonita's trailer.

Roland's Durango was parked kitty-corner to the steps. I didn't see the dogs, or hear them.

I parked but left the ignition on.

Denny said, "Be right back." He rounded the front end of Roland's car and stopped abruptly. I could only see the back of Denny's head as he bent down. Then he straightened up; his face resembled a wax carving.

My gun was in my hand and I jumped out of the cab. "Denny? What's going on?"

He stepped aside.

And I saw it.

A body splayed in the dirt just below the steps.

Face up.

Roland.

His throat had been sliced from ear to ear. His eyes were wide open. Filmy. Milky white like he'd developed cataracts overnight.

I shuddered. Jesus. Just like in my dream.

But in my dream he'd been whole. His calves hadn't been gnawed to the bone, except for a few sinewy strips, dangling in the dirt. His feet still had skin and muscles and tendons.

In my dream starving dogs hadn't found him.

CHAPTER 36

I MADE MYSELF LOOK AT DENNY, HOPING HE STILL WORE the same shocked expression.

He did. When he started to gag I knew he wasn't responsible for Roland's near beheading. My thoughts flashed to the gruesome crime scene Martinez and I had stumbled on last summer. Martinez literally had to clamp his hand over my mouth to keep me from throwing up. With Roland's body between us, I couldn't get to Denny in time.

I needed a different tactic.

I pointed the gun at Denny's head. "Don't fucking move."

He froze, then swallowed hard.

Good, that would keep the bile down. "Talk to me. Swear to me you had nothing to do with this execution,

Denny."

"I-I didn't. Oh, man," he glanced down at Roland's remains and shuddered. "Oh, Jesus, I'm gonna be sick."

"No! I said, look at me!"

His head snapped up and he gaped at the barrel of my Browning.

"Did you kill him?"

"No!"

"Did you hire someone else to kill him after he beat the shit out of your mother?"

"No."

"When was the last time you saw Roland?"

"Th-that day he used the stunner on us in Sturgis."

"You're sure?"

"Yes, I'm fucking sure. Jesus. What's wrong with you?"

"Okay. Listen to me. Don't look at him. Don't think about what those dogs did to him. Turn around and get back in the truck. We're getting out of here right fucking now."

Denny didn't question me; he just obeyed.

I waited until he'd shut the door before my gaze strayed. First to the bloody carnage that'd been Roland Hawk, then to the dogs, still chained to the tree, lying in the trash next to the metal skirting of the trailer. They were lethargic after their unexpected feast. I suspected if I got too close to the body, they'd see me as a threat horning in on their prize and try to attack me, even when they hadn't actually made the kill on Roland, just reaped the benefits.

I covered the distance to my truck in three steps, climbed in, and we roared off. Once we'd cleared reservation land, I pulled over on the shoulder, opened the door and threw up.

After I wiped my mouth, I faced a petulant Denny.

"What the fuck was that shit, Julie? Pullin' a gun on me?"

"Sorry. I used it as a diversion to keep you from blowing chunks all over the scene."

"Well, it worked, 'cept I almost crapped my pants. I thought you were gonna shoot me!" He was completely panicked. "Oh, God. What do we do now?"

"I don't know.

The legal parameters were different on tribal land. People who'd done business on White Plain told horror stories about glitches in the legal system. Add in the sovereign nation angle? I'd rather not spend months in the White Plain jail on a suspected murder rap while my legal rights were questioned and legal parameters defined.

Once again I'd lit out of a crime scene like a mad bull was chasing me. I hated that this shit was starting to become habit.

Would the tribal police even investigate? Blame it

on the dogs? Chalk it up to good riddance? I doubted anyone would mourn him. Might seem harsh but I wasn't sorry Roland was dead, just sorry about my bad luck in finding him.

Tough talk. I knew the final vision of Roland, as a dog's chew toy, would haunt me for many years to come.

"Can I ask you somethin'?" Denny said.

"Sure."

"Did *you* have anything to do with him getting killed?"

The question jarred me, but not as much as the question running round in my brain I'd refused to acknowledge until right that second: Had Martinez done this to Roland? In retaliation for Roland cutting and zapping me?

Then again, the list of people who wanted Roland dead was mighty long.

"Julie?"

"Not intentionally."

Denny didn't comment.

"I have to call Kevin. He has a clearer head than both of us right now."

Kevin picked up on the second ring. I recited the details. The silence was unbearable as I waited for his advice. Finally, Kevin sighed. "I know I gave you a rash of shit last time this happened to you, Jules. But I have to be honest. I don't see any other way for you to deal with this besides call it in anonymously and drive like hell away from there."

"Can't they track cell phones?"

Beside me, Denny snorted. "*Shee.* The rez police don't got enough money for gas for their patrol cars. They sure as shit don't got no kinda super spyware that can track you down."

"He's right," Kevin said. "Call it in, then get back to Rapid City. Fast."

"I don't have the number for the tribal PD."

Denny rattled it off.

I gave him a skeptical look.

He shrugged. "You surprised I had to call the cops a time or two?"

I dialed the White Plain Tribal Police Department before I lost my nerve. Yeah, I disguised my voice—poorly—and ranted about Roland driving his Durango, obviously drunk, on the wrong side of the road. Throwing beer bottles on the highway and then cruising along home.

Lame? Totally. Hopefully they'd check it out before the dogs needed another snack.

Denny and I didn't talk at all as I cruised straight to the office. I'd use drudgery to block out the horror of my morning. Maybe it'd work on the rest of the nasty things I'd dealt with in the last week too.

I buckled down and had done a fair job in forgetting about my hellish morning, when the door clicked open and Kim shuffled into my office.

Her pasty complexion didn't scare me as much as the way she inched across the room. I pushed back my office chair and skirted the desk. She looked ready to topple over.

"Kim?" I clutched her shoulders. "What's wrong?"

She sagged against me. "I'm bleeding. I think I'm having a miscarriage."

"Oh, shit. Sit down." After I'd situated her in the chair, I asked, "Who's your doctor?" She whispered the name and I found the number and dialed. I explained the situation and received instructions.

I hung up and glanced at her. Tears streamed down Kim's cheeks. My throat closed. I knew—I remembered—exactly how she felt right now. "I'm taking you in. Sit tight while I tell Kevin I'm going to be gone for awhile again."

Kevin, being the (nosy) helpful sort, brought my truck around and helped me bundle Kim inside.

At the doctor's office, Kim watched the pregnant women waddling in and out of the reception area with the most forlorn expression. She'd wanted this baby way more than she'd ever let on.

I clasped her hand in mine. "You need anything?"

445

"No."

"Do you want me to come in with you?"

"I-I don't know. What's going to happen, did they say?"

"They'll do a pelvic exam and an ultrasound. If everything is okay, they'll send you home and tell you to rest."

Her voice dropped to a whisper. "What if it's not okay?"

"If it's no longer a viable pregnancy then they'll do a D&C, send you home and tell you to rest."

Kim studied me strangely. "They just told you this?"

No.

The nurse called Kim's name and she opted to go in alone.

Sesame Street didn't take my mind off what might be happening to Kim. Or what'd already happened to Roland Hawk. I suspected nothing would erase the images besides booze.

My stomach rumbled. Food was out of the question.

Another hour later Kim emerged. I scrutinized her face but couldn't detect a damn thing about her diagnosis. She didn't speak until we were in my car and I demanded, "Well?"

"Everything is fine. I'm just spotting a little. Things are normal. So is this constant nausea. Apparently I freaked out for no reason."

446

"I'm glad everything is okay." I signaled and turned right onto 5th Street, past Rapid City Regional Hospital. The Emergi-Flight helicopter sat on the pad like a big, hungry bird of prey, eager to swoop down on misfortune.

I hung a left on Minnesota Street and followed it past the clusters of single-family homes and generic apartment buildings until I reached the rows of condos, neatly lined up like something out of a Martha Stewart magazine.

Inside Kim's place, I tucked her in bed with a cup of herbal tea. Fluffed her pillows. Brought her crackers and juice.

"You don't have to do this, Julie."

"Let me fuss a little, will you?" I mimicked in her southern drawl.

She smiled and sank back into the mountain of pink pillows. Chiffon, lace, silk, satin, velvet. All different shapes, all different sizes, all different shades . . . of pink. Be interesting to see how Kim would handle having a boy.

"How did things go with Murray?"

"Good, I guess. We're taking it day by day. No major changes. He wants to be involved in everything."

"There are worse things, Kim."

"I know." I knew she knew, but she had something else on her mind.

447

I straightened the puffy coverlet. "Anything else you need?"

She said, "No," but was strangely hesitant.

"What?"

"Can I ask you something?"

I almost pulled a Martinez and said, "Sure. Doesn't mean I'll answer." Instead I shrugged. "I guess."

"What happened in the last few days?"

Revelation and revulsion. Disenchantment and dismemberment. She didn't need to hear my woes in her current frame of mind so I shrugged again and said, "Some stuff I can't talk about."

An angry pause.

I sighed and searched for patience. "What?"

"I thought since we'd both been burned by bad friendships in the past, that we'd made some progress in willingly sharing things about ourselves in the last few months."

"We have. But this isn't something you want to hear about, Kim."

"Okay, then why didn't you tell me you had a miscarriage?"

I backtracked so fast I plowed over a beaded floor lamp.

Kim snagged my wrist. "Have you ever talked to anyone about it?"

No.

"I know how you hate being vulnerable, and how you never let anyone in—"

"If you're all right, I have to go." I didn't need her prodding at another thing in my screwed up psyche after what I'd been through today.

"Julie, please stay. Don't run away. Talk to me."

No. "Is Murray coming by?"

"Probably after work."

"Good." I slipped out of her hold without having to resort to a forearm strike. But I would have done anything to escape. "I'll call you tomorrow. Get some rest."

"Julie, I didn't mean—"

I said, "Take care, Kim," and bolted from her pink palace.

CHAPTER 37

I COULDN'T FACE THE OFFICE. KEVIN HAD TOLD ME NOT to worry about coming back, so I didn't. I drove aimlessly. Nickelback's *Animals* blasting from the speakers couldn't drown out the thoughts spinning in my head.

I'd had a miscarriage about five months before Ben's murder. If I'd carried the pregnancy to term, my child would be about the same age as Jericho. Was that the reason I felt a need to cling to him? Because of my own sense of loss?

No time to dwell on it. I shoved it in the dark recesses of my mind where it belonged. As I passed the turn-off to June Everett's house, I realized, with all the other stuff going on in my life, I'd forgotten about Jeff Colhoff.

The red Dodge truck was parked out front. I didn't see the ancient Chrysler Lebaron from the other day.

When I pulled up I noted a little dark-haired boy playing alone in a big tractor tire that'd been recycled into a sand box. Tonka trucks and other miniature construction equipment surrounded him.

I cut the engine, palmed my gun in my jacket pocket and slowly approached the kid. "Hey. What's your name?"

He didn't look up. "I ain't 'sposed to talk to strangers."

"But I'm not a stranger. I was here talking to your mom the other day, remember?" He kept rolling the mini-dump truck in the same set of tracks. "And I know your Aunt June."

"She's dead. Now she ain't gonna be sad no more 'cause she's where she wanted to be."

"And where's that?"

"Up'n heaven with Uncle Lang."

Well, hell. I didn't know what to say to that. Had June's death officially been ruled a suicide? "So, what's your name?"

"JJ."

"Wow, JJ. You have quite the selection of cool machines. I bought one just like this for my nephew." I tapped the cab top of a road grader.

"My mama bought that for me. Does he got one like this?" JJ held up a tiny bobcat with a bucket on one side, and the cab swiveled to the claw arm on the other side.

I shook my head.

"We gots a real one of these, too." JJ pointed to the hobbled machine, missing a left front wheel, stuck alongside the metal barn. "My mama used to run really, really big trucks when she worked in the coal fields. Sometimes my mama takes me for rides in that one."

"Yeah? Where do you go?"

"Out in the pasture." His little chest puffed out. "I even got to sit on her lap and drive."

Something mighty strange was going on in my head. "Awesome. Did you get to drop the bucket?"

JJ nodded. "And the claw. It digs really big holes." He scowled. "'Cept last time she went by herself and made me watch the crybabies. She was gone a long time and Dougie pooped everywhere." He clapped a grubby hand over his mouth. "That's 'sposed to be a secret. Doan tell her, 'cause I'll get inta big trouble."

The truth hit me like a Wyoming coal train. Jeannie had dug up those bones and dumped them in the stock damn. Why? Who was she protecting? Her husband? Or herself?

The metal trailer door banged and Jeff inched down the steps with a baby on his hip, and a two-year old hiding behind his leg.

"What are you doing here?"

"I was in the neighborhood and wanted to see how you were holding up. And to apologize for my rudeness at the sheriff's office the other day."

Jeff relaxed and nodded somberly. And for the briefest second, I caught a glimpse of the handsome man June claimed he was before marriage and children sucked the life out of him. But was he a monster? Like Ted Bundy? Using his charm to lure and then kill?

"I noticed the Bobcat over there by the barn. How long has the wheel been off?"

His pale green eyes met mine head on. To JJ he said, "Take Dougie and Stevie in the house."

"But, Daddy—"

"Now." He passed Dougie to JJ and the tiny boy clung to JJ like a bald monkey.

No further questions from JJ. He just trooped by, grabbing Stevie's arm and hauling him inside.

When Jeff and I were alone, out in the middle of nowhere, I was mighty glad I'd pocketed my gun.

"Why are you doing this?"

"Doing what, Jeff? Trying to find justice for a murdered woman, whose body was hacked to bits and buried in a shallow grave on your land? Oh, and then her remains were desecrated *again* and unceremoniously dumped in a stock dam like trash."

He winced.

"Did you have that Bobcat hidden someplace when the sheriff came out here to question you?"

LORI ARMSTRONG

"He never came out here to question us. Every interview was done at the sheriff's office."

Was that my fault? Because I'd been trying to pin Maria's murder on Roland Hawk? That was a mistake I'd have to live with.

"You do know I'm working as an independent investigator for the Bear Butte County Sheriff's Department? And if you don't answer the question, I can take you in and have you talk to the sheriff?"

"Yes."

"So, was the Bobcat hidden?"

"No. It's been sitting there since the wheel fell off."

"When was the last time you used it?"

"Couple of months ago."

"Let me rephrase that: When was the last time the Bobcat was used by *anybody*?"

His hand came up and he rubbed his forehead.

"Jeff?"

"Three or four weeks ago."

"Jeannie?"

"Yeah."

Mentally, I belted a shot of Don Julio. "Did you kill Maria Dove?"

"No." The pointed toe of his cowboy boot dug into the hard-packed ground. "I was crazy about her."

When he glanced up at me it seemed as if he'd aged

454

ten years in ten seconds.

I said, "Tell me what happened. From the beginning."

"Jeannie and I were separated. We'd been living in Gillette. I came home and found a job at a repair shop in Rapid City. I fixed bikes for some of the Hombres members and started hanging out at Fat Bob's. Those guys said I oughta join up with the Hombres, so I did. I passed the initiation pretty quickly. It was the first time I ever felt like I . . . *belonged* anywhere. I made it through the pledge ceremony."

My thoughts flashed back to the faded T-shirt he'd worn the first time I saw him at June's, the letters LED visible beneath his jacket. I'd bet he'd kept the pledge shirt as a memento from his past, looking upon it fondly like an old concert T-shirt.

"Part of the pledge initiation was working security at Bare Assets. When I met Maria, it was like I'd found the other half of myself."

"Had Maria really talked about moving to Denver?"

He nodded. "Once I became a patched-in Hombres member, I planned to transfer to the Denver chapter and we were gonna live there."

"What happened?"

"Two things. My dad died and then we had the whole mess with the ranch. June didn't want to sell it, I did, and she didn't have no money to buy me out, so I was stuck.

Then Jeannie showed up and told me she was pregnant."

Jesus. Secret babies and jilted lovers; shit like this happened every fucking day, who needed to watch soap operas?

"I told her I'd support the kid but I wanted a divorce because I was gonna marry someone else." His sour laugh nearly pickled my innards. "I even told Jeannie Maria's name. Can you believe how fucking stupid that was?"

My mouth had gone bone dry.

"Maria and I had a fight after I told her about Jeannie being pregnant. She said some dumb shit about never seeing me again. I gave her a couple of days to cool off. Then she disappeared. I thought maybe she'd taken off for Denver, like we'd talked about. It wasn't like I could call up her folks and ask, and Maria didn't have no friends. After a couple of months, I knew Maria wasn't coming back and Jeannie had JJ, so I married her.

"I swear to God I didn't know. All these years she was right there . . ." He shook his head as if he were trying to get the idea to stick in place. "Something started to bug me when the hunters found them bones. Then Lang died. Somebody dug that hole and made them bones disappear. I noticed the wheel was off the Bobcat, like it'd been sittin' there broken for months. Only I knew it hadn't been broken."

"Did you have any idea what Jeannie had been up to?"

"No. Lang wanted to do the right thing and it should've tipped me off back then when Jeannie argued the loudest we should forget about it. Then Maria's name was released. And I knew.

"So here's the truth hittin' me in the face. I look at my little boys . . . and I don't know how I can tell them what kind of evil she is. She's their mother. She's my wife."

"Jeff—"

"Not only that, I'm pretty sure Jeannie killed my sister."

"How?"

"I found June's cell phone in Jeannie's jacket pocket this morning. I know June had her cell with her when she died because she'd called me that afternoon from the bluff. Drunk. Saying she knew Jeannie was a cold-blooded killer. And if I didn't tell the sheriff 'bout her murdering ways, she would."

What the hell? "June knew you were seeing Maria?"

"Yes." And then he broke. Through his heartbreaking sobs, he stammered, "If it's not b-bad enough she f-fucking murdered my sister, she's actin' all happy, like now we c-can move into their house, get their share of the land, get the insurance money, like it's some goddamn . . . *b-blessing* instead of a horror show." Jeff squeezed his eyes shut. "I just wanna wake up from this nightmare. But I have, and I realize I been married to the monster all along."

I couldn't offer him any kind of comfort. I struggled to maintain a professional distance, even when my heart hurt for the ugly reality he'd faced and the horrors yet to come.

I waited to speak until he had some semblance of control. "I have to take you in, Jeff, so you can tell this to the sheriff. You do realize there's no way around it?"

He nodded.

"Where is Jeannie now?"

"She went to Wal-Mart in Spearfish." He lifted his head. "I can't leave my boys here. I got no one to look after them."

"Would it be better if I called the sheriff and had him come out here?"

"Yeah. Jeannie'd get suspicious if I wasn't home anyway. She don't trust me, always thinks I'm up to something. Ain't that ironic, when she's the one . . . ?" He choked and couldn't finish.

There was that overwhelming urge to run again. "Is there anyone I can call? Maybe your uncle?"

He shook his head.

I dug my cell phone out of my right rear pocket and called Sheriff Richards.

Sometimes things play out that way. No big confrontations. No AHA! moments. Jeff talked. The sheriff jotted notes. When Jeannie Colhoff pulled up and got out, and Sheriff Richards approached the vehicle, she dropped the bag of frozen chicken nuggets and took off across the field.

I don't know what possessed me to give chase and tackle Jeannie, but I did. It felt goddamn good to grind her face in the dirt and listen to her cries as I waited for the sheriff to catch up. He cuffed her and read her the Miranda.

Jeff hadn't allowed let his sons watch their mother get taken into custody. I don't know if I could have acted so selflessly, given the circumstances. Just another indication I'd be a lousy parent.

As I drove home, I didn't get a sense of victory that I'd solved the case the sheriff had hired me for. I felt absolutely heartsick. Why was jealousy called the green-eyed monster? It should be called the red-fisted monster, because of the rage and blood that follow in its wake.

After the epically awful day I'd had, I didn't want to talk to anyone so I shut off my cell phone. I just wanted to curl up in my bed, alone, with a bottle of anesthetic. Tequila couldn't erase the bad images but I'd settle for blurry. Really blurry.

In my state of distraction, I didn't notice the vehicle in my driveway until I'd nearly rear-ended it.

Kevin paced on my front steps, waiting for me. He enfolded me in a hug I didn't know I'd needed. Tears poured out as the emotions I'd held in all day exploded like a dam breach.

CHAPTER 38

KEVIN AND I DIDN'T TALK.

I drained the remainder of the Don Julio. I panicked when I realized I was out of booze, a clear sign I was far too dependent on the tasty stuff. But I didn't give a rat's ass about my future membership in AA. Getting drunk tonight wasn't a luxury; it was a necessity.

Kevin lined up the remaining treasures from my liquor cabinet. Ooh, choices, choices. Peppermint schnapps? Rum? Jack Daniels? I decided on the Jack. The hangover would be minimal. Mixing the whiskey with soda caused blood sugar problems so I drank it straight up. I chased the shots with beer. My stomach acid did a fine job churning the contents into an acceptable boilermaker.

I hadn't eaten all day so the booze hit me quickly.

I smoked and drank. Kevin alternated between watching me and *Star Trek* reruns. What seemed like 100 shots later, I was totally shit-faced. The room tilted. I welcomed the wavering eyesight and the way my body started listing to the left. I snickered.

"Hey, now I'm off balance inside and out."

"Jesus. You're babbling."

"So?"

"So, enough booze already," Kevin said and heaved himself out of the recliner.

I squinted at him as he cleaned up the empty beer bottles and dirty shot glasses. "Are you leaving?"

"I don't know. Why?"

"Just wanted to say goodnight before I passed out."

"How considerate."

"You're welcome." Even in my blurry state I could see he had that look. "What?"

"Do you want me to call Martinez?"

"Why?"

"So he's here to make sure you don't choke on your own vomit."

I got my mean on. "I'm not exactly a lightweight, Kev."

"True. But you're getting a little old to do this."

"To do . . . what?" I threw my arms out. "Too old to find a dead body gnawed on by rabid dogs? Too old to sit in the waiting room while my friend bawls her head off because she might be losing a baby she didn't know she wanted? Too old to watch a man realize the person he pledged his life to has purposely destroyed damn near everyone he loved? Too old to lose the last goddamn link I have to Ben?"

I closed my eyes. *Don't cry. Don't be a fucking crybaby. Jesus Christ, suck it up, Julie.* I was sick of crying.

My tear ducts didn't appreciate being berated; moisture leaked out anyway.

"So, yeah. I feel every single minute of this awful day sinking into my bones like poison. It's making me old. It's eating me alive. It's sucking my will to do anything but suck down liquid courage so I can go on for yet another sucky day."

Kevin didn't respond. Good. I'd shamed him into silence. The drama that'd become my life in the last week *was* getting old.

"Jules—"

"Go home. I'll be fine. I'm a tough girl, remember? I don't need anyone. And if I wake up in a puddle of cold barf tomorrow morning . . . well, you can't say you didn't warn me."

No argument from him. He just kissed me on the forehead and left.

I tottered off to bed and passed out.

❧ ❧ ❧

I woke up feeling like shit. Martinez breathed deeply in my ear. He'd wrapped his big body around me like a 200-pound blanket. Huh. I didn't remember anything from last night. Did we have sex?

Clouds of steam and the pounding spray of hot water beating on my face in the shower stall helped my hangover. A half pot of strong Columbian, and four Excedrin helped the rest of the way into making me human.

What fun thing could I do today? Track down Abita and demand she keep her life the way it is to suit mine? Go to the sheriff's office and rehash the brutal realities of the Dove case? Crash June's funeral? Check on Kim and have her grill me about something painful from my past that wasn't any of her damn business? Ask my lover if he'd murdered a man?

My dismal list of choices brought back my sense of futility.

The cupboard door squeaked. I automatically smiled at Martinez, but it dried up when I remembered I'd have to ask him about Roland Hawk. Specifically if he'd *killed* Roland Hawk.

"You don't look hungover," he said.

"I am. What time did you roll in last night?"

"Early. Shortly after Wells called me at Fat Bob's."

"Kevin called you?"

"Yeah."

"Why?"

He shrugged. "He was worried about you."

My eyes narrowed. "I don't need a goddamn baby-sitter, Martinez."

"No kidding? Well, I guess I'll pack up my toys and go home." He disappeared from the kitchen.

Yeah. I'd handled that with tact. I followed Martinez into my bedroom.

He gave me a flinty-eyed stare as he yanked on a Deadwood Jam T-shirt. "What?"

"I'm an asshole, okay? I'm sorry."

In two quick strides he loomed over me. "That was a record apology for you, blondie."

"Don't get used to it." I studied his dark eyes. "I have to ask you something. I don't want to but I have to."

"What?"

"Did you have anything to do with Roland Hawk ending up in a body bag yesterday?"

Not a single change in his expression. "And if I did? What would you do? Turn me in?"

"No."

"Then why do you care?"

"I just do, okay?"

"Not good enough. Why does it matter?"

"Because I saw it . . . It was awful; it was like someone tried to remove his head from his neck with a hacksaw. And it looked like a crime of passion, brutal, personal, and done out of extreme anger."

"Jesus. You *saw* him like that?"

"Yes, before the tribal police did. So I have to know if you did it."

Stoic Tony appeared.

I pushed the issue. "If so, why? For revenge? Hombres retribution? As a warning? Was any of it about me? And while you're formulating your answer, I'll silently berate myself about morphing into one of those women who lie and cheat and cover for their man."

He grinned slowly. "You admitting I'm your man now?"

"Shut up. I'm serious, Tony."

Martinez sobered quickly. "Am I supposed to lie and tell you we never do shit like that?"

My turn to stare at him.

"It's a moot point this time because I didn't have anything to do with it. In fact, this is the first I've heard of it."

I ignored the *this time* portion of his response. "Kevin didn't tell you?"

"The only thing Wells told me was that you'd had

a monumentally shitty day, you'd crawled into a bottle and he didn't want to leave you alone to drown." He crushed a handful of my hair and brought it to his lips before he let it fall through his fingers. "You were out of it when I got here."

"Sorry. I don't remember anything from last night after I hit the sheets." I looked at him expectantly.

He lifted a brow. "Nothing to remember."

"Good. I hate to have to stroke your ego unnecessarily."

"You didn't stroke my ego or anything else last night."

"Oh, poor baby."

"You can make it up to me."

"Deal." Wow. That was almost . . . easy. Were we figuring out this relationship thing? "What's on your agenda today?"

"I can cross 'killing Roland Hawk' off my list of things to do since somebody beat me to it."

My jaw dropped. "You made a joke? An actual joke? Albeit a sick one." I noticed the tight set to his jaw and remembered I wasn't the only one with problems. My fingers smoothed the stubble on his cheek. "What happened with Jackal yesterday?"

"He groveled. And . . ." He sighed, tilting his head into my hand for a more complete touch. "Just pretty much groveled and apologized. He's on probation. If he fucks up again, he's gone."

467

I didn't want to know what *gone* meant. "Is he still the chief enforcer?"

"No. Cal is temporarily filling in."

"Who's Cal?"

Martinez said, "The guy you call No-neck."

"Ah. Is he qualified?"

"Immensely."

"What's his first order of business?"

"Dealing with Dave."

I suppressed a shudder. "Can I ask Dave's punishment? Since I helped bring him down and all."

Martinez rolled his eyes. "Dave has a video lottery gambling problem, which isn't earning him the sympathy he's expecting from me or anyone else. Everyone has addictions. Shoving 300 bucks in an electronic machine every goddamn night ain't the way to solve it."

"How much did he take?"

"He fessed up to every penny of the 15K from the last two months."

"Holy shit. How's he gonna pay it all back?"

"I'll get my fifteen thou, even if I have to take it out in pounds of flesh, trust me."

I had nothing to say to that.

He locked his gaze to mine and roughly pulled me against him. "Make time for me tonight. Better yet, let's take a couple of days and hide out at my house. Think you can get things arranged for time off by this afternoon?"

"Yeah." I curled my arms around his neck and pressed my cheek into his chest. "Thanks for staying with me last night. I'm glad you're here, Martinez."

"Same goes, blondie."

The moment, while brief, was enough.

"Big Mike will jump my shit if I don't get going. I'll call you later and let you know what time I'm picking you up."

After he left me with an entirely too chaste kiss, I felt even more at loose ends.

☠ ☠ ☠

The paper didn't have any information on the Roland Hawk situation. No surprise. They usually lumped all the bad news from the reservations together, once a week, and it encompassed an entire page. Funny, how little of the good things going on the rez were chronicled with such regularity.

Which reminded me I should probably give Sharon Dove a call. No doubt Jeannie's arrest would make the paper.

Maybe this was the sheriff's job, but I felt I owed Sharon a personal accounting since I'd found Maria's remains and worked on the case.

Sharon answered on the third ring. "Hello?"

"Sharon? Julie Collins. I just wanted to give you a heads up on Maria's case. We finally had a break."

"You did? When?"

"Sheriff Richards made an arrest late yesterday afternoon."

Silence. "An arrest? But . . ."

"But what?"

"Isn't Roland Hawk dead?"

I frowned at the receiver. How did she know that? "He didn't arrest Roland Hawk. He arrested Jeannie Colhoff. Remember the guy Maria had been seeing, the bouncer from the strip club? Well, I tracked him down. The suspected killer is his wife." I detailed everything I knew.

Utter silence.

"Sharon?"

"Yes. I'm here. I-I can't believe it. Sorry. It's just such a shock."

"I imagine so."

"The sheriff is positive Roland didn't have anything to do with Maria's murder?"

"I don't know if Jeannie has plead guilty. It appears she killed another person while trying to cover her tracks. I doubt the case will go to trial. If anything, she might take a plea bargain. Good defense attorneys are pricey and her husband isn't about to lend his support, financial or emotional."

An old murder, plus a new one pretty much guaranteed Jeannie Colhoff would spend her life in prison. Gave me a warm fuzzy feeling justice had been served. Too often bad deeds go unpunished. Bad people get away with bad stuff all the time. Hence the appeal of vigilante justice. No one was immune to it. No one.

Reality washed over me like a frigid December wind.

No wonder Sharon Dove had known Roland Hawk was dead. She'd killed him.

The bloody butchery of Roland's body flashed in my memory. A crime of extreme anger. Frustration. A mother who'd avenged her daughter. Problem was, she'd avenged the wrong one.

No one would argue Roland Hawk had scraped the bottom of the barrel of humanity. Preying on people. Causing problems with anyone who crossed him. He'd put Bonita in the hospital half a dozen times. He'd been the bane of the tribal police for years.

If Roland wasn't around the rez wreaking havoc, how could that be a bad thing . . . for anybody? No more wasted manpower for the tribal cops. Bonita might actually become a productive member of society without Roland sucking her into the cycle of abuse. Denny could leave White Plain permanently, without fear for

471

his mother's safety.

Could my conscience let me hand over Sharon Dove to the sheriff? What would throwing her in jail prove? Who would it help?

Not your job to act as judge and jury.

Then I heard her crying and I knew I wouldn't make the call. She might choose to turn herself in, but it wouldn't be at my urging.

Her sobs were getting louder.

"Sharon, listen to me. We all have demons. Sometimes we listen to them when we shouldn't. You've finally got that demon off your back. Move on. I realize that's cold comfort when you've buried your daughter, but the truth is, you've got *another* daughter who needs you. She'll need you more than ever now. Think about that."

"How can I live with myself?" Her voice was scarcely a whisper.

"If you're looking for absolution, I can't give it to you."

Sniffling pause.

"Whatever you decide is your business. My part officially ended when the sheriff arrested Jeannie Colhoff. Far as I'm concerned the case is closed." I quietly hung up.

Maybe I should take my own advice. Maybe I should try and get the demon off my back. Maybe it was time to admit I'd never have the answers as to why Ben was murdered. Maybe it was time for me to move on too.

CHAPTER 39

WITH MY POTPOURRI OF POISONS LAST NIGHT I FIGURED Kevin wouldn't expect to see me at the office. I wouldn't want to disappoint him by showing up.

But after an hour of my mind replaying Roland's final grisly image, the utter defeat on Jeff Colhoff's face, and the niggling truth about the high price of revenge, I decided work would numb my brain. I'd file; perfect punishment for a hangover. I'd file, and goddammit if I wouldn't act happy as a fucking clam about it.

I had my coat on, my keys in hand when the phone rang. I hesitated to answer it, but maybe Martinez had gotten away earlier than he'd expected. Ooh. Then I could avoid filing altogether.

"Hello?"

Abita blurted, "I-I'm sorry about the other day."

I slumped against the wall. "Me too."

"Look. I know it's short notice, but is there any chance you could meet us at the park today? It's important."

"When?"

"You tell me."

"Now? It'll take me at least a half an hour to get there."

"That's okay. I'll wait. Same place as last time?"

"Sure."

"Good. See you in a bit."

Something funky was going on.

But hey, like that was any big stunner in my life.

💀 💀 💀

I pushed aside the ugliness of my recent adventures as I racked my feeble brain for clues to Abita's phone call.

The second Jericho saw me he bounded over. "Hey! Didja bring me any more trucks?"

The image of JJ and his trucks flashed in my head, and the utter decimation of his young life. "Afraid not. Does that mean you're not gonna be my pal if I don't buy you stuff?"

He looked torn, then a smile creased his chubby cheeks. "You're funny," he said before he scampered to the sandpit.

I faced Abita. "Why the summons? I figured you'd

take off and I'd never see you again."

"I thought about it. But I wanted to explain. You caught me off guard," Abita said. "I'd hoped to work my way up to talking to you about John."

"Well, the fiancé is out of the bag so to speak; I'm listening."

Abita blushed. "John is a great man."

"I'm sure he is."

"Compared to Ben I'm sure you wouldn't think so." She cocked her head and looked at me. "Then again does *any* man compare to Ben for you?"

Martinez immediately popped into my head. Her testy comments notwithstanding, I pasted on a benign smile. "If this is where you chastise me for putting Ben on a pedestal, I'll leave. I've heard it before."

"I'm sure. From Yvette?"

"And Reese. And Owen. And Leticia." And Kevin and Sheriff Richards and my ex-husband and my father . . . could there be something to this I wasn't seeing?

"Ironic, isn't it, the Standing Elk family has decided to come around now that Jericho and I are returning home."

My belly muscles jerked like a log chain. "When are you going?"

"The next couple days."

"Is your weaving seminar finished?"

"Almost."

Getting information out of her was almost as hard as dragging it out of Martinez.

"I saw Yvette and Owen and Reese for dinner last night. Leticia popped in for coffee and dessert. I-I didn't tell them about John. I probably won't. I'll just leave without saying goodbye."

"Is that why you called me? To say good-bye?"

"Partially. But I wanted to show you something first."

Abita dug a small wooden box out of her purse.

The top had intricate tribal carvings. "What is that?"

"Remember the box I told you about? Ben made it while he was in Arizona. My uncle was teaching him how to carve. He was getting pretty good."

My blood pumped faster, making my head throb and my guts twist into tiny knots as she lifted the lid.

"I was sorting things before I came here and I'd completely forgotten about this." Abita untangled a worn necklace.

My heart alternately soared and sank. I recognized that necklace. I'd given it to Ben the summer I turned thirteen.

I was sucked back in time to the blistering summer day Ben and I had attended the Oglala Lakota Nation Fair and Rodeo in Pine Ridge, one of the largest outdoor powwows in the Midwest.

Scents of dirt, sweat, onions, livestock, and cooking grease hung in the humid air as we wandered from booth to booth, drinking lukewarm Gatorade. Vendors circled the outdoor arena. I checked out the dreamcatchers, crafted from chokecherry branches, sinew, deerskin leather, and finished off with red, black, yellow, and white beads. I lingered at the stalls with colorful Indian art and T-shirt stands touting NATIVE PRIDE. In essence the *wacipi* was part flea market, part spiritual ceremony, part family reunion, part Indian taco feed.

While I'd been pawing through the racks, Ben had haggled over the price of a necklace. The necklace was just a simple woven leather strap with silver accents. In the middle rested a small charm of a lone elk carved out of elk ivory. It was beyond his range and the trader wouldn't lower his price.

After Ben stomped off, I tossed down all my money. Not enough. The guy eyed my Swatch and let me use it and my Black Hills Gold earrings to make up the price difference. I was absolutely giddy.

In his truck heading home, I drummed up the courage to give him the necklace and waited for his reaction; he could blow up from the slightest bruising of his pride just as easily as me, a trait we'd both inherited from our father.

But my gesture had touched him. Ben put on the necklace, letting it fall right next to the other necklace he always wore.

"Julie?" Abita prompted.

I refocused. Managed a slight smile. "Thank you for showing it to me again. I wondered what had happened to it."

She watched Jericho. My gaze followed hers.

He sat at one of the stationary sand diggers, pulling the handles, digging and then swiveling his chair to start a new hole, making machine noises.

The sun shone on his dark hair. With him growing up in the desert I'd expected those glorious sun-washed red highlights. His skin wasn't the same dark hue as Abita's, but a tawny gold. Even if I'd seen him on a hard-packed red clay street in the middle of a barrio I would've known him. His eyes and his smile were all Ben. Humbling to think I'd been worried about the necklace, when Jericho is what Ben had really left behind.

"I didn't bring him here to hurt you."

I wrapped my arms around my updrawn knees. "But you are, Abita. You're hurting me, you're hurting Ben's family, but most of all you're hurting Jericho."

"By giving him a father?"

"No. I'm happy you've found someone you want to spend your life with. But you're doing the same thing to Jericho Ben's mother and my father did to Ben. What happens when Jericho discovers John is not his biological father?"

Abita opened her mouth. Closed it without comment.

"Don't think for a second he won't find out. He'll look in the family photo album and see John didn't enter his life until he was three. Or you'll have another baby, and he'll realize there are no pictures of *him* as a baby with his father. And while it's true you can tell Jericho his real father is dead, he's a curious little boy. He'll want to know more. And if you hide it from him . . ."

Neither of us said anything. A chilly breeze blew off the water; the leaves swirled in a maelstrom. Wintery bluish-gray clouds scuttled in and blocked the sun, reminding me it was the end of October.

Jericho raced over. "I wanna go now."

"In a bit. First let's check the speed of your new tennis shoes. Run to that bridge." Abita pointed. "I'll time you. Ready. Set. Go."

He darted off like a ten point buck during hunting season.

Abita faced me and grabbed my hand. She locked her too-wise eyes to mine, put the necklace in my palm and curled my fingers around it. "I want you to have this. *Ben* would've wanted you to have it."

I couldn't speak. I just stared at her, my expression somewhere between awe and skepticism.

Her delighted laughter trilled around me like music.

"I'm assuming its not often you're rendered speechless, Julie Collins."

I squeezed the necklace until I felt the blood pulsing in my closed fist. Yep. It really was there.

Jericho raced back and said, "How long?"

Without glancing at her watch, she said, "Thirty-seven point two. You can do better. Go again."

He added a war whoop and tore up the distance.

I smiled and admired his exuberance. Little boys.

"—had the other necklace and I knew it was only fair you should have this one."

My head whipped around so fast my neck cracked. "What did you say?"

"That it's only fair you have a necklace too."

"What other necklace?"

"Remember the one Ben wore all the time? He'd taken that one off"—she pointed to my clenched fist—"for some reason, and forgot to put it on before he left for South Dakota."

"But he had the other necklace, the one with all the funky pieces on it, when he left Arizona?"

"Yes. I teased him because I always thought he had an unusual attachment to it."

Jericho zoomed back, putting on a burst of speed the last two yards, panting, "Faster?"

I almost yelled at him for the interruption.

"Yep. Thirty-six point nine. Go again. Go faster. I could probably beat you today, slowpoke."

I didn't bother to watch Jericho's antics. "When did you see Ben's necklace?"

"Umm. This week."

Omigod. I was starting to hyperventilate. My blood pounded. I broke out in a cold sweat. "Where? Who had it?"

A loud cry of pain rent the air. Abita was on her feet racing toward where Jericho rolled on the ground.

I followed as fast as my smoker's lungs allowed.

Tears tracked Jericho's face. Abita soothed him as she brushed dirt and pulverized leaves from his palms.

I had to wait. I had to stand there and fucking *wait*. Logic asserted itself even as I ground my teeth. I'd already waited three and a half years, what was another few minutes?

Those minutes were the longest of my life.

If I didn't calm down I'd have a heart attack. Or an aneurysm.

When Jericho settled down, Abita picked him up and jacked him on her hip. He buried his face in her neck.

Déjà vu. Reminded me of the first time I'd seen them.

"He's tired. I should get him back to the dorm for a nap."

"Abita—"

"I doan wanna nap," he mumbled.

I inhaled. Exhaled.

Was it possible Abita didn't recognize the importance of seeing that necklace?

Or maybe I'd attributed way too much importance to that damn trinket.

No. Ben never would have willingly given it up. It'd meant too much to him. Someone had taken it. Who?

Abita had seen Yvette, Owen, Reese, Leticia, and my father recently. One of them had killed Ben.

Another deep breath and I was ready to use a calm tone, even when my insides quaked 9.9 on the Richter scale. Spots danced in front of my eyes. "Abita. Who did you see wearing the necklace?"

"Didn't I tell you?"

NO! TELL ME RIGHT NOW! my head screamed, but I managed a civilized, "No. You didn't tell me."

But even before she said the name, an awful realization clicked in my brain and I knew.

"Oh. Leticia was wearing it that night we had dinner with her and Yvette. I almost didn't see it. But she bent down to get her purse, and where her shirt gapped, I saw that oddly-shaped bear tooth charm had gotten caught on the lapel. Remember? It was orangish-red and looked like amber? There could only be one of those in the world. Anyway, she had the necklace on, tucked inside her shirt. I guess it didn't match her outfit and she didn't want anyone to see it or something."

Or something. Or that fucking traitorous bitch had taken it from our brother Ben after she'd slit his throat and left him to fucking die.

And now I knew.

I fell to the ground and heaved up my soul.

CHAPTER 40

THE LAST FACE BEN HAD SEEN WAS LETICIA'S. WAS THAT worse for him? Knowing his sister had put an end to his life? Were his last thoughts about the ultimate betrayal?

I was paralyzed. Numb. Filled with hatred and sadness. And horror. Everything in my life, everything I'd known spun out of control. I'd been living for this moment. Now that it was here I couldn't believe I'd ever looked forward to it.

Out of the corner of my eye I saw Abita lean down beside me. "Julie? You okay?"

I think I moved my head. In affirmation or denial? Did it matter?

I threw up again.

Abita retreated.

Dry heaves followed. I squeezed my eyes shut as

my stomach continued to spasm. My heart to constrict. My blood to freeze, then boil. I don't know how long I stayed like that, poised on my hands and knees, facing the chilly, filthy ground. Dizzy, blind, deaf, and dumb.

I wanted to die.

"Julie?"

Go away, go away, go away, go away, go away, go away

"Do I need to call an ambulance?"

Jericho's whimpers brought me out of that dark place quicker than a slap to the face.

I swallowed. Once. Twice. Three times. I managed to push myself upright, but I couldn't open my eyes. God. I didn't want to see Abita and Jericho standing in front of me. I wanted to wake up in my bed in a pool of cold sweat, clutching my star quilt, freaked out and pissed off by another one of those epic nightmares that haunt me.

Not real, not real, not happening, not happening

"Julie, you're scaring me."

I had to find control. "Must've been something I ate." I peeled my eyes open and hoped to hell I didn't look like the drunken zombie Harvey had been the day he'd taken after the man he believed had killed his sister.

He'd gone off the deep end. Would I?

Yes. I already had.

Abita's brow furrowed. "Are you okay to drive? Or

do you need me to take you home?"

"I'll be okay to drive. I just need a minute to catch my breath."

"If you're sure . . ."

"I am. Jericho needs a nap. You go on."

"I'll call you later and check on you."

I couldn't watch her carry him away. Not when I suspected it'd be the last time I'd ever see them.

Wind rushed across the lake. The damp breeze cooled my heated face and brought the scent of stagnant water. Car doors slammed. Logging trucks whooshed down Rimrock Highway, jake-brakes grinding. Children's laughter echoed behind me. An ambulance sped by on Jackson Boulevard. My pants were soggy; my knees cold from the ground. I was there. Yet I wasn't. I'd drifted into a realm of sub-reality.

When I was sure my legs would hold me, I stood. I lifted my face to the sky, hoping for the sun. Cold, wet wind stung my cheeks, but it wasn't as painful as the coldness imbedded deeply in my bones.

I trudged to my truck and hoisted myself up into my seat. I began that staring out the window process I couldn't seem to stop.

Leticia had killed Ben. I repeated it out loud. "Leticia killed Ben."

Never in a million years had I suspected Ben's sister.

Why had I discounted her so quickly? Because *I* couldn't imagine killing him and I'd somehow applied my honor and accountability to *her*?

In murder cases family members are always prime suspects. It didn't make sense Leticia hadn't been on the short list. And I finally had a moment of clarity: there had been no short list; no list at all.

The scant file on Ben's murder hadn't listed a single suspect or motive. That's why I'd been so damn frustrated for so many years. I'd thought the "powers that be" hadn't cared. I'd cried *conspiracy!* because that word garnered attention, especially when jurisdictional and controversial racial issues were involved.

The more I sat in stupefied horror, the more I realized there *had* been a conspiracy. A conspiracy of one.

Leticia had contacts in the BIA, and the Native American Gambling Commission, the FBI, and the tribal police. How had she managed to get Ben's murder case set aside? And then ignored completely?

Easy. By telling the assorted agencies *not* to devote excessive time trying to solve her brother's murder, or they'd be accused of preferential treatment because of Leticia's position within the tribe. With the backlog of other issues, those agencies probably were more than happy to let the case fade away.

Her seemingly selfless action might've even changed

tribal members perception of her. A woman faced with tragedy sets aside her personal issues to work harder on the gaming compact, to create better opportunities for *all* members of the tribe.

Yes. She'd known how to spin it. I could almost hear it: *"Ben's murder was a terrible thing. Our family is devastated. The circle is broken. But we know our* tiblo *is walking with the* Wakan Tanka.*"* Then she'd go on, business as usual, and concentrate on getting the goddamn casino up and running.

I was glad that fucker had blown up. For the first time I wished I would've been the one holding the match.

What did I do now? There wasn't a cop in the county or on the rez who'd arrest her on such circumstantial evidence. She'd just claim Ben had *given* her the necklace before he died and she wore it in remembrance of him. Other members of the Standing Elk family wouldn't contradict her, not when I knew her earnings were the only thing keeping the family ranch afloat.

If by some miracle I actually convinced anyone to listen to me, Leticia had an easy counterargument: she'd point out my obsession with Ben's case. She'd claim I'd do or say anything to find the culprit — which was true — including accusing an innocent family member. No doubt she'd mention I'd been around when the casino blew, the casino she'd spent the last four years of her life trying to build for her people.

Yeah, I'd come off as a vindictive psycho.

Was that what she wanted? I'd bet a million dollars she'd worn Ben's necklace the day we met at Mostly Chocolates. Had she hoped I'd recognize it? Had she been taunting me with it, letting me know I couldn't touch her? Or bring her down?

Wrong.

I had a Browning that would bring her down just fine.

My blood frothed. I dialed her number.

It was the hardest thing I'd ever done, acting normal. I must've pulled it off because Leticia agreed to meet me to hang Ben's prayer bundle.

I drove to the place this had all started, and where it would finally end: Bear Butte.

CHAPTER 41

MATO PAHA LOOKS THE SAME IN THE FALL AS IT DOES IN the summer. The only time the face changes is when it snows. White covers the toffee-colored rocks, erasing the hillsides and the 1400-foot laccolith disappears into the gloomy winter skies like a mirage.

I parked away from the blown-out casino shell. The visitors' center was boarded up. No one here but me and my ghosts.

I secreted my gun in my right pocket, a bottle of water in my left, and my cell phone in the back pocket of my jeans.

A wind blew off the depression where the creek flowed and whistled through the bare branches. I forced myself to walk over to the ledge. The riverbed was bone dry, save for a stream running down the center about a foot wide. The water hadn't frozen yet. Everything looked dead. Forgotten. Forlorn. Strangely enough, I finally felt like I fit this place.

I ducked under scrub oak branches and emerged in the creekbed. It smelled dank, even though the rocks nearly crunched beneath my boots. I wandered upstream, the gurgle of the water solace in the immense shadow of Bear Butte. I didn't know exactly where Ben had died. It'd been spring and the snowmelt made the creek run higher and he'd washed downstream.

A chill snaked through me. My mother would've said a goose had crossed my grave. Could the opposite be true? Could I just have crossed my own grave? Was I destined to die here today? I glanced down at the ugly gray rocks coated with black scum and mint green-colored moss. Dead vegetation. Cigarette butts. Stray food wrappers. All in all, a piss-poor resting place.

I craned my neck and looked up at Bear Butte. Didn't Indian people come here for guidance? I mentally shouted: Give me an answer!

Not a single sound rumbled from the sleeping giant.

I sighed and turned around.

And Leticia Standing Elk stood behind me ten feet away.

I jumped before I caught myself. *Play it cool, play it loose.* "Hey. I didn't hear you."

"My people were scouts for a good reason. We excel in matters of stealth." Her hands were in the pockets of her long wool coat. My stance mirrored hers. Did she have a gun in her pocket too?

"Thanks for coming."

"Thanks for asking me."

Weren't we polite? "You ready to go up?"

"I suppose. My legs are already aching anticipating the climb." Leticia eyed my Timberland boots. "I wouldn't have thought you were much of a hiker."

"I'm not."

"You been up there before?"

"Yeah. Last summer." I paused, let my finger run along the top of the gun barrel. "You?"

Leticia smiled. "We can follow the riverbed until we reach the bridge and use the shortcut to get to the main trail."

She hadn't answered my question.

"You have the prayer bundle?"

I could hedge too. "Think it might snow?"

"Maybe up at the top."

"Looks like the clouds might wreck the view anyway."

She huffed a little. With her extra poundage and my smoker's lungs we were pretty evenly matched.

We didn't talk, just lumbered on.

We'd reached the bridge. We were both panting.

The path diverged, one each side of the wooden bridge, a steep climb through the raggedy bushes. She arced left; I headed right.

Once we exited the underbrush, we cut across the blacktop road to the information center, a shelter made of painted logs that held up sheets of plywood. Plexiglas covered the different maps of the area and pictures of the kinds of vegetation, along with warnings about rattle-snakes in the summer. Reptiles wouldn't be a problem now, with the exception of the snake at my back.

I pulled my water bottle out of my left pocket. I wondered again if she was armed. I wondered if she'd shoot me in the back. Or if she'd sneak up behind me and slit my throat. That sick, helpless, rage-fueled feeling returned. I stared at the tips of my boots until I regained control. I had to let her think I trusted her.

Leticia said, "Are you sure you want to do this?"

I nodded. "How about if I pace us for part of the way, and then we'll switch?"

"Lead on, MacDuff."

Hikers are supposed to sign in with a brief description of their destination and then out when they come back down. In case they get lost or hurt, then the GF&P would know where to look. We bypassed the login station and beat feet for the rocky path.

My increased heart rate owed nothing to the

493

strenuous climb.

The first tree we passed was weighted down with prayer bundles and ties in every color of the rainbow. I kept going. More scrub oak and chokecherry bushes curled over the trail as it straightened. Then the path jogged to the right, the incline increased drastically, and the trees were scarce.

Leticia breathed down my back.

Odd, that Leticia didn't ask why I didn't pick one of the trees closer to the information station. I'd let her think I trusted her. She'd make her move on the backside of Bear Butte. The steepest section without barricades to keep hikers from tumbling down the mountainous drop like Jack and Jill on meth. Or from being pushed over the edge.

Friendly conversation was conspicuously absent.

We rounded the first rock outcropping that overlooked the camping area. From this distance the white stone rings around the firepits stared up at us like blind eyes. Creepy. No tipis either. We really were all alone.

"How about if we switch now?" I panted.

She nodded. Leticia's pace was slower. We'd started the first set of switchbacks. Before I could curse RJ Reynolds, we were making our first descent.

No trees back here to tie the prayer bundle to. She didn't stop; she kept trekking along, even through the precipitous parts, where off to the right, deadfall clogged the ravine. It was unbelievably cold. I shivered again. This would not be a fun place to be after the sun set. I spied the first official stopping point, a large wooden deck.

Leticia turned and smiled through the heavy puffs of air leaving her mouth. "I'm ready to stop for a minute."

"Me too."

"You want to go all the way to the top?"

I didn't answer, pretending to catch my breath.

We heaved ourselves onto the platform. Bench seats were lined around the perimeter.

I walked to the railing and looked over.

We had a perfect view of the destroyed casino. It was a serious blight on the landscape. I'd feel the same way even if it hadn't blown to pieces.

"How much longer are we going to continue this pretense?" Leticia asked.

"As long as it takes for you to tell me why you killed my brother."

She sniffled. "It was an accident."

Fury filled me. How fucking stupid did she think I was? I said, "Bullshit," and whirled around to see her pointing a gun at my head.

"I didn't think you'd buy it, but it was worth a shot." Leticia's reptilian eyes didn't leave mine. "That gun is useless in your pocket, isn't it? Having second thoughts about using it on me?"

"Not anymore."

"Too bad. I believe I'll be taking it." She approached me, putting the barrel of her gun against my temple. "Move and I'll kill you where you stand."

Sweat slithered down my back, creating ice on my spine.

Her hand crept in my jacket pocket and out came my Browning. Then she aimed both guns at me.

"Didn't you ever consider I'd eventually figure it out?"

"You *didn't* figure it out." She smirked. "I have to tell you, it's been amusing watching you chase your tail like a retarded bloodhound these last few years."

"Maybe it did take me a while, but I pretty much nailed why you killed him when you were in my office last week."

"Right. You don't know squat."

"Wrong. See, I was working too hard creating conspiracy theories. Looking for political motivations within the tribe surrounding the casino and gaming issues. But the bottom line is this: You slit his throat because you were jealous of him. Classic Cain and Abel, right? Mommy loved him best no matter how much *you* accomplished."

"Shut up."

"Ooh, I'll bet it burns your ass that you're still not Mommy's favorite. That my half-*white* brother ranks above you even though he's *dead*? What finally set you off, Leticia? Why'd you do it?"

I feared she wouldn't answer me, but the noxious words poured from her mouth.

"Ben returned from Arizona, flush with his new Native spirituality, his sudden adherence and reverence to the 'old ways.' He'd brainwashed my mother into believing his bullshit that he'd changed into something beyond another lazy fucking injun. He told me I was hurting *our* people by bringing in gaming. He said he couldn't stand to be around me and the 'negative energy' I used, and he'd be moving to Arizona permanently.

"My mother blamed me. She said it was my fault he'd gone down there in the first place and my fault he was staying away. She told me she wished *I* was the one leaving, not Ben.

"That mealy-mouthed motherfucker was so self-absorbed he didn't care about the problems he'd caused. I asked him for forgiveness. I asked him to meet me here at this Lakota holy place, to meditate, so I could get on the right path." Leticia snorted. "Pompous asshole couldn't wait to prove how much better he was than me. As he lit the sage and closed his eyes to commune with the Great Spirit, pretending he was something more than a miserable fucking *half-breed*, I snuck up behind him and gave *Mato Paha* the ultimate sacrifice: blood of the profane."

I didn't realize I was crying until an icy wind froze my

tears to my cheeks. "You're a sick, self-serving bitch."

She thumbed the safety on my gun; her gun was ready to fire. "And yet, I still got the jump on you. You been slacking on your training, Miss PI." She'd kept her hostile gaze locked on mine the entire time. "Where's your cell phone?"

"In my truck."

"You lie. Try again."

When she asked me to take it out I'd rush her. "It's in the back right pocket of my jeans."

"Turn around."

I did. Slowly the right side of my coat was swept back with the barrel of the gun, while once again the other barrel made an intimate acquaintance with the side of my face.

Leticia said, "Take it out with your right hand and keep your left arm straight out."

Shit. I dug the phone out of my jeans.

"Hold it out and drop it."

I did.

Leticia kicked it hard and it slid across the deck like a silver hockey puck, then dropped into oblivion.

"Turn around and walk backward to the bench."

I shuffled until the crease of my knees met solid wood.

Leticia put her gun in her pocket and aimed the Browning at me. "Be ironic, wouldn't it, if I shot you with your own gun? I could probably even make it look like suicide."

"You're going to shoot me? A little hint from Detecting 101: Bullets are a dead giveaway that foul play was involved."

She laughed again. "Oh, I'm not going to shoot you. You're going to jump."

CHAPTER 42

I STARED AT HER. LOOKED OVER THE LEDGE. THEN I laughed. Mine sounded slightly more hysterical than hers had.

"Fuck you, Leticia. I'm not gonna jump."

"You're going to do whatever I tell you to do. Stand up on the bench."

"No."

I could sense she was getting agitated. Good. Agitated people made mistakes and the second I glimpsed the tiniest opening I'd take it.

"Last chance."

"No. You'll have to shoot me."

"Fine. Have it your way." She fired.

The first bullet grazed the outside of my coat, blowing a hole in the sleeve. She corrected her aim and I felt a hot sting as the second shot lodged between my shoulder and collarbone.

I screamed. Surprise and the bullet's momentum knocked me back, and then the immediate throbbing pain leveled me to the ground.

Oh shit oh shit oh shit it hurt.

A hand grabbed my hair and she cranked my head back. I looked at Leticia's placid face set against the backdrop of the swirling storm clouds in the darkening sky.

"Get up."

I whimpered. My shoulder was on fire; the pain receptors in my brain were going haywire.

"I said, *get up*." She jerked me to my feet by my ponytail with enough force that sections of my hair were ripped from my scalp. I swayed; my fingers automatically tried to touch the spot where I'd been shot. Leticia batted my hand away. "Stand still or I will shoot you again."

My heart was beating so hard I expected it to explode. I gritted my teeth against the searing agony and the stickiness I could feel spreading under my shirt.

"Change in plans. Which means I have to rough you up a bit."

The grip of the gun connected with my jaw. She followed through with a crack to the other side of my face between my ear and temple.

I shrieked. At least I think I did. I couldn't hear anything out of my left ear. The pain was so unbelievably intense I sank to the deck, momentarily forgetting about the bullet wound until my arm and shoulder met unforgiving wood.

Another scream burst from my throat even as I curled up in a protective ball and blinked the blood out of my eye.

She laughed. And kicked me in the ass.

All the breath left my body. I prepared for the next blow, forearms blocking my face, familiar with the drill. I'd been in this position plenty of times with my father. If I laid there motionless for long enough, not fighting, not crying, not responding, he'd go away.

Would she go away?

Not until I was dead.

The taste of blood filled my mouth. I couldn't swallow. I couldn't spit. I opened my lips and let the saliva and blood run out onto the wooden slats before I choked on it.

With my eyes squeezed shut, I was that helpless fifteen-year-old girl. Waiting for the next punch to land.

Stand up. Don't let her win.

I stopped breathing entirely. *Ben?*

No answer.

Fuck. Now I had hallucinations in addition to the

excruciating bag of pain my body had become.

Stand up. Get away. Live to fight another day.

That *was* Ben's voice. He'd preached to me that I couldn't win the fights with my dad; I just had to survive them. Did hearing Ben's voice mean I was close to dying?

No.

Ben?

Get away.

I heard Leticia's footsteps circle around behind me. Would she kick me again? I tightened up my stomach muscles and flexed the fingers on my right hand.

Leticia bent close enough I felt her sour breath on my cheek. "You should've jumped when you had the chance."

Out of the corner of my eye I saw the edge of her long coat. I grabbed it, jerking with every ounce of strength I had. She wobbled. I swung my legs around and knocked her feet out from underneath her. She landed flat on her back. My action caught her by surprise.

But not as much as the fist I plowed into her ugly face.

Blood spurted; she shrieked and let go of my gun. I rolled to my right side and wobbled to my feet.

Whoa. Head rush. Speckles of light and dark spots wavered in front of my eyes.

She grunted and scrambled for my gun. I reached it a split second before she did.

Leticia's gun was in her right hand. I didn't stick

around to see if her aim was still good. I dove for the stairs and caught my ribs on the bottom tread. I didn't manage to keep my left shoulder from striking the ground, but I bit my tongue hard to stop the scream from escaping.

Get away.

Thoughts of vengeance vanished. My adrenal system kicked into overdrive as survival became paramount. Leticia would kill me. Guaranteed. I struggled to my feet and hit the ground running.

Two gunshots echoed somewhere to my left. Shit. My red coat was a bull's-eye. I couldn't move my left arm to hold onto the sleeve while I removed my right arm. I jammed the Browning in my back jeans pocket and shrugged my shoulders up and down as I ran like a drunken sailor.

I clamped my teeth together and crossed my right arm over the center of my body. Jesus fucking Christ that hurt. My frigid fingers caught the sleeve and somehow gripped the cuff as I jerked. In one quick painful movement my arms were free. I rolled the coat up in a ball and chucked it into the ravine.

I kept running.

Blood dripped in my eye. I stumbled on the flat rocks and almost took a header over the edge of the embankment. A cool mist pressed down. Not fog, just a gauzy veil that made this surreal situation even more so.

Footsteps pounded behind me. Or was that the thudding of my own heart? Didn't matter. I didn't have the luxury of stopping to see if Leticia was close.

I stumbled through the rock cut where the path angled upward, sending me over the hump between the two sides of the butte, which separated the back from the front.

Every footstep jarred my shoulder, a hot poker jabbing my flesh. My scalp stung. My jaw throbbed. I swiped blood from my eyebrow before it dripped into my eye.

The descent would take less than half the time than the ascent. The path smoothed to hard-packed dirt. I rounded an enormous pine tree dripping with prayer ties. Below the exposed root structure was another narrow, steep path, which disappeared between two big white boulders. Probably led directly to the private Indian campground area with the firepits and the tipi skeletons.

Or maybe it didn't.

Did I chance it? Head into the unknown? Find a safe hiding spot until nightfall?

No. Stay the path.

I shivered. Why was Ben in my head now? Was it my subconscious' last-ditch effort to retain my mental acuity by grasping onto the one thing guaranteed to get my attention: my dead brother?

Leticia knew the layout of Bear Butte much better than I did. Which meant even if I turned around, gun drawn, and faced her down like an Old West gunslinger, she still had the upper hand.

But if I made it to the bottom first, I had a chance.

That thought spurred me on and I increased my pace, only to trip in a sinkhole and go flying ass over teakettle past sagebrush bushes.

My injured shoulder slammed into a rock. Another sickening rush of wetness coated my skin beneath my shirt, while I got a face full of yucca. Two razor sharp spikes pierced my neck; another one grazed my cheek below my eye. I hit with such force the gun jiggled in my back pocket.

I wanted to lie there, catch my breath and formulate a plan. Pretend I was a chameleon and Leticia would zoom past me as I became one with the landscape. My eyes started to drift shut.

Stand up. Get away.

Shut up, Ben.

His laugh inside my head vibrated down my spine and brought a fresh rush of tears.

Why are you here now?

Because you need me now.

But I've needed you for years.

No. You've always been strong enough on your own.

Don't let her win again, tanksi. *Stand up. Quickly*

I didn't argue with the phantom voice. I slid on my butt until my feet were on a fairly flat spot, rolled on my right side and crouched. I scrambled up the embankment like a three-legged dog and was stumbling on the trail, running for my life.

My lungs burned. My legs were half-cooked noodles. My face had gone numb. I wished my arm would. Sweat soaked my back, my head, my chest. Hell, even my earlobes were sweating from pure fear. Blood dripped down the side of my body. I wasn't cold without my coat, but once I stopped I knew I'd be frozen to the bone.

If I lived that long.

The low level of light signaled dusk's fast approach. I identified the roof of the visitors' center through the skeletal trees. Nearly at the bottom. Tears of pain, frustration, and relief clouded my vision.

I added a burst of speed, vaulting over the last jog in the path. I couldn't afford to take the long way and follow the road. Leticia would assume I'd travel the road. A shudder broke free and I knew she and I weren't finished. I removed my gun from my back pocket.

As quietly as possible I cut through the underbrush by the bridge. Part of me wanted to wait until full dark to creep along the bank. Part of me wanted to play troll and hide under the bridge forever.

I hunkered down, dodging a low-hanging elm branch, which snapped back and smacked my shoulder. A cry of pain escaped, extraordinarily loud in the ghostly stillness.

Lavender light deepened into prunish-black as darkness fell. I humped along the left side of the bank, scanning the trees for sign of Leticia. Numbness settled in my shoulder. The fingers gripping the gun were so cold I didn't know if I was physically capable of pulling the trigger any more.

Chills racked my body as I began to measure the distance in inches. Nothing seemed familiar. Would I even recognize the break in the treeline that led to where I'd parked my truck?

Resting my gun on my thigh, I stopped to take a breath. When I straightened up Leticia stood downstream about 20 yards.

How the fuck had she gotten here so fast?

Leticia adjusted her stance and I saw it: Ben's necklace. Wrapped around her wrist. The bones practically glowed in the near darkness.

The necklace wasn't a good luck talisman; it was a harbinger of death. The old man's. Ben's.

And now, Leticia's.

I raised my gun and fired. The shot went wide and skimmed the side of her head. The kickback nearly threw me on my ass I was so weak.

She stumbled, then righted herself. "This is better than I'd planned. Now I have a bullet wound to prove self-defense when they find you shot to death. It'll be a sad thing. Poor Julie Collins finally tipped over the edge of insanity over her sainted brother Ben."

I willed my wavering hand to steady; it flopped to my side like a dead trout.

"I wish I could scalp that blond hair."

Jesus. *Shut up and fucking fall down already.* She kept coming at me with a sneer on her face like some goddamn B-grade horror movie zombie.

I thought, *why isn't she firing at me?* and then she did. *Pop.* The bullet tore into my thigh. My knees buckled. What little blood remaining in my head drained, making me dizzy. I wanted to stay down. I had no fight left in me.

Don't let her win.

Leticia picked up her pace. "There'll be no prayer bundles or ties for you. No—"

I gritted my teeth and straight-armed my gun, aiming for the black hole where her heart should have been and squeezed off two shots.

She landed flat on her back amidst the dust and mud of the rocky creekbed.

Resting on my knees in a puddle of water, I wheezed like a kicked dog, bled like a stuck pig, and whimpered like a trapped wolf from the injuries riddling my body.

Before I gave into the pain I had to make sure she was down for good. I swayed to my feet and had taken two shuffling steps when Leticia sat up.

On automatic, I emptied the rest of the clip into her neck.

The buzzing in my ears from the gunfire overpowered the silence.

Leticia would never get up and come at me again.

I spit blood. I'd faced her with a ruthlessness only surpassed by what I'd witnessed in her eyes.

I waited.

For what?

An easing of my sorrow?

An awareness of justice?

A sense of absolution?

For *Mato Paha* to forgive me or punish me further for spilling blood on sacred ground?

Nothing changed.

There'd be no vindication for me. No moment of clarity. Leticia Standing Elk was dead by my hand. I'd avenged my brother's murder. I should be whooping a war dance around her dead body. I should watch to see if her soul was as black in death as it'd been in life.

I did none of that.

Instead I bent over her body and snatched Ben's

necklace. It seemed fitting to have the necklace in my hand when I died.

Crying in relief, I stumbled backward until I fell down.

CHAPTER 43

Tanksi.

Go away. I'm tired.

Listen to me.

You're not real.

I'm here, aren't I?

*No. You're an illusion. I'm cold. And I hurt. I'm dying.
Or am I already dead? Is that why I can hear you, Ben?*

You can hear me because you never forgot me.

I never will.

So don't give up on me now.

Too late. I'm so tired. Will it hurt when I die?

You are not dying, Julie.

I want to die.

No, you need to live.

Why?

You have more to give.

I'm tired of giving. It hurts too much.

It will stop soon. The time has come for you to fill the void I left in your life.

I don't want to fill it. It reminds me of you.

Instead of letting it hurt you, use it to heal yourself. Use it to tell her about me. Let her fill it.

Who?

Mitanksi. *Your* tanka.

My tanka? *Brittney?*

Be to her what I was to you. She needs you.

But I need you.

No, you need to let me go.

Silence.

Ben? Are you there?

I'm going now.

NO!

Be at peace, tanksi, *my little sister, be at peace.*

I let the darkness and pain overtake me completely and let go.

CHAPTER 44

THE CALLER ID ON KEVIN'S CELL PHONE READ: *PRIVATE number.* He'd been avoiding phone calls all day, but answered it anyway. "Yeah?"

Martinez said: "About time you answered the goddamn phone. Have you seen Julie?"

"No, why?"

"Because she's missing."

"You're sure?"

"I wouldn't be calling you if I wasn't sure."

That explained the restless feeling Kevin hadn't been able to shake all day. He looked at his watch. 6:00. "What makes you think she hasn't gone off to shoot her bow? Or to get drunk?"

"Because this just feels . . . wrong."

"Gotta give me something more, Martinez."

"Fine. I came to her house around 5:00 because I'd been trying to get a hold of her for four goddamn hours. We were supposed to go out of town this afternoon. While I was here, Abita called to check on her. Evidently they'd met at Canyon Lake Park and Julie had gotten sick. Abita tried her on her cell phone and got no answer. Then she called the house phone to make sure she'd gotten home okay, only I know Julie hasn't been home all fucking day."

Heavy silence.

"What? Spit it out, Wells."

"Did you have a fight?"

"No, we didn't have a fucking fight. What does that have to do with anything?"

"Don't deny you two haven't been having problems."

"How the fuck do you know that?"

Kevin counted to ten. "A) Julie is my partner. B) I've known her a lot longer than you have, Martinez. I know when she's upset, I know when she's hurting, and she's been messed up by whatever shit is going on between the two of you."

"Damn." Deep breathing, followed by a sigh. "Things were fine this morning when I left."

"Did you call Kim?"

"Yes. And Jimmer. Neither one have heard from her. I even called out to her dad's place and talked to her

515

little sister. Nada."

Christ. If Martinez had been calling all over the county, including the Collins ranch, he really was losing it.

But the other scenario Kevin came up with was one sure to piss off El Presidente, big time. "Does anyone in your organization have a reason for wanting to hurt her or make her disappear?"

No answer.

But when Martinez spoke, his words dripped ice. "Has Julie been talking to you about Hombres business?"

"No, Jimmer has. He didn't go into the details; he's concerned about Julie being used as a pawn or caught in the crossfire of Hombres politics. As am I."

Another moment of silence.

"Martinez? You still there?"

"Yeah."

"Is that a possibility?"

"Maybe. I'll have my guys check into it."

"In the meantime, I'll have the cell phone company put a trace on her phone. Then I'm calling Sheriff Richards."

"Why do we need to bring in the cops?"

"Because that's the way I do things. You can sit on your ass and protect your fucking secrets and your organization, Martinez, but I guarantee if Julie is anywhere in Bear Butte County, the sheriff will find her."

Martinez sighed. "All right."

Kevin said, "One other thing. If anything's happened to her, and I find out any of your guys were involved? I won't call the cops. I'll fucking kill them all."

Martinez laughed softly. "You'll have to beat me to it."

The dial tone buzzed in his ear. Kevin tamped down his panic and started making calls.

💀 💀 💀

Jimmer sat silently in the passenger seat, staring out the window into the darkness. It was scarier than shit, seeing his stealth military training kick in. Wearing monochrome night camo, he blended into the shifting shadows. If Kevin turned his head just right, Jimmer wasn't there.

The sheriff had gone on instant alert after Kevin had explained the situation. He'd promised to send out a deputy to Julie's usual haunts: Dusty's, and The Road-kill Café, and out in the county proper to see if she was having car trouble on some off road somewhere with no cell service.

Kevin's eyes kept straying to his cell phone, willing it to ring.

Two Cadillac Escalades, one silver, one black, were

parked in Julie's driveway. No sign of her truck. Kevin and Jimmer tromped inside.

Martinez paced in the living room, phone glued to his ear. The bodyguard, Big Mike, was perched on the sofa arm, training a Sig on them, which he dropped beside his thigh after Jimmer scowled at him.

"Anything?" Martinez said.

"Not yet."

Jimmer and Big Mike talked guns. Too agitated to sit, Kevin leaned against the wall. Another bodyguard poked his head around from the doorway to the kitchen.

Martinez clicked his phone shut, mirroring Kevin's position on the opposite wall. "All my guys check out. None of them have been anywhere near Julie today."

"What exactly did Abita say?"

"She met Julie in the park. They talked about Jericho. Then Abita gave her some kind of necklace that'd belonged to Ben and Julie started throwing up." He shrugged. "Mean anything to you?"

"Was she sick this morning when you left?"

"Slightly hungover, but besides that, no."

"Any other messages on her machine?"

"Just the half dozen or so from me."

The tension in the room heated the air to an unbreathable level.

Kevin's cell phone rang. "Wells. No, that's fine. You're

sure? Okay. No. Keep the trace on. Call this number if anything changes. Yeah. Thanks."

"What?"

"They traced Julie's cell phone to Bear Butte."

"What the fuck would she be doin' up there? She hates that fuckin' place," Jimmer said.

Kevin looked at Martinez. "Gotta have something to do with Ben."

"Let's go." Martinez slipped on his leather jacket.

Big Mike stretched tall and shrugged into his coat.

Jimmer shook his head. "No. You ain't comin'. This ain't Hombres business. If you think Tony's in danger then you'd better stop him from comin' with us."

Big Mike waited for Martinez to respond.

"Jimmer's right. Stay here."

He sat like a trained dog.

Kevin pocketed his phone. "I'll drive. We'll update the sheriff on the way there."

🏍 🏍 🏍

The silent trip to Bear Butte seemed to take an hour. The moon was a silver scythe, offering little illumination. As they rounded the last curve before the visitor's center, the Jeep's headlights swept the back end of a black pickup, parked at a picnic area.

Martinez was out of the Jeep before it'd come to a full stop. Jimmer pursued him, disappearing into the night like smoke. Kevin parked behind the Ford and climbed out.

A patrol car putted into view, the searchlight methodically sweeping the roadside. Sheriff Richards rolled down the window. His gaze zoomed to the pickup. "Any sign of her?"

"No. Maybe you should start at the top and work your way down and we'll start down here and work our way up."

He nodded and kept the snail's pace up the narrow road.

At the treeline Kevin saw two shapes crouching by a gnarled scrub oak.

Jimmer said, "Follow the creekbed up to the bridge. Keep an eye along the banks. Split up."

No question Jimmer had taken charge. Kevin didn't argue. Neither did Martinez.

Kevin pushed through the foliage until he balanced on the lip of the dry creekbed. Between the lack of flashlights and moonlight, it was pitch black, leaving the river stones a ghostly shade of gray.

The water seemed unusually loud. The area felt closed in. Tight. Angry. Frigid. Unwelcoming. Like their presence destroyed the sanctity of the holy place.

Up ahead Jimmer said, "Fuck."

Kevin ran until he saw Jimmer and Martinez standing side by side over a body.

First thing he noticed was the long hair rippling in the creek waters. The lips were peeled back from the teeth in a snarl. Eyes were wide open and dulled. The body was riddled with bullets.

Leticia Standing Elk.

What the hell was she doing here? Had she and Julie confronted Ben's killer together? If so, where was Julie?

Frustrated, he looked at Martinez. Martinez looked back at him. Kevin turned to Jimmer, but Jimmer was already running to another body sprawled in the rocks about 50 feet away.

"Ah, Jesus Christ, *no*."

Kevin didn't know if that'd come from him or Martinez; he only knew he'd never been more afraid in his life.

He sprinted, yet felt as if he were running in molasses.

Martinez reached the body first.

It was Julie. No coat, clothes covered in blood. Her face cut up. Dried blood on her cheek, her temple, her chin. Chunks of vegetation tangled in her hair. Her eyes were closed, her gun on the rocks next to where she'd fallen. A necklace dangled from her fingertips. No sign of her cell phone.

Jimmer's hand was on her throat. "She's alive. In shock and probably suffering from hypothermia, but alive."

Kevin dropped to his knees and automatically reached for her hand, a hand usually so strong looking that was now lifeless and milky white against the stark ground.

"Don't touch her," Jimmer warned. "She's got a bullet in that shoulder. One in the upper leg too. Take off your coats, let's get her warmed up." He whipped off his flack jacket, gently tucking it around her seemingly lifeless body. She didn't stir. He touched her cheek. "Julie? Can you hear me?"

No answer. No movement. Kevin couldn't tell if she was breathing. He leaned closer.

Martinez did too. "Come on, blondie. Talk to me."

"Like that's gonna help," Kevin replied sharply.

"Back off, right fuckin' now, both of you, or I'll shoot you where you fuckin' stand," Jimmer snapped. "She's not a goddamn bone. Do something to help her. Flag down the sheriff. Jesus Christ, someone call a fuckin' ambulance before she dies."

Martinez slanted over Julie's body while Kevin called the sheriff.

Jimmer tested her pulse again. "Julie? Can you hear me? Darlin', if you can, squeeze my hand."

No response.

"Her breathing is too shallow," Martinez said.

Kevin couldn't see her chest rising and falling at all beneath the coats.

"Come on, little missy. Stay with us. Prove that tough girl act ain't an act."

A cough, then Julie croaked, "Ben?"

"No. Jules. It's Jimmer. Don't talk."

"Ben, don't go."

Silence.

"It's okay. We're here now."

Awareness seemed to settle on her. "Ben isn't really here. He's dead."

Jimmer answered, "Yeah."

Pause.

"She killed him." Julie attempted to move and gasped, "Hurts."

"I know. Stay still."

"I shot her. I—"

"Ssh. Don't move."

"I hurt." She whispered, "Everything hurts."

"We got an ambulance comin'. Stay with us, little missy."

"I'm tired."

"I imagine."

"Wanna let go. Just let me go."

"No, goddammit, I will not let you go," Martinez said, his face hovering inches above hers.

"For Chrissake," Jimmer hissed, "Give her some fuckin' space, Martinez—"

523

"The fuck I will." He dragged the back of his knuckles down her cold cheek, back and forth. "Come on, blondie. Stay with me."

"Tony?"

"I'm here."

"Don't leave."

"Not ever again."

Julie calmed when Martinez continually smoothed her hair from her bloodied face, and murmured in Spanish.

Kevin remembered the last time he'd felt this helpless, when he'd watched Lilly die.

The sound of sirens grew louder.

Despite the fear gnawing his innards, Kevin pushed to his feet. "I'll direct them this way."

The crew had Julie loaded on a stretcher, covered up and in the back of the ambulance within minutes.

Martinez clambered in beside her and Kevin swallowed his fear, watching the blue and red lights swirl until darkness engulfed him again.

It was like a punch to the gut, the realization that Martinez *was* the perfect fit for Julie. He was strong enough to be the type of man Julie needed, and he wouldn't balk at the demons that dogged her, because it appeared Martinez had plenty of his own. Maybe Julie would let Tony be the one to finally help her heal now that her crusade to find Ben's killer was over.

Instead of feeling resentment, Kevin felt a heavy weight slip off his shoulders. Julie could move on. It was time for him to move on too.

CHAPTER 45

EVERYTHING BEHIND MY LIDS WAS DREAMY. FLOATY.
Ethereal.

Weird damn dreams. Weirder than usual.

My body went rigid. Were they dreams?

What if they weren't?

What if I was dead?

Did I dare peek and see if I'd ended up in heaven or
hell? I slowly opened my eyes. No fiery red pits. The
light was dim, and soothing, not divinely bright. Soft
music played in the background. I blinked away the grit
coating my eyes. Looked to the left. And saw him.

Definitely heaven.

Martinez' rough fingertips caressed my jawline. "Hey."

My lips parted but no sound came out.

"Don't talk. I'm glad you're awake." He briefly

squeezed his eyes shut and pressed his mouth to the back of my hand. "Jesus, Julie," he whispered hoarsely, "I'm glad you're alive."

I looked around. Industrial wallpaper. A rolling tray table with a Styrofoam pitcher. The constant hum and beep of machinery. Antiseptic scents. A hospital. Again.

It all came rushing back to me. The climb up Bear Butte. My terror-filled trip down with a bullet lodged in my shoulder. Bleeding. Beat up. Scared. Hiding from Leticia along the creek as I tried to make it back to my truck. The simple understanding that it boiled down to her or me.

And I'd chosen me.

I'd watched as she died with an ugly sneer on her face that matched her black soul.

From that point on things had gotten blurry. I'd been in a dream-like state talking to Ben. Then nothing but coldness and pain. Faint voices. Everything hurt. Yet, I felt hollow. I felt the finality of what I'd done. How had I ever thought killing would be easy?

I looked at Martinez.

As he looked back at me, *into* me, he knew exactly what I'd done, what I was feeling, and he was still here.

I started to cry.

He let me, crowded into my narrow bed and held me. When my tears ran dry, he whispered, "We'll get through this. I swear, we will get through this."

Exhaustion set in and I drifted off again.

💀 💀 💀

Someone digging in my collarbone with a razor blade woke me from the blessed nothingness of slumber. I jerked away. "Do you fucking mind? I'm trying to sleep."

"And I'm trying to check your wound for an infection."

I forced my eyes open. "Who are you?"

"Dr. Blair. I did your surgery two days ago."

"You're just getting around to checking on me now?"

"I've checked on you twice. You were out both times and I'm beginning to think that's the best way to deal with you. Looks good. How's your mobility?"

"Slow."

"Then I'll increase your physical therapy time."

Great.

He dropped the side railing and lifted the blanket covering my lower half. "Let me look at your thigh."

"You have to buy me dinner first, doc."

"Oh ho. I haven't heard *that* one before." Dr. Blair slid my stunningly attractive faded blue cotton nightgown up my leg. More poking and prodding. It reminded me my ribs hurt. He muttered to himself as he rearranged the covers. "How do you feel?"

"Fuzzy. Everything is pretty good when I'm sleeping. When I wake up . . ." I glanced at the foot of the bed, away from his earnest assessment.

"Let's focus on your physical injuries first." Gloved fingers brushed my hair from my forehead. "Another nasty little gash I stitched up here. Now it matches the one on the other side."

"I'd hate to be off balance."

Dr. Blair chuckled. "Firecracker, aren't you?"

Then he did the oddest thing: He perched on the side of my bed, his gaze scalpel sharp. "Here's the deal. I'll discharge you tomorrow if you promise to keep up with physical therapy on a daily basis."

"Okay."

"*And* if you promise to talk to a mental health professional about the trauma you're suffering from." He stopped my protest. "The external physical injuries will heal. You need to make sure you're healing the psychological ones also."

"I'll think about it," I lied.

"Excellent. You can go home tomorrow. Do you have someone who can stay with you a few days?"

I opened my mouth to tell him I didn't need a damn nanny, only to hear, "I'll be staying with her, Dr . . . Sugar, what did you say your name was?" Kim winked at me. "Since I'll be doin' her daily physical therapy, maybe we oughta go over the instructions again, just so I don't get confused," she cooed as she drew him out of the room.

I didn't want to look Kim in eye after what I'd done. I didn't want to see or talk to anyone. I faced the wall and feigned sleep.

        💀   💀   💀

"Collins. Wake up."

Déjà vu.

Couldn't ignore Sheriff Richards' summons.

I scowled at him. "What?"

He rubbed the brim if his hat, balanced on his knee. "I need to talk to you."

I noticed he hadn't brought me flowers. "You're here in official capacity, then?"

"Yes, I am."

An awkward moment ensued as my heart rate monitor spiked and beeped loudly

"First, I'm here to tell you you've officially been cleared in the shooting death of Leticia Standing Elk."

Where was the relief I should've felt?

"It's on the record as justifiable homicide by self-defense. No charges will be filed against you. The case is closed."

No sense of relief yet.

"Second, because of the inability to question the deceased Ms. Standing Elk over the allegations of her involvement in the homicide of Ben Standing Elk, that case will officially remain open for the time being."

Bitter tears stung the back of my eyes.

Sheriff Richards leaned forward. "Off record? I wish I could stamp 'case closed' and file it away once and for all. I'm damn proud of you, Julie, for sticking with it, if only for your own sense of justice for Ben."

"Doesn't feel as good as I thought it would, Sheriff."

He studied me, sadness and understanding filled his eyes. "It never does."

My shoulder started to throb and I knew it was close to time for more pain meds. "What else?"

"The missing persons case involving Maria Dove."

With all that'd happened, I'd forgotten about that and Sharon Dove's confession about killing Roland Hawk. Had the guilt eaten at Sharon, forcing her to confess? "What about it?"

"Jeannie Colhoff admitted she killed Maria. I don't know if it will matter." His sigh went beyond exasperated. "Jeannie's gotten herself an attorney. He's filed for a mental evaluation because she's claiming temporary insanity due to rampaging pregnancy hormones at the time of the murder."

"This is a goddamn joke, right?"

Sheriff Richards frowned at my language. "No. Since Jeannie hasn't had so much as a parking ticket in the last five years . . ."

He didn't have to spell it out for me. "Then how the hell does she explain killing June Everett? She isn't pregnant now, is she?"

"No. She's denying she had anything to do with June's death. Frankly, we've got no evidence to tie her to it, besides Jeff Colhoff's statement about finding June's cell phone in Jeannie's belongings."

"Isn't that enough?"

"You'd think so. But Jeff has filed for divorce, for sole custody of the kids, and it's his word against hers. Jeannie's attorney is claiming the only reason Jeff Colhoff wants June Everett's death listed as a homicide instead of a suicide is because her life insurance policy pays double for accidental death. He's listed as sole beneficiary."

"You gotta be fucking kidding me."

"Nope."

"Who's her attorney?"

He scowled. "Charles LaChance."

It figured.

"I'd rather have her convicted of a murder she confessed to than take a chance on losing it all."

We chewed on that for a minute.

"Last thing. Roland Hawk was found dead outside

his place on the rez a couple of days ago. The BIA and FBI contacted me because of the loose connections to the Dove case and the Standing Elk cases." He studied me intently. "Hawk's throat was slit, just like Ben's. You think Leticia might've had something to do with it?"

"I don't know. Why?"

"They're leaning that direction, just to get the case closed. No one's too broken up about Roland Hawk being dead anyway."

I didn't feel guilty no one cared about his demise.

"That's it. Don't forget to send the county a bill for your investigative services. I appreciate everything you did."

I said, "You're welcome," even when I knew I'd never send the bill.

Sheriff Richards stood and jammed his hat on his head. "Don't take this the wrong way, Collins, but maybe you'd better rethink staying in the PI biz. This is the fourth time you've been in the hospital in the last seven months. It's not normal, it's not healthy, and your luck is gonna run out one of these days."

"I know."

"But if you ever wanna come back to work for me, all's you hafta do is ask." He grinned. "It'll have to wait a couple of weeks, though. I'm taking your advice. Bernice and I are bound for Hawaii. Aloha."

I almost asked him to send me a postcard, but the nurse came in with my pain meds and when I looked up, he was gone.

💀 💀 💀

A few hours later the chair next to my bed chirked.

I stayed still, silently willing the interloper to leave.

"You ain't sleepin'."

Jimmer. I slowly turned my head.

His paws were wrapped around the metal side rail. "You look better than you did. Almost lost ya there, little missy."

"Seems to be the consensus." In the farthest corner of my mind, I remembered his voice. Cool. Determined. A lifeline to my future, not a hallucination from the past.

I dropped my gaze to the NRA logo on his T-shirt. He knew. He'd seen it.

His voice was oddly gruff. "You done what you had to, Jules. No shame in that."

Don't cry. For Chrissake don't cry in front of Jimmer.

He cleared his throat. "So they're cuttin' you loose tomorrow?"

"I guess."

"Between Wells, Martinez, and the one-eyed wonder, you'll have plenty of people to snarl at for takin' care of you."

I nodded.

"Good." Jimmer paused and I watched him struggle. "I'm sure you're gonna wanna trade that gun off after you get it back from the sheriff. There's a couple of real sweet ones at the shop for you to try when you're ready. I can make you a helluva deal."

I set my hand over his and squeezed. "Thanks."

"No problem." He towered over me, a gentle giant. "Oh, I brought this." He unrolled a *Bowhunter* magazine from his rear pocket. "You'll need something for wastin' time after you escape from this sawbones motel."

"Why couldn't I have fallen for you? You do have an incredibly sweet side, Jimmer."

A horrified expression creased his face. "Jesus Christ, don't say that. And for fuck's sake, don't tell no one."

"I won't."

Relief made him grin. "Not fallin' for my special charms is your loss, little missy. I'm twice the man he is." Cocky male smirk. "Literally."

Yikes.

After he left I called the nurse and told her no more visitors. Period. Then I downed my pain medication and returned to my safe haven: sleep.

CHAPTER 46

KEVIN BROUGHT ME HOME AND HANDED ME OFF TO Martinez while Kim clucked around, a mother hen in training.

I explicitly told them all to leave me the hell alone and slammed the door to my bedroom.

Except no one listened. Appeared they'd all decided to move in instead.

Didn't matter. I didn't see anyone unless they barged into my room because I couldn't get out of bed.

I couldn't do anything but cry.

I cried until I fell asleep from sheer exhaustion. I cried until I ran out of tears. I cried until it felt like my tear ducts were bleeding. My body just made more. As my tears fell, I wondered what had happened to the tough girl who sucked it up. The chick who kicked ass and led with her fists and her chin. I cried for the loss of her too.

Martinez wasn't cowed by my behavior. Every night he wrapped himself around me and attempted to chase my demons away.

Kim, that cheerful little torturer, forced me to do the physical therapy exercises every morning. When she suggested I'd feel better if I talked it out, no holds barred, I crawled back in bed, tunneled under the covers and ignored her.

My waking world was full of gruesome images. Every time I closed my eyes I saw her. Leticia. Saw me pulling the trigger. Saw her bloody face. Saw me killing her. Over and over.

I wanted to forget. To hide. I went back to sleep.

Days passed. A week. Two weeks. Nothing changed, inwardly or outwardly. I felt the impatience of those who'd taken on the burden of caring for me. I heard their whispers, questions on how long I'd be like this, wallowing, miserable. Lost.

Maybe forever.

Another epic daymare woke me. My room was dark even when the alarm clock read 2:00 in the afternoon. I scrambled back and smacked my head into the headboard. "Fuck!"

The door flew open, the lights came on. Kevin

looked at me and scowled as Martinez shouldered his way past him.

"I'm fine," I said to no one in particular.

"No, you're not fine," Kevin said.

"Enough," Martinez said. "She's been babied enough by all of us."

"Babied? After what she's been through?"

"I know exactly what she's going through."

"Then why aren't you helping her?" Kevin demanded.

Martinez stared at him without comment.

"Got no answer, Martinez?"

My throat closed and I couldn't breathe.

"Get out," Martinez said in that deadly tone.

"Fine. I'll go." Kevin shoved a hand through his hair. "Get through to her somehow. Jesus. Just . . . fix her, okay?"

God. Even Kevin thought I was broken.

Kim bustled in to run interference and Kevin stormed out.

Martinez said, "Pack her a suitcase."

"Where are you taking her?"

"Away."

He rummaged in my closet, tossing a pair of jeans and a turquoise cashmere sweater on the bed. "Get dressed. Got five minutes or you're going in those ugly-ass pajamas."

"No."

"Don't fucking push me. I'm not in the mood."

"I don't give a shit what you're in the mood for."

"Glad to see that temper back, but move it."

"I'm not going anywhere with you."

"Wrong."

"Fuck you, Martinez."

"Best offer I've had in days. I'll take it under consideration."

I fumed. Didn't budge an inch.

"Tick tock, blondie." He spun on his heel and exited the room in a cloud of testosterone.

Kim was frantically jamming my clothes in a duffel bag she'd balanced on the rumpled bed.

"You don't have to do what he tells you."

"I know."

"Then why are you?"

"Because he's right." Kim lifted her head. Black mascara tracks lined her face. "I miss you."

"Kim, I'm right here."

"That's not you. I miss the real Julie. Find her and bring her back to us, okay?"

I didn't know what to say. Next thing I knew, my bags were in Martinez' SUV and we were on the road.

💀 💀 💀

A gorgeous, sunny day beckoned and I forewent sleep to drink in the sights of the great outdoors. Once we were in Rapid City, we drove down Jackson Boulevard and hung a right on Sheridan Lake Road. Past the housing developments, condos—finished and in progress—until the city limits and the suburbs were behind us.

In late fall, pine trees lose their green tone and can look faded, washed out, and dead. Some of the beauty returned after it snowed. I wished it would snow. Maybe the blinding whiteness would perk me up too, and keep me from fading away forever.

Finally I asked, "Where are we going?"

"Home."

"I was home."

"Not your home. Mine."

Guess I'd get to see his digs after all.

He hung a right on a rough gravel road —scarcely a step above a Forest Service firetrail— that seemed to go straight up. Around a sharp curve we stopped in front of an enormous black steel gate connected to an electric fence. Whoa. Serious security measures here too.

Martinez flipped his sun visor and poked a garage door opener. The gate opened. We inched forward. I couldn't see anything the forest was so thick. Once we reached a small clearing I caught sight of his house.

Holy shit. He'd totally been slumming with me.

His place was a sprawling Spanish grotto-style house with native stone siding, instead of stucco or adobe, and accented with rough-hewn pine timbers. Solar panels protruded from the concrete roof. A walkway, crafted from river rocks and slate, curved from the garage to the front door. It was stunning.

"Wow."

He smiled.

The inside was even better: earth-toned walls, terra cotta tiled floors covered with colorful rugs. An oversized chenille sofa, loveseat, and chair faced an immense rock fireplace. The kitchen wasn't huge, but the den was, and it housed the largest flatscreen TV I'd ever seen.

The house teetered on the edge of a cliff. In the great room, floor to ceiling windows overlooked a spectacular canyon. Sheer rock walls in shades of shimmery silver amethyst and charcoal, hundreds of feet high, gave way to a sea of green-black pine trees and a golden, sun-kissed meadow.

His hand cupped my good shoulder and he kissed the back of my head. "You like it?"

"God, yes. It's amazing. You have great taste, Martinez."

"In all things." He clasped my hand and led me down a darkened hallway. "I want to show you my bedroom."

My stomach jumped.

His bedroom was a masculine space, neutral colors, brown and tan, dark wood and a king-sized bed. A sliding glass door opened off the master bathroom onto a covered redwood deck with a hot tub.

"Kinda small for all those wild biker hot tub parties."

"The only person that's ever been in that thing is me."

"Really?"

"Really. Very few people know about this place."

I followed him out of the bedroom into the living room. "How few?"

"Half a dozen. Give or take."

"I'm in the inner sanctum now?"

"The inner inner sanctum since you're the only woman I've ever brought out here."

Before I could process the truth of that jarring statement, he was in my face, his dark eyes a morass of confusion.

"I know I'm not supposed to push. I'm supposed to give you time to heal and deal or whatever, but dammit, I want you to talk to me about what went on up there."

"I can't."

A beat passed.

"Try."

"Drop it, Martinez."

"Not a chance."

"I don't have the emotional energy to deal with this right now."

His cynical, almost inaudible laugh made me cringe. "*You* don't have the emotional energy? I was there, remember? I saw what she did to you. I see what she's *still* doing to you and she's dead."

"Stop it." My chin fell to my chest, allowing my hair to hide the shame coloring my face.

"Jesus, I look at you and see you are filled with so much . . . goddamn *remorse*, and I don't understand why. She killed your brother. For Chrissake, Julie, she almost killed you. How can you feel *any* guilt?"

I went rigid. "I don't owe you any explanations."

He waited. Calm, cool, collected.

I preferred his temper to his coolness. My temper— my goddamn backbone—seemed to have disappeared. It pissed me off. "What gives you the right—?"

"The right? Because I laid myself fucking bare for you. You think I do that for everyone? For anyone *besides* you? You're telling me that doesn't matter?"

Tears clouded my vision. "It does matter. But what is it that you want from me?"

"Jesus Christ, Julie, let me help you. I want you to let me in."

Terror flitted in my chest. "I can't."

"You owe me a better answer than *I can't.*"

543

"Goddamn you, Tony, please, don't do this. Just drop it. Leave me alone."

"Not on your fucking life."

Rage, fear, aggravation, and humiliation broke free from that dark place inside me and I lost it. Frustrated, I shrieked at the top of my lungs, like a wounded animal caught in a trap. When that didn't faze him, I pushed him away and yelled, "What don't you understand? I always deal with this kind of shit by myself. Always. I can't let you in because I don't know how to let you in, okay? I just . . . don't know how."

Martinez said, "Finally," and reached for me.

After my hysterics subsided, I tried to squirm away. "Don't. Just let me go."

"No." His arms were steel bands. "Look at me."

I locked my gaze to his, reluctantly, afraid of what he'd see in my eyes.

"Don't let the choice she forced you to make in a split second change who you are. You have the strongest sense of self of anyone I know."

His hand shook as he gently brushed my hair from my tear-stained face. "I didn't know how to let you in either. Let me show you, like you showed me."

Stunned, and wary, I watched him.

"I need this as much as you do, Julie. I gave you a chance to walk out on me once. You didn't take it. And

I sure as hell am not walking out on you."

Martinez knew how to ground me, knew how to get through to me when no one else could. As the truth of how he felt about me stared me in the face, I realized that needing him didn't make me weak; it strengthened us both. At another time in my life I might've made tracks for the closest exit. Not now. Probably not ever.

Those dark eyes watched me. He didn't move.

I disentangled from him, turned and stopped in front of the windows. I basked in the sun's warmth, needing the heat to drive away the coldness inside me. Needing the beautiful scenery as a focal point away from the ugliness inside me.

Martinez didn't allow the distance, emotional or physical. He circled his arms around me and held tight.

If I wanted to heal, I had to let go. So I did.

I took a deep breath. "For all those years, as tough as I talked, planning, scheming on the ways I'd torture the person who'd killed Ben, the cold reality is it wasn't easy. Even as she came at me, I hesitated. Even as I hated everything about her and what she'd done, I hated killing her. Yet, I'm so goddamn glad she's dead." I paused. "Does that make me a monster? Does that make me a liar? Am I just a fake? A tough girl poseur?"

"Jesus, no." He squeezed me tightly. "Come on, let it all out. I've got you."

I sagged against him and I didn't flinch in the rest of the retelling of what had happened with Leticia. Within my brutal honesty and Martinez' unconditional acceptance of it—of me—I found strength. I found concord. I found myself again.

When my storm of emotions subsided, he was strangely quiet.

And still I spoke in vague generalities. "Don't you feel guilty? After the fact? Even if your action or reaction was justified at the time?"

"Not as often as I used to. Maybe that's why I don't understand your guilt, blondie. But I'm gonna try like hell to change that."

Try to change not feeling guilty? Or try to change the behavior? I knew he'd explain the comment to me sometime, and I could live with that.

We existed in easy silence. A first, I hoped, of many.

After a time, I angled my head and rubbed my cheek along his smooth jaw. "What now?"

"You should probably rest." He nuzzled the side of my neck. His cool lips trilled a path down my throat.

"But?"

Martinez sighed against my damp skin, sending a delicious shiver through me. "But if I get you in my bed, the last thing I'm gonna let you do is sleep."

I smiled. I could live with that too.

CHAPTER 47

AFTER A FEW DAYS OF R&R WITH MARTINEZ, I returned home. In the last few weeks he'd actually hung a couple of changes of clothing in my closet, and stored some tools in the spare bedroom. That almost qualified as a declaration of love from him.

When I finished physical therapy, I tried to resume my normal life. Working with Kevin. Listening to Kim detail the horrors of morning sickness. Knocking back a beer or two with Jimmer. Accompanying Martinez to Hombres functions. And most importantly, attempting to establish a relationship with Brittney without the self-pressure of immediately becoming to her what Ben had been to me.

I still have nightmares about Leticia. I expect I always will. The bottom line is: Killing another human being changes you, regardless if the killing was justified.

The hardest part of letting go of Ben and moving on was coming to terms with Jericho's permanent departure from my life. I hope at some point, when he's older, he'll contact me.

But I realized I couldn't live on hope any more than I could dwell on the past.

Come spring, after the snow melts and when the chokecherry trees burst with sweet-scented buds, I'll take my little sister on a long overdue hike up Bear Butte. We'll talk about Ben, hang Ben's prayer bundle, and create a new family bond. I may not ever make my peace with *Mato Paha*; but hopefully, by then, I'll have made peace with myself.

Don 't miss the next Lori G. Armstrong book from
Medallion Press:

Snow Blind
LORI G. ARMSTRONG

ISBN#1933836598

ISBN#9781933836591

Mass Market Paperback

US $7.95 / CDN $9.95

Mystery

OCTOBER 2008

www.loriarmstrong.com

BLOOD TiES

LORi G. ARMSTRONG

Blood Ties. What do they mean?

How far would someone go to sever . . . or protect them?

Julie Collins is stuck in a dead-end secretarial job with the Bear
Butte County Sheriff's office, and still grieving over the unsolved
murder of her Lakota half-brother. Lack of public interest in
finding his murderer, or the killer of several other transient Native
American men, has left Julie with a bone-deep cynicism she
counters with tequila, cigarettes, and dangerous men. The one
bright spot in her mundane life is the time she spends working
part-time as a PI with her childhood friend, Kevin Wells.

When the body of a sixteen-year old white girl is discovered in
nearby Rapid Creek, Julie believes this victim will receive the
attention others were denied. Then she learns Kevin has been
hired, mysteriously, to find out where the murdered girl spent her
last few days. Julie finds herself drawn into the case against her
better judgment, and discovers not only the ugly reality of the
young girl's tragic life and brutal death, but ties to her and Kevin's
past that she is increasingly reluctant to revisit.

On the surface the situation is eerily familiar. But the parallels end
when Julie realizes some family secrets are best kept buried deep.
Especially those serious enough to kill for.

ISBN#1932815325
ISBN#9781932815320
Mass Market Paperback / Mystery
US $6.99 / CDN $9.99
Available Now
www.loriarmstrong.com

HALLOWEd GROUNd

LORi G. ARMStRONG

Grisly murders are rocking the small county of Bear Butte where Julie Collins has spent the last few months learning the PI biz without the guidance of her best friend and business partner, Kevin Wells. Enter dangerous, charismatic entrepreneur Tony Martinez, who convinces Julie to take a case involving a missing five-year-old Native American girl, the innocent pawn in her parents' child custody dispute. Although skeptical about Martinez' motives in hiring her, and confused by her strange attraction to him, Julie nevertheless sees the opportunity to hone her investigative skills outside her office.

But something about the case doesn't ring true. The girl's father is foreman on the controversial new Indian casino under construction at the base of the sacred Mato Paha, and the girl's mother is secretly working for a rival casino rumored to have ties to an east coast crime family. Local ranchers — including her father — a Lakota Holy group, and casino owners from nearby Deadwood are determined to stop the gaming facility from opening.

With the body count rising, the odds are stacked against Julie to discover the truth behind these hidden agendas before the murderer buries it forever. And when Julie unwittingly attracts the attention of the killer, she realizes no place is safe . . . not even hallowed ground.

ISBN#1932815740
ISBN#9781932815740
Mass Market Paperback / Mystery
US $6.99 / CDN $9.99
Available Now
www.loriarmstrong.com

A CALCULATED DEMISE

Robert Spiller

Bonnie Pinkwater, a veteran teacher with a knack for finding trouble, is at it again.

This time sadistic wrestling coach Luther Devereaux is found murdered, and her mentally challenged aide, Matt, is found with blood on his hands. She enlists the help of Greg Hansen, student council president, to pursue her investigation and exonerate Matt . . . and then Greg's marijuana-dealing brother and father are killed as well. And it looks like Matt's dwarfish brother Simon is the culprit. That is, until Simon is shot and killed by an amorous millionaire rancher pursuing Bonnie. Can it get any worse?

Oh yes. The rancher's son is now the prime suspect. And Superintendent Xavier Divine, AKA The Divine Pain in the Ass, demands Bonnie cease her investigation or lose her job.

Maybe Bonnie should have listened to him. Because things are about to get a whole lot worse. The murderer has now kidnapped Bonnie's beloved dog, and unless she wants to see him alive again, well . . .

ISBN#9781933836157
Mass Market Paperback / Mystery
US $7.95 / CDN $9.95
Available Now
www.rspiller.com

THE SAUCY LUCY MURDERS

CINDY KEEN REYNDERS

Dan Lightfoot's wandering eye has finally gotten the best of his wife, Lexie. Bereft, she moves with her teenage daughter Eva back to her hometown, Moose Creek Junction, Wyoming, to be near her sister Lucy, and they open a small business, The Saucy Lucy Café. It sounded like a good idea. Hometown. Family. A career and an income . . .

But Lucy is a staunch churchgoing woman who believes her sister must remarry in order to enter the kingdom of heaven, and the reluctant Lexie finds herself dating again. Trouble is, all her dates wind up dying and visiting Stiffwell's Funeral Parlor. Gossiping townspeople begin to mistrust the sisters and café customers dwindle . . . along with the town's menfolk.

Although Detective Gabe Stevenson, with whom Lexie has a love/hate relationship, and Lucy's husband, the inept town sheriff Otis Parnell, warn the sisters not to get involved, Lexie just can't let things be. Business is down the toilet and, according to Lexie, the police simply aren't getting the job done. It's time to intervene.

And so begins the hilarious and half-baked investigation of The Saucy Lucy Murders.

ISBN#9781933836249
Mass Market Paperback / Mystery
US $7.95 / CDN $9.95
DECEMBER 2007
www.cindykeenreynders.com